SWEET GUM

www.**booksattransworld**.co.uk

Also by Jo-Ann Goodwin

DANNY BOY

SWEET GUM

Jo-Ann Goodwin

BANTAM PRESS

LONDON · TORONTO · SYDNEY · AUCKLAND · JOHANNESBURG

TRANSWORLD PUBLISHERS
61–63 Uxbridge Road, London W5 5SA
a division of The Random House Group Ltd

RANDOM HOUSE AUSTRALIA (PTY) LTD
20 Alfred Street, Milsons Point, Sydney,
New South Wales 2061, Australia

RANDOM HOUSE NEW ZEALAND LTD
18 Poland Road, Glenfield, Auckland 10, New Zealand

RANDOM HOUSE SOUTH AFRICA (PTY) LTD
Isle of Houghton, Corner of Boundary Road and Carse O'Gowrie,
Houghton 2198, South Africa

Published 2006 by Bantam Press
a division of Transworld Publishers

A catalogue record for this book is available from the British Library.
ISBN 978 0593 045244 (from Jan 07)
ISBN 0593 045246

All extracts from *The Faerie Qveene* by Edmund Spenser are taken from the
Longman Annotated English Poets edition, edited by A. C. Hamilton (Series General
Editor F. W. Bateson, assisted on *The Faerie Qveene* by R. J. Manning) London: 1977.

Typeset in 10½/13½pt Sabon by
Kestrel Data, Exeter, Devon.

Printed and bound in Great Britain by
Clays Ltd, Bungay, Suffolk.

1 3 5 7 9 10 8 6 4 2

Papers used by Transworld Publishers are natural, recyclable products made
from wood grown in sustainable forests. The manufacturing processes conform to the
environmental regulations of the country of origin.

For Gilmar Cruz Silva,
and my sister, Susan Goodwin Lidgett

SWEET GUM

CHAPTER ONE

A Gentle Knight was pricking on the plaine,
Y cladd in mightie armes and siluer shielde,
Wherein old dints of deepe wounds did remaine,
The cruell markes of many' a bloudy fielde;
Yet armes till that time did he neuer wield:
His angry steede did chide his foming bitt,
As much disdayning to the curbe to yield:
Full iolly knight he seemd, and faire did sitt,
As one for knightly giusts and fierce encounters fitt.

Edmund Spenser – *The Faerie Qveene,* 1596:
The Legende of the Knight of the Red Crosse,
or of Holinesse: I.i.1

Eugene cut the phone halfway through the second ring. The idiot had been ringing all night, every fifteen minutes. Waste your time for real. What did these people think he was? Some kind of runaround? Eugene didn't appreciate that sort of pressure. Did not respond well. As he passed the Seven Sisters junction, the Holloway Road opened up clear and free before him. Eugene clicked his tongue and the silver Puma surged forward, flying Northward, heading for the next piece of business.

They stopped at Tollington Road – a one-off drop at the

house. Then headed towards Finsbury Park where another handful of desperados were awaiting Eugene's attention. The cocaine was packaged into grammes and ready to go; Eugene didn't waste time talking, didn't want to know these people. Just tolerated the job, the mad phone calls and hysterical punters, because he knew he must – though hopefully not for much longer.

The last customer was up at the Archway. Which suited Eugene because it was close to home. This time he had to go in – swap pleasantries, take a cup of tea and a line – because this guy spent serious money on a weekly basis, and if he wanted to chat, well, that was cool. Eugene was happy to let him chat away – up to a point.

Eugene saw himself as star of the movie, top of the bill. He liked sauntering into clubs, acknowledging the chorus of greetings. He was a face. People recognized him, pointed him out, whispered his name as he passed: 'Geno, it's Geno B.' Yeah, he walked tall – local kids looked up to him. You could say he was something of a hero.

Gladys Burnside had always known her son was something special. Thirteen years since her husband had died – Gladys remembered it like yesterday. Eugene had been just a boy. A gangling adolescent. A boy, who, like all boys, had big ideas. Then his dad fell ill and got worse. Within weeks Jean-Baptiste was off work, at home, dying on the front-room sofa. Part of Gladys had wanted to die with him. Her handsome Jonny, so young. Cancer in your thirties – Gladys couldn't believe it.

She took Eugene off school for the last two weeks. Afterwards, he became the man of the house. Looking after her, and his little sister, Simone.

Tall, handsome, clever Eugene. Gladys's friends and neighbours knew the story by heart – how Eugene's father had died when the boy was scarcely fourteen. What a help Eugene had been in those troubled and desperate times.

How he'd left school to 'look after the family'. How he should have gone to university – if his teachers hadn't let him down. How he battled against racist employers, the police who picked on him, and the friends who tried to lead him astray. How lucky Gladys was to have such a son.

As Eugene was the first to admit, Gladys was prone – like most mothers – to selective blindness when it came to her children. Not all of her mythologizing was nonsense though. Eugene was clever, very clever, although at school he had done his level best to disguise it. It was fair to say that the teenage Eugene had been a teacher's nightmare. Mouthy, insolent and utterly allergic to making the least effort.

But Gladys was right, his father's death had changed everything. Eugene had hero-worshipped his dad. Looked just like him. Father and son were close, spent a lot of time together. Jean-Baptiste was proud of Eugene and told him so – and told all three of them – Gladys, Eugene, Simone – how much he loved them. 'Us four: complete and sweet,' he used to say, laughing. 'Can you tell me what more the world can offer?' And then he broke their hearts and left them.

Gladys was desolate. Little Simone became angry and withdrawn. At school Eugene's playful clowning turned to rudeness and aggression, when he bothered to turn up at all. He was no longer interested in exams and careers. He had responsibilities now. He needed to make money.

That was all a long time ago. Now Eugene had his feet firmly on the ladder and climbing. For a couple of years he'd been consolidating his position in the Firm's middle ranks. Gaining a reputation, steadily building up credits. Soon he intended to make a move, Eugene reckoned it was time he stopped running about doing deliveries and donkey work. Time his talents were properly recognized.

By the time the Puma swung into Wentworth Road and Eugene returned home it was close to dawn and he was well and truly shattered. The coke affecting not much more than his heart rate as the rest of his body screamed for sleep. He walked softly down the hallway and avoided switching on the house lights. The very last thing he needed right now was a visit from the Minimonster. The slightest noise, the least disturbance, and the little bastard would be up and creating chaos – and at this time of the morning he just couldn't deal with it.

When he'd been on the powder, Eugene had a bedtime routine going, always the same thing in the same order. With a drug like cocaine it was important always to keep to certain rules, cos otherwise life would spin off the deck. You lost all direction, became trapped in a gibbering, paranoid mess of your own making. He'd seen it happen – seen friends go AWOL, grip on reality sliding. The whole performance getting more and more ragged. Until finally gravity took over, and the slow descent turned into a pell-mell free fall. And all you could do was watch as the hurtling corpse tumbled down the mountainside. A human avalanche pulling to destruction anyone mad enough to stand in its path. No, Eugene was having none of that. Much too smart for that game.

He had to keep a grip on things, so when he reached the kitchen, he did the same as always. Cup of tea, glass of vodka, then off upstairs. Half the vodka he swallowed – to help him sleep. The rest he carried to the bathroom. First off he would meticulously sort out his clothes – dirty in the basket for his mum, the rest to be folded, hung up, straightened, properly put away. Then clean the teeth and into the shower. Luckily the Minimonster slept on the opposite side of the house, so the bathroom was something of a safe haven. The shower relaxed him and made the next bit easier. Once out of the shower, Eugene leant over the sink, poured a pool of vodka into the palm of his hand, brought his hand up beneath his nostrils and sniffed. There was no denying it was agony. The alcohol shot up his nose and through his sinuses. If he felt brave enough to really give it a go, and snort it, he could feel the icy liquid burning across his eyebrows, and for two or three seconds the intensity of the pain would rock him. He always did it three times, each go got a bit easier, and despite the torture there was a perverse pleasure.

He'd learnt the trick from a customer, ages ago. The guy was a nurse, so he obviously knew what he was about. He explained that the alcohol washed out any remains of the cocaine lodged in the nasal recesses, whilst also acting as a disinfectant and countering the cocaine's corrosive, nose-eating properties. Dual action as the ads say.

Eugene thought it made sense. He kept the vodka in the fridge, and always bought the good stuff – Smirnoff Blue Label, or Absolut. The top-of-the-range gear, none of your supermarket-own-brand £7.99 per litre crap. And definitely none of your corner-shop tackle, Dirtcheapikoff, so crap we can't even give it away, guaranteed pure lighter fuel, straight from Siberia. No thanks. There was absolutely no way Eugene was going to put that sort of shit up his nose.

The vodka had caused a degree of domestic disharmony in the Burnside residence, not that Gladys was any part of the problem. Mrs Burnside regarded her son's possessions as sacrosanct. Once a week she'd be back from the bingo on Essex Road. Hopping off the bus around 10 o'clock. Moira from next door would be with her, regular as clockwork, but sometimes there'd be a wee party. Dennis and Gerry Q, both long-time unrequited admirers, who bickered over Gladys; Maria Caridad from down the road and maybe a few of the old crowd, from the Saracen's Head – the pub on the corner of Wentworth Road.

Everyone would push into the kitchen, carry-outs on the table, plus a communal bottle of whisky. The whisky came from the Saracen's and could only be drunk by those who'd chipped in, so frequently became the focus of furious argument as the party wore on. But no matter how desperate the drink situation became, no amount of begging, shouting or cajoling could persuade Gladys to touch the vodka. 'That bottle belongs to my son,' was the start and finish of the matter. Anyone who thought different was banned from the house.

No, the challenge to Eugene's personal vodka stash had come from another and entirely predictable direction. Number forty Wentworth Road was home to four people. As Gladys would say, when she'd had a whisky too many, 'I'm blessed by God, and a lucky woman. All my children under my roof, all my babies in one nest.' Eugene saw things differently.

Three years younger than him, Simone had been a disappointment at birth – he'd wanted a baby brother – and twenty-four years of shared existence had merely sharpened the mutual antipathy. Eugene kept hoping some chancer would take a shine to her, whisk her away to set up home in Harlesden or somewhere – Eugene wasn't fussy, as long as it wasn't North London. He could see Simone doing well out west – say, Stonebridge Park: wall-to-wall hoodlums and a crack den on every corner. Plenty of men to flirt with, plus ongoing turf wars offering the possibility of causing serious mayhem. Yeah, the girl would fit in fine.

Unfortunately though, Simone hadn't been whisked. Nor did there seem much chance of it. Eugene accepted that it would take a lot of luck. He reckoned his best hope was introducing her to one of the Yardie boys, on the run and straight off the plane. Too fresh to London to know the girl's rep. His sister might be stunning – or so everyone told him – but she was mouthy, awkward and – this was by far the worst bit – the Minimonster came with her.

Simone was just turned eighteen when she got caught. All tight white Lycra, silver polish on fingers and toes, and hair weave funded by a month's serious shoplifting. She hadn't noticed at first and was almost five months in when the struggles with the Lycra alerted her to the big event.

14

She'd been worried about putting on weight. The bigger tits hadn't been a problem, bursting out of her dresses with gravity-defying ebullience, the tits had been something of a temporary triumph. A real pair of scene-stealers they were, pissing off all her girlfriends with the attention they generated. The growing stomach had not been so funny. It's hard to hide in Lycra, and some of the girls enjoyed sweet revenge. The jealous bitches hadn't failed to point out that Simone's amazing figure was becoming a thing of the past. Finally, her boss had had a word. She'd taken his advice and bought the kit. She couldn't believe the price. Near enough a tenner; Simone thought the NHS paid for things like that. Gladys spent another tenner, after her daughter raced downstairs waving a white plastic wand. Second time around the result was the same. Simone was pregnant.

Aided by the hospital scan, Simone's 'secret diary' (a five-year, lock affair and a sixteenth birthday present) and Eugene's mental arithmetic, the Burnside family were able to pin down the guilty man. It might have been better not to have bothered. Simone had a long and dispiriting list of past loves but, even amongst such sorry company, Carl disappointed. He said his parents were from Jamaica. Said they'd done well in business, sold up and gone home to retire – describing a palatial residence just down the coast south of Negril. But like a lot of things about Carl, his background was all a bit vague. In fact, Carl was something of a man of mystery. The boy from Nowhere, hard to pin down.

Simone had bumped into him when she was out dancing with her girlfriends in some club up Tottenham way. The girls had clocked him straight off, the three of them exchanging glances. They'd gone into a huddle by the bar to discuss the thing properly. Carl was new; Simone, Chenelle and Tanya were all adamant they'd not laid eyes on him before. 'If I'd seen something that good,' said Tanya, 'I'd remember, believe it.' The problem was how to share the spoils. He was looking over their way, and the three of them knew it. The

15

girls began discreetly manoeuvring, trying to present their best. Hands going up to check the hair was OK. Shoulders back, breasts pushed out, stomach pulled in, hands moving downwards now, smoothing over the hips, accentuating the curves, showing what was on offer.

Simone was wearing shorts: skin-tight, silver stretch shorts. Her mother said she'd catch her death of cold. Much she knew. Simone caught Carl instead.

Carl's looks worked best from a distance. He wore his hair in locks, tied back with a loose band. His clothes were on the exotic side, velvet trousers, silk jackets, poetic shirts with lace on the cuffs. He had regular features and exceptionally long, thick eyelashes. In the half-light of clubs and bars he looked good. Inevitably the girls came running; all he had to do was decide which one he wanted. He had a great line in chat too. Bohemian adventures, tales of decadent parties attended by the rich and famous. A year living in LA hanging with the black aristocracy. Hopping over to Jamaica for Ziggy Marley's party. He was going to go back to the States, he said. Probably some time next year.

Because of all the travelling, Carl didn't have a regular address. No point when he didn't know when he'd be moving on. He stayed at friends' houses, and with girlfriends, but much of the time he simply disappeared. A regular invisible man.

Simone and Carl lasted around three months. She couldn't find him to tell him she was pregnant, so Eugene took on the job. It was like looking for a ghost. Carl's life had collapsed in upon itself like a black hole. Those closest to him preferred a mobile number, now redundant. No one knew his second name. No one knew where he was. And that was as far as Eugene got. To be honest, he wasn't that sorry.

Anyway, Carl's no-show meant there was no option on the birth certificate. Under 'father', the registration clerk wrote 'Unknown' in flourishing black ink. Simone called her little boy Nero. 'It means "no one",' she explained, 'because of his father.' Simone, by this time, had decided to present Carl's disappearance as mysterious and exciting, which seemed more romantic than the alternative reading, which was that he'd simply fucked off and left her. It was Eugene – 'my clever boy,' said Gladys – who pointed out Simone's mistake. 'It's NEMO, you fool,' he said. 'Not Nero. Nemo, N-E-*M*-O, you get it?'

Simone said she didn't care. Nero was 'a beautiful name for a beautiful boy. And anyway,' she added, 'I think Nero suits him.'

Eugene started laughing and then shook his head. 'Nero suits him? You'd better hope not little sister. You'd better hope not.'

Simone, however, proved unwittingly prescient. From the very beginning, Nero lived up to his name. Simone was two weeks overdue when the contractions finally started. She went by minicab to the Whittington, which was only ten minutes up the road. The Turkish cab-driver had enjoyed the drama, headlights full on and horn blaring as he careered round the Archway roundabout. He needn't have bothered with the rush. Thirty-six hours later, Simone was clutching her mother's hand and screaming in agony. The contractions were coming in great spasms, wrenching through her body so that her screaming redoubled, but all to no avail. The baby wasn't breech. There were no apparent problems, but the birth just wasn't happening. As the labour continued through a second night Gladys told her daughter she'd be back in a minute and headed for the hospital pay phone. Eugene was halfway across town when his mobile rang, he listened to what his mother had to say, then told her not to worry. Forty minutes later he was running down the Whittington's endless corridors. He didn't need to ask directions. He'd heard his sister screaming from the car park.

Simone's skin had turned the colour of wet ashes, her eyes were yellow and beginning to roll in her head. Her

17

body seemed dislocated, loose-limbed and skeletal, entirely subsumed by the hugely swollen belly. Eugene couldn't take his eyes away: his sister's skin was so tightly stretched, he thought she was going to explode. Every time the contractions came you could see them rippling through her, you could see the exhausted, flailing efforts as she tried to expel this monstrous thing inside her. And the screaming. Eugene thought it sounded like her soul was being ripped apart. Simone needed a Caesarean, but it turned out that there was no anaesthetist. One bloke had gone home, the other wasn't due in until nine-thirty the next morning. Gladys thought her daughter was dying.

Eugene got on the case. His mother had called on him, he wasn't going to let her down. He shouted, threatened, cajoled and created. He rang local newspapers. He accused the hospital of racism, of torturing his sister. He addressed the other waiting relatives and expectant mothers. He went down to Accident and Emergency and told the story. After two journalists and a *London Tonight* TV crew turned up, it was game over. The anaesthetist arrived shortly afterwards, and Simone's agony ended. Nero appeared from his mother's womb dripping with blood but otherwise entirely unperturbed. He weighed a gigantic thirteen pounds six ounces. 'Isn't he just a bonny big boy?' said the midwife. Eugene thought he was the most horrible thing he'd ever seen.

Simone was in hospital for eight days, recovering. It was noticeable that the nurses' initial enthusiasm for the 'bonny big boy' had quickly waned. Nero was a nightmare baby. He yelled the ward down. He fed voraciously and packed on weight at an alarming rate. He disliked being picked up, and pinched, kicked and struggled until put down. He was also very dirty, soiling mountains of Babygros and bedclothes. The nurses were, frankly, glad to see the back of him.

Over the course of six years, Eugene saw little to alter his first impression of his nephew. Adored and indulged

18

by his mother, little Nero achieved the distinction of being expelled from both nursery and primary school. The second incident had almost initiated criminal proceedings. Nero had been caught attacking a fellow pupil. He was holding four-year-old Alison by the neck, using his superior size and strength to throttle her. By the time the teacher pulled him off, the little girl had lost consciousness. Nero said he was 'only playing'. He was 'only playing' when he set fire to the rabbit hutches in a neighbour's garden. Likewise when he hung a kitten from the washing line.

Unusually tall and strong for his age, he would eat anything and began shoplifting sweets before he could walk. Often Simone had arrived home to find the folds of the pushchair bulging with Kinder eggs, Hula Hoops and Swizzlers. And Nero's malevolent presence turned the house into a kind of open prison. Eugene and Gladys soon learnt to lock their bedroom doors as a matter of habit. There was a padlock on the fridge and a Chubb lock on the pantry door. No one ever left an unguarded wallet or handbag around, and Eugene was careful with his car keys. They had a phone lock installed following a police visit. Nero had been phoning random numbers and shouting, 'Fucky, fuck, fuck,' when anyone answered. At five years old he was too young to face charges.

Sometimes just looking at the boy made Eugene's flesh creep. His chubby little face and sharp pointy teeth. The way his hair curled down his neck. Eugene would never admit it, but sometimes Nero unnerved him. It was something in the kid's expression. He'd glance up at you, super-long lashes fringing grey-black eyes, a knowing, sharply calculating look, it seemed. At such times he appeared more malign dwarf than child. A video-nasty made flesh.

To be fair, Eugene didn't waste too much time worrying about his nephew. When all was said and done, at six years old the Minimonster was still well manageable if push came to shove. No, life presented other, more pressing problems, unavoidable day-to-day stuff that just had to be sorted.

Eugene's progress through the Firm's ranks had brought with it commensurate responsibilities. Now in the higher echelons of what might loosely be termed 'middle management', Eugene shouldered a number of onerous duties. The most unpleasant of his tasks was unfortunately the most important. The Firm's drug empire was extremely profitable. The small circle of those closest to the Brothers – what might be termed the 'company executives' – sorted out the supply side. They dealt with South American and Caribbean contacts. But when the merchandise reached the UK was when the real risks started. And at that point the Firm's top men withdrew. The British wholesale business was franchised out. And for the past five years or more, the lucky franchisee had been a bloke called Shifter. Eugene was responsible for ensuring weekly collections of the Firm's merchandise from Shifter, which could then be divided and split amongst the Brothers' various sales staff. So Eugene had no choice. Every week he went to Shifter's house to sort out the necessary. He hated it.

Mr Malcolm Shifter lived in Acre Row, a narrow cul-de-sac on the edge of Camden. There was a padlocked barrier across the entrance prohibiting traffic, and the lack of vehicles always struck Eugene as slightly eerie. He sensed a kind of deadness about the place, a crippled inertia which weighed upon him. Acre Row was a small street, with maybe half a dozen three-storey Victorian semis on either side. The tall, dark stone houses rose up to cut off the light, standing blank and impassive behind front gardens choked with mammoth weeds and piles of litter. Eugene always hurried to and from Shifter's house. Walking past the rows of opaque sash windows with their dead, sightless stares unnerved him.

If there was something lifeless and inert about the buildings, the long-neglected gardens were almost frightening in their aggressive vitality – their burgeoning determination to grow, thrive and prosper. In summer the gardens of Acre Row went feral, overflowing across the pavement. The thick broad leaves making a squishy sound if you trod on them; and the sap oozing along the Tarmac made you watch your step. You wouldn't want to take a skidder into that lot.

Naturally, the luxuriant plant life was home to a wide and unpleasant variety of insects. Eugene thought the slugs of Acre Row were probably a distinct genetic strain. A race of super-slugs, grown strong through generations of gorging on the green, fleshy abundance. Huge things they were, black, brown and a pallid grey. Their skin shining and bodies plump, slimy trails following in their wake, a self-secreted glistening history. The things made Eugene shudder; the thought of touching one was unbearable. 'Why do women have legs?' – he'd first heard the joke at school – 'Because otherwise they'd leave a trail like a snail.' Even as a teenager he'd winced with revulsion. The last time he'd heard it, Eugene had taken the would-be comedian outside and threatened serious damage. It wasn't that Eugene was oversensitive on the sisters' behalf. He'd heard the one about the Irish abortionist who lost his ferret more times than were worth counting, and he could still manage a half-smile. But the snail-trail, he wasn't sure why, but it just wasn't funny.

Another thing Eugene hated about Acre Row was the smell. Around August the smell would start as the piles of vegetation began to rot and die down. A sweet, pulpy smell it was. So strong you could taste it. It made Eugene nauseous, and sometimes took days to get rid of. It lingered in his hair, seeped into his clothing, coated his trainers. Whenever he'd been to Shifter's he would always strip off and shove everything in the washing machine the moment he got home – then straight upstairs to shower the rest of it away. He'd skipped the shower once, a few months back,

21

when the hot water was out. Just had a quick cat lick at the sink instead. Big mistake.

At 5 a.m. the following morning, as the dawn rose over London, Gladys found Eugene frantically pulling the sheets from his bed. She had woken with a start to the sound of her son screaming. He'd had a nightmare; dreamt of clingfilm being wrapped around his head, every breath drawing the plastic tighter across his mouth and nose. And all around him was the sickly-sweet smell of blood and decay.

When Eugene screamed himself awake, he found the whole room was full of the stench of decomposition. The smell had come off his hair and soaked into the pillows. It was on the sheets, the duvet, on his skin – it was everywhere. So thick he could almost see it, coiling through the air. Eugene felt himself choking, starting to hyperventilate, heartbeat racing. Then his mother had appeared and taken charge. Eugene felt weak with gratitude and relief.

Gladys dealt with changing the bed whilst Eugene went to shower. She opened the bedroom window and made the boy hot milk with sugar and a dash of whisky. She sat beside the bed as he drank it, singing quietly and stroking his head. She stayed a while after he'd fallen asleep, listening to the slow regular breathing, making sure that he lay quiet and the night terrors wouldn't return. He was holding her hand, like he had when he was a baby. He was twenty-seven now, her boy, but asleep he looked much younger. And so much like his father.

It should be said that this little episode was an aberration. Eugene did not make a point of screaming nightmares, and in general tried to look upon his regular trips to Shifter's as nothing more than a minor trial. So he carried on doing the job as before. It was widely accepted that Mal Shifter was a weirdo and a creepy bastard, but he was also the man with the gear, and therefore his weirdness had to be tolerated.

*   *   *

22

This week Shifter had rung him and, as usual, told him to be round at 9 o'clock sharp. Punctuality was one of Mal Shifter's little quirks. If you didn't turn up on time he wouldn't answer the door, simple as that. If you started banging and shouting, leaning on the doorbell and creating to be let in, the big front door would swing open, and the three dogs would silently surge forward. They never barked, never made a sound. Shifter had paid a dodgy vet to cut the dogs' vocal cords. 'It's the Ladies upstairs,' he explained. 'Their condition, you know. I couldn't risk anything up-setting them.' The vet had also gone in for a bit of cosmetic surgery, docking tails and cropping ears, 'So as to get the look right,' Shifter said.

According to Shifter, the dogs were Rhodesian Ridge-backs. Huge reddish-coloured things with a stripe of raised hair running counter along the spine. They were called Faithless, Hopeless and Loveless – 'my little joke,' said Shifter. Normally, Eugene didn't mind dogs, but these things were different. Following you with their narrow brown eyes, perpetually surrounding Shifter like a canine hit-mob. And always so utterly silent.

Eugene rang Shifter's bell bang on 9 p.m. and prayed it would be a quick one. Sometimes it was all spot on. The gear would be weighed and waiting. The money handed over. The dogs barely present, hovering behind Shifter, subdued and ghost-like – the memory of a bad dream. Ten minutes and Eugene would be back in the Puma, shoving the gear down his Y-fronts. He knew it would be sensible to sort the gear-stashing in the house. But for some reason Eugene couldn't bear the thought of fiddling around in front of Shifter. And the trip to the bathroom was too hazardous to contemplate. The bathroom was 'upstairs'. Upstairs was where the Ladies lived.

Eugene didn't know how old they were. It was impossible to tell. Shifter was, at a guess, somewhere between late forties and early fifties. Letitia and Dolly were some sort of

23

relation – aunts? cousins? – and they could, in Eugene's view, be anything from sixty to ninety.

As Mal Shifter would explain to you, both the Ladies were invalids. Their complaints were manifold and invariably required complex treatment, but despite age and infirmity, they seemed almost indomitable. Serious illness came and went, but the sisters remained. Eugene suspected they were immortal. He'd seen something on BBC2. He liked the Learning Zone, and the timing – 2 a.m. to 6 a.m. weekdays – suited perfectly. Anyway, the thing he'd seen was a 'drama module', as they like to call them. This one concentrated on some play from ages back where the main character sold his soul to the devil in return for the gift of eternal life. As Eugene had easily foreseen, the bargain went sour. But it had been one of those programmes that start you thinking. And he couldn't help playing around with the idea, pretending – or was it just pretending? – that the Sisters had made the same deal. They'd go on, Eugene imagined, getting every disease invented. Rotting away, bit by bit, but never quite dying. Come back in a hundred years' time, and they'd still be there, upstairs on Acre Row, because the devil keeps his word.

Shifter opened the door a good minute after Eugene's ring. Then, with the three dogs circling him, Shifter gestured for Eugene to go through to the kitchen. Eugene nodded and walked down the narrow Victorian hallway. He kept his face blank, although he knew full well what was coming. The kitchen meant the sisters were up. Which meant he'd be lucky to get away much before midnight. Dead lucky.

The kitchen was right at the back of the house, where the original servants' quarters would have been. It was a bleak room, smelling slightly of damp and mould. If Letitia, the elder sister, was alone, she would remain in semi-darkness in her tall-backed iron chair at the head of the big wooden table, sitting immobile for hours, oblivious to the cold. Eyes closed, whilst on her lap her fingers danced in a blur of speed. She didn't need light to work, she said. She knew what she was doing. She knitted Mal's jumpers and socks. She crocheted shawls, tablecloths, antimacassars and bedspreads. Made shirts, patchwork quilts, embroidered seat- and cushion covers. She also did appliqué and macramé and tapestry work – but the complicated stuff was only undertaken when upstairs.

Dolly never came down alone, she only appeared when chaperoned by Letitia; but her presence changed everything. The fire was lit in the kitchen grate and piled high with logs, table lamps with coloured bulbs appeared, casting pools of pink, green, blue and red light. Scented candles and tea lights placed inside Chinese lanterns. Sometimes fairy lights would be strung up. And finally, there was music. Shifter had installed a state-of-the-art sound system, which Dolly adored. Donna Summer, Barry White, Shaggy, Frank Sinatra, Mary J. Blige, Elvis, Take That, Snoop Doggy Dogg, Dizzee Rascal – the list was eclectic to say the least. Whilst Letitia sat with her one cup of tepid Earl Grey tea – no milk, no sugar – Dolly hit the cocktails. Shifter made them for her – silver shaker a go-go, crushed ice, olives, Tabasco, limes: he had the lot. After a couple of drinks, Dolly would start dancing, twirling and cavorting, singing along to the music. Throughout all this, Letitia never moved. Between songs you could hear the frantic chattering of her needles.

The sound of 'Love To Love You, Baby' pouring out of the kitchen confirmed the sisters were in situ. Eugene was a particular favourite, especially with Dolly. She called him Mr Gorgeous, or just 'Gorgeous', for short. In other circumstances Eugene might have been flattered. But not here, though. Definitely not here.

Because the sisters' liking for him translated directly into time spent. As far as Shifter was concerned, 'The Ladies' wishes are my commands.' If the Ladies wanted Eugene's company, well, Mal was happy to ensure they got it. No deal would be done until the sisters retired, exhausted by the excitements of the evening. Usually that meant Eugene was stuck for a couple of hours of agony. He did his best to take the occasional Ladies' Night in his stride. Tried to see it as a kind of fitness test, on-the-job training, if you like. Eugene prided himself on his ability to cope, to deal with the nonsense that his chosen line of work inevitably entailed.

But a little under a month ago Eugene's forbearance had been stretched to the limit and beyond, and the fall-out from the events of that night had a major effect on Eugene's prospects.

Jogging down Acre Row that night, Eugene had been thinking only of a swift handover of money and drugs. He had no clue to the torment that lay ahead. Shifter told him the bad news the moment he opened the door. 'Young Geno,' he sang out, 'the guest of honour. The face we've all been waiting for. Come in, come in, my boy.' Shutting the door behind him, Shifter pulled Eugene aside and began speaking in a stage whisper. 'It's her birthday, you know. Dolly's been like a cat on hot bricks all evening. Worrying. Thought you might not come. You're such a favourite of hers. Talked about nothing else all day.' Shifter winked and nudged Eugene's ribcage. 'Better not to tell you what she was saying about you. Make you blush, it would. Little bit cheeky, it was.'

Eugene could feel his face going hot even as Shifter spoke. He took a deep breath and followed as Shifter beckoned him into the kitchen. In honour of the occasion, Shifter had hung streamers and bunches of yellow, red and purple balloons. Dolly was wearing a short, chiffon, halternecked dress patterned with red and yellow flowers. She gave a little scream of delight as Eugene came through the kitchen door.

'Happy Birthday, Dolly,' Eugene said. 'Forgive me for arriving empty-handed, but the man Malcolm gave me no warning. A lady has the right to expect flowers on her birthday, at the least, but I'd no idea it was a special day, so now I'm embarrassed. Hope you accept the apology.' All said with respectful sincerity and a dazzling smile. Eugene possessed Olympic-level charm and had good manners drilled into him at an early age. As Letitia had previously remarked, 'That tall darkie is in a different class, Malcolm, from the rest of the scum you have dropping round the house. Twice the man you'll ever be.' As Shifter spun round on her, she'd resumed her knitting and sharply shaken her head. 'Sit down, Malcolm, and be quiet. You don't want to wake up with a darning needle in your eye, do you?'

Already half-cut on strawberry daiquiris, Dolly was in party mood. 'I'm Aries,' she laughed. 'The sign of the ram. Fiery, impulsive, sexually demanding. What do you think, Gorgeous? Is that me? I'll bet you're a Scorpio. Magnetic, fiercely possessive, strongly passionate by nature. Am I right? Go on, tell me.'

She was right, but Eugene lied and said he was Libra. 'Fair-minded, even-tempered and good at friendships,' he quickly filled in. It was his mother's sign, so he knew the gen.

It was the start of a night of torture. Friends and neighbours dropped by with cards and presents. There was a Marilyn Monroe birthday cake, non-stop music, and endless alcohol.

'Can't do business in the middle of a party,' Shifter said, giggling happily. 'Disrespectful to the Ladies. Just relax, we'll sort it out later.'

'Later' was the apposite word. Eugene left at precisely 4.30 a.m. So furious, he'd done the unthinkable. He'd rung the Firm – more than that – afterwards he couldn't quite believe it himself – he'd rung the Brothers. Rung George and Archie Faron on their personal mobile just before 5 o'clock in the morning. He must have a deathwish.

Eugene had been lucky, dead lucky. George was in the middle of a party, slightly off his face and feeling at one with the world. He'd laughed a little as Eugene ranted. 'Shifter,' he'd said, 'he's a strange cunt right enough. Here, explain it to Archie.' Then the other brother was on the phone and Eugene had to say his piece all over again. Only the second time around, all the anger had evaporated, replaced by the cold realization of just what he'd done – was still doing.

'What?' was all Archie said. And Eugene began to tell him, all the while the nerves building, tightening around his throat and threatening to choke him. As his voice got quieter, so Eugene's legs began to shake, to judder so that he had to sit down, resting on the Puma's bonnet. But it turned out that Gladys wasn't off the mark, like she said, her boy was special, had star quality. Because Eugene had gone on with the story. Stoically labouring through Archie's contemptuous silence, like a man wading through glue.

When Eugene finished talking Archie said nothing. Eugene knew he was being offered rope to hang himself. He was sharp enough to understand that to start apologizing now would be fatal. So despite the fear rising inside and the overwhelming desire to beg and babble, he'd bitten his tongue and held back the 'Sorry to ring so late' and the 'Sorry, shouldn't have bothered you' and the thousand other 'sorrys' he longed to say. He waited as the silence ballooned, lengthened, then he took his chance: 'Look, I'm trying to do this job properly,' he said, striving to keep his voice steady and even. 'Thanks to Shifter's lunatic games, I've wasted the entire night and let down half a dozen punters who'll probably fuck off and take their money elsewhere. I don't call that good business.'

Finally, Archie spoke, 'Get off the phone, cunt,' he said, and then the line went dead.

Eugene heard nothing for forty-eight hours. He was sure he'd fucked it. Thought there'd be a squad out for him. Didn't know whether to stay or to run. It made more sense to get the hell out of North London, but he had this awful scenario playing in his head: saw the chosen envoys turning up at Wentworth Road, dragging Gladys out of bed. His mum in her quilted dressing-gown and the headscarf she

28

wore to sleep in . . . So he stayed put, and then the phone rang.

It was Talus, Gerry Talus, the Brothers' right-hand man. Talus told Eugene that Shifter had been spoken to, told to behave himself, to keep within limits, given to understand that the Brothers had an eye on Eugene, had things in mind for him. Talus said that George Faron had been amused by Eugene's nerve and Archie had liked the way he handled himself. There was a party on next month, up at the Halcyenda. Eugene was invited. Details nearer the time. Then Talus told him never, Never, Not Ever to ring the Brothers' personal mobile again, let alone at five in the fucking morning. 'If it happens again,' Talus said, 'I'll come round to see you. I'll cut your dick off and then I'll make you suck on it. Clear?'

'Well clear,' said Eugene.

'And don't get carried away,' Talus went on. 'George and Archie said to remind you that Mal Shifter is an important man. You need to understand that, to tolerate his little ways, up to a point. Also clear?'

'As crystal,' Eugene replied. It was hard to keep the excitement out of his voice. He'd just been promoted.

After that little episode, Shifter had kept within boundaries, albeit boundaries of his own making. And Eugene found the Acre Row nightmare easier to deal with, because despite the manifest irritations and annoyances of the whole thing, he was increasingly confident that his penance was coming to an end. All the signs were that Eugene's star was ascending. He no longer did the delivery jobs. Driving round London doing customer drop-offs was now someone else's responsibility. Eugene still ferried the occasional major deal, but that was all. He had a feeling that if he played his cards right, he would likewise be saying adios to Shifter. So although it was clear that he was in for another dose of the sisters on his latest visit to Acre Row, Eugene was reasonably light-hearted as he followed Shifter down the hallway.

In the kitchen Donna Summer was in MacArthur Park and Dolly was dancing freestyle amongst the pools of coloured lights. Letitia nodded stiffly in response to Eugene's greeting. Dolly tossed her head and did a touch of Michael Jackson-style moonwalk. 'Hi, Mr Gorgeous,' she said. 'Hi, Foxy,' Eugene replied. 'Would you ladies mind if I took a seat?' It was always the same, Eugene sometimes asked himself why he played along with them. Why he flattered and appeased. They were not, on anyone's reckoning, nice old ladies. Not by the furthest stretch.

Shifter followed Eugene into the kitchen and gave him a beer before applying himself to the cocktail cabinet. Between spins and shuffles, Dolly requested 'a very bloody Mary with all the trimmings'. Letitia still had a full cup of Earl Grey, by now stone cold. 'The way I prefer it,' she said.

Cocktail duties temporarily over, Shifter took his place at the table. He held a large triangular-shaped glass filled with creamy yellow liquid and chunks of fresh pineapple. 'Home-made pina colada, my young friend. Go on, try a little taste.' Shifter fished about and produced a box of straws. 'Exotic, Bizarre and Very Naughty!' said the packet. 'Stiff-Stuff Straws for Party People – Come On! . . . Suck It and See.'

'Here we go,' trilled Shifter, 'an Anaconda straw for you, I think. Nothing too risqué, we all know what a sensitive soul you are.' Such remarks were Shifter's only recognition of the Brothers' intervention on Eugene's behalf, but it was enough. Sucking cocktails through a coiling green and yellow 'Anaconda' straw wasn't the peak of dignity admittedly. But Eugene knew what the box contained. Shifter and the sisters loved Stiff-Stuff straws. Shifter bought them in bulk, somewhere down Soho. As Eugene acknowledged, they were very well made, which at £20 a box they ought to be. And there were a number of very intriguing designs.

There were Finger and Toe straws to suck on. French Kiss straws, with plump red lips and a pink tongue poking out. There was an impressive range of snake and insect straws. But entirely predictably, and by popular demand, a good 50 per cent were Dick straws. The phallic models came in every size and colour, circumcised and uncircumcised. There was even one sporting a very realistic Prince Albert piercing, which always made Eugene wince. Dolly invariably requested her favourite Stand-Up straw, which, when bobbing in a sea of bloody Mary or margarita, resembled with commendable detail a small and flaccid penis. However, as Dolly started sucking up her drink, the straw changed dimension and filled out until it reached twice its original length and girth. No longer resting pallidly against the side of the tumbler, the Stand-Up straw now justified its name, its newly acquired buoyancy causing the thing to bob up and down in a hilariously suggestive manner.

When Donna Summer gave way to the Spice Girls, Dolly decided to take a break from the dancing and moving the chair closer, settled down on Eugene's left-hand side. For the next few minutes she concentrated on the enlargement of her straw.

'She should be on stage, you know,' said Shifter admiringly. 'That's a lifetime of technique on display, sheer poetry, especially with the tongue. Look! Look my boy and learn. Like a butterfly that tongue is. Can you appreciate the skills you're seeing? Watch her . . . see . . . now she's surging like a dolphin, soaring like an eagle. Ooh . . . can you imagine? She's an artist, pure and simple. An artist, no other word will do.'

As Dolly finished, she leant back against Eugene, flushed and slightly breathless but pleased with her achievement. 'One day I'll do the same for you, Gorgeous,' she said, hand sliding along Eugene's inner thigh.

Letitia's pale grey eyes snapped open. 'Leave the boy alone, you dirty old bitch,' she hissed, 'and get your filthy hands away from him. Otherwise we're going straight upstairs.' Eugene remained still as Dolly disengaged. Shifter grinned and shook his head. 'Women, eh!' he said jovially. 'The eternal mystery, the unexplored dark continent. Now come on, ladies, sheathe those claws. We've got visitors, you know.'

For the next hour or so Dolly danced, sometimes alone, sometimes with Shifter. The Spice Girls had segued into Hot Chocolate's Greatest Hits, and as Dolly shimmied and smooched, Letitia worked on rapid-fire overstitch, whilst updating Eugene on her full medical report. The arthritis was no better and she was booked in for a second hip replacement. The waiting list was over a year, but it was pretty likely she'd be fast-tracked for early treatment because now they'd diagnosed brittle bones and osteoporosis. The pain was excruciating, Letitia explained, worse at night and in damp weather, pulling up her long wool skirt to reveal her swollen knees. Red and puffy with infection, they sat incongruously atop her white, razor-thin shins. One knee had a streak of discolouration running towards mid-calf. Letitia said, with some satisfaction, that amputation was a possibility. Otherwise, she said, her health was fairly stable. Neither the stomach ulcer nor her gallstones had played up much recently, and the alopecia was no better, no worse. 'Comes out in clumps,' she said. 'Look, see what I mean?' She nudged Eugene, proffering a sizable lock of freshly plucked grey hair, flakes of scalp still attached. 'You can hold it if you want,' she added. Eugene smiled tightly and shook his head.

'Is it painful?' he asked.

'Painful!' snorted Letitia. 'Watch.' She wound her fingers around a second clump and tugged lightly. To Eugene's horror, the hair broke from the scalp immediately, leaving a bald patch the size of a ten-pence piece above the left temple. Letitia waved the fistful of hair across the table. 'Like picking flowers,' she said. 'Go and put it in the bin for me, will you? Can't get up, it's my bones.'

Eugene held his hand out and refused to look. It was like touching a dead animal, and when he threw the stuff away, strands of hair remained stuck to his palm, clinging until peeled off, one by one. He went straight to the sink and began washing and rewashing his hands. Behind him, he could hear Letitia laughing. 'You don't need to do that, you know,' she called. 'What's the matter, think you might catch something, eh?'

Dolly after another bout of dance moves returned to sit at the table. Initially she nudged her chair alongside Eugene, leaning into his body, hands wandering. But one furious glance from Letitia put an end to all that. Instead, Dolly hogged the limelight with her own catalogue of ailments. Eugene always found Dolly's recitation of her medical symptoms particularly excruciating. He tried to tell himself there was no need to get embarrassed, tried to distance himself, but it was no good. Dolly was the queen of mortification.

They'd done all the tests, she told him, and the lump on her breast was definitely benign, no more than a cyst apparently. Dolly's disappointment was palpable. It had been such a let-down, she told him, especially after all the initial excitement. They were still intending to operate, but now there was no rush, and no chance of a mastectomy. Dolly paused theatrically and closed her eyes. 'It was all a bit of a shock,' she said. But luckily, she had other fish to fry. She'd got a definite diagnosis for irritable bowel syndrome, 'extreme bloating and flatulence,' she confided, but the real bonus was them managing to sort out her trouble 'down there'. Just in case Eugene hadn't cottoned on, Dolly nudged his elbow, 'Down there,' she said, pointing and nodding. 'You get my drift?'

Eugene nodded vigorously. 'Been giving me hell,' she continued. 'I scratched myself raw, but it just got worse. Ooh, Gorgeous, I can't tell you. Worst at night. It itched to blazes, couldn't keep my hands away.'

There was a sharp crack of sound as the elder sister slapped the table, and then Shifter was hurrying to help Letitia as she levered herself out of the chair. 'I'm going to wash your mouth out with soap tonight, you little scrubber,' she hissed. 'You're not fit for company, you filthy, dirty, dilapidated toolshed. We're going to bed, gentlemen,' Letitia announced. 'My sister is overtired. Dolly, we're leaving.' They both disappeared through the kitchen door as Eugene called 'Goodnight.' Neither he nor Shifter said a word as the sound of footsteps slapping on the hall lino subsided into the muffled thump of the stair carpet. Both men jumped when Dolly's tousled head reappeared round the kitchen door. 'I wanted to tell you how it ended,' she said, casting nervous glances behind her. 'Couldn't believe it. Nothing more than a yeast infection. Cure it by painting on yoghurt. Two days on I was as right as rain. Thought you'd like to know.' Then she was gone. Shifter smiled benignly. 'Marvellous,' he said. 'They don't make them like that any more. Real women. That's what they are. One hundred per cent female.'

Eugene knew he'd got off fairly lightly. Just gone 10 p.m., and both sisters out of the picture. But now Shifter was centre stage. Pratting about with the scales, breaking off to organize more drinks and clearly in no hurry. Whilst the sisters were present, the dogs had remained in the hallway. Now they padded forward and positioned themselves round Shifter. Their small hot eyes fixed on Eugene.

'My boys,' Shifter crooned, caressing the broad heads. 'Fascinating breed, the Ridgebacks. I don't think I ever told you, about the history, that is? How the breed came about?' Shifter looked at Eugene, eyebrows raised. 'Have I? No, I'm sure I haven't told you?'

Eugene kept his face blank. He had a good idea of what was coming. 'No,' he said quietly. 'You haven't told me.'

Shifter beamed. 'Oh, you'll love this,' he said.

First he got the gear weighed, wrapped and ready.

Counted the money Eugene gave him and put all the equipment away. The big lump of cocaine stayed on Shifter's side of the table. All that remained was to hand over to Eugene, but first there was a tale to tell. Shifter settled back in his chair, two dogs on his right-hand side, one on his left.

'Well,' said Shifter. 'Where shall we begin? At the beginning, I suppose.' He giggled for a moment, then composed himself. 'The Rhodesian Ridgeback,' he announced, 'is one of the few breeds to come out of Africa considered pure enough for Kennel Club registration.' He described weight, height and colour. And the famous ridge of spinal hair. Talked of the dog's ferocity, loyalty and strength. Moving on to explain how the dogs were bred to fit a particular purpose. 'They were bred by white settlers, you see,' Shifter told Eugene, smiling slightly. 'In Rhodesia. White farmers who had to guard their property. Some people say the dogs are racist, but that's silly, isn't it? Silly. Yes. Though some people, people who study these things, say it's in their genes, a hatred of blacks. Selectively bred for it apparently. Something to do with their sense of smell.' Shifter's smile widened as he leant confidentially towards Eugene, 'You see,' his voice was so low it was almost a whisper, 'I don't credit it myself, but these experts, well, they say we smell different. So that's how the dogs can tell. Nothing to do with sight at all. They tell by the smell.' Shifter gave a little laugh and leant back in his chair. He shook his head and giggled again. 'Tell by the smell,' he chanted, 'Tell by the smell, the smell will tell, so run like hell, if you want to stay well.'

Eugene didn't say a word. He knew Shifter did it on purpose, insulting him, winding him up, waiting for the moment when his temper would snap. Mal Shifter loved playing this game, did it to everyone. Did it to show who was boss, and because he liked it, revelling in the humiliation he inflicted, soaking up the pain and embarrassment. Eugene took it, sitting immobile, expressionless. At the moment, he had no choice, but he knew it wouldn't always be like this. He'd always known he was something special, and his call from the Brothers had confirmed it. This boy's future was looking good. And if Shifter was the Brothers' chosen wholesale distributor, well, as Eugene saw it, there was no point in arguing. He would keep patience, and one day, oh, one fine day, Judgement would come.

So as Shifter continued his story of canine carnage in the African bush, Eugene daydreamed about the day of reckoning. As Shifter took the piss, Eugene allowed his imagination to fly. He allowed himself to think what it would feel like to hit Shifter straight in the face. To feel his fist connect, the crunch of the nose cartilage giving way, and the hot wet blood. Shifter's voice, begging and pleading, grovelling and apologizing. Eugene was half smiling, far away on fantasy island, when he sensed movement. Shifter wasn't talking any more. He was looking straight at Eugene. So were the dogs. All three had risen and were moving around the table. Triangular bat ears pricked, top lips drawn back in voiceless snarls.

'What's happening?' Eugene asked. 'Mal, what's with those fucking dogs? They're supposed to know me.' Shifter gave a half-shrug, as the dogs continued their advance, moving stiff-legged, with tiny half-steps, saliva dripping from the long white teeth. 'MAL!' Eugene's voice was louder, his panic discernible. 'Mal, I'm not joking, get them away from me. Tie the fuckers up or something. Look at them, they've gone loopy.' They were less than a yard away from him, and unconsciously Eugene raised his arms, protecting his face and throat. 'Mal, please, please, I mean it. Call off the dogs.'

'Enough.' Shifter spoke softly, but the response was instant. The dogs returned to their master.

Eugene looked at Shifter and shook his head. 'What the hell was that about? It's not on, man. Those things are dangerous.'

Shifter caressed the nearest dog, stroking the silky head

36

and gently pulling the cropped ears. The other two dogs pushed closer to the chair, jostling for attention. Shifter crooned to them as he stroked and petted.

'Hopeless, Faithless, Loveless,' he carolled. 'Oh, I am triply blessed/ Hopeless, Faithless, Loveless/ The three that are the best.' The dogs were pushed up against his legs, eyes shining with adoration, aquiver with the joy of their master's touch. Finally, with a last patting session, the love-in was over. Shifter sat up in his chair, and the three animals moved back to their original positions. Then Shifter turned his attention to Eugene.

'"What was that about?", you ask me. A good question, young man, yes, a good question.' He suddenly looked sharply at Eugene and pursed his lips. 'I hope you weren't thinking bad thoughts, were you now? Because they can tell, you know. They can tell if someone's an enemy.' Shifter gave a tight little smile. 'Mm, you haven't been ill-wishing me by any chance, have you? P'raps having a bit of trouble seeing the funny side to my little jokes, yes? Lost your sense of humour, Geno? Is that what my three boys are telling me? Is that the answer to your question – is that "what it's all about"?'

Eugene told Shifter not to be stupid. When had there ever been a problem between them? He didn't know what had got into the dogs. The animals had gone mental, that's all there was to it.

Shifter shrugged. 'I know my boys,' he said. 'They always have a reason. I'd watch my step, if I were you.'

The three animals continued to stare blankly at Eugene. He desperately wanted out of there. Shifter was strange at the best of times, but this was genuinely and scarily weird. Eugene's eyes went from the dogs to the cocaine and back again. Finally Shifter scraped back his chair.

'I think you'd better go,' he said. 'I was looking forward to a nice evening, but it's been spoilt, completely spoilt. I'm in a bad mood now, and that's your fault.'

Eugene said nothing. Such displays of petulance weren't unusual. He got up, reached over for the cocaine and, keeping his eyes on the dogs, left the kitchen and walked up the hallway. 'OK,' he said, as he reached the door. 'See you next time.' In the kitchen Shifter was still muttering on: 'Yes, yes, a really bad mood. That's it, everything's spoilt. Spoilt, spoilt rotten. Well, boys; we know what to do. No good moping. Just have to try and cheer myself up. Make the best of a bad job. Give myself a treat.' Shifter's high-pitched laugh rang out. 'Yes, just like we planned. A nice treat. That's what I'll do. Cheerily, cheerily cheerily, eh, my boys. Put a smile on, shall we?' He was still chuntering away as Eugene let himself out.

As the Puma headed back down the Camden Road, Eugene told himself to get a grip. He tried to rationalize it, to construct an explanation for why the three animals had suddenly risen and turned on him. But the dogs' display of psychic powers worried Eugene. He thought about it all the way home. He supposed it must have been some kind of weird coincidence, but it hadn't felt that way. It seemed to him that the dogs had known – that somehow they had read his mind. As if Shifter's trio of silent protectors were some kind of succubi, and not like normal dogs at all.

It was an early night for Eugene. Back in the house just gone eleven. He sat in the kitchen with Gladys, chatting over a drink. He enjoyed these quiet times with his mum. She talked sense, which was more than you could say for most people. Just after one, Gladys said she was off to bed. Eugene went to watch TV, something on National Geo about the Lost World of the Incas. He liked the archaeological stuff and was quickly immersed in the story of the 'lost princess'. The body of a fourteen-year-old Inca girl had been discovered buried in the ice up in the Andes. She had been a sacrificial victim, it was thought. A virgin chosen to assuage the anger of the gods. The programme did a particularly convincing reconstruction of how she'd been dressed in the finest clothes, decked with gold, hair braided and oiled. Then she was frog-marched up the mountain by a handful of priests. There was much speculation about how the little party had got up to the peak – it was still a nightmare of a climb with all the modern gear – the TV guys had down-filled jackets, oxygen masks, ropes and spikes and anything else you cared to think of. The little princess was bare-legged, wearing leather-thonged sandals. Anyway, when they finally got her up there, she was given a ceremonial final meal and a drink laced with sedatives. Then she was forced to sit in the snow whilst the priests used rocks to smash her head open.

The noise when it came was so loud and sudden that Eugene's first move was to grab his baseball bat. Seconds later, the cause of the disturbance became apparent, as a small but solid figure came pelting down the stairs. It was the Minimonster. He was shouting and waving his arms. At the bottom of the stairs he carried on running, hitting the front door full tilt. He hardly seemed to feel the impact, rebounding, then smashing straight back into the door. Next he turned round and raced for the kitchen, kicking out at anything in his way. 'Blood, blood, blood,' he screamed, 'she wah full of blood an' funny snakey bits. I can see her thing. All blood, bloody blood.' The child was beside himself, but to Eugene's eyes he appeared excited, even exhilarated, rather than upset or fearful.

At first Eugene had to physically restrain the little boy, who continued hammering and kicking at the kitchen door and lashing out at anything else within reach. Eventually, the worst of the fit subsided and Gladys, woken by the crescendo of screams and shouts, took charge of Nero, whilst Eugene sorted out the child's bedroom. As usual, he'd peed the bed, but this time he'd done something else as well. Did six-year-olds have wet dreams? Eugene tried to remember how old he'd been when his started – surely Nero was much too young? The child also seemed to have had some half-conscious fit of rage. A fluffy toy littered the carpet, ripped into a hundred pieces of fur and foam; there were blots of red felt-pen staining the walls, and the Power Ranger now sported a pencil, stuck straight through its stomach.

It took almost an hour to get the little boy back to bed. His explanations were incoherent, but it seemed he'd had a particularly gruesome nightmare. When they finally got him settled, Eugene told his mother about the carnage in the bedroom. Gladys shook her head. 'Sometimes I think that boy's unnatural,' she said. Eugene knew exactly what she meant.

Simone was dropped off from work just after 4.30 a.m. She didn't like walking at that time of night, but the free lift saved her a tenner taxi ride, so she wasn't going to argue, though next time she'd think twice. She was ready to leave and kicking her heels for half an hour before they finally got on the road home. And dropping her off here wasn't something Simone appreciated either. The place made her nervous, pitch black and deserted.

Archway Tower stands no more than quarter of a mile from the Burnside house. In the car Simone had swapped her dance stilettos for trainers and, swinging her costume bag across her shoulders, she walked rapidly. She didn't relax until she was halfway home, and the black Tower had disappeared behind a bend in the Holloway Road.

But in the dark overhang beneath the Tower, down among the shadows, the rubbish and the concrete pillars; down in the dark, someone had been having fun. Quite a lot of fun, by the look of things. The body was discovered by a London Underground employee coming off the nightshift. He was taken to the Whittington and treated for shock. The case was assigned to Detective Chief Inspector Arthur Gale. It took a day or so, but they found out her name was Stella, and that she was nineteen years old.

CHAPTER TWO

Whilst round about them pleasauntly did sing
Many faire Ladies, and lasciuious boyes,
That euer mixt their song with light licentious toyes.

FQ: The Legend of Sir Gvyon, or of Temperance: II.xii.72

Simone had worked in loads of clubs, but for the past five months she'd been back at SweetHearts. 'He begged me to go back, said I'd be top girl, I couldn't say no really. I mean he was, y'know, desperate,' was how she explained her decision to return to Mr Barry. For once, Simone was almost telling the truth.

Back in early November, Mr Barry's plans for the festive season had taken a nasty knock. Sherry and Kenya – two of his most popular girls – had waltzed into his office and told him they were resigning from SweetHearts – as of now. It turned out they'd been booked for a three-month stint in a club just opened in Marbella. They could talk of nothing else but yachts, millionaires and what chance of meeting Adnan Khashoggi.

Mr Barry had barely kept his temper as they'd giggled and preened, telling him how sorry they were to go – but it was the chance of a lifetime after all – and they knew he'd understand, right? They both planted big lipstick kisses on his cheeks and promised to send a postcard. Then they sashayed their way out of the building. Mr Barry stood at his office window and watched them go. He was breathing heavily. The stinking, selfish, stupid little slappers, he thought. Bloody ungrateful bitches.

Mr Barry understood full well that Sherry and Kenya must have known for weeks about the Marbella contract. Known they'd bugger off a month before Christmas and that would leave him well and truly stuffed. If they'd told him earlier, he would have had a chance of finding proper replacements. But that wasn't their problem, was it? So the little cows had left him in the lurch, and done it now, of all times.

Mr Barry was frantic. He rang round business acquaintances and pored through the contact files. After half a day of near-hysterics, he found her. 'Perfect,' he shouted. 'Get her on the phone.' Mr Barry had not enjoyed the subsequent interview with Simone. She'd made great play of needing more time to consider his offer. She was *really, really* happy at Peccadillo's. And the money was *fantastic* and she felt really, y'know, *valued*. Really *respected*, so it was a bit difficult to say.

Mr Barry spent fifteen minutes engaged in what his Mancunian mother would have called 'flannelling'. He'd been in the business over ten years, he told Simone. Must have seen hundreds, thousands of girls. But there was something about Simone. Something different, something special. It had been a big mistake to let her go in the first place. He'd always regretted it. So many customers had asked about her.

They were rehearsing a new centrepiece 'extravaganza' for Christmas and New Year, Mr Barry explained. All about a band of Amazon warrior maidens. The maidens 'capture' one of the men in the audience, who of course would be a plant. Probably, they'd use Shaun, a dancer and male stripper who often did 'guest' appearances at SweetHearts. Anyway, Mr Barry went on, the two loveliest Amazon princesses both want the man for themselves. The finale is this big fight scene, very dramatic, very sexy. Then the whole show closes with the winner and Shaun in a romantic moment as she unties him and leads him to her hammock. We've got this amazing see-thru hammock. In fact, all the sets are amazing, Simone, we've put a lot of money into this.

This was true. Kenya, whose parents were in fact Nigerian, was to have played one of the fighting 'princesses' opposite Ulrika, a German girl with white-blond hair and skin to match. Mr Barry considered the juxtaposition of the black and white limbs of the fighting girls would be 'very artistic'. However, as of now he had only one black dancer left. And she, quite frankly, wasn't up to the job.

Simone, however would be perfect. She was, as Mr Barry would say, 'a real knockout'. Halle Berry's double, sleek and classy. Simone had star quality. So Mr Barry made his financial offer, droned on a bit about terms and conditions and played his ace: 'I know you need to think, love, but make it quick. You see, The Extravaganza casting has to be sorted by tomorrow, latest, and I had you in mind for the star role. If you're going to be my winning princess, I need to know. There's the promo pictures and magazine shots to do, never mind the rehearsals.' Simone asked for an hour to think. Ten minutes later she rang back and said yes. Mr Barry had been euphoric with relief, the Christmas 'Extravaganza' was safe. Ulrika paid the price for Simone's return. She was supposed to have been the 'winning princess' and was none too thrilled at the prospect of demotion.

Before Simone arrived, Mr Barry exercised his managerial skills. He called Ulrika up to his office and said something about not being able to make an omelette without breaking eggs. He then presented her with a 'pre-Christmas bonus'. This, Mr Barry explained, was in recognition of her positive and cheerful attitude and her highly professional approach to the job. Ulrika got the message, took the money and put a smile on her face.

So Simone had returned to SweetHearts and proved an

enormous hit as 'Electra, Warrior Princess'. The Christmas Extravaganza was featured in a glossy lads' mag and was so popular it ran through February. There was talk of a summer 'Spectacular' set in a Turkish harem.

Increasingly, Mr Barry dreamt of escape from SweetHearts. He wanted out. Other blokes thought it was a dream job – 'What? Manager of a lap-dancing club? You jammy bastard. You get to interview the girls personally, eh? Check out their credentials, do you?' Mr Barry played along with it, protesting, with a wink and a smile, that they'd got the wrong idea, that the club was run on entirely professional lines. Shrugging and smirking at the inevitable cries of 'Come off it!'

But Mr Barry wasn't a happy man. He was good at the job and knew it, widely regarded as one of the best in the business. But Mr Barry had had enough. OK, so he wasn't short of shagging opportunities, the money wasn't bad, and he was the boss. But the longer he did the fucking job, the more he asked himself if it was worth the stress. Because stress there was, by the bucketful.

SweetHearts was officially owned by a Portuguese businessman – a Senhor Ninho de Vazio. Mr Barry had never met Snhr Vazio, and didn't expect to. Instead he dealt with the owner's 'agents', George and Archie Faron. Mr Barry had a healthy respect for the Faron brothers. During the course of his tenure at SweetHearts, Mr Barry had developed a real admiration of the Brothers' business acumen. In addition to their dealings in the entertainment sector, the Brothers had a surprisingly eclectic portfolio of investments: a chain of mobile-phone shops, shares in a couple of high-profile car-dealerships, a company specializing in wholesale imports of exotic plants and flowers, three retail florists and even a small supermarket in Dalston – to name but a few. Mr Barry often wondered just how much they were worth but found it impossible to calculate – beyond the certainty that it was a hell of a lot.

What really impressed him, though, was the way they handled the club. Archie could read the books quicker than most people read the *Sun*. His ability with all things financial was akin to genius and he did the annual accounts personally. The previous manager of SweetHearts had been interviewed by Archie when discrepancies had been discovered – Mr Barry understood it had been to do with the wages bill – and given the opportunity to explain himself. His explanation failed to convince, and the man was sacked on the spot. He was escorted from the club and given seven days' grace to find £56,384.13. Cash. Which was Archie's estimate of money stolen, inclusive of lost interest. Mr Barry never found out whether the money was given back or not. A few weeks after leaving SweetHearts, the ex-manager was found floating in the Regent's Canal. The coroner's verdict was death by misadventure.

Mr Barry learnt from the mistakes of his predecessor. SweetHearts' yearly audit had taken place four weeks ago, at the beginning of March. Archie worked through the endless lines of figures with silent speed. Mr Barry knew better than to distract by talking, so he tried to get on with other jobs, to ignore the cold sweats and the way his hands were shaking. Then Archie stood up. 'Job's done,' he said, gesturing towards the papers. Mr Barry nodded. He'd tried to speak, but no sound had come out. The Farons had that effect on people. 'Good,' Archie said. 'Six per cent up, very good. Here's your end-of-year bonus.' He reached into his briefcase and pulled out a brown-paper package. 'Congratulations,' he said, and left.

It had taken ten minutes of deep breathing and steady drinking before Mr Barry was in a fit state to investigate his 'bonus'. The brown-paper packet contained £5000 in brand-new fifties. As someone once said: with the Farons, it was all or nothing.

The brothers were in the habit of dropping in at Sweet-Hearts for a spot of r&r when the mood took them, often accompanied by 'business associates'. They would settle down in the VIP enclosure, champagne, brandy, cocktails and beer would be delivered at a sprint, after which Mr Barry would appear saying how thrilled he was to see everybody. The party would choose a handful of girls, and after a few more obsequious remarks, Mr Barry would effect a tactful withdrawal.

He absolutely dreaded such nights. He drilled the staff, laid contingency plans, constantly checked supplies and personally supervised, but remained haunted by the fear of disaster. George and Archie didn't like it when people let them down. He tried to cover every angle, but life had a way of throwing up nasty surprises. Take Sasha, for example. He'd employed her six months ago, and sitting through her audition, he'd been well chuffed. She was Croatian or something – Mr Barry was a bit unclear on anything east of Germany, there were so many countries springing up out of nowhere and disappearing just as quickly. He'd interviewed dozens of girls claiming to be Hungarian, Lithuanian, Ukrainian, Albanian, plus a whole gaggle of Serbians, Bosnians, Kosovans and Moldavians. Mr Barry ignored the detail. He instructed Mae – SweetHearts' Malaysian-born House Mother – to file the blonde ones under 'Scandinavian' and the dark ones were 'Mediterranean'.

Sasha was blonde, twenty-two years old with huge blue eyes and great dance moves. Mr Barry had been well pleased with his new acquisition. She started on a Monday, so as to work herself in gradually before the weekend. Entirely coincidentally, George and Archie, plus a couple of 'the boys' had chosen that very Monday night to drop by. There were no accompanying clients to be entertained, it wasn't a business visit. Just a bit of low-key relaxation on the way home.

Sasha had been picked to join the party, and everything was fine. The Brothers and their favoured lieutenants drank,

46

talked and fondled the girls, who gulped champagne and giggled. Then George shoved Sasha off his knee, took a couple of fifties from his pocket and told her to dance for him. Halfway through George lost interest. By the time Sasha was peeling off her G-string, he was deep in conversation with Archie. As she danced nude, three feet from his chair, he didn't even look. When she threw a glass of Cristal in his face, George's undivided attention was secure.

George slapped Sasha's face, Sasha slapped him back. She screamed he was a rude pig of a man. He had no class, no manners. He was not a gentleman, just a pig. There was more, but it was lost in the mayhem and the screaming as the bouncers carried her out.

Mr Barry started to hyperventilate even thinking about the events of that night. Luckily George had calmed down quickly, even seen the funny side, whilst Sasha, naturally, had been sacked on the spot and chucked out of the building. Even so it had been a close one. So small wonder Mr Barry felt stressed. And the last thing in the wide world he needed was an 11 a.m. phone call on a bright Tuesday in April telling him Detective Chief Inspector Arthur Gale was on his way to SweetHearts. Or that DCI Gale wanted to speak to him regarding 'a very serious matter'. Mr Barry called the Farons immediately. He was instructed to be helpful and polite, and to say nothing; how to accomplish this feat of social contortion was left to Mr Barry to fathom.

DCI Arthur Gale had spent the previous morning down at St Pancras morgue at the postmortem on the girl whose body had been discovered in the shadows beneath the Archway Tower. Nineteen-year-old Stella Jane Hope. As they wheeled her in on the metal gurney and pulled back the sheet, he'd felt an unexpected heave of revulsion. This one should have been all right. The body was fresh, discovered an estimated two to four hours after time of death. There was no smell, no sickly-sweet scent of decomposition. She hadn't been in the water – bloated and spongy with sodden, tripe-like flesh – and although young, she was most definitely adult. In common with most detectives, DCI Gale found child murders difficult. But Stella Jane Hope was a grown-up. DCI Gale had done car-crash autopsies. He'd attended a wide variety of postmortems and seen what some of us get up to with knives and the like. So really, Stella Jane Hope should have been a doddle.

Unfortunately, the pristine state of the corpse served only to clarify the desecrations inflicted. The clean, unblemished white skin provided a perfect canvas, a fine contrast to the dark colours of furious degradation framed within. DCI Gale had seen many terrible things in the course of his career, but never anything approaching the carnival of obscenities visited upon the naked body of nineteen-year-old Stella Hope.

DCI Gale believed in order. For without order there was only chaos. And DCI Gale knew all about Chaos. Knew the fellow liked to party, liked a bit of a laugh. He'd followed Chaos's dancing red footsteps cavorting across the autopsy table. Pursued his litter-strewn trail through the underpass and up the concrete stairs. Heard the screams when Chaos got down on the carpet and played with the kids. Cleared up the mess when Chaos played rough. And with Stella Hope Chaos had really gone for it – was playing to big boys' rules. And, Gale was sure, he'd had such a good time, he'd be looking for another girl to play with, some time soon.

Mr Barry was at the door of SweetHearts as DCI Gale's car pulled up. They went straight upstairs to the manager's office. Like most clubs, SweetHearts looked sick in the daylight. A little tawdry, scuffed at the edges. The rich hues of night lost their promise and turned heavy and sullen. And under the electric lights, the cleaners seemed to be making little headway. 'Sorry about the row,' called Mr Barry, as they climbed the stairs under a barrage of vacuum cleaners and dance music. 'Got a rehearsal going on. Our summer show – "Harem Nights", it's called. I could probably sort out a few tickets for you and the lads?'

DCI Gale shook his head. 'No, thank you,' he replied.

'Oh fuckin marvellous,' thought Mr Barry. 'I have to get the detective with the Blue Peter badge, don't I? Fuckin marvellous. Say fuckin nothing, my arse.'

DCI Gale didn't waste time. He began by explaining the reason for his visit. For a couple of seconds he thought the manager was going to faint, his face waxy-pale, eyes blank and unfocused. DCI Gale suggested a glass of water might help. Mr Barry agreed, although he felt brandy would have helped a lot more. Mae came in from the outer office with the water and asked her boss if he was all right. Mr Barry nodded grimly. DCI Gale noticed the manager had begun to rock himself, making tiny, rhythmical to-and-fro movements. His normal colour had returned, and he was beginning to sweat heavily.

'Stella,' said Mr Barry. 'You're quite sure it's her? Little Stella? I mean, it's definitely her?'

'Yes, sir,' Gale replied. 'There's no doubt. The identification has been confirmed and checked. If you don't mind, I would like to ask you some background questions. We are trying to find out as much as possible about Ms Hope.'

Mr Barry always made it his business to find out about the girls he employed. Such attention to detail took time and effort, but in Mr Barry's experience, the approach paid dividends. Thinking back, Mr Barry did a rapid mental check over all he knew of Stella Jane Hope. As far as he was aware, there was nothing at all about Stella likely to cause the club a problem. Considering the line of work she was in, Little Stella was surprisingly clean. No drugs or petty crime. No 'escort' work. Stella was basically a decent girl. And she'd got herself killed miles away from SweetHearts, which was another bonus. The Farons wouldn't need to get involved. Mr Barry felt light-headed with relief on one hand

and shock on the other. But with a senior copper sat opposite him there was no time to get all emotional. He was supposed to be shit hot at his job. Now was the time to show it. Mr Barry could almost hear his mother's voice telling him to 'pull yourself together'.

So Mr Barry got a grip. Looking at the bigger picture, he thought, it was well manageable. He'd have to tell the Farons asap, and then have a talk to Mae, because the press would need to be handled properly. And there were a couple of potential problems that needed tidying up. But all in all, it could have been worse. There was nothing that couldn't be handled. Of course he'd need to find a replacement for Stella, he quite fancied one of those specialty acts – like the Bangkok bar girls who could blow smoke rings. Those Asian girls were tiny, almost like kids. He told Stella only the other day she'd have to lose weight. Too much of a tummy on her. Mr Barry phoned through to Mae and asked her to bring Stella's 'personnel file'.

'Well, officer,' said Mr Barry brightly, flourishing the file as Mae departed. 'Ask away, anything you like, just ask away.'

DCI Gale nodded, then began. 'Can you remember the last occasion on which you and Miss Hope had sexual intercourse, sir?' he said.

Simone got home early that night. Everyone had seen the police car pull up outside the club and all the girls had been agog. Anyway, there wasn't long to wait. The police were no more than ten minutes gone when an announcement was broadcast summoning all SweetHearts' staff to the main dance floor.

When the gathering was complete, the lights dimmed, there were a couple of seconds of near black-out, and then a dramatic, single spotlight sent a stab of white light cutting across the nightclub shadows. Everyone fell silent. There, illuminated at the top of SweetHearts' 'Staircase of Mirrors' was Mr Barry. His sombre expression reflected in each one of the thirteen mirrored steps below.

Something akin to Moses coming down from the mountain, clipboard folder standing proxy for tablets of stone, SweetHearts' manager slowly descended. Halfway down he stopped, head bowed. Finally he looked up. 'I want you all to prepare yourselves for some shocking and terrible news,' he said. After that there was no stopping him.

Simone tried hard to convey just what it had been like. To explain to her mum and Eugene how amazing it was to have actually been there. 'Like watching those people when they pulled down the Berlin Wall. "Witnessing history," they said. I know Stella wasn't famous or nothing, but I'll tell you for a fact, this is going to be big.'

'Why?' said Eugene. 'No, no. Hang on, Simone. No disrespect, none at all. It's a terrible thing to happen, I'm not denying it. But you only have to pick up the local paper to see that people get rinsed round here every day of the week.'

Simone shook her head. 'It's not like that, smartboy. It's not like your normal kick-offs. Not from what I've heard.'

Eugene held up his hand. 'Fair enough. Go on, girl, tell me, cos I'm listening.'

Simone paused, glanced round the kitchen table and was satisfied: her mother and brother were silently attentive, waiting for her to continue. Nero had been sent to his room. The child had been watching when reports of Stella Hope's murder came on the regional evening news. He'd become totally hyper, bouncing up and down on the sofa and asking over and over to be taken to the Archway Tower. 'I wanna see blood. Lego Tower, show me dead lady. Please, please, please, wanna see her. Lego Tower and see lotta blood, now. Now.' After five minutes of this Gladys had marched him upstairs.

'OK,' Simone said, looking pointedly at Eugene, 'If you let me finish, you'll understand what I mean about Stella's murder being big. If you're interested, y'know.'

Eugene smiled. 'We're listening and we're interested. Go ahead.'

Mollified Simone continued. She explained how Mr Barry had announced Stella's death, how shocked everyone was and how upset. 'He even cried, Mr Barry, when he said about her being really nice-natured, and said how everyone was her friend. "Even in the jealous whirlpool that is the world of high-class table dancing," he said, "little Stella did not have a single enemy."

'He called her Little Stella a lot, because she was quite short. Only about five foot two, which is really no good for a dancer: that's why she was only chorus in Harem Nights.' Gladys and Eugene nodded.

'And he asked us to observe a minute and nineteen seconds' silence as a tribute to her memory. That's when I started to cry, when Mr Barry said the nineteen extra seconds were "for every year of her brief, brief life", that's exactly what he said, and a lot of people lost it then.' For a moment Simone seemed about to burst into tears all over again. 'It was really emotional,' she continued, voice wavering. Gladys reached over and passed her a paper hanky. 'Thanks. It's OK, Mum.' Simone blew her nose. 'Honestly. It was just so sad.'

Simone took a deep breath and went on. 'So after that they played that old Commodores song. Mr Barry must have arranged it, cos it came on over the sound system exactly as the one minute nineteen second silence ended. You know the one, it's really beautiful – "Three Times a Lady" – dead slow and sad. After that we were all in bits; even some of the security men were upset. Then Mr Barry said he'd cancelled all rehearsals and the club was closing tonight as a mark of respect. "In honour of Stella's memory," was how he put it. It was really nice. I know it's only Tuesday, but it's the thought that counts and it's the proper thing to do.'

By now Gladys was on the verge of tears herself, and

Eugene's eyes were suspiciously shiny. Gladys told Simone to wait before saying any more, and got up to make tea with sugar and whisky. 'Good for the nerves,' Gladys maintained. When everyone was settled back round the kitchen table, Simone got on to telling them the bad stuff.

Simone explained how she'd been one of the last to leave the building and on the way out had run into Mae, the House Mother. Simone and Mae were old friends. They decided a drink would be good for the nerves, and together they headed for the nearest bar. Mae bought two large brandies and ushered Simone into a quiet alcove.

'Well,' Simone said, dropping her voice so that Gladys and Eugene leant forward to hear. 'Mae said that she'd been called by Mr Barry cos the police wanted to interview her about Stella. Mae told me the police as good as said that Stella wasn't the first. They think there's been other girls he's done. The police said Mr Barry had to warn everyone at the club to be careful. He said Mr Barry ought to set up a taxi service to get the girls safely home after closing. Anyway Mr Barry just laughed and said, "We're not made of money," so this police guy nodded, then he got a photograph out of an envelope and passed it over to Mr Barry. Mae said she thought he was going to black out.

'Afterwards Mr Barry told Mae what they'd shown him was a photo of Stella's body. Apparently he was in a really bad state. He kept saying "Oh, Christ" over and over again, and asking for brandy. She said it was a good few minutes before he got himself together enough to do his speech. You've got to admire the way he pulled it off though. Y'know, he was totally professional.'

Simone pushed her chair back from the table and began clearing plates. 'And that's it really. Mae was dead nice and gave me a lift in her taxi, right to the end of our road. Wouldn't take anything either.'

Gladys joined in the clearing-away. 'Simone, if you can't get a proper lift home, I want you to promise me, promise me, you pay a taxi. You hear me? I don't want you walking around at that time of night no more.'

'I promise, Mum, no worries at all. You've got my word, I'm not walking any more.'

Eugene left his mother and sister to the washing-up and headed up to his bedroom. Passing Nero's room, he could hear a steady thudding as the little boy kicked and hammered at the locked bedroom door. 'Little bastard,' Eugene muttered.

Propped up on his pillows, his bedroom door firmly shut, Eugene searched channels before deciding on National Geographic. The programme was about the customs of a tribe living hundreds of years ago somewhere in East Africa. Archaeologists had discovered a large baked-clay tomb, like a miniature house, with domed roof and walls four feet thick. When the chief died his body was ceremonially escorted and laid out in the tomb, then his wives were led in and bricked up alive inside. This ensured the chief would have plenty of company when he crossed over into the other life.

And they'd found some bits of writing. Markings scratched into the stone which seemed to relate to a very elderly chief who'd married a girl of fifteen when he was already very sick. The unwilling bride had tried to run away, but they'd caught her. When the old chief died it had taken four men to carry the struggling girl into the royal tomb. They said that experts were currently working on deciphering a number of other stone tablets.

Eugene was utterly lost in it all. The archaeologist said that chiefs could have as many as twenty wives. They thought the women would have died within hours through lack of oxygen. And heatstroke. They reckoned the daytime temperature inside the tomb would have been above 40 degrees. Fragments of human tissue had been discovered embedded in the clay walls – fingernails and shreds of skin. Hundreds of years old, but still there.

Eugene didn't hear the mobile at first. It was a short call, no more than a few seconds. From Gerry Talus – the Farons' right-hand man. Eugene couldn't quite believe it – Gerry Talus calling his mobile. Like getting a Christmas card from Prince Charles. 'There's a party up at George's place. Saturday. The Halcyenda,' Talus told him. 'Get there at 11 p.m. Don't come early and don't be late. And don't turn up with some slapper girlfriend. It's a smart job, suit and tie. Got it?'

Eugene didn't blow it, kept calm and steady. 'Yeah, all heard,' he said. 'See you Saturday.' Then he realized the connection was already dead.

CHAPTER THREE

But he their sonne full fresh and iolly was,
All decked in a robe of watchet hew,
On which the waues, glittering like Christall glas,
So cunningly enwouen were,

FQ: The Legend of Cambel and Telamond, or of
Friendship: IV.xi.27

Eugene spent the rest of the week panicking about
clothes. He ended up going down the serious shops and
paying serious money. Back home, posing in the mirror, he
decided the cash had been well spent. The mega-glam man
and no doubting. One of the shop guys had told him he was
a born clotheshorse, had the height for it, and the shoulders.
'Perfectly proportioned,' the shop assistant said. Eugene was
glad to get away from him.

Gladys had ironed the creases from his new shirt and
polished his shoes. The entire outfit now hung inside plastic
cleaning-bags in his bedroom. Perfect and ready to go. The
Puma was booked in for full valeting, wax and polish on
Saturday morning. He would get his hair trimmed whilst he
waited. Already a nervous wreck by Thursday, God knows,
Eugene thought, what state he'd be in come the party.
He comforted himself with failsafe preparations, checking

and planning every last detail. Obsessive, maybe – but Eugene had a great deal riding on Saturday night.

On Friday, party business well in hand, Eugene was back doing the runnings – but it was getting bigger and better. Only one delivery, a major quantity, with a drop-off in Luton. The drive out was fine, the Puma galloping down the M1, glad of a chance to stretch its legs in the spring sunshine, skimming the miles like it was flying. Coming back was a different story, the road clogged and crowded, the pace reduced to a crawl. Passing Highgate Tube Eugene was relieved to see it was still only 4 o'clock. He'd made arrangements to go out early and wanted a shower and some tea. Gladys was doing stew and dumplings, on the table for 5 o'clock sharp. Eugene had stayed off the coke all day in anticipation.

The Puma loped down Highgate Hill and over Archway roundabout, passing the yellow police noticeboards stationed at every exit. They all said the same thing:

MURDER
– ARCHWAY TOWER –
STELLA JANE HOPE AGED 19

The police asked anyone with information to ring the murder squad hotline. Eugene wondered just how many wankers had done just that – proffering some or other garbage for the thrill of being involved; murder, people just loved it, didn't they?

Eugene had seen the curious crowds hanging round all week, leaning over the yellow-tape crime-scene barriers, peering into the shadowed depths beneath the Tower, speculating on what might be going on as police and crime-scene personnel did their work. A while ago, he'd seen something on Bravo, or maybe Channel 5 – anyway, it was about women who fell in love with serial killers. The women were almost all Americans, which meant there was the added excitement of possible executions and a cell on death row to factor in. Eugene found it incredible. The women would start off by writing to the convicted multiple murderer of choice, quickly progressing to visits, and within six months or so he'd proposed and she'd accepted, undeterred by his sentence – if not death, it would inevitably be ninety odd years and more – the glow of romance undiminished by thoughts of the rapes, assaults and murders her hero committed before the forces of law and order caught up with him. And there were loads of these mad women. Eugene watched open-mouthed as one after another was interviewed explaining how the police had got it all wrong, and her man was innocent, or the victim of a frame-up, or the suffering product of a cruel childhood. Eugene wondered if it worked the other way round: had Myra Hindley received hundreds of marriage proposals? Was Rose West overwhelmed by love-struck letters from impassioned male admirers? Somehow, he doubted it. Which probably said something about society, something unpleasant.

Eugene was worried about Stella Hope's murder. Worried because of his sister. It was her life and her decision, but Eugene didn't relish the fact that his sister was a lap-dancer. He thought the job was degrading and dangerous – fine for other girls, but not something you'd want to see your sister – or your daughter, or your mother – doing for a living. And Stella Hope had worked at the same club. Probably just coincidence, but it made him nervous.

He hoped they caught the maniac double quickly. And all the more so because he knew the dead girl. Not very well, just to say hello to, but he sometimes used to see her when he came to give Simone a lift home when the club closed. Stella would be hanging around the foyer – waiting for her own lift, Eugene presumed. Long blond hair and eager expression. 'Naive', Simone had called her.

Eugene shook his head. He wanted to relax tonight, to stop worrying about Simone and the murder, to forget about tomorrow's party at the Halcyenda and spend a few hours enjoying himself. As the Puma turned into Wentworth Road, Eugene made a conscious attempt to clear his mind. In two hours' time he was picking Ralph up from the shop – then it was straight down to the Sports Bar to bag a decent view of the big screen before the place started filling up. It was going to be a big night – Champions League: Real Madrid *v.* Arsenal, kick-off 7.30 p.m.

He was really looking forward to it. Watching his team, having a couple of drinks, and hanging with his star boy – his mainman. You couldn't deny it, Eugene and Ralph Palmer were practically brothers. The two boys had met, aged four, in the playground of Seven Sisters primary school. Within a week they were inseparable. All through secondary school it was the same story, Eugene and Ralph, a single unit, never apart. They smoked their first weed together, committed petty crimes and went on joyriding sprees together. They received their first unofficial police caution in tandem; and lost their virginity – aged thirteen – within the same week. Though not with the same girl.

After leaving school, joint ventures in petty crime gave way to a steadily increasing involvement with drugs. Then Ralph got a letter. Just a few weeks after celebrating his twentieth birthday, Ralph Palmer trailed unwilling down the job centre. He'd been selected for a compulsory interview.

Two weeks later, wearing a nylon uniform, name badge and permanent sneer, Ralph began twelve months' work experience at Thomas Cook travel agents – Archway branch. It was pointed out to Ralph that he was very fortunate to have this opportunity. Learning about travel and tourism whilst simultaneously absorbing office administration and interfacing with clients – the man from the job centre told Ralph that with a bit of luck, he could probably make something of this. Ralph rolled his eyes and sneered some more.

But entirely unexpectedly, and despite his best efforts,

Ralph took to travel and tourism and interfacing with clients and proved to be extremely adept at office administration. He liked the job, liked Thomas Cook – Archway branch, and liked Matthew Roberts, the branch manager. The feeling was mutual and when the year ended Mr Roberts asked Mr Palmer to come to his office for a chat.

That evening Ralph Palmer bounced down the Holloway Road, sprinted across the adjoining estate and up the steps to the second floor of St George's House, and began shouting to his parents before he was halfway along the walkway. His dad went out to buy a bottle of Martell to celebrate his son's appointment as trainee Asst Manager for Thomas Cook – Archway branch. His mum said he'd made her very proud, and immediately started phoning every relative she could think of to pass on the news.

It was the beginning of the separation. Eugene tried hard to understand why Ralph was so over the moon, tried to feel the same way. But didn't and couldn't. By now Eugene had started small-scale dealing. He had crept in on the bottom rung of the Firm's ladder. It was about this time that people started calling him Geno, that he began to get recognized around local clubs. That people began to whisper that Geno B. was a Farons' man.

And Eugene was beginning to make money. Proper money, not some pathetic single-figure salary minus tax, for fuck's sake. But Ralph was all made-up and thrilled. His mum and dad, Auntie and Uncle to Eugene, well, Uncle Joseph and Auntie Una looked like they'd just found the Holy Grail. Beaming they were. Forget 'glowing with pride' – the Palmers were white-hot with it.

Eugene had always thought he'd be in it with Ralph, a team, looking out for each other, taking care of the business. Well that wasn't going to happen. Eugene was on his own. He tried, made a genuine effort to be pleased for Ralph, to see it all from his point of view, but inside he felt betrayed, frightened and angry. He got a new mobile and told his mum to tell Ralph he'd moved and that she had no address.

Eugene neither saw nor spoke to Ralph for almost three years. Their reconciliation was effected amidst the echoing Victorian corridors of the Whittington hospital. There'd been a spot of bother, a bit of a territorial disagreement, which eventually had been settled in the Brothers' favour. The argument cost Eugene a punctured lung and three weeks in hospital. It also cemented his relationship with the Firm. Lying helpless in Reckitt ward, Eugene was given an object lesson in how good management practices can secure employee loyalty.

One of the Firm's representatives visited daily. Whatever he wanted was provided swiftly and free of charge. What Eugene appreciated still more was the way they took care of his mum.

Eugene gave Gladys £500 per week – supposedly for rent, bills and food. Both parties knew Gladys was ludicrously overpaid. That was how Eugene wanted it. Whilst he was in hospital, his mother had a visit. One of the boys, smartened up and besuited. He told Gladys he'd come on behalf of Eugene's employers. 'We work for the same company,' he explained. He'd given her £2,500 – in cash – then asked her to sign an official but entirely bogus form, explaining the money was owed to Eugene in sick pay. When Gladys questioned the amount, the Brothers' rep explained that Eugene had sensibly been paying in to his employer's sickness and injury scheme. 'My clever boy,' Gladys said, and ran up to the hospital to tell her son.

It was during his second week in the Whittington that Eugene got a surprise visitor. It was about 9 p.m. and he was half reading and half dozing. Then out of the corner of his eye he saw a young black man walking down the ward. Eugene struggled to sit upright, slipped back down on his pillows and cursed. A second later, he was looking up at Ralph, who said nothing but put his hands under Eugene's armpits and gently pulled him up, then supported his back while he arranged the pillows. When Eugene was comfortable, Ralph sat on the bed, and the silence stretched.

'Christ, man.' Ralph's exclamation drew the attention of the entire ward.

Eugene returned the stares of his fellow patients, then waved at them. 'Hello, everybody,' he said brightly. The entire ward immediately looked away. Ralph started to smile, then looked back at Eugene.

'Christ,' Ralph said again. 'You know you nearly died? They nearly killed you, man. I'm not kidding. You stupid fuck. You stupid fuck, Eugene. Don't do this, spar, don't do this . . .' They got as near to embracing as Eugene's bandages allowed, and the love affair started up again.

When Eugene came out of hospital and felt near enough back to what he should be, arrangements were made. Hair fresh from the barber's, shaved and showered, dressed in Issy and Moschino – the full clip – Eugene arrived at Ralph's new Crouch End address. Sitting by Eugene's hospital bed, Ralph had proudly told him that just over a year ago he'd married Belinda Sykes. Whereupon he'd invested his savings – (Savings? thought Eugene. Married? What the fuck is he on at?) – and bought a shop on Crouch Hill. Ralph and Belinda lived in a flat above the shop, and DCT Travel Agency was starting to do well.

DCT stood for Dreams Come True, Ralph explained, as he, Eugene and Belinda drank wine in the flat. 'That's what holidays are, you see – dreams, fantasies, escapism. I see my business as all about making those dreams a reality, so that's how we chose the name.' Ralph looked across to his wife and smiled. Eugene sat very still.

It had all been a bit of a shock. The flat with rugs on polished floorboards, framed black and white photos of Mandela, Muhammad Ali and Malcolm X in the hallway and African carvings. Since when had Ralph been into that shit? And then there was the wife.

Belinda wasn't Eugene's kind of black girl. Not his kind of any girl, come to that. Ralph seemed to think she was some sort of paragon of loveliness. He had that 'aren't I just the luckiest man in the world?' little smile on him every time he looked at his wife. Which was like 90 per cent of the time.

Eugene tried hard to stay civil. To keep smiling whilst Belinda interrupted and contradicted. Why the fuck didn't Ralph tell his woman to shut her mouth? That's what Eugene couldn't understand. What was his friend doing, letting his wife show him up like this? Talking shit about politics and racism and the whole bollocks. Eugene had met them before, middle-class girls with their university degrees and posh jobs. Their 'authentic' hair weaves, ethnic jewellery and endless opinions. Poor Ralph getting stuck with all that.

Thankfully, after an hour or so, Ralph suggested going out for a beer. Incredibly, he actually asked Belinda if this was OK with her. Eugene was having trouble believing his ears. In the old days he'd have got Ralph alone and put him straight. Told him to bounce the mouthy dog quick time. But things were different now, and Eugene knew enough to keep patience as Ralph sang Belinda's praises all the way to the bar and halfway down the first drink.

Getting the second round in, Eugene admitted to himself that this was all a waste of time. He had nothing with Ralph any more. Sad but true. No use pretending. He was cold with disappointment. Embarrassed and angry about how much he'd hoped. He felt like a fool.

He was in the toilets washing his hands and thinking about telling Ralph he'd need to be going soon when he felt a hand on his shoulder. 'I shouldn't ask, and don't tell Belinda, she'll go ballistic.' Ralph was beside him, grinning sheepishly and talking in Eugene's ear, 'But I couldn't buy half a gramme, brother, if you're carrying, that is?'

Eugene was always carrying. He refused the money, gave Ralph a gramme for old times' and chopped out a line apiece in a cubicle. Twenty minutes later, the two of them were on a roll. Talking and laughing like always. Tagging each other's jokes and swapping stories. Best friends. After the bar closed Ralph took Eugene back to the flat. Belinda said pointedly that it was almost 1 a.m. and tomorrow was a work day. She was going to bed. 'Nightie night,' said Eugene, before he and Ralph started giggling.

From that moment, the two of them never looked back. Ralph's business continued to prosper, and he and Belinda bought a house just off Crouch End Broadway. No more than ten minutes' walk from the shop. Belinda taught Race and Ethnicity Studies at Holloway University. She and Eugene detested each other. Eugene's impression of a stuck-up, know-nothing megamouth hadn't changed. He was honestly shocked that someone with Belinda's take on life was allowed to teach. Even university students, he felt, should not be exposed to this sort of malign drivel. All at the taxpayer's expense. Eugene thought it was a total disgrace.

Belinda in turn saw Eugene as a no-good. Far too bright to be fooled by her husband's half-truths and evasions, Belinda had a fairly good idea of what Eugene was about. She regarded him as a drug-dealing gangster. She had no proof but suspected Ralph took drugs when he was out with Eugene. This infuriated and frightened her. And there was something else, a subconscious niggle. Belinda wondered what her man got up to on Friday nights when he was out with Eugene. Where had he been till 2 a.m.? Who with? She tried not to ask too many questions. Frequently talked about trust and honesty. And every Saturday morning, before he woke, she silently checked her husband's wallet, pockets and mobile phone.

Eugene knew nothing of Belinda's fears, and wouldn't have cared. Friday nights with Ralph were sacred to him. Nothing got in the way of Friday night. He knew Belinda didn't like it, but, you know – Jesus – she had Ralph every other day and night of the week. One night out of seven wasn't too much to ask was it? Eugene – as endless past girlfriends could testify – wasn't too bothered about being late, keeping people waiting. But he had little enough time with Ralph as it was. He wasn't up for wasting any. Eugene had agreed to pick Ralph up at the shop just after closing time. So, dead on 7 p.m., the Puma was parked up and Eugene was at the door of DCT Travel Agents.

Ralph was almost done. Computer screens dead and wrapping up his last customer. Passing over bits of paperwork and telling her the flight tickets should arrive within the week. Eugene flipped the door sign to 'closed' and stood quiet. 'Final thing,' Ralph was saying, 'because I know people worry about this. If by any chance the tickets aren't through your letterbox by next weekend, look, here's my card and my numbers. You call me and I'll sort it. It's always fine, but sometimes they'll send out only three or four days in advance. It's totally understandable that people start panicking – hell, if it was my holiday, I'd be panicking.' The girl laughed, said thanks and, picking up her bag, turned to go. Mainly because he was standing slap in the way, Eugene stepped back and opened the door for her to leave. She smiled at him and said thank you. Eugene smiled back. Closing the glass door, he watched her walking up Crouch Hill. She was lovely, he thought. Really gorgeous.

'I know what you're thinking, bro.' Ralph's voice came from the stockroom where he was rapidly changing out of his suit and into the new Arsenal shirt plus matching jacket. Eugene had the identical combo.

'Come on then, man. You tell me – what am I thinking? Go on, bro, surprise me.'

'Well.' Ralph emerged grinning from the stockroom, transformed from go-ahead young entrepreneur into Gunners die-hard. 'My guess is that you were thinking that my last client was, what should I say? That she was a very attractive young lady, and that you would welcome an opportunity to become more intimately acquainted. Am I right?'

Eugene smirked. 'Yeah – more or less got the gist.'

Ralph nodded. 'Course, those weren't the exact words running through your head, but let's not go there.'

'Beautiful eyes,' said Eugene.

'Lovely,' Ralph agreed. 'Third time she's been in. Seems nice as well, friendly and dead polite. Works in some media thing, she told me.'

'Course' – Eugene nudged Ralph with his elbow – 'you, my longstanding, and oldest and best-ever friend, you, were you so minded, could lay your hands on the lady's phone number?'

'No chance,' said Ralph. 'Come on, Eugene, get out the shop and let me lock the frigging door, man. No. Can't do it, bro. Would, if I could, but I can't.'

Eugene moaned, cajoled and flattered all the way to the Sports Bar. Ralph didn't budge.

'Anyway,' Ralph said finally, 'not that it makes any difference about me giving you the number, because I just won't. There's an end to it. But come on Eugene – you know it's a waste of time. Yeah, she's really nice, but she's not for you. You know that.'

Eugene shook his head. 'No, I don't know. You think she's above my level or something? What you trying to say?'

'No, you fool,' Ralph said. 'It's not about that. I don't think she's "above you" or any of that shit. But come on, Eugene, think about it, man. Those beautiful eyes – beautiful blue eyes, yeah? That's what I'm saying.'

Eugene said nothing for a second, checking the Puma was safe and secure before they did the short walk to the Sports Bar.

'You know what I mean?' Ralph said.

'No, except you've got a problem with blue eyes. Tell me, exactly why is this girl no good for me?'

Ralph shrugged and glanced across at Eugene. 'She's no good because she's white and you're black. That's it. I know you mess around. That's up to you. If the women are up for it – fair enough. But if we're talking serious – well, you asked for my view, and now you have it. Listen, Eugene, London's full of beautiful girls. Girls with education, style, girls with everything going for them. Girls with beautiful brown eyes, the same as you.'

Eugene shook his head. 'This shit is from Belinda, right? This is the kind of bollocks she's always on at. Well, I don't buy it, spar. And come to that, I can remember a few years back when you didn't seem to find white girls a problem yourself. So I know where you've picked up this rubbish. No disrespect to your wife, star boy, but I hate all that stuff. It really pisses me off. And I'll tell you something for real, I'll marry the woman I fall in love with, right? I'll get married when I find a girl like my mum. Nah, fuck off.'

Ralph was laughing and telling Eugene there were laws against that kind of thing. 'Oh, sorry, bro,' he said, between snorts of laughter, 'I get it. You don't mean nothing pervy, you're just worried about the home comforts, yeah? Looking for someone to do the washing, eh?'

'Very funny, Ralphie boy. No, you know I don't mean cooking and stuff. I'm serious, bro. If I get married I want someone I can talk to and listen to. Someone with class. It's got to be a lot more than a good ride and a bit of a laugh. It's hard to explain.' Eugene shrugged and grinned. 'Anyway, if she's got that special thing, plus a gorgeous face and a body to stop the traffic – well, what I'm saying is I don't care what colour she comes in' – Eugene's grin widened – 'and no double meaning intended.'

Ralph held up his hands. 'Enough, enough, point taken, spar. OK, here's the deal – I'll tell you the girl's name, and the local she sometimes hangs in Saturday nights. No numbers, no address. The rest is up to you.'

'That's my top man,' Eugene said. 'A real friend never lets you down. I owe you, spar, big time.'

Ralph grinned. 'Mine's a double vodka and Red Bull,

seeing as you're buying. Oh, Eugene, just wanted to ask, how would you feel then if Simone came home with a white boy?'

Eugene didn't hesitate. 'I'd fuckin murder him,' he said. 'But anyway,' he added. 'Simone wouldn't dream of doing that.'

CHAPTER FOUR

And euer as he rode, his hart did earne
To proue his puissance in battell braue
Vpon his foe, and his new force to learne;
Vpon his foe,

FQ: The Legende of the Knight of the Red Crosse: I.i.3

Eugene was seriously late home that night. Arsenal had pulled off a total shock victory, and the celebrations had been euphoric. The Sports Bar had recognized history in the making and stayed open and serving well past midnight. It was near 1 a.m. when Eugene and Ralph left for home.

'Fuckin amazin bro,' said Eugene, as the two of them headed, arm in arm, towards the patiently waiting Puma.

'Amazin,' Ralph agreed. 'I mean, you know. You know man I thought I was up for a fuckin coronary watching that. I mean, those last ten minutes . . .'

'Oh tell me brother – tell me,' Eugene agreed.

'Yeah,' Ralph nodded. 'I felt sick man. Shaking. Incredible. Really and truly.'

Arsenal had scored a fluke goal ten minutes in. The London team had spent the remaining eighty minutes of the game hanging on for grim death. Unbelievable luck, missed chances, frantic defending and goalkeeper heroics had somehow maintained Arsenal's ill-deserved lead. The Sports Bar clientele had oohed and aahed and blasphemed their way to the verge of a collective nervous breakdown. Then, just three minutes from full time, the inevitable came about and the Spanish galacticos' fortunes finally changed. They were awarded a penalty.

'You cheating, diving, dago bastard,' yelled Eugene, as the bar erupted in a crescendo of abuse.

'Get up you wanker,' screamed Ralph and a hundred others, but to no avail.

The referee blew his whistle and pointed to the spot. Eugene could hardly bear to watch. It was too cruel, getting your hopes up, going through all that agony, only to get stuffed at the last minute.

Some hugely expensive Argentinian superstar sauntered out to take the kick for Real. 'Big-headed bastard,' muttered Ralph, as the Sports Bar seethed with projected hatred. The Arsenal goalkeeper checked his gloves, jogged on the spot and looked immensely serious. Then the referee blew his whistle and total silence descended.

Even in slow motion it looked impossible – just how the Arsenal goalie had got there. How he'd flung himself across the height and distance – fingertips stretching, contact barely made. But that touch was enough. The ball clipped the corner of the crossbar, bounced back on the pitch and was booted into infinity by an Arsenal defender.

There was a moment of utter silence. Eugene felt it physically, the suspension of time. Then the roar of collective triumph shook the Sports Bar from end to end and the celebrations began.

Any reasonable woman, Eugene reflected later, would have understood. Would have heard the match report on TV and deduced the obvious; and, anyway, Ralph had sent his wife a text: 'HISTORIC VICTORY – V. CLOSE AN NERVES SHREDED. CELBRG WTH E! MGHT B LTE. LVE U XXXXX.' So everything should have been cool. And it wasn't that late – about 1.15 a.m. – when the Puma strolled into Crouch End. 'Come on, bro,' Ralph said. 'It's a night to remember, come in – only half an hour – I'll make coffee. Come on, friend, tonight is something special.'

They went up to the house arm in arm, trying to be quiet but failing. Then Ralph couldn't remember which key for the deadlock on the front door. Giggling and telling each other to 'keep it down', Ralph dropped the keys and lost them. Then the door swung open and the shouting started.

Belinda hadn't gone to bed. She had expected Ralph's return midnight at latest and whiled away the time reading and swallowing glass after glass of wine. When the bottle finished she hit the brandy – brought back from Cyprus last year and still unopened. Shortly after, she began poring over mobile-phone bills and Ralph's credit-card receipts. She tried to call him, but just got voicemail. What the fuck was he doing?

Eugene said his goodbyes on the doorstep and made a run for the Puma. Why, oh, fuckin why, couldn't the woman loosen up? Eugene was astounded at the amount of crap Ralph took from Belinda. Couldn't understand for the life of him why his star boy put up with the amount of grief he got. Anyway, as Eugene saw it – you win some you lose some. After his team's historic and heroic victory he had nothing to complain about. So Ralph had got lassoed by the missus at the last minute – but all in all it had been a good night.

With the Halcyenda party ahead, Eugene planned to take it easy on Saturday afternoon, to enjoy a bit of peace and quiet. On Saturdays the house was empty. Gladys out shopping, Simone ditto, or round her girlfriends'. The Mini-monster at the Buzzi Bee Centre – he went every Saturday, one till five. The Buzzi Bee was part of the Islington 'Special People Have Special Needs' project. With a ratio of one staff member per child, on-site swimming pool, computers a go-go and a refreshing 'best that money can buy' approach to facilities, the Buzzi Bee was the focus of some local resentment.

But the Council never wavered. They appointed a press and public liaison officer to help journalists and residents alike understand the importance of 'support services for children with underdeveloped social skills and/or pathological impulses'. At Buzzi Bee, the tiny would-be serial killers were expertly assessed and encouraged. Some small psychopaths showed marked behavioural improvement. Some did not. Nero had been allocated a place eighteen months previously. Shortly after he'd tried to strangle the little girl at school.

When the gladsome news had come through, Gladys, Simone and Eugene were, frankly, euphoric. As far as the Burnsides were concerned, the Buzzi Bee Centre was worth every penny of council taxpayers' money. And cheap at twice the price. Every Saturday – four hours – entirely Nero-free. It was a gift from God.

So Eugene spent the afternoon half dozing, half watching telly. Quite good, he thought – the History of Britain, BBC Knowledge. All about the rivalry between Mary Queen of Scots and Elizabeth I. One of them had finished up murdering the other, but he didn't know which. He'd fallen asleep and missed a big chunk at the end. Hadn't woken up till gone seven-thirty, when his mum knocked on the door with a cup of tea. Eugene had promised Gladys that he would show himself before setting off for the party. 'Me and Moira want a bit of a twirl,' she'd told him.

Gladys and Moira. For more than ten years it'd been a Saturday-night ritual. Around sevenish – tap, tap on the door – and there was Moira. Bottle of Bell's whisky in one hand, forty Superking Black in the other.

They would settle at the kitchen table, kicking off with a cup of tea apiece, but fooling no one. After half an hour the whisky came out and the music started. The two of them would sit for hours, drinking and laughing. Talking over news and scandal and what was happening family-wise. Singing along and remembering the old days.

It had gone nine-thirty, and 'Tears of a Clown' was playing in the kitchen, Moira and Gladys both following word for word. Eugene's yells went unheard until a bellow of 'MUM!!' stopped Gladys's finger-clicking crooning. Apologizing to Moira, Gladys headed upstairs to tend to her son. Eugene was in a state. He'd been trying to shave for nigh on twenty minutes, but it was no good. He was shaking too much. He knew that if he didn't pack it in his chin would be slashed to bits. It was a miracle he hadn't drawn blood so far.

A mass of foam from nose to chin, Eugene was desperate for help. Gladys pushed him in the bathroom, picked up the razor and took charge. She sat the boy on the laundry basket, tied a towel round his neck, and set to. She had the job done in minutes. Eugene could have screentested for the next Wilkinson Sword ad.

Just before half-past ten, groomed and ready, Eugene came into the kitchen to say goodbye.

'Look at him, Moira,' said his mum. 'Just look at the boy. You look top notch, my son. You look the full ticket.'

Moira nodded. 'So he does, Gladys. He looks the business and no denying. Turn around, Eugene lad. Let me see the back of you.'

'Auntie Moira . . .' Eugene began, but obediently spun around nonetheless. Gladys told him to stand still whilst she got a tissue to clean the shaving-cream blob she'd missed behind his ear. Moira twitched imaginary threads and hairs from the suit. Then they both stood back for the full effect. 'You'll do, my boy,' said Gladys. 'You think, Moira?'

The Irishwoman nodded emphatically. 'He'll do, Gladys. And I doubt you'll find many better.' And wasn't that the truth?

'Go on, my boy,' said Gladys. 'And be careful driving, and

mind your manners with these rich friends. Let them know you've been brought up properly.'

'Bye, Mum,' said Eugene, kissing her. 'Bye, Auntie Moira. Come on, a kiss for luck. I might be late, mum, so don't wait up. Have a good night, you two – oh – and make sure you behave yourselves. I know what you get like on the drink.' Eugene skipped out the front door before they could make a grab for him.

Moira had been in and out the house since Eugene was old enough to remember. Jimmy and Moira Haley came to live next door three months after the Burnsides arrived in Wentworth Road, bringing with them the three Haley daughters – all teenagers: Gráinne, Caitlin and Siobhan. Moira had been just seventeen when she got caught with Gráinne.

The Haley girls were fascinated by the little Burnsides. They spoiled, cuddled and played with them. Gave Eugene the status of adored baby brother, and treated Simone like a tiny princess. The Burnside toddlers loved it, happily lapping up the endless attention and praise. Gladys was forever fetching her children back from next door; 'Wanna go 'Ay-ees',' was their endless whining refrain. Within a year the sisters were babysitting on Friday nights. Liberated from responsibility and worry, Gladys put on her tight dresses, did her make-up, and with her husband's arm around her waist, was off down the dance hall. After a while Jimmy and Moira began to join them – they went out dancing, or for a drink. When the men were feeling flush it was a meal with a bottle of wine. Midweek they'd go to the pictures. Eventually, the two families spent more time together than apart.

So when Eugene's dad got sick, the Haleys were there to lend a hand. The last two weeks – his father lying in agony on the front-room sofa, a skeleton wearing a nappy and pyjamas. His dad. When he died Eugene helped his mum prepare the body. Fetched the clean clothes she'd got pressed

and ready for him. Lifted his dad's hips and shoulders as his
mum got him properly dressed. So his dad was all ready for
when the funeral people came. His mum said his dad
would've been proud. At night, sleepless and crying into
her pillow, Gladys would hear it, 'Daddy, Daddy, Daddy,
Daddy, don't leave me, Daddy, come back, Daddy, come
back.' And she'd go in to her son, a teenager, already near
on six foot, his face wet with tears, curled on the bed,
begging his father not to go away.

About two weeks after they buried his dad, Jimmy Haley
had called round to ask if Eugene was interested in the
football. After that, Jimmy was there every other Saturday to
take the boy down the Arsenal. Walking back from the
match, Jimmy usually nipped into the Roger Casement Club
for 'a quick one'. Eugene was allowed a half of lager, and
Jimmy would talk about how they'd be in serious trouble if
they got found out. 'Best keep this between ourselves,' he'd
say, adding how there was 'no need to mention anything to
the women folk'. It was all nonsense, but Eugene had loved
it – and when Jimmy introduced him to acquaintances in the
bar: 'Like you to meet a pal of mine,' he'd say. 'Eugene
Burnside, Jean-Baptiste's son. You remember Jonny? Great
friend of mine. Very great friend of mine.'

Eugene felt proud of his father. And proud that he was
Jimmy's friend, just like his dad had been.

Jimmy Haley had a heart attack at work a month before
Eugene's fifteenth birthday. Eugene sat with Simone and the
three Haley girls for the funeral mass. They all held hands,
and he'd been embarrassed, but when Caitlin felt him pull
away, she'd let go. He grabbed her hand back and kept hold.
And held on all the way. Even when they walked out first
behind the coffin, and everyone was looking – Simone,
Siobhan, tall Graínne, Caitlin and Eugene – hand in hand at
slow march, unwavering. Still in step up to the very hearse.

And his mother and Moira all in black. The two widows,
side by side. Watching as the shovels of earth rattled down

on the coffin. 'Dust we are. And to dust we shall return,' said the priest on Ash Wednesday. 'Man that is born of woman is few of days, and full of trouble. He cometh forth like a flower and is cut down: he fleeth also as a shadow and continueth not.' The priest said that at both the funerals – Jimmy's and his dad's. 'And God shall wipe away all tears from their eyes,' he'd said, 'and there shall be no more death, neither sorrow, nor crying, neither shall there be any more pain.' The first time – come on, he was only thirteen – Eugene had half bought it. Standing in the winter sleet by Jimmy Haley's grave he knew different. Bollocks, man. Pure bollocks.

They could say what they liked about resurrection and eternal life – it made his mum feel better, so why not. But Eugene was crystal clear on one point – his father and Jimmy Haley were gone, and they wouldn't be back any time soon. He'd just have to get used to it. And besides, he had responsibilities now. He was the man of the family, both families, if you liked. He needed to make money.

And he was proud of the way he looked after them all. Proud of how he did stuff and got things sorted. That showed bottle, the way he'd shouldered the weight.

It kept Eugene warm, the glow of unselfish love and bright virtue. The way he took care of the women. Jesus, the Haley girls were all married now. Kids and the lot. They still rang him though. And if ever real trouble came, it was Eugene they turned to. He knew it. Encouraged it. That time he'd driven through the night with Moira and the girls. London to Glasgow – the Puma racing flat out, flying through the dark down the endless miles. Dropped everything in an instant he had. Got them to the hospital forty minutes before the end, in time for Moira to see her sister and say good-bye. 'No one else would have done it,' said Moira. 'No one else could have done it – only Eugene.' All the Haleys – Scottish branch included – said Eugene was a hero. Gladys radiated pride. 'Just what your father would have done,' she told him.

Eugene held on to the thanks and praise. Hung on very tight, because it made it better. In his desolate hours, playing on the Web, flicking through the channels, alone in his room – the whole house asleep – he felt it drawing near, the creeping panic closing in. He would debate about another line, OK, it was gone five, he should have a joint and get to bed. But it would be better if he took a line, then had the joint with a sleeping tab, because the coke would lift him up – it would all be OK again. Then he could be in bed before the panic came back. He'd be up and running – as in asleep and unconscious – before it had a chance to get a proper grip.

And ninety-nine times out of a hundred, that's what he would do. And the coke would give him a buzz, and he'd mess around on the Web some more, or maybe put on a tune, or watch more cable. Then, half an hour later, having forgotten all about bed, he'd be back to square one, sensing the darkness behind him, getting anxious. Of course, this kind of game could go on for ages.

But Eugene was aware that there was a limit. That going completely off on one wasn't an option. He had to think about his responsibilities. And about how proud his mum was and what he'd done for her. What he didn't think about, not at all, was what his father and Jimmy would have said. What their take on the Farons would have been. He didn't wonder what his dad would have thought about his son's 'job'. He already knew full well. It spoilt things.

The Saturday party wasn't Eugene's first trip to George Faron's HQ. He'd been a good half a dozen times on one sort of business or another, although he'd never seen the house itself – he'd been left waiting outside the gates until one of the boys was sent down to do the necessary. The Halcyenda stood in two acres of landscaped garden.

Ten-foot walls topped with razor wire kept outsiders outside. Waiting roadside, all you got was a three-second glimpse of Tarmacked driveway before the automatic gates swung shut. Privacy was important to the Farons.

On party night the steel gates swung open the moment the Puma's nose turned off the road, then a group of heavies, all walkie-talkies and lumpy jackets, walked across and barred his way. He'd seen a couple of the faces before. The Firm's muscle, payroll boys. Frighteners, minders, security. Very professional, capable. Eugene flicked the window down.

Two men walked across and leant up against the car. Eugene hated people touching the Puma.

'Do us a favour, off the car.' Eugene didn't know why he said it. Couldn't believe how stupid, his stomach tightening even as the words came out. The silence lasted for maybe three seconds. Then the heavies moved. 'No offence,' said one.

'Fuck me,' thought Eugene.

They asked his name. 'Geno,' he said, 'Geno B.' They got the walkie-talkies out. Seemed that someone inside was describing him. 'Yeah,' the heavies were saying. 'Puma, yeah. Uh? Right, hang on. Yeah, spot on, OK.' The static crackle died down.

'Who phoned the invite?' one security man asked.

'Talus.'

'Sound, mate,' he said. 'Go on, Geno, up the hill and park to the left. Take care, mate.'

At the top of the drive, a man in uniform took the Puma keys, and a waiter appeared with a tray of pink champagne. Glass in hand, Eugene took a deep breath and followed a winding stone path which disappeared beneath an archway entirely covered in pink and yellow blossom. He passed through and, emerging from the curtain of hanging flowers, caught his first sight of the dream house.

* * *

George Faron had bought the Halcyenda two years previously. It was an engagement present – a declaration of love, a fairy castle for his queen. The place had cost millions, but that was as it should be. Nothing but the best for his Gloria.

George met the love of his life at a charity dinner. Tickets a grand apiece, proceeds to Comeback, an outfit allegedly dedicated to the care of disabled ex-boxers. Al Acrasiafi was honorary treasurer of Comeback and also the Firm's senior lawyer. He introduced George to his only child. 'This is my little girl, Gloria.'

The moment he saw her, George was lost – couldn't eat a mouthful at dinner, barely uttered a word. He couldn't stop looking at her.

George Faron said it was love at first sight. The minute he saw her he knew. She was the one. And eighteen months of marriage had changed nothing. For George, the sun rose and set in Gloria's dark eyes. All the women in the world were garbage next to his Gloria. His heart and soul, buried deep for so many years, came clambering out into the light.

George was clumsy – it was all a bit new and difficult, loving someone. So he floundered around and made mistakes. Said and did embarrassing things. But if his dance of love was lacking finesse, it was more than redeemed by sincere passion.

Gloria found his efforts sweet and entertaining. And OK, he was a bit of a lump, not dead porky, but love handles and slightly flabby. And she knew he dyed his hair, and so did every other fucker, because no one, but no one, had blue black hair. But never mind. She could have done a lot worse. He treated her like royalty and he had money – real, serious money – and she was fond of him. In fact, increasingly, she surprised herself, because she really had a soft spot for George. She stopped taking the piss out of him in front of her girlfriends. He didn't deserve that. She'd become quite protective of him. Because, as she told her girlfriends, she saw the other side of George, the vulnerable, private side. He was a big teddy, she said, trying to be a growly bear, but inside, all sweet and cuddly. Most people listening to this would have said Gloria was off her trolley. But that was the whole point. George Faron didn't give a fuck for most people. He would have cheerfully laid down his life for Gloria. 'My Queen,' he called her; and meant it.

It was a mark of her genuine feelings that in the main Gloria had been faithful to her husband – that and the practical difficulties involved. Marrying a Faron turned adultery into a very high-risk venture – potential lovers tended, she found, to lose their nerve.

Gloria liked escaping from the all-encompassing Faron empire and the attendant restrictions, so she took a lot of holidays. Abroad she could be just another anonymous rich person. While George was tied up with business she headed off to the Caribbean, South Africa, the Seychelles. She always went with a girlfriend, usually Sandy. The two of them got on really well, had the same outlook, liked the same kind of things.

George was happy enough. He knew he could trust Sandra to take care of his Glor. She was a Faron was Sandra, his and Archie's cousin. And since two years past – lovely civil ceremony at Westminster Reg; all the footballers go there – Sandra was also Mrs Gerald Talus. Roots didn't go any deeper. No – George didn't fret at all. Put the two girls in five-star suites. First-class flights. Platinum Amex and spare cash. 'Just relax and really enjoy yourself, sweetheart. I'll be waiting for you.' And wherever she went, his Gloria, even the arse end of third world nowhere, she always managed to phone him to say goodnight. Saying how much she was missing her big man, blowing kisses down the line.

Eugene had heard about Gloria, heard plenty, but he'd never seen her. He'd never seen a house like the Halcyenda either. Like a sugar castle, it was, all in white with towers and turrets and balconies, and climbing vines twisting elegantly up the walls. All around were pink and gold Chinese lanterns, lighting the terraced gardens and encircling a large sunken pond. Strings of golden fairy-lights marked out the pathways and led directly to the house. The doors were open and, inside, Eugene could see a woman with long dark hair. As he approached she turned and smiled at him. 'Thanks for coming,' she said. 'You must be Geno? Yes, I thought so. Well, come inside and enjoy the fun. And I must introduce myself.' Her backless gold dress clung and shimmered as she moved. Eugene knew it. It had to be her. He tried to drag his eyes away from her body, but it was a real battle. Especially when she came so close. The woman smiled again. 'I'm Gloria Faron,' she said. 'George's wife.'

Half an hour later, Eugene was starting to sweat. Gloria had taken him to see George. After a brief chat, George had been called away, and Gloria had stuck with Eugene. She'd shown him round the gardens, they'd inspected the swimming pool, the Jacuzzi, the sunken pond and koi carp. She'd steered him round the buffet and ordered and re-ordered champagne cocktails for two. Finally Eugene found himself inside the conservatory.

The conservatory was huge and kept at tropical heat. Lush, broad-leafed plants, shiny and turgid, ranged across the glass walls. Monster ferns waved like ostrich plumes, strange flowers gave out musky odours, and exotic orchids in brilliant colours hung from their trellises. The atmosphere was full of moisture and drenched with heavy scents. Eugene felt almost faint, gulping air like he was under water. Gloria Faron's gold dress shrank in the damp air, clinging to her, semi-transparent and soaking. She was leaning into him as they walked. Eugene could feel her body, tight and hot, curving into him, hip riding against him, her breast just touching his arm. He was half erect already, and ready to go all the way at any second. She was beautiful, and so, so sexy.

Like Arsenal's heroic goalie, Eugene's sense of self-preservation pulled off a miracle save. Even as he leant his body against her, as his hand began to stroke her bum – Jesus, she was gorgeous – even as he ran his hands over her buttocks, it started. Getting louder all the time. Refusing to go away. 'She's Gloria FARON,' the inner voice was shouting. 'Gloria FARON, you idiot. George Faron's wife. Get away from her – get the fuck away from her. Now, Eugene. Stop now. Cos any minute someone's going to see you.' The voice got louder. 'And then you're dead meat. Leave her, you fool. Move it, boy. Now, please, you're running out of time, for Christ's sake, NOW!' Eugene stopped dead on the path. He disengaged and moved away from her.

'It's a bit hot for me in here,' he said. 'Let's go back to the party and see what's happening.' He sounded like a wanker and he knew it.

Gloria smiled, standing in front of him, hands on hips, 'What's a matter Geno? Lost your bottle?'

'Something like that,' Eugene answered, and opened the conservatory door to let her pass.

Gloria was far too clever and classy to bear a grudge. Back inside the house she gave Eugene a wink and a smile and disappeared. He felt relieved – very relieved. But, Jesus – you just knew she'd be red hot in bed. The way she rolled her bum as she walked. Fantastic tits as well. Eugene shook his head. Forget her, he told himself. Shagging Gloria Faron was suicide. Guaranteed. Come on, he decided, time to enjoy the party.

Eugene discovered that aside from the buffet and a gaggle of old boys playing on the snooker tables, the party revolved around two main locations. First off there was the ballroom: acres of parquet floor, crystal chandeliers and a live band up on stage. The band wore bootlace ties and played a mixture of country and western, Irish folk and the usual popular requests. The first Abba cover encouraged a mass outbreak of deeply dodgy dancing, but Eugene acknowledged the musicians were real class at what they did – which was to be expected, Eugene thought, cos they'd hardly be playing the Halcyenda if they were your usual pub crap.

The alternative to ballroom bliss was the 'salon'. Lit by candles and furnished with chaises longues and padded armchairs, the salon had a small dance floor, 'romantic' music provided by a self-effacing DJ and lots of snogging, groping couples. Eugene spotted a few of the Boys lurking – waiting to move in on some silly bird when she was too drunk to resist. A couple of the lads saw him and waved. He waved back but didn't stop.

Back in the ballroom the band had been replaced by another, flasher DJ, and the music had moved up-tempo. The floor was absolutely heaving. Eugene avoided the entire scene. He hated drunken free-for-alls. Why didn't they just sit down, girls who couldn't dance? They must know it: you either can or you can't. What – for fuck's sake – makes them think that getting totally smashed on Bacardi Breezers will change anything? It won't. It just makes it all much worse. From the sidelines he could see them at it. Legs splayed, hips rotating, breasts pushed out. It was meant to be dead sexy, but it was just dead stupid. He found it painful to watch. In truth he almost felt sorry for the silly cows.

Anyway, he hadn't come here to dance. Eugene had other fish to fry. It took a good while to fight his way around the throng before he found him. Standing unnoticed in the far corner of the room, watching the dance floor. The man Eugene wanted to see. Before setting off, Eugene had promised himself he wouldn't duck out. He'd thought it through time and again. The party offered an opportunity, and Eugene was determined that if the chance came, well, he would go for it. And opportunity had knocked. There he was – no mistaking. Eugene flexed his shoulders then, chin up and face purposefully blank, he walked across.

Talus watched him all the way. He'd been waiting for the

boy to make a move. Seen him arrive, seen Gloria latch on. Only to be expected. Gloria had a thing about black men, she did. And by any standards, Geno was a looker. Talus knew she'd make a play, no question about it – he'd seen it all before. More than once. What he wanted to see was how the boy behaved himself. Because he had plans for Geno B. Talent should be recognized and rewarded, was the way he looked at things.

So unbeknownst to Eugene, Talus had watched, and watched closely, every second he'd spent in Gloria's company. Talus thought the boy had done well. George Faron thought his wife was utterly loyal and faithful beyond compare. Talus knew different. He had Gloria's measure: BMW she was – Black Man's Woman. That's why the dirty cow was always on holiday, and why she was so bloody keen on Africa and the Caribbean. Sandra had filled him in. The entire script in Technicolor detail: Gloria's holiday fun.

In the near future he was going to have a word with Mrs Gloria Faron – a word to the wise. Explain exactly what kind of conduct was expected of George Faron's wife. But for the minute he had other fish to fry. Talus looked up as Eugene approached, and smiled.

'Geno, just the man I want.' He snapped his fingers in the face of a passing waiter. 'You – yeah, you. Kir royale – OK for you, Geno? Good. Two kirs, got it? I want them back here in one minute, yeah? So shift it.' The waiter shot away and Eugene moved alongside Talus.

'I want to ask a favour,' Eugene said.

Talus grinned. 'Ask away, my son,' he said. 'Ask away.'

Eugene knew what he wanted to say. Had rehearsed the whole thing. He paused as the hyperventilating waiter returned, took his drink and said his piece. Talus sipped his kir and said nothing. Eugene did likewise. He had to keep his cool. If he got knock-back, well, so be it. Babbling nervous rubbish wasn't going to help his case. And at least he'd had a shot at it. Who dares wins, faint heart never won sod all – and all of that.

Eugene was six foot two. Gerry Talus was probably an inch shorter but stockier in build. Six or seven years older than Eugene, he carried heavy muscle. Serious muscle, not wanky stuff from the gym, but the real McCoy, earned from years of grafting and frequent violence. Talus kept his red-gold hair short. Tried to cut the curls before they could really get going. The colour was beautiful. 'A girl would die for that hair,' his wife would say. But never mind the red-gold curls. The thing people always remembered, anyone who met him, was always the same. It was the eyes. Jesus, God, those eyes. They were turquoise. Not blue, not green, but clear and true and dazzling aquamarine. Beautiful eyes and beautiful hair, and the face of a psychopath.

Halfway down the kir, Talus broke silence. He looked up – a brief half-smile showing the small, square teeth. 'I think you're talking sense, my son,' he said softly. 'I think we might well go with that – once we've had a bit of a chat. Ring me Monday, about three o'clock. Sorted, yeah.'

Eugene took the hint. 'Three, Monday. Sorted,' he said. And still holding half the kir, he headed across the dance floor. Eugene had no intention of trying to pull. The Halcyenda party was all about work and opportunities to do better. Being noticed by George, dredging up the confidence to take his chance with Talus; even just putting his face about with the people who mattered. That was the point of it all. Normal party stuff – drinking, dancing, finding a half-decent girl to shag – it hadn't even crossed his mind. And by the time the pitch to Talus was done, it was near two in the morning. Trouble was the success of his Talus encounter had left him totally buzzing and high as a kite. He intended to wait ten minutes or so and then start making his goodbyes. In the meantime he grabbed another glass of champagne and strolled back to watch the dance floor.

Halcyenda parties always offered plenty of pretty girls, and the dance floor certainly had its share, but even so she stood out. She really did. In more ways than one. She was a Liz Hurley lookalike, thought Eugene. Long glossy red-brown hair, big green eyes and long dark lashes. Fantastic tits, nipples pointing skyward – you could tell because the girl had no bra, just a virtually see-through white halterneck dress. A dress which finished a good inch below her bum. Eugene wondered if the tits were real. Surely real never looked so firm and bouncy? She was dancing to Bryan Ferry – 'Love is the Drug' – and she could move, which made a change. She turned round, caught him looking and looked straight back.

With a big come-on smile. He didn't need asking twice.

After two more songs Eugene knew the girl's name was Lucy and they were going back to her place. Ten minutes later they left.

Lucy was drunk and the fresh air made her giggle and stagger on her heels. Eugene hoped she'd sober up – if she was sick in the Puma she was out the car and on her own, no joke. He had to help her get in and fasten her seatbelt. If the worst came to it, he could always dump her on her doorstep and do a runner.

Within five minutes the Puma was back on home turf, cruising down the Holloway Road, heading for Lucy's Islington flat. Eugene was concentrating on the road, only saw him out the corner of his eye, but that was all he needed. He reacted without thinking – throwing the Puma across the road and shooting after him. The Puma shot down the maze of narrow sideroads in a mad, reckless pursuit, leaping over junctions and careering through the turns and bends.

It was to no avail. The man had vanished. Eugene couldn't be sure. It was dark and late and he'd had a bit to drink. But he was almost certain that the guy with the hoodie, the guy who'd veered off, almost like he knew Eugene was there, turned off the road and just vanished – Eugene was positive that the man he'd seen walking down the Holloway Road, well, if it wasn't Carl – the Minimonster's father, the invisible man – well, if it wasn't him, it must have been his twin brother.

CHAPTER FIVE

Thus when she had his eyes and senses fed
With false delights, and fild with pleasures vaine,
Into a shadie dale she soft him led,
And laid him downe vpon a grassie plaine;
And her sweet selfe without dread, or disdaine,
She set beside, laying his head disarm'd
In her loose lap.

FQ: The Legend of Sir Gvyon; The Bowre of Blisse: II.vi.14

Eugene's handbrake-turn, tyre-burning pursuit of the phantom Carl seriously impressed Lucy. Prior to all the excitement she'd been dead to the world, swinging comatose in her seatbelt. As the Puma leapt into action, Lucy was flung sideways, cracking her head on the window. She snapped awake and perked up immediately. Eugene could hear her yelping and whooping as they careered round the dark sidestreets. Twice he caught the flick of a long coat and thought he'd got him. But although the Puma sped with cat-like agility down the narrow backstreets, they never closed on their quarry. The man – whoever he was – had melted into the darkness.

Eventually Eugene gave up the ghost, and the Puma turned back on to the Holloway Road, headed for Islington.

Lucy was on fast-forward and talking non-stop. Eugene was surprised at the posh accent – it was the first time he'd really heard her speak.

'You're mad, d'ya know? No joking, you are seriously crazy. I mean I thought I was dead. Like really I did. I thought I'd bought it, seriously, like – you know, when you pulled that one. Cool stunt or what? And right across the fucking Holloway Road, like suddenly you were in some Hollywood skit, you know, big car-chase scene.' Lucy was laughing, 'Wow,' she went on. 'I mean, that was beyond amazing and madder than most mad. Oh! Left, left, left, sorry wasn't paying attention.'

The Puma screamed in outrage as Eugene threw a lurching left turn. Lucy gave a contrite shrug. 'I know, I know. Stop the rattling and look where you're going, girl. Eyes shut, mouth open, that's me. Can't keep quiet, that's my trouble, but you know – oh, oh, hang on, next left, I think, no, next but one, here, here, here.'

Lucy lived close to Highbury Corner, on a tree-lined serpentine road full of sleeping policemen. Edwardian villas stood either side, each with an imposingly ornate door-way atop flights of balustraded marble steps. The marble gleamed soft and cold under the moonlight. Eugene was surprised a second time. What with the tiny dress and easy-lay behaviour, he'd had her for a slapper.

There were hundreds of them – gangster groupies, nameless and interchangeable girls. They were models, or so they said. 'Glamour' models mostly. Teenagers with big bouncy tits, in tiny dresses and five-inch stilettos. Raucous loud girls from nightmare backgrounds, the cocky gobshite daughters of teenage mothers and disappearing dads. Seventeen-year-olds gobbling up the free drugs, the champagne and cocktails, thrilled to be in the orbit of all that power and money.

Eugene couldn't get enough of them at first. He couldn't believe how easy it all was. And initially he'd been shocked by their cheerful lack of self-respect. Get them in bed – or in a carpark or a nightclub toilet – and they'd do anything: threesomes, up the bum, porno-photo poses – anything at all. The shock wore off, slowly replaced by disinterest. Eugene had shagged enough to last a lifetime – nowadays, he left the Firm's parties mostly sober and alone. And he knew his restraint had not passed unnoticed. It was important. Self-possession, control – it all spoke volumes. The boy had class.

And he had fully intended going home alone from the Halcyenda party. Naturally the girls invited to George Faron's private dos were miles above the blonde-hair-big-tits lookalikes wheeled out for the Firm rank and file. For the Halcyenda, it was actresses and catwalk merchants, sleek and shiny with hair like silk and designer gear. But basically desperadoes all the same.

To tell the truth Eugene couldn't really remember how he'd ended up dancing with Lucy or why he'd picked her up. The last hour had been a bit of a blur. He should have left earlier. Should have gone home. Anyway it was too late now. And it could have been worse. The girl was gorgeous, no denying it.

Eugene followed Lucy up to the flat. It must have been gone 3 a.m., but there was no stopping her. Talking at the top of her voice all the way. He bet the neighbours just loved her. Inside her flat and she was still babbling on about the roof terrace she'd show him some time and how she loved being high up, cos the views were so great, and how she wanted to do loads of work on the place but hadn't got around to it. Eugene said nothing – there wasn't much point.

After running around the kitchen Lucy emerged with two glasses. 'There you go. My own recipe. You'll love it, everyone does. I call it Juicy Lucy. Look, relax, put on a tune, whatever you feel like. I'm going to change.' She blew him a kiss. 'Back soon, promise.'

Left alone Eugene took stock of the place. Victorian

mirrors in ornate gilt frames were on every wall, their shadowed depths reflecting in infinity the green and gold fairy lights which curled vine-like around various objects before flowing into a flickering pool of light beside the marble fireplace.

He shouted through to ask Lucy for the bathroom. It was up on the second floor. It was a huge flat. Like a tardis, Eugene thought. Bigger inside than out. And the layout was deceptive – he got lost coming back from the bathroom and almost fell down the stairs, catching himself just in time. When he found his way back to Lucy she was smoking a joint. 'Where've you been?' she said. 'I've missed you.'

Eugene woke up in a tangle of silky sheets and underwear. Lucy sprawled next to him, still sleeping. He felt like absolute shit, but it had definitely been worth it. He started to extricate himself from the bed and winced. What the fuck happened to his wrists? Bruises and friction marks. What had she done? He couldn't remember. The drink and drugs had reduced most of the night to a euphoric blur.

Eugene stumbled around trying to find the bathroom again, opening doors and tripping over rugs and discarded clothes. He felt like he was dying – hungover, exhausted, aching and sore as hell. Even so, the legs were the worst – it hurt just to walk. The shower, when he found it, helped a bit, but not much. Putting on last night's clothes didn't improve matters. His suit was fucked, a screwed-up raggy heap which had somehow ended up under the bed. As he scrabbled about on the floor retrieving jacket and trousers, Lucy sat up, yawning and stretching.

He was almost dressed before she spoke. 'What you doing?' she'd said. 'Don't run off and leave me, come back to bed. Come on, just for a while.'

Eugene tried to explain – about his mum, Sunday dinner, family – all that. Lucy listened, shrugged and picked up her tiny mobile. 'Bye, then,' she said and blew him a kiss. Eugene said he'd phone her. 'Fine,' she said. Not angry, not hurt, not interested. She was chattering down the phone before he was out of the bedroom.

The Puma was loping towards home when the mobile rang. Eugene knew who it was . . . 'Yeah. I know, great, Mum. Don't worry. Home in five minutes, at most. Love you – OK?' The Puma picked up speed in earnest.

Gladys was smiling, her son's confident voice chasing away the worries. She knew it was foolish but she fretted over her boy. Couldn't really settle when he was out and about, however big and strong he was. Gladys smiled. Her boy, what mother could wish for a better son?

She was turning down the oven when Simone shouted, 'Mum! Mum! Quick, come on. It's another murder, Mum. Oh, Jesus, it's round here again. Come on, before you miss it.' Gladys straightened up and ran through to the sitting room.

The three of them sat side by side in silence. Gladys, Simone and Nero, lined up on the sofa as the TV news cameras tight-focused on DCI Arthur Gale. The policeman wore a dark suit and a black tie – which Gladys thought was a gesture of respect.

Eugene walked into an empty kitchen. Moving through the hallway, he saw them – the whole family struck dumb, staring at the TV. Like they were hypnotized or something – even the Minimonster – rapt, silent and unmoving. 'Shush,' said Simone before Eugene had time to open his mouth. 'Another murder, found her just down the road.' Eugene nodded and took his place on the arm of the sofa. Four of them now, quiet and attentive as the policeman explained the details of desecration.

She'd been killed on Saturday night or early Sunday morning. Police were still waiting for the precise time of death. She was fifteen years old and had lived in care for nine years. Her name was Amy Fiddeler and she had convictions for drugs and shoplifting. The police wanted to talk to anyone who'd been around Peter Pan Park between 11 p.m. Saturday and 3 a.m. Sunday.

'Why,' said Eugene. 'What's the park got to do with it?'

'You missed it,' said Simone. 'That's where they found the body. They think that's where it happened. In the middle, by the slide.'

'Jesus.' Eugene couldn't quite take it in. 'When, what time did he do her?'

'You heard, man.' Simone rolled her eyes. 'They want people around there from eleven to three. Odds on, she caught it late on, like two or three in the morning. No one around, you know.'

Eugene was early to bed that night. He was exhausted. Desperate to sleep. Really, *really* tired.

He couldn't remember falling asleep, but he knew all about it when it came to waking up. Eugene awoke in terror some time in the early hours. He'd had a nightmare. A real shocker.

He dreamt he was driving the Puma. Hunting for Carl off the Holloway Road. And the streets growing darker and narrower. And in the dream he could feel the fear inside him growing like fungus. Then he was out of the Puma – why the hell did he get out of the car? The Puma was safe, he shouldn't have left the car. He was trapped now. Couldn't get away from the footsteps which were coming closer by the second. He started running. He knew they mustn't see him. So he sprinted down the dark streets. Went through the little wrought-iron gate at full stretch and threw himself sideways. Now he lay on his belly behind a small grassy rise, camouflaged beneath the dense shrubs. He was totally hidden but able to see out beyond the shrubbery, to see the asphalt circle and the slide and swings. He could see the crappy statues of Wendy in her nightdress, Captain Hook and the crocodile and, bang in the middle, perched up on a plinth, was the lost boy himself – Peter Pan in his very own park. Eugene could hear the footsteps. They were coming.

Eugene could vaguely sense his conscious mind. A distant voice urging him to wake up. Telling him he didn't need to be a witness. Arguing that there was no need to get involved. And he could hear the tearing of fabric, the whispered obscenities. He heard the snap when they broke her arms.

They didn't hurry. Eugene could not look away. He watched it all. But somehow, he never quite saw their faces. Just backs and shoulders and hands. Especially hands, hands up to unspeakable things. He thought it would go on for ever.

Eventually the screaming stopped, and then he saw she was nearly dead, her struggles reduced to agonized twitches. When the two men gathered up their tools and left her, she was no longer human. A mess of blood and slime. A heap of glistening offal spreading over the asphalt.

Eugene was thrashing with panic when he woke up – the sheets were soaked with sweat. It took him a good half an hour to get everything cleaned up.

Talus suggested they meet 5 p.m. Monday; Eugene said fine. It would be the usual venue. The King's Head belonged to the Farons. A scruffy pub on the Caledonian Road, the King's was what you might call a non-profit-making enterprise. The place was a dump. Green leather bench seats round the walls, tatty wooden tables, wobbly stools in threadbare Draylon. A pool table at the far end, and fuzzy satellite sports endlessly on the telly. The entire shebang covered in a layer of seamless grime. It's almost like someone has sprayed the place, Eugene thought. Blasted the entire King's Head interior with polyurethane, non-chip, non-removable grime. Guaranteed to last and last.

Vinnie, the King's landlord, wasn't in the Firm as such. He was more like an aged retainer, pensioned off after years of faithful service to the Farons' cause. Eugene heard tales of how Vinnie'd done a lengthy stretch years back, and how he'd kept his mouth well shut: kept important names to himself; stood alone in the dock; and taken ten years straight on the chin.

The Brothers had rewarded him with a pension – a lifelong sinecure as Mine Host of the King's. Vinnie was probably knocking sixty now, and as dirty and dilapidated as the pub. He had made a career of discretion, and the Farons trusted him. Gerry Talus regarded Vinnie as 'staunch', the Victoria Cross of crim accolades. Indeed, Vinnie was the only living recipient of the Talus 'staunch' award, which tended to be bestowed posthumously.

The Farons cared nothing for the pub's turnover, profit margins or annual takings. The King's Head was a useful asset in the running of Firm business – the last thing the Farons wanted were customers. This suited Vinnie well enough. He was a solitary soul, sullen and sour-tempered.

Vinnie lived alone above the pub – he'd never been married, never had a girlfriend. Wasn't interested. But Vinnie wasn't gay, not in any sense of the word. You could tell a mile off that Vinnie had no truck whatsoever with tight T-shirts, poppers and mutual masturbation.

Vinnie was one of the old school. He'd been around for donkey's, had known Old Man Faron and dandled baby George on his knee. He still had a soft spot for George – and if the Farons came in the pub, his tight-lipped grimace lifted slightly. He treated the rest of the Firm's boys with contempt – excepting Talus: Vinnie was always polite to Talus. Vinnie knew about Talus, knew more than enough.

Talus and Eugene settled at a table by the back wall whilst Vinnie set things up. First he closed the curtains. Job done, he locked the pub doors and shut off the lights above the bar. Then Vinnie disappeared out of earshot and out of sight. He'd come back only if called. 'That's a good man, Geno,' Talus said suddenly. 'He's solid. One hundred per cent. A good man is Vinnie.'

95

Eugene nodded. 'Sound,' he said. 'Like you said, solid, all the way.'

'Loyalty, Geno. Rare commodity.' Talus was checking his mobile messages as he spoke. Eugene said nothing. Finally, Talus sat back, jewel-coloured eyes looking straight at Eugene. 'So Geno,' he said. 'Why don't you tell me all about it?'

Eugene kept it short. Outlined the Nottingham set-up, ran through the names involved, the quantities, expected profits. He spoke with confidence, handled questions with authority. 'I think it's a goer,' Talus said eventually. 'But first off I want to check it out myself. Tell your friends in the North you and me will be paying them a social visit later on this week, so we can all get to know each other.'

'Sorted,' Eugene replied.

He got straight on the case the minute they left the King's. Put in some serious effort and arranged it all. On Thursday Eugene drove Talus to Nottingham and the two of them spent a very rewarding afternoon. It had all gone smooth as silk, and the deal got the final OK. Talus bought Sandra a present of Nottingham lace.

Next thing the Puma was skipping home back down the M1. Staying in style – ice-cool Geno B. clear on your screen. He'd come so far so fast and couldn't quite believe it.

CHAPTER SIX

Her name was *Ate*, mother of debate,
And all dissention, which doth dayly grow
Amongst fraile men,

FQ: The Legend of Cambel and Telamond: IV.i.9

Friday night and Eugene was still high with triumph. April was nearly May, the trees were out and birds were singing as the Puma strolled down Crouch Hill. Eugene and Ralph usually hooked up at a local bar. But this week was different.

Ralph had called earlier and explained. Belinda was kicking off major. Sick of spending Friday alone with the telly. Couldn't Ralph cancel – just this once? Ring his lowlife friend and call it off? It was unbelievable, it really was, Belinda had said – especially after last Friday, or had he forgotten already? Ralph told Eugene she just wouldn't let it drop. 'You risked your life in that fucking car,' she said again and again. 'Your drug-dealer so-called friend could have killed you. He was wrecked. I mean, how irresponsible is he? Think about it Ralph, just think. What if a child had run out after a ball or something?'

'Belinda, it was one in the morning,' Ralph interrupted.

'Not many children about.' As he told Eugene, he was just trying to keep things in perspective.

'Come round the flat an' pick me up,' Ralph had said. 'She won't throw a wobbly in front of you. You can ring the bell, say hello, then we'll be out of there in thirty seconds max.'

Eugene didn't fancy the idea at all. 'Belinda hates me. No, no, you know it's true. If she's going to lose it, then me hanging round is exactly what you don't want. Just looking at me fucks her off. No, bro. You need to review your tactics. Can't you wait till she's cooking or something and then do a runner?'

'You my friend or am I getting confused?' Ralph said. 'I mean I'm asking for your help here. And don't tell me how to deal with my own wife – cos I think I know best on that score. Come on, my man. Nothing to it – or is it you scared of her or something?'

'Like you're not,' Eugene retorted.

'Me, scared of my own woman? You joke or what?' Ralph was indignant. 'Look, I asked a tiny favour. But I don't want to be worrying you or putting you under no stress.'

'Belinda no stress to me, star boy,' Eugene said. 'I'll pick you up nine o'clock, yeah? In and out, no hanging round.'

'My top man. No worries, Belinda's cool with it,' said Ralph.

Eugene doubted that – Belinda loathed him, although Ralph refused to acknowledge it. Eugene knew exactly what Belinda thought of him, he had heard it all before: 'Coke-head, gangsta, crackhead, junkie, streetboy, pimp, social parasite, robber, sadist, pathetic self-hater. No courage without a gun and a gang. Uneducated and vulgar. Showing off his stolen money. Screwing cheap white trash – lap-dancers, strippers. Violent lowlife scum.' It was just a crying pity she was his best friend's wife.

So, as promised, Eugene settled the Puma just off Crouch End Broadway and at ten past nine was sitting on the new sofa in Ralph's front room. Ninety minutes passed. Eugene and Ralph still hadn't moved an inch. Belinda made mango cocktails – new recipe from Mali. And they had to hear this new recording. Totally brilliant band.

Eugene thought the DVD could wait for another time. Belinda couldn't see his problem. Couldn't Eugene hang cool for half an hour? So the tunes were played and Belinda opened a bottle of wine. Eugene fidgeted, sighed and shot pissed-off meaningful looks at Ralph – who responded with helpless what-can-I-do shrugs.

When Belinda got the Scrabble board out, Eugene felt his temper going. He glanced at his watch – quarter to eleven. That was it. Enough. Selfish silly cow. It was only one night a week, but even that was too much for her.

Eugene stood up, jacket in hand. 'Are you coming, Ralph?' he said. 'We gotta move, look at the friggin' time.'

Ralph took his cue. 'Yeah, bro. Let's go, let's move it.' Grabbing his jacket, he followed Eugene to the door. Before he left, he turned to his wife. 'Belinda, please,' he said. 'I love you. You know that. Come on, baby, please. I'll be back in a couple of hours.'

Eugene heard the slap and the door slamming. 'God, she caught me a real one,' said Ralph, holding his jaw. 'Christ, she really got me. Shit, man, what's a matter with the woman?'

'They're all the same, bro,' said Eugene. 'Fuckin loopy. Let's just get out of here.'

They stayed local. The Isis was ten minutes from Ralph's and didn't shut till 2 a.m. It was a tenner on the door and drinks prices were astronomical but Eugene was cool with that. Kept the street-shite out, didn't it? If you can't afford it then fuck off. Fair enough, Eugene thought.

It was clear from the start that Ralph wasn't going to go the distance. All he could do was bang on and on about Belinda. How unreasonable she was, how difficult, how hard she'd hit him. Eugene didn't want to hear about

Ralph's marital troubles. Not tonight. Tonight Eugene had specially wanted to talk with his best bro.

Eugene was upset. The murders – both so close to home – seemed almost personal. Simone had worked with poor Stella, hadn't she? He'd met her himself. It had unnerved him somehow, and the thing about Peter Pan Park made it worse. He kept thinking about the Puma skimming flat out through the dark empty streets as Lucy laughed and shrieked encouragement. They'd shot past the park a couple of times. Eugene, obsessed with finding Carl, remembered nothing out of the ordinary. But he couldn't rid himself of the tinge of guilt. The belief that he could have saved her. That as the Puma leapt past the park railings in mad pursuit – he didn't know why but he was sure – at that moment they were in there, killer and victim. And he should have stopped because she was still alive. And he could have saved her.

He needed to talk about it. To get his head straight. Because the murders had taken over – it was everywhere and all over – murders, dead girls, sex and serial killers. Every newspaper had pages and pages on the terror stalking the capital. The murders were splashed on TV as well. And naturally enough the whole of North London could talk of little else. Eugene read every word of the crime reports. Bought all the papers, local and national, trash and posh, the lot. Police were saying that the girl under the Archway Tower wasn't the first he'd done, not by a long way.

And another thing Eugene couldn't stop thinking about was how the girls were killed. Early in the week he'd given Simone a lift home from SweetHearts. It was gone three in the morning but Gladys had videoed the latest murder prog for them. Brother and sister watched the documentary in the dark. 'Whoo! Spooky!' Simone had joked. The documentary said it looked like another Ripper was on the loose. The victims were 'obscenely mutilated'. The killer 'committed unspeakable acts of violent perversion'.

Eugene had wanted to check with Ralph about that as well. Because it had really got to him. And they never said if the girls had suffered – if he had tortured them or done the cutting and the rest of it after death. OK, Ralph wouldn't know any better than Eugene himself, but it would help to talk about it, to get it off his chest, sort of thing.

But no chance of that. Belinda had seen to that fine style. And sure enough, within half an hour of arriving, Ralph was off home. Apologizing as he gulped his drink and checked his mobie for the umpteenth time. 'She hasn't rung. Fuck, Eugene. What's going on with her?'

'Go home, star, and sort it out,' Eugene said. 'It's cool. You're stressed, man. Go home talk to your woman. Make it sweet between you.' He was totally fucked off, but getting moody with Ralph wouldn't help any.

Besides, Ralph looked utterly pissed off himself. 'I'm really sorry, man,' he said. 'Look, bell me tomorrow and we'll make another night.'

'No sweat,' Eugene said. 'I mean it.' As they left the bar Ralph touched his jaw, which was now visibly swollen. Eugene shook his head. 'Look, there's just one thing before you go,' he told Ralph. 'You tell Belinda, now you just say it loud and clear; tell her she goes beating up my mainman again I'll have to come round and have a talk. I don't care what the upset is, I'm not having you slapped around none. Yeah, you tell her, she starts again I'll be straight on her case.'

'Yeah, yeah,' Ralph said. 'You know, bro, I think somebody's been winding you up.' Ralph threw an arm around Eugene's shoulder. 'Some trickster's been tellin you you're funny, right?' he went on. 'Top word man an all that, sayin what a witty individual? Well, no worries, star boy. You just give me the name and I'll go mash him. Setting you up like that so as you make a fool of yourself, mugging off my brother. I'll more than mash him, I'll iron the fuck.'

Eugene shook his head. 'Nice try, Ralphie boy, with

practice and application, you'll be quite smart one day. Go on then, let's move it.'

They walked down the road together, then split, Eugene heading the opposite direction. It wasn't yet midnight, too early to pack in and go home. He fancied seeing Lucy, but her mobile was off.

And Lucy wasn't the only girl on the planet. Eugene paused, weighing the options. He didn't feel like driving into town, wasn't up for a big night. A couple of drinks would do him. That's it then, he was staying local.

The Mirror Bar had once been a Wesleyan chapel – Eugene had been impressed when he'd first heard this, but his first visit had been a let-down. There were no stained-glass windows, towers and transepts were completely absent. Just a thick-set oblong of a building, with a diminutive spire squatting atop the front gable.

Eugene walked straight past the queue and on up to the three heavies guarding the purple-neon doorway. The Firm had a monopoly on security North London-wise. Eugene didn't remember the last time he'd paid to get in a club and heading through the glass doors he barely broke stride to acknowledge the muscle. Didn't have to – they knew who he was.

'Straight through, Geno, mate. On the house. Enjoy yourself.' Eugene nodded and said nothing.

The club was busy but not heaving. Eugene sipped vodka and coke and watched the action. It was a salsa night – some dancers were good, some were awful. Looking across the club Eugene could see his own reflection in a huge gilt-framed mirror. The night-club half-light made the image flicker in white and purple neon, so the mirror showed two Eugenes endlessly splitting and merging.

The spliff he'd smoked walking to the club was doing its stuff. Eugene caught himself slipping into a half-trance staring at the mirror in vacant fascination. Classic reefer-wreck conduct. He shook his head and snapped to. A quickie line in the cubicle and ten minutes later he was back on top of his game.

Leaning back on the wall, sizing up potential options, Eugene didn't see her. Too busy checking the dance-floor talent. It was when he turned back to the mirror – and then by accident – that he recognized her and caught her eye.

He got another drink and watched her. She was leaning back against the wall, head half-turned to the mirror, her gaze flicking back and forth. She was with a friend, a lean sinewy-looking woman with long dark hair. When dark-haired friend went to the bar, Eugene moved in.

He didn't push it. Told her he'd just worked out where they'd met before. Sorry if she'd caught him staring, but he knew he knew her face. Couldn't think how. She joined in – played the game with him. Admitted his face was familiar but wasn't sure why. She failed to solve the puzzle. 'Dreams,' said Eugene. 'That's where it was. My spar owns the place – you know, the travel agents.'

She laughed. 'DCT. That's right. They were almost closed. You opened the door for me.' She laughed. 'I remember now.'

Eugene asked her to dance. She said yes and told him her name – Brittany. 'My parents loved it there, that's why. It's the French holidays, not the teenage diva, but I really wish they hadn't.' When the track ended he held on to her until the next song began. Then it was over and she said thanks for the dance and headed back to her friend. He asked her again ten minutes later. Then she had to leave because her dark-haired friend was tired and they were sharing a taxi. He asked for her number. She said they could exchange mobiles. And that was it.

Eugene left ten minutes after the two women. Cruising home he keyed her number in whilst the Archway traffic lights were on red.

CHAPTER SEVEN

Redounding teares did choke th'end of her plaint,
Which softly ecchoed from the neighbour wood;

FQ: The Legende of the Knight of the Red Crosse: I.iii.8

Saturday afternoon was Eugene's chosen time to chill. He needed to relax some – to recover after the full-on frenzy of last week. Granted it had all gone like clockwork – the trip North, the intros, the handover of gear and payment for same: all of it completely sweet – just as Eugene had wanted. But pulling it off had cost Eugene stress and grind aplenty. Hours of phone-work plus a dummy-run face-to-face trip up the motorway: and then the coke-fuelled all-nighters, poring over the numbers involved. Attention to detail and all that. Absolutely necessary as Eugene well knew – but fuckin exhausting all the same.

If all this wasn't stress to factor ten – well, just throw in half a dozen calls from Archie Faron demanding all the deal's potential profit figures in nano-detail. Nightmare or what? But he'd passed the test – pulled off the big one and kept everything sweet and easy. He was a serious player now.

After this hard-earned triumph, Eugene was looking for some well-earned downtime. Now he was going to unwind. Simone and Gladys were out shopping. The Minimonster was at Buzzi Bee. Eugene stretched full length on the sofa. Three grands' worth of plasma-screen-state-of-the-art TV dominated the Burnsides' front room – a Faron knock-off which cost Eugene £500. Remote in hand, he flicked straight to Nat-Geo. 'Oh, fuck you,' said Eugene to the TV. 'Mount fuckin Everest again. I don't want to see no more snow.'

Ten minutes of channel-flicking and he found *The Killing Fields of Cambodia* – part of the Most Evil Men in History series. Eugene had no idea what or where Cambodia was, but thought it worth a try. Too right it was – Eugene was glued, entranced from the off. Sixty minutes was way too short for such a blockbuster. Eugene needed more. Cambodia – he could hardly believe what the lunatics had done. It was unreal. Pol Pot – even the name sounded weird and made up. He wished he'd videoed it – maybe you could buy the DVD? He wanted to look again at the eerie footage of the deserted capital city – unbelievable – he must tell Ralph – and the skulls. They'd shot all people with specs; what the fuck was that about? Pol Pot's madness amazed Eugene – he was shocked, blindsided. It was unbelievable – but it was on the TV. They didn't make things up.

Cambodia had finished and Eugene was on to the Discovery Channel and human cloning when his mobile rang. He checked the number – Simone – then he heard his sister's voice, incredibly loud, sobbing and screaming. A tumble of nonsensical sound. Incomprehensible – Eugene couldn't get a word. Then suddenly it was his mum on the phone. 'Go on, Mum,' he said.

He listened in silence. He could hear Simone still crying in the background. They were both down at Buzzi Bee. His mother sounded frightened and upset. Eugene told her he'd be there in ten minutes.

Saturday afternoon and the Holloway Road was chocka with traffic. The Puma dodged from lane to lane, twisting

105

and turning, desperate to move on. Eugene made up his mind quickly. After a hundred yards or so, he pulled into the empty bus lane and let the Puma fly. He half-hoped he would get a pull – 'Yes, officer, but this is an emergency, a child's life is at stake.' Shooting across traffic lights and junctions, Eugene saw his mum talking to a WPC by the Buzzi Bee gates. People – mainly police – were everywhere. Squad cars parked on pavements and across the road. And at least two unmarked serious-crime Sierras – which Eugene could spot blindfolded on a foggy day. There were two ambulances, paramedics and a bunch of Buzzi Bee social-workers drinking tea from plastic cups. There was no sign of Simone. 'Shit, shit, shit,' Eugene said, as he sprinted towards Gladys. 'What's the little bastard done now?'

His mother looked terrible, her face grey and bloodless. 'Thank God and all the angels,' she said. 'You're here, my son, you're here.'

Eugene took her hand. 'It's all OK now. I'm here and it'll be sorted, no worries now. Mum, first off, where's Simone? Where's my sister?'

A WPC told him Simone was 'inside, being looked after'. Gladys went to find her. A police officer then explained to Eugene 'the events of this afternoon – as far as we currently understand'.

The twenty or so Buzzi Bee Saturday kids always spent from four till five at 'free play' in the Adventure Arena, watched over by staff – a final hour to 'let off steam', which inevitably degenerated into a maelstrom of noisy aggression. This week had been worse than usual. Amidst a mêlée of fighting and stone-throwing, one of the kids – a five-year-old girl – had somehow fallen from a climbing net, knocking herself unconscious.

In the resulting hoo-ha, the kids 'might have been' unsupervised for a 'few seconds' – in which time all nineteen children had disappeared, leaving the Adventure Arena empty. 'What's really troubling us,' the policeman said, 'is

106

that the gate seems to have been deliberately opened by an adult stranger.'

Eugene was told that social workers and police had managed to round up eighteen children without too much public grief – petty thieving, broken car-windscreens and the usual screaming and swearing hardly counted. On their return to Buzzi Bee, the children appeared manic, highly aggressive and hyperactive. They were shouting about 'the man', all babbling and contradicting each other as they told how 'the man' had opened the gate and beckoned them outside. 'The other children all say Nero was the first through the open gate. Some appear to think he knew the man, and talked to him. One boy says Nero held the man's hand and walked away with him. However, the boy in question is highly disturbed and difficult, so we aren't putting too much weight on his testimony. We have a similar problem with the man. Every one of the eighteen children says they saw him open the gate – and we have eighteen different descriptions. He looks like Dracula, or Prince William, or Fred West. He's black, white, Asian, red hair, bald. I won't go on. You'd expect a degree of contradiction, but this is ridiculous. I'm beginning to wonder if the man exists outside their imaginations.'

'And one child's still missing,' said Eugene. The officer nodded. 'Yes. I'm sorry, but Nero hasn't come back yet.'

Eugene found his sister inside the centre. Simone had a blanket over her shoulders, a WPC on one side, a female paramedic on the other. For a second he didn't recognize her, his beautiful sister Simone – a walking advert for weaves, nails and labels. Simone, heels so high they could stand proxy for the Twin Towers. SweetHearts' top girl. This Simone was entirely different, and Eugene could hardly bear to look at her.

Despite the blanket and the tea and the valium, Simone was shaking. Juddering from top to bottom. Whilst shaking she was rocking in her chair, swaying back and forward, just like a mental case. The sobbing had given way to low-level crying, little mewlings, intense and unbearable. Her hair was a mess and eye make-up made black and purple tracks down her face. Her face so swollen that her eyes were barely visible, nose running and mouth trembling. The paramedic told Eugene a doctor had been called and should be here to see Simone any minute now. A second later, Simone grabbed at Eugene and disintegrated into agonized sobbing. There was nothing he could do but hold on to the convulsing body of his little sister.

It was close to three in the morning when the Burnside family finally reached home. Nero had been found just after half-past eight. A sharp-eyed policeman spotted a boy's training shoe in the playground in Peter Pan Park, and his subsequent search of the rhododendron bushes revealed the Minimonster. He'd been there all the time, apparently, sustained by shoplifted sweets. Headed there straight after his escape from Buzzi Bee and managed to dodge under the police tape cordoning off the scene of the crime. For the next four hours or so he'd squatted silently under the bushes in the park, enjoying an unrivalled view of the murder spot. 'I was there,' he kept saying proudly. 'I saw. Can we go back tomorrow?' Simone didn't answer; she was zonked on the doctor's tranquillizers – even in her stupor, she had tight hold of Nero's hand. Both Eugene and Gladys told the boy to be quiet.

They'd had to spend hours down at the police station after Nero was found. Statements were needed, medical checks ditto, social-workers' assessments; the whole performance took ages. All Eugene and his family wanted to do was go home. It was close to 4 a.m. when Eugene finally hit his bed, and tired as he was, one thing was nagging at him. The man who opened the gate: Nero was the only child not to have seen him. He insisted the others were lying. The gate was broken, that's why they got out. No one could budge him.

Before the Burnsides finally left Holloway police station, there was a last piece of news. The little girl who'd fallen and knocked herself out – the hospital had just confirmed she'd suffered an unspecified degree of brain damage and was on a life-support system.

CHAPTER EIGHT

... the euill donne
Dyes not, when breath the bodie first doth leaue,
But from the grandsyre to the Nephewes sonne,
And all his seed the curse doth often cleaue,
Till vengeance vtterly the guilt bereaue ...

FQ: The Legend of Sir Gvyon; Prince Arthur: II.viii.29

E ugene's relaxing weekend was well and truly out the
window – Nero's little escapade had seen to that.
Normally Eugene looked forward to his Sundays. Gladys
always cooked a massive dinner, to be eaten around the
kitchen table, not in front of the TV like weekdays. The
adults took their time over it; the Minimonster gobbled at
top speed, wriggling off his chair the second Gladys nodded
permission. With Nero gone, Gladys, Simone and Eugene
would lean back and relax, swapping news and laughing or
tutting over the latest gossip. She wasn't often in the mood,
but sometimes Eugene and Simone could persuade their
mother to talk about her life in Guyana, and how she met
Jean-Baptiste and fell in love. Sundays were special.

But not this Sunday. By 11 a.m. the police had arrived,
complete with specially trained child interviewer and a case
full of anatomically correct dolls and similar gadgets. Gladys

made mugs of tea whilst Eugene went to get Simone, who was still in bed, wiped on last night's tranqs. Twenty minutes later, the social-services crew turned up on the doorstep, accompanied by a child psychologist. The object of all this attention was in the front room. The Minimonster was perched on a chair back, watching *Forensic Detectives* on The Discovery Channel with rapt attention. The little boy's face was tilted so close to the screen he was almost touching it.

Back in the kitchen the specially trained police interviewer explained to Simone that officers were 'very concerned' about yesterday's breakout at the Buzzi Bee. Police were 'treating the matter very seriously'. Simone drank more coffee and said, 'Great – that's great.' Simone paused, then looked up. 'So what are you doing here then?' she asked. The policewoman explained briskly. They needed to re-interview Nero about the strange man – if he really existed. Role-play with the dolls would 'facilitate reconstruction of a worrying sequence of events'. Her 'colleague in social services' – the child psychologist – apparently intended to make an 'initial assessment'.

Simone was indignant – her son wasn't mental or anything. Nero was hyperactive, high-spirited. He'd got attention deficiency, same as loads of kids that age. 'I'm not having this. It's just victimization. What about all the other kids? Picking on him . . . it's not fair.'

The child psychologist sat shaking her head as Simone said what mothers always say. She had heard it all before, and didn't waste words. 'Ms Burnside, yesterday, your son spent four hours in hiding, staring obsessively at the exact spot where seven days ago Amy Fiddeler was raped and butchered. If you think that's normal behaviour, then I suggest you think again.'

Simone gave in. As Eugene said – the woman wasn't wrong.

The rest of the day was a total horror show. Eugene had

never taken to his nephew, but by the end of Sunday he could have killed the little bastard. Nero had blanked the police interviewer – ignoring her questions, still glued to the TV. Eventually the policewoman lost patience and offed the telly, triggering a fit of violent hysterics from Nero. The commotion brought Simone rushing in from the kitchen, with Gladys close behind her. Familiar with the physical damage the Minimonster was capable of inflicting in a temper, Eugene went after them, tailed in turn by the child psychologist and another WPC. With such a crowd jammed into the front room, Nero's kicks and punches scored a considerable hit rate.

It took for ever to calm him down. But when, at last, he'd stopped shouting, lashing out and screaming obscenities, when they'd got him sitting quietly sipping his juice, the interviewer began again. It took ages, and was, in Eugene's view, a complete waste of time and energy. Nero mostly refused to say anything, but when he did cooperate, his answers were fantastical rubbish. When asked about the strange man, he insisted there was no man. The child psychologist fared little better.

When everyone finally left Simone tried to cuddle her son. Nero pushed her off: 'I want TV, le-go. Le-go-me. Want TV.' The moment he escaped his mother's embrace, the Minimonster was off. Eugene followed; grabbed the little bastard halfway down the hallway, held tight and steered him into the front room, shutting the door firmly behind them. In a millisecond Nero shot across the carpet and grabbed the remote; with equal speed and superior force, Eugene snatched it off him and zipped it in his pocket. Nero's mouth opened but, before the screams started, Eugene took hold of the child's shoulders and turned him round so they were face to face. Eugene crouched down, still holding the boy's shoulders, looking straight at him.

'I want my mummy.' Nero's voice was small and frightened. 'Le-go. You hurting. I want MUMMY, MUMMY!'

Nero's voice had risen to a high-pitched shout. 'I WANT
. . .' Suddenly he stopped.

Eugene's face was an inch away. 'You shut the fuck up
NOW,' he hissed.

Nero had never been spoken to like this. His entire life
had been about doing what he wanted. Getting his own way
was the whole of Nero's law. Eugene's adult fury shocked
and frightened the boy. He lapsed into stunned silence.

Eugene told him it was game over. Nero had had his
fun, involving the usual trail of emotional and physical
casualties. But funtime was over, and the immediate future
looked bleak. 'I've had it,' said Uncle Eugene, still gripping
the child's shoulders. 'I don't want to hear or see anything
more of you tonight – you little fucker. Got that?' Nero
nodded emphatically. 'One foot out the front-room door,
one shout. Just annoy me once' – Eugene leant in, an inch
from Nero's ear – 'and then we'll see what goes down. Any
more of your crap; well, then, you just wait till Mummy goes
to work tomorrow, and see what I do. You catch my drift?'
The Minimonster nodded. 'I asked you a question,' Eugene
said. 'I want to hear a proper answer. You understand me?'

Nero looked up through tarantula lashes. His voice was
small and high. 'Yes, Uncle. I be good now. OK? Telly now?'

Eugene nodded and stood up slowly, stretching his
cramped leg muscles. He pulled out the remote and held
it out. Nero grabbed it immediately. When Eugene left
the room, the boy was giggling happily, zapping through the
channels.

Back in the kitchen, Simone was crying; she couldn't seem
to stop. She pulled herself together at Nero's bedtime.
Reading and singing to him, staying, as usual, for the hour
or more it took to get him settled. But once back downstairs,
Simone was crying again.

Monday morning she was still red-eyed and upset.
Monday was rehearsal day at SweetHearts: the preparations
for Harem Nights were well advanced, and Simone – as top

girl – naturally had the star role. Eugene had some running around to do, so he told his sister he'd give her a lift in. Sitting beside him in the Puma, made-up and hair perfect, Simone looked much better. He'd suggested she ring in sick, but Simone said she was a professional and professionals honoured commitments.

Eugene dropped his sister at SweetHearts' door. He had business matters to attend to, and a lot on his mind. Even so, as he turned the Puma northward he clocked the unmarked police car parked on the sidestreet. Serious-crime squad, was Eugene's guess. What did they want with SweetHearts? He let the Puma run and rang Talus.

And it was a useful phone call, because Mr Barry had been caught on the hop. DCI Arthur Gale had turned up un-announced half an hour earlier, and – sneakily, in Mr Barry's view – had simply strolled through the club's side door, up the stairs and straight to Mr Barry's office. Ignor-ing Mae's instructions to 'Wait here, please', DCI Gale had marched through to the inner sanctum, knocked on Mr Barry's door and walked in. 'The shock,' Mr Barry told Mae afterwards, 'was terrible.'

As he discovered, worse was to come. DCI Gale had some very bad news for Mr Barry. And some more photographs for the SweetHearts boss to look at. They were before and after photos this time. Amy Fiddeler when alive and nomi-nally living in local-authority care – Amy Fiddeler when very dead. 'Do you recognize her, sir?'

The awful thing was that Mr Barry did recognize the girl. Had auditioned her, been more than willing to give her a job – she looked so young, absolute jailbait, the punters would love it. She hadn't called herself Amy though, told him her name was Lola Faith – not that Mr Barry was going to argue. The employment deal had collapsed when he demanded to see her birth certificate. She said she was seventeen, but Mr Barry thought different, and using an underage girl in the club was just begging for trouble. He'd told her to come back after her sixteenth birthday. 'Too right I will,' she'd said. Cheeky, she was, confident.

Mr Barry said he'd never seen the girl in the photos. DCI Gale asked him to take another look, because the girl was connected to SweetHearts. She had been a runaway, disappearing from the care home on a regular basis. She had found somewhere else to stay, a friend's place – she was always round there. A friend working at SweetHearts. Mr Barry knew what was coming: Amy's mate – Canday Sweete, had to be. He would get hold of her the minute this cunting copper fucked off out the club.

'The friend's name is—' DCI Gale paused a moment and checked his notes. 'She's Canday Sweete – aged seventeen years. Employed as a SweetHearts dancer. Is that correct, sir?' Mr Barry nodded. Teenage Canday, who wasn't much of a looker but, at her age, that didn't really matter. She had long hair, good tits and could move a bit. Came on in school uniform. Proved popular. A few weeks back Canday had asked Mr Barry if her friend Lola could audition for the club – chattering on about how Lola lived with her, and how they were closer than sisters. 'Great, bring her in,' he'd said.

Mr Barry found it hard to concentrate – he was desperate to get to a phone. He had to ring the Farons. He needed advice. Some help dealing with this bloody mess, none of which was his doing. The Farons must understand that surely. They couldn't blame him. Bloody stupid whores and their dirty bloody lives. What the fuck was he supposed to do?

Mr Barry had temporarily lost the thread. DCI Gale was still speaking – something about going clubbing . . . Suddenly Mr Barry was listening and listening hard. Oh, shit. He couldn't believe it. The stupid, mouthy little cow. The fucking silly tart. Canday knew the rules – so why had the bitch given a fucking voluntary statement – behind his back – a police statement. All about her and Amy – she'd gobbed off the lot. Told them every last detail – about her and Amy, the things they did together, what a laugh they had. Mr Barry listened in nauseated silence. The Farons – what the fuck would he say to them?

Afterwards Mr Barry told Mae all about it. How it was torture, pure torture. Answering, as best he could, question after question relating to Canday's babbling indiscretions, dreading what came next, wondering just what else she'd told them.

Canday had not been shy. She'd explained how clients in the club would approach her and arrange to meet for sex, and how Amy – aged fourteen – would go with her. For fifty quid more the man got both of them – which Canday thought was 'very fair'. And on she chattered, happy as Larry. Mr Barry was incredulous at the blithe imbecility of the girl. Her chirpy take on prostitution, drug addiction, paedophile sex. The complete absence of shame: 'They liked us because we both look dead young. We do schoolgirl stuff, y'know. Or we work together, do a lesbian thing. We do it really well, actually.' She had told police about their regular clients – City boys, middle-aged executives and 'this creepy old bastard who made us call him Daddy.' Amy used to meet Canday at SweetHearts after work. 'We'd go out clubbing or to parties sometimes, whatever was going.' Canday said they were dead close. Sharing clothes, talking endlessly, always together. Like sisters.

Canday told the police that Amy had a new boyfriend. She wouldn't even tell Canday the guy's name. Which was weird, because like she said, they were so dead close.

Bombarded with DCI Gale's endless questions, Mr Barry could only keep a straight bat. He quoted club rules: no one to perform under sixteen years, clients eighteen years and over. Girls totally forbidden to 'fraternize' with clients. Rules strictly enforced. Knew nothing of Canday's outside activities. Never seen the other girl. Couldn't think why Canday said different. Couldn't remember any audition.

Couldn't think of any special clients. Canday had always been a bit unstable. Fully licensed, very strictly run. Glad to help if we can, but can't see how. Sweat was pouring down his back and his heart was pounding. What a fucking mess. He had to call the Farons.

Finally, DCI Gale stood up. 'Oh, before I go, sir, one last thing. It concerns your relationship – or relations – with the previous victim.'

For a second Mr Barry looked blank then it came to him. 'Little Stella,' he said.

DCI Gale nodded. 'Stella Jane Hope, that is correct.' The detective paused before continuing. 'Were you aware that Ms Hope was four months pregnant, sir?'

Mr Barry shook his head. 'No. Hadn't a clue. Told her she needed to lose a bit just before . . . thought she'd got a bit of a tummy. She never said. Didn't say a word. Oh Christ. Oh fuck.' Mr Barry looked up. 'Was it mine?' he asked.

'Can't say for sure, sir. There was no other boyfriend we know of, so it's possible. Thank you for your cooperation.' As DCI Gale knew, it was doubtful the paternity of Stella Hope's baby would ever be confirmed. You could keep your DNA tests and the rest of it. Because Stella's murderer had fancied a souvenir, a keepsake, you might say. So he'd cut the foetus out of her and taken it with him.

Mr Barry watched DCI Gale leave. Watched him down the stairs from his office window. Went across the corridor and watched him get in the car. Waited until the police driver pulled out into the stream of traffic, followed the car until it disappeared. Then he asked Mae for a large brandy, which he drank in one. Mae fetched another which went the same way. Next, he knew, he should phone the Farons. But not just yet. Before he faced the dreaded phone call Mr Barry went for a piss. When he'd finished he locked himself in a cubicle. He sat quietly, arms wrapped around his body, rocking back and forth, back and forth.

CHAPTER NINE

And euery head with fyrie tongue did flame,
And euery head was crowned on his creast,
And bloudie mouthed with late cruell feast.

FQ: The Legende of the Knight of the Red Crosse: I.viii.6

The death of Amy Fiddeler was still hot news. Throughout the following week the media was full of speculation. 'Reliable police sources' talked of a number of similar 'unsolveds' around Manchester and the North-West.

The press declared that a new serial killer was on the loose – 'a vicious maniac who prowls the streets for his chosen prey'. They talked of 'a psychopath consumed with perverted bloodlust'; dispatching victims in 'an orgy of violence'. No one was sure who coined the nickname, but it was taken up by police, press and public alike. They called him 'The Meatman'.

The headlines and TV bulletins invested the mutilated corpses of Stella and Amy with a sheen of celebrity and glamour. Predictably, SweetHearts' staff were agog with excitement. Monday's Harem Nights rehearsal was a shambles of missed steps and inattention. No one could concentrate, not with all this going on. Off stage the girls talked of nothing but the murder. Everyone claimed to have known Amy. Likewise Canday was every girl's 'close friend' or 'best mate'. The girls huddled together in groups, spending every spare minute discussing and dissecting murder minutiae. It was obvious; all agreed. Stands to reason, they told each other – the killer had to be connected to Sweet-Hearts. The dancers joked about it backstage – had a laugh guessing who the Meatman might be – outdid each other with stories of weirdo clients, gossiped about the steroid-fuelled security heavies, discussed jealous exes with violent tendencies. 'There's so many nutters out there,' someone would say, and everyone else would nod in agreement.

The girls incessantly begged Mae for more details and seized on any new scrap of murder news. The obsessive interest showed no sign of flagging as the days passed but, imperceptibly, something changed. As the weekend approached the atmosphere backstage became strained and oddly febrile. The girls continued to swap weirdo tales, but their laughter dwindled and the jokes disappeared. Like children with a ouija board, they were beginning to frighten themselves.

Canday turned up for work at SweetHearts on Thursday, creating an enjoyable drama of supportive hugs and kisses. She had a scant half an hour to enjoy all the sympathy and attention backstage before being summoned to Mr Barry's office. Mr Barry said very little. Talus did the talking. Two hours later, Canday was at Holloway Road police station asking to withdraw her statement. DCI Gale's boys were less than thrilled. There was threatening talk of charges for wasting police time. But it made no difference. The statement was history. Canday wouldn't budge.

Simone naturally relayed all the SweetHearts news back home. Gladys was worried sick. Eugene felt uneasy and gave his sister £100 taxi money. 'And if you spend it on designer Lycra or whatever, I'll be seriously out of countenance, girl – understand?'

119

Eugene had a lot of business on that week but, none-theless, Simone's daily bulletins from the club seemed to stick in his mind. He felt tired and did more coke than usual to keep himself moving. Looking at the picture of the murdered girl on TV he wondered if he'd seen her. Thin face, thin hair, mouth curled in teenage defiance – local-authority residential-care photo taken a year ago. Simone said it looked nothing like her. Simone said Amy was a regular fixture – always hanging around the club at closing time, waiting for Canday to finish. Eugene reckoned he must have walked past her, must have seen her waiting by the door when he dropped by SweetHearts to pick up Simone. His sister said more than likely he'd passed the poor girl dozens of times. Eugene tried to recall the face, but there were so many girls – and he had no reason to remember her – not before all this, anyway.

All in all it had been a bit of a shit week, Eugene felt; and the final fuck-off came Friday morning. He was expecting Ralph to call. They had arrangements to make. Instead, when Ralph rang, it was to cancel. His bitch of a wife had finally flipped out big style. Eugene could have predicted it, could have written the script. Wanted to tell his star boy to stop pandering to the skinny dog – get himself a decent woman. But tragically this wasn't possible, because Ralph was in love – properly, really, in love. If Belinda walked, it would break the man's heart. Absolutely no doubt about it. It was rough, but there was nothing to change. Eugene knew it, so he kept his mouth shut. Listened to his bro talk it through – what she'd said and done, how she'd got it all totally wrong. No change there, Eugene thought.

It had all kicked off Thursday night. 'She just started on me,' Ralph said. 'Delivered this big fucking ultimatum. After dinner. Turned the TV off and said we had to talk. There was no "we" about it, man – I didn't get a fuckin word in.' Belinda informed Ralph it was his decision. He was welcome to run around clubbing and doing drugs with his gangster

120

friends. He could enjoy his usual Friday-night safari, she said, come home at 2 a.m. or stay out all night for that matter. Do what the hell he wanted, because she wouldn't be waiting there when he came back. She'd be gone the minute he set foot out the door. She knew what he was at. So he could cruise around clubs being the bachelor boy or he could save his marriage. His choice.

Ralph said Belinda was out of order. 'She has to stop this stuff, you know,' he said. 'I mean it. It's too much. I'm so far fucked off, man, I can't tell you. She's not said it straight but she thinks I'm shagging. No, E., man, I mean it. She bought me some stupid fuckin book about the pressures on black relationships. Keeps going upstairs and crying – I can hear her. Look, I'm really sorry man. But I can't risk it tonight – I've got to straighten this out with her, make her realize everything's cool. I'll catch you soon – yeah? Sorry bro.'

Eugene told Ralph, no worries – what else to say? Next he contemplated what to do with the wreck of Friday night. He occasionally saw a girl up in Wood Green, but he was bored with her. Then there was Lucy – Eugene thought about ringing her but decided against. Sense told him Lucy was odds-on to have Friday night plans of her own, and he wasn't risking a knock-back. Anyway, he wasn't sure he was in the mood for it – Lucy's special brand of lunacy and high-octane drama.

So he rang Brittany. Apologizing for calling her at the last minute. As he'd hoped, she was going to the Mirror Bar with her friend – same as last week. Eugene said he'd meet her there. She agreed.

When he strolled up to the club she was near the front of the door queue. Dark-haired friend beside her. Eugene smiled, steered Brittany out the line, the friend following on their heels. Eugene did his usual free breeze-through, accompanied by the usual chorus of respect: 'All right, Geno? The ladies with you? No sweat. Good to see you,

Geno.' Brittany was astonished – 'old school friends,' Eugene told her. Found a place on the edge of the dance floor and left her with the friend whilst he went to the bar. Brittany wanted a glass of wine. Unasked, the friend jumped in and said she'd have the same. So Eugene bought a bottle and returned with three glasses. It looked like he was stuck with the mate. She'd barely uttered a word, but the face was enough. Eugene reckoned if the bitch was riding him for free entry and free drink, she could at least stick a smile on it and make herself scarce.

The music was too loud for any three-way conversation. Eugene learnt that the friend's name was Rhoda. He also learnt that she stuck like glue.

As the evening wore on Rhoda showed no inclination to practise her salsa. The only soul brave enough to ask her for a dance received a brusque 'no'. Instead she whispered endlessly to Brittany, and ignored Eugene. When he and Brittany went to dance Rhoda's sharp eyes followed their every move. Eugene could feel her brooding presence tracking him. Was she loopy or what? Why didn't she get the message and give her mate some space? Normally Eugene would have chucked the towel in – given up and fucked off to greener pastures. But tonight there were no greener pastures on offer. The pity of it was that he was getting stronger on the Brittany girl. Alone they could have had a good time. But with Rhoda there was no chance of that.

Unbelievably, the ferret-faced bitch even forced him to dance. 'Aren't you going to ask, then?' she demanded. 'Or do you keep your manners in your trousers?' Eugene could have slapped her. Instead, he pointedly asked Brittany to excuse him and led Rhoda out on the floor. What was she at? Acting well ignorant all night – and suddenly she's after dancing.

Eugene had Rhoda all worked out soon enough. Holding on to his hand, she had pulled him almost to the centre of the packed dance floor. Surrounded by bodies they were effectively hidden from view. Then, as the music began, Rhoda wound her arms around his neck and closed against him. Some Colombian was singing about his girl 'like a jewel, a flower'. Eugene felt Rhoda's breasts swelling against him, and the sway of her hips. She danced pretty well. The Colombian's heart was on fire, his girl was a queen, more beautiful than the stars. Rhoda rested her head on Eugene's neck; her hair was soft and smelt of sandalwood and musk.

On another night Eugene might have gone with it. Would have taken her phone number, arranged to meet. Taken full advantage of a free shag with no worries. But now, he wasn't in the mood. To start with, he didn't like the bitch, her sour mouth and darting dark eyes. The crimson-red top with lipstick to match – black hair, pale face – a cross between Carmen and The Addams Family. No thanks. He supposed a lot of men would have gone for her, but she wasn't for him. She wasn't much of a friend either.

So Eugene spent three minutes on the floor moving Rhoda in every direction excepting close to him. His wrists ached with the effort. When the purgatory finally ended, he said thanks to Rhoda and headed straight back. Brittany smiled when he reappeared from the crowd.

Half an hour later, Rhoda said she had to think about leaving. She was in work Saturday at 9 a.m. 'We live in the same street,' Rhoda told Eugene, 'so Brittany and I always walk home together. It's really unsafe walking at night as a single woman. And now there's a serial killer roaming the neighbourhood.'

Eugene was politely sympathetic. He offered to pay Rhoda a taxi – so he and Brittany could stay in the club. Rhoda wouldn't accept. 'I can't afford to pay you back, and I would feel awful taking the money.' Eugene nodded. Fine, he'd drive her home in the Puma and return with Brittany. Rhoda said she thought Eugene was over the limit, and wouldn't feel safe in the car with him. She kept repeating that she wasn't trying to be awkward. Brittany veered between guilt and resentment. Eugene accepted the inevitable and got the coats. The two women lived right on the edge of Crouch End, a crescent of Edwardian semis opposite the Texaco garage.

Rhoda disappeared into her house, leaving Eugene and Brittany alone together. He put his arm around her, pulling her closer as they walked. He knew already he had no chance of sex, and he was right. She was embarrassed, avoiding his eyes when they got to her door. 'You can't come in,' she said. Eugene told her it was cool. Then – against the garden wall – they started kissing. By the time she finally broke away and went inside, he was so hard it hurt. Her body was all curves and dips. She was just lovely, he thought, walking the half-mile back to the Puma. Beautiful eyes. And she had class. He sent her a text as he walked along the Broadway. Said he was missing her already and wanted to see her again (provided she promised to get rid of the skankin friend, that was). The Puma was in sight. He finished texting and sent, 'WL RNG THS WK 2 ARRNG 2 MT. XXX E'. He didn't really like 'Geno', he'd told her in the club. Preferred Eugene. 'Good choice,' she'd said.

Eugene slept like the dead that night. He reckoned he needed the rest, anticipating a day of Minimonster hell.

After the traumatic events of the previous Saturday, the Buzzi Bee Centre had notified its 'clients' – including Nero – that it would be closed for a week. The Burnside family was unhappy but, as Gladys said, it was only one week. It could have been worse. Anyway, it turned out not to matter, because Simone spent the day accompanying her son to a succession of interviews, assessments and investigations. Nero saw psychiatrists and psychologists, paediatricians, dieticians, child-protection workers and a second specially trained police officer – male this time. Nero behaved just as before, alternating between profound silence and bizarre lies, punctuated by the odd tantrum. It was gone six-thirty when Simone arrived home, exhausted. Before his mother had got her coat off, Nero took advantage of Eugene's absence to throw another tantrum.

Eugene spent the day cruising the shops and hanging out with friends in Portobello. Then as the Puma was heading home his mobile rang.

'Hi, sweetie pie. It's me, sugar boy, Lucy in the Sky. So how you feeling?' It turned out Lucy was calling him on the look-out for 'a bit of the white stuff'. If Eugene had supplies, maybe he could come over to the flat – have some champagne, a couple of lines, you know, a fun evening. Eugene said he'd be there around 9 p.m.

Lucy had champagne, vodka, brandy, Baileys, Benedictine, Cointreau and quality weed. Eugene dished the powder. Lucy dressed up for him – stockings, boned corset, high heels. She danced, provoked, used handcuffs, a vibrator, blindfolds. Anal sex, oral sex, normal sex. She got on top, they did it doggy, in the shower, over the table downstairs, she dominated him, he smacked her. The coke prevented Eugene from coming, so he was hard for hours. And they couldn't stop, tore at each other until, utterly exhausted, they collapsed on the wrecked and tangled bed.

Eugene had no idea of the time when he awoke. Had left his mobile in the flat, but God knows where, ditto his watch. As expected, he felt like shit, weak and shaky, with a ringing headache. Well, he'd known the score, hadn't he? It had been an amazing night, the bits he could remember – flying-time for real. Fantasy Island, everything you want and much much more. Eugene reckoned a hangover-headache and the rest of it but a small price to pay for such pleasures.

Showered and dressed, he found his watch in his trouser pocket. It had stopped. When he saw the clock downstairs, he noticed that had stopped, too. Likewise the digital in Lucy's bathroom. It was when he checked the display on

Lucy's mobile that he understood: watch, clock and digital were fine. Eugene was the one out of sync. It was six-fifteen on Sunday evening. Using Lucy's phone he rang his mobile; tracking the faint cries of response he found it in the fridge – frosted at the corners, but still working. He had nine missed calls and three messages. His mother had called seven times. The other two were Simone. His mum's message was a 'Where are you son? What about dinner?' He could hear the anxiety in her voice, the unspoken fear that 'something must have happened' to him. 'It's now four-thirty.' Simone's voice on the second message. 'We've finished dinner, Mum's gone to bed. She's worried sick about you. Waited dinner till three o'fucking clock, boy. Couldn't even stress you to call her, eh? Proud of yourself, are you?' Message three was Simone again. 'And I don't expect much from you – know better. But just thought you should know that I've had about the worst week of my whole life, so thanks, bro, today's fuck-up has been just what I needed.'

Eugene went back in the bedroom and said he'd have to go. Lucy smiled and stretched. 'OK lover-man,' she said, nestling back into feather pillows. 'Have fun, kissy-kiss.' As he headed for the door, she sat up. 'Hey, angel-boy, can I have a micro-mini tiny favour?'

'Course,' said Eugene. He was desperate to move.

'We-ell, it would be really cool if you could leave me a little something for later. Is that OK, or am I being a real cheeky chancer and making you hate me for ever?' Eugene said that was fine. Filleted a page of *Wallpaper* magazine, did some speedy origami to make a wrap, poured in over a gramme from his personal stash, said, 'I'll give you a call,' and left. Lucy was squealing with delight over the free coke. 'Thank-you everso, everso,' she called after him.

He let the Puma dawdle and took the long route home. Even so it was no more than fifteen minutes from Lucy's flat to the Wentworth Road. Eugene spent every second agonizing over what he could say to his mother. He was just parking up when he got Talus's call. 'Need you to go down Shifter's place tomorrow – he says 9 o'clock as usual . . . No, not back to that. Listen, will you. Shifter's got something for you to take a look at. We've agreed on the paper and the weight, so get round there and check it's what he says it is – that he's not stuffing us with ten key of moody bollocks. Give me a call when you've seen it and had a taste.'

Eugene thought he'd left all that behind – the running, late-night deliveries, dealing with Mal Shifter. Had delegated all that crap to his juniors. And so he had. Tomorrow, he'd be doing serious business – acting for the Firm, with the Farons' authority. Talus had said it. But Eugene had one overriding thought: no matter how far or how fast he'd travelled, come Monday night, he'd be back in Shifter's kitchen.

CHAPTER TEN

Lewd *Losse of Time*, and *Sorrow* seeming dead,
Inconstant *Chaunge*, and false *Disloyaltie*,
Consuming *Riotise*, and guilty *Dread*
Of heauenly vengeance, faint *Infirmitie*,
Vile *Pouertie*, and lastly *Death* with infamie.

FQ: The Legend of Britomartis, or of Chastitie: III.xii.25

Sunday at Wentworth Road was a total nightmare. Hung-over, shaky and exhausted, Eugene was in no shape to cope with all the upset back home. His garbled apologies – lost the mobile . . . got stuck out at this mate's house . . . car got clamped . . . did phone . . . operator said line was faulty – cut little ice. Gladys had made herself ill fretting over his non-appearance, and after the initial relief that her boy was safe home, she went back to bed. Simone took care of her mother, running around with aspirin, cups of tea and extra pillows. She took time out from the ministering-angel routine to tell her brother he was a lying, low-life bastard.

Come Monday night Eugene was glad to get out of the house. Simone was bad enough, lecturing him about how selfish he was, how thoughtless and uncaring. But it was his mother who really upset him. Seeing her face as she struggled to believe his improbable excuses. 'These things happen, son,' she said repeatedly. 'I know you didn't do it on purpose.' Over and over, as if she was trying to convince herself he was telling the truth. Eugene couldn't look at her. Couldn't bear to think what he'd been doing with Lucy when he should have been at home. Flinching as he pictured his mum preparing dinner, a little ruffled when she couldn't raise him on the mobile, steadily worrying herself sick as the dinner congealed on the hotplate and the hours came and went . . . Eugene couldn't understand how he had let it happen.

So by Monday he was relieved to escape – away from the guilt and the torment, letting the Puma carry him through the fine spring night towards Acre Row and Chez Shifter. Renewing his acquaintance with Mal and the Ladies was not top of his wish list. But as things stood, it was preferable to staying home – well, just about.

In late April the voracious vegetation of Acre Row was in adolescent phase. A couple of months away from the dark maturity of high summer, but green and growing and full of life and energy. Heading towards Shifter's house, Eugene noticed the pale teenage creepers, young but true to type, their lime-green tentacles stretching towards him. Some of the pallid new leaves already bore tell-tale bite-marks and silvery trails, stalks swollen with burgeoning colonies of greenfly and blackfly. Eugene felt queasy, catching the familiar scent of decomposition, and quickened his stride.

As he rang Shifter's doorbell he could hear the dogs panting, and sure enough, there they were, Faithless, Hopeless and Loveless surrounding their master when the door slid open.

Shifter giggled. 'Ooh, look, my fine fierce boys, it's our old friend. Young Eugene. But not any more – oh, no, not now, my handsome young men. Oh, no, not at all.' Shifter giggled again as the dogs wound and pressed more closely around him. 'No – young Eugene has become a Very Important

Man, he has. Show respect, boys. Come in, then, Geno, come in.'

Eugene could have predicted it. Shifter would spend the next hour, or however long it took to sort the business, capering about trying to take the piss. Mad little fucker that he was. Shaking his head, Eugene followed Shifter down the hallway towards the kitchen.

'Oh, I should have said before,' Shifter said over his shoulder. 'The Ladies missed you so very badly, really didn't take it well, your absence, that is. They were quite thrilled that you were coming back to us. They are so looking forward to seeing you again. Talked about nothing else.'

Shifter opened the kitchen door with a theatrical flourish: 'Here he is, Ladies. Sidney Poitier's double. Are you old enough to remember Sidney Poitier, Eugene? *Guess Who's Coming to Dinner*? Marvellous film. Hilarious. The black boyfriend. Oscars, I think. Seen it, have you?'

Eugene gave a tight smile and nodded. 'Yeah – classic.'

'Mind you,' Shifter continued. 'Times have changed. I mean, half the young ladies in London are running after a bit of chocolate nowadays it seems. Bet you're in demand, eh, Geno? Although they're not what you'd call "decent" girls, are they? Scrubbers in the main, or so I'm told.'

Eugene was saved from replying by Dolly's ecstatic squeals of welcome. 'It's Mr Gorgeous!' she shrieked, bouncing up from her chair. 'Why have you stayed away so long? You want to break a girl's heart completely? Eugene, Eugene, ooh . . . if you knew the dreams I dreamt of you.' Dolly tossed back her red curls and mimed a shiver of ecstasy. 'So – have you missed me, Tiger?' she continued, moving around the table and taking Eugene by the hand. 'Have you pined for me – just a tiny bit? Come on, pin-up boy, sit down and let's have some fun.' Eugene found himself dragged along behind her. She was much stronger than she looked. 'Come on, sit here, Gorgeous,' she said. The chair was pulled up so close he was practically sitting in her lap.

'Don't let Dolly embarrass you. Move that chair, Malcolm. Let the boy breathe.' Letitia's voice silenced her sister's babble. Seated, as always, at the head of the table, Letitia wore a grey cardigan over her customary black dress. She was working on a large-scale tapestry, weaving the thread in and out as she spoke. The table in front of her was covered with skeins of coloured yarns in reds, purples, browns and black and an array of awls, thimbles, scissors and needles of varying styles and sizes laid out in neat rows. 'So?' Letitia raised an eyebrow as she looked across at Eugene. 'You've gone up in the world. The Big Man now – that's what I'm led to believe?'

'Oh yes,' Shifter interrupted. 'Quite right. Fairly scampered up the greasy pole has Eugene. No, not the dogsbody, nobody he used to be. Not at all. Our dark friend is up there with the boss men.'

Letitia paused, needle in hand, and tied off her thread. 'I wasn't talking to you, Malcolm,' she said. For a few seconds, there was total silence, then Shifter stood up. 'Right then,' he said brightly. 'This calls for a celebration drink. What will you have? Ladies first, I think.'

Shifter's dogs followed their master from the table and continued to swarm round him as he busied himself preparing three champagne cocktails and a mug of black tea. Dolly giggled and shimmied and tried to catch Eugene's eye whilst Letitia gave him a comprehensive medical update:

'How am I? you ask. Well, seeing as you want to know . . . the alopecia – you remember?' Eugene nodded emphatically '. . . the alopecia is unstoppable. "Chronic" is the term. This' – she gestured to her iron-grey hair – 'it's a wig. Whole thing. Look.' Letitia took hold of the coiled bun at the back of her head and pulled. Underneath, she was almost bald, just a few long, greying wisps hanging around her ears. 'Alopecia totalis – it's been a blessing. Wig's easier to wash. Take it off at night. Wouldn't go back to my own hair if you paid me.'

131

'It looks very realistic,' Eugene managed.

'Yes, so it should. It's real hair, my boy. Expensive, I'll tell you. Want to stroke it? No?' Letitia laughed. 'Still squeamish, eh? Go on, touch it. Doesn't bite.' Eugene shook his head. The thing sat on the table, hair-grips holding the bun in place.

'How's the legs then?' Eugene said, desperate to avoid the wig. 'Oh, the osteoporosis just gets worse,' Letitia said. 'Only to be expected. Hurts to walk. But Malcolm helps me stay mobile. Better than crutches, he is, eh? Eh, Malcolm?'

'It's an honour to be of use,' Shifter said, still faffing with the drinks.

'Do you think Malcolm means that?' Letitia looked straight at Eugene. She cackled. 'Don't know what to say, do you? No, course he doesn't mean it, do you, Malcolm? But he has no choice. It's his duty. And we have to do our duty, don't we?'

Letitia smiled and selected a dark red yarn. 'So there you are.' She threaded her needle and nodded as Shifter brought her tea before glancing across the table. 'As I'm sure she'll tell you, my sister's had her own health problems.'

Dolly nodded emphatically. 'Terrible—' she began, then stopped short as the elder sister spoke.

'Decorum,' Letitia said.

After a five-second silence, Dolly tossed her head and gave a winning smile. 'As I said, terrible trouble. Could be the uterus, but they just don't know. I've had so many explorations, lost count.' Dolly paused for more hair-tossing and leaned closer towards Eugene. 'Anyway,' she said conspiratorially, 'I'm in for an overnight next week, Gorgeous. The Whittington. Ooh, all those doctors in white coats. I'm getting quite excited. They're doing another probe, internal.' Dolly's hand touched Eugene's thigh. 'And you ought to see my new naughty nightie, got it specially. Mixed wards at the Whittington, you know. I've heard they get up to all sorts.'

Letitia's chair scraped across the stone floor and Dolly

subsided. Shifter giggled. 'So lively, our Dolly, eh, Eugene. A regular little minx. The eternal temptress – the daughter of Eve, she is, seducing us men into sin and wickedness with all her charms and winning ways. Delightful. Do you want a straw? Oh, I forgot. Too important for straws. A bit above our silly little games nowadays.'

Dolly pouted. 'Oh not Eugene, he's not stuck up, are you darling? Not like the new one, mind you, I've always loved dark men. And he's another handsome one – and all brooding, oooh. Makes me go all shivery he does.'

'That's enough,' Letitia said sharply.

Eugene suppressed a smile. Following his own rapid promotion, the role of liaising with Shifter had fallen to another of the Firm's middle-rankers. Omar was the chosen one – an acne-scarred Sudanese guy permanently wired on khat. Eugene supposed it was chewing the khat leaves that had done Omar's teeth in. Handsome? You what? But if Dolly had taken a shine to the poor fucker, then Omar had Eugene's deepest sympathy.

''Nother drink, Ladies and gent?' Shifter enquired brightly.

'Ooh, yes, please!' Dolly responded.

'I've still got mine,' Letitia said, before flourishing her needlework. 'Come here a minute, Malcolm, hold it whilst I move the frame. That's right.'

Released, Shifter turned to Eugene. 'Drink?' One by one, the dogs, which had been resting in the hallway, got silently to their feet and moved towards their master. 'There's hope and faith and love, all three/And less, and less, and less for me,' Shifter chanted, caressing each dog in turn. The animals pushed each other aside, snapping and shoving to get closer to their master. Shifter was singing now: 'Hope and Faith and Love, you see/Oh, they make a trinitee/And Dad an Son an Holy G/But LESS and LESS and LESS for me!' He stopped suddenly. 'Drink?'

Eugene looked up. The winding movement of the dogs and Shifter's ridiculous jingles had put him in a near-reverie, staring fixedly at the beasts' red-blond coats and the strange ridge of reverse hair running up their spines. For a second his mind was blank then he snapped to. 'Yeah. That's really kind, Mal. But we need to sort the business sharpish. I've got to bell Talus when I'm through.'

Shifter gave a thin smile. He couldn't keep Eugene pissing about all night if Talus was waiting on Eugene's call. 'Very grown-up, aren't we? One more little drink, and then we do the necessary. It won't take long. I'll go through in a moment and get everything ready. That suit, young sir?'

'Perfect,' said Eugene.

The dogs followed Shifter as he messed around making cocktails. Eugene noticed the elaborate leather collars they wore. 'Nice collars on the dogs, Mal,' he said, for want of anything else to say and because Dolly was whispering to attract his attention.

'Nice?' Shifter gave Eugene an arch look. 'Those are more than nice, young man. They're unique. Quite unique. Money can't buy them or their like. The finest, very finest materials, fashioned and crafted by an artist. A specialist unrivalled in her field. Have a look, have a closer look . . .' Shifter laughed at Eugene's reluctant approach. 'Not too close, you're thinking, eh? Remembering the bit of trouble between you and my boys, eh? Don't worry. You're quite safe as long as I'm here. I'd advise you not to touch though.'

Eugene had not the least inclination to touch. Nor any interest in the finer points of dog-collar fashion. He nodded appropriately as Shifter warbled on about the marvellous workmanship involved and the individual merits of each particular collar. Turned out Letitia made the bloody things. He should have guessed. 'Upstairs work,' said Shifter. 'Demands total concentration.' Loveless was apparently wearing last year's collar. 'The Ladies are waiting for materials. The minute they arrive, it will be creative frenzy.' Shifter tickled Loveless. 'Not long, my young hero. Soon, I'm sure.'

Eugene looked at the dog's murderous little eyes and then at Shifter, still prattling on as he displayed embroidered stars and other collar highlights. 'He's mad as a badger,' Eugene thought. A split second later he jumped back, as Loveless's teeth flashed past him, just missing his hand.

Shifter chirruped, and the dog spun back to his side. All three dogs were staring at Eugene now, hackles erect, teeth bared. Shifter looked at Eugene, then back at the dogs. He shook his head, eyebrows raised and half smiling. 'Uncanny,' he said. 'Uncanny.'

Eugene stared back at Shifter, uncertain. 'What's uncanny?' he asked.

'The dogs,' said Shifter briskly. 'Rhodesian Ridgebacks. Uncanny, the way they hate you blacks.'

As the dogs began to bristle, Eugene turned away, frightened to provoke them further. 'Yeah,' he said flatly. 'Just uncanny, Mal. A freak of nature.'

Shifter giggled. 'No offence intended, Eugene. I know some people are very sensitive. Tactless, that's me. Tactless, Loveless; Thoughtless, Hopeless; Graceless, Faithless,' he chanted. 'Apologies, Eugene. Apologies.'

'No worries,' Eugene replied. He desperately wanted to get out of the house and away. He looked at his watch and told Shifter he would need to be moving before long. Shifter shuffled off to sort the gear and told Eugene he'd shout him through in a couple of minutes.

Letitia was using a dark purple thread. To escape Dolly's wandering hands Eugene moved across to look. The tapestry was three-quarters done. Distorted by Letitia's work frame, it was difficult to make out the exact subject. 'What is it?' he asked.

Letitia paused and looked up. 'Siege of Caffa,' she said, releasing the frame and spreading out the square of fabric. 'Got inspired watching the news. Chemical Ali.'

Eugene tried to make sense of what he saw. To the left were people standing, sitting and lying down. Dividing the picture was something like a big wall, which people appeared to fly over. To the right of the wall were different-looking people. And down in the corner were black ships, sailing away on a wine-red sea.

'Ready,' called Shifter. Eugene didn't need telling twice. Twenty minutes later he was back in the Puma telling Talus the deal looked sweet and arranging a meet at the Halcyenda to brief George and Archie.

When he got home that night he went straight up to his room and on to the Net. '1346 – Siege of Caffa. Genoese merchant town on banks of Crimea. Besieged by Tartars. Siege collapsed due to Tartar army becoming infected with Bubonic plague. Before leaving, the surviving Tartars catapulted their former comrades' plague-infected corpses over the city wall and into Caffa. The Genoese threw the corpses straight into the sea, but the plague began to spread inside the gates. Those who could fled by boat, via the Straits of Bosphorus and into the Mediterranean. The refugees carried the infection with them. By 1349 it had wiped out a third of the population of Europe.

'Shifter's Fuckin House of Horrors or what?' Eugene said to himself.

After such a start the week could only get better, and within a couple of days Eugene was feeling considerably brighter. He'd been on his best behaviour at home and chauffeured Simone back from work three nights running. His efforts were rewarded. Gladys calmed down and stopped fretting every time he left the house. Simone left off telling him he was a sad pathetic loser who cared only for himself. The Minimonster was still shuttling around various experts who had the unenviable task of deciding on 'a comprehensive care and assessment plan' for the little bastard. Nero, meanwhile, carried on as usual, except for nervousness and improved behaviour when Eugene was around.

CHAPTER ELEVEN

In whose sad time bloud did from heauen raine.

FQ: The Legend of Sir Gvyon: II.x.34

Now everyone at SweetHearts was murder mad. At first it was just the girls, the dancers and their perpetual talk of dead girls, torture and perversion. The rest of the staff took the piss, told them they were well weird and should lighten up. But it turned out that the girls were simply quick on the uptake, because soon everyone had caught the bug. Murder mania spread like contagion – it became an endemic infection seeping through the club, all-pervasive and unavoidable. Kitchen staff, barmen, cleaners, secretaries – even the security hardmen – succumbed to the serial-killer obsession. Inevitably, Sweet-Hearts was quickly awash with rumour and competing claims of 'confidential information'. Everybody knew somebody whose friend's sister married a copper. Everybody speculated on the details of death. Where and what had been slashed, cut out, or penetrated? Everybody wanted to know how the killer was linked to SweetHearts.

Nor was Mr Barry exempt from murder mayhem. The manager seemed to spend half his life talking to Talus or Archie Faron about the two deaths. Discussing strategies and damage limitation and how to handle the coppers – especially Gale, who was becoming a total pain in the arse.

Mr Barry – when relaxing – was keen on American detective shows. Unfortunately DCI Arthur Gale was nothing like the homicide cops featured in Mr Barry's blockbuster series. The Americans were all laid-back mavericks with deadpan expressions and a fund of quirky one-liners; DCI Arthur Gale possessed no trace of jokey cool and ran investigations by the book. He believed in rules. It was his job to uphold society's rules – and to punish those who sought to flout them.

Gale's murder-squad team were committed, well organized and efficient. They were now working flat out on the Meatman murders, trying to catch the bastard before he did another one. And their attention focused on the SweetHearts connection.

And as a result, Mr Barry had been showered with demands: they asked for employment files, tax returns, proof of VAT and national insurance payments, copies of club membership lists, details of SweetHeart employees, including all personnel records, past and present. You name it, DCI Arthur Gale wanted it. Every last scrap of it.

Unfortunately for the police, Archie Faron was the custodian of the club's financial records, which he kept firmly under lock and key. As DCI Gale's multiple requests were, according to Ali Acrasiafi, Gloria's dad, and the Firm's top legal, totally bona fide and all present and correct – well, then, there was only one thing for it: if DCI Gale wanted documents, then documents he would have.

Mr Barry, working under Archie's direction, had spent night after night fabricating sanitized – and entirely bogus – versions of the required paperwork. Since Amy Fiddeler's murder, the SweetHearts' manager had averaged three hours' sleep a night. It was beginning to get to him.

DCI Gale was proving a major headache. But Mr Barry had other, and more personal, concerns. He was sure that it wouldn't be long before the press caught on. It was public knowledge that Stella had been a SweetHearts dancer, but no one had connected Amy to the club. Her audition and friendship with Canday Sweete were, as yet, undiscovered, but – as Mr Barry and the Farons well knew – any minute now some fuckin journalist would wake up to two plus two making four. Then it would be pure pandemonium.

So the Farons were preparing defences. Mae was already acting as press liaison officer – handing out free drinks, complimentary tickets and lots of flattery and attention to target journalists. The girls were told to keep their knickers on and clean up their acts. Private dance sessions were – for the moment – off limits. Any girl seen leaving with a client would be sacked on the spot.

The prospect of publicity terrified Mr Barry. He was well aware that the story was a tabloid dream. An irresistible mix of murders, lap-dancers, under-age prostitutes and teenage junkies: Amy Fiddeler's toxicology tests had come back, indicating that on the night of her death she had taken heroin, cannabis and a large amount of crack cocaine. Plus enough alcohol to float a battleship. But Mr Barry had expected as much.

Dead girls, drugs – it was all very unsavoury and bad for business. Mr Barry could cope with that – it would be no more than a few weeks of tabloid sensation, then another scandal would take over. Takings in the short term would, naturally, suffer, but the punters would soon be back. The notoriety might even be good for SweetHearts in the long run.

No, Mr Barry's worries were of an altogether more personal nature. The fear started off as a mere niggle, now it was an ever-present headache. He knew the vermin journos would find out about him and little Stella.

He could picture the centre-page spread – 'Club Manager

Barry (46 years) Was Murdered Teen's Love Rat'. There would be a deeply unflattering snatched photo of him, looking ten years older and a stone heavier, set alongside Stella's last publicity shot, a big-eyed eighteen-year-old smiling through a curtain of long blond hair.

Mr Barry had nightmares about it. The papers would tell the story of how he and Stella 'fell in love' and how she adored her 'nightclub boss'. Then, appalled readers would learn how Stella's lover abused and cheated on her. How he'd never known that she was carrying his baby.

All the girls had heard him when he said Stella was getting too fat for the job. 'Do some sit-ups or something,' he'd instructed. 'Tone up, girl, and get the weight down.' She must have been about three or four months by then. Why hadn't she said? Why the fuck hadn't she told him?

It had been that Saturday afternoon – the murder day – when Mr Barry had looked in on the Harem Nights rehearsals. Stella's stomach was bigger than ever. 'You look like a pig in a fucking wig,' he'd told her. The other girls tittered. Stella just stood there. The tears pouring down her face, looking straight at him. 'I'm telling you for your own good,' Mr Barry had said, embarrassed and annoyed by her overreaction. 'Lose the gut and you'll be mint, all right, love?' Then she was sobbing, crying like her heart would break. One of the other dancers took her off stage. Mr Barry shrugged and rolled his eyes, miming total bafflement. The other girls laughed on cue. It was the last time he ever saw her.

Mr Barry usually met Stella after work on Saturday nights. The two of them would organize takeaways and drink and head back to Mr Barry's place.

But that Saturday he didn't feel like it. The silly cow had shown him up – all that crap, turning on the tear-tap. Couldn't she take a joke?

She had started to get clingy, and he wasn't interested.

140

So he asked Mae to tell Stella he couldn't make it. 'Tell her something's come up. I'll see her Monday,' he'd said.

That Saturday he'd cashed up and finished by 3.15 a.m. Walking out through the foyer, he'd looked for her, half-expecting, half-hoping, to see her waiting for him as usual. But no Stella. She was obviously having a strop, he thought, and carried on, out the club door and into a taxi. And now, he kept thinking about it. About how it was his fault she was dead – because if he had kept to the usual plan, she would have been with him, not on her own. And she wasn't fat either. It was the baby. That night, Stella ought to have been in the taxi, with him. Not walking alone down to the dark of the Archway Tower.

With SweetHearts staff, and especially in front of the Farons, Mr Barry was all business-like efficiency. He drew up plans for 'crisis management' and impressed every-one with his firm but calm demeanour. Only Mae knew different.

It was Mae who found Mr Barry under his desk, knees clasped to his chest. It took a long time and multiple brandies to coax him out. Mr Barry told Mae about Stella's baby. Mae already knew – Mae knew everybody's secrets at SweetHearts – but she didn't let on. Just listened quietly as Mr Barry talked and cried.

Thursday the same week the Puma was skimming down the hill towards Crouch End Broadway. It was 7 p.m. and the light was fading. Eugene was meeting Brittany at her new house. She had told him when he phoned that she had finally been able to move in, after months of waiting. He'd asked her out for dinner and she'd refused. 'I'll cook, then you can see the house.' She was clearly thrilled with the place. Eugene was mainly interested in the bedroom.

Brittany's new flat was in a sideroad. Red-brick villas stood on a tree-lined road, which coasted over the brow of a small rise. Front gardens were full of early flowers and eager spring leaf and the evening carried a faint scent. As the Puma purred to a halt, Eugene could see the pale new moon rising. Walking up to number three, the two bottles of Pol Roger clanking beside him in a plastic bag, Eugene wondered how the hell the girl could afford this.

CHAPTER TWELVE

All things, as they created were, doe grow,
And yet remember well the mightie word,
Which first was spoken by th'Almightie lord,
That bad them to increase and multiply:

FQ: The Legend of Britomartis;
The Gardin of Adonis: III.vi.34

Eugene heard her coming, just seconds after he'd rung the bell, the rapid sound of her feet on the stairs, changing to a slower beat as she hit level ground. A moment later, the door opened and there she was. Smiling at him – but definitely nervous. To Eugene, the nerves were a relief. He was more than a bit jittery himself, truth be told. Eugene wasn't used to this 'nice girl', come-round-to-dinner stuff. His 'romantic' life generally revolved around a tight locus of wine bar–nightclub–bedroom. Familiar territory, where he kept control and knew the plot.

This was new ground. Eating and talking – he didn't talk to girlfriends, just shouted the odd remark above the babble of voices and multidecibel music. Couldn't hear what the girl was mouthing in reply and didn't care. He was after a shag. If he'd wanted to revive the lost art of conversation, he'd have gone elsewhere. So no wonder he was a tad edgy now. What the fuck would they talk about? It worried him. And it was just him and her. Alone. Eugene's idea of one-to-one intimacy concentrated on girls who were naked and horizontal.

So what? he told himself. It was no big deal whichever way. He felt oddly self-conscious, all the same, returning Brittany's nervous smile as she invited him in. Crossing the threshold, Eugene paused – he felt very strange, and the house felt stranger still.

The sense of disembodied dizziness lasted a split second. Then Eugene was inside; telling himself to relax as Brittany led the way across a tiled hallway which seemed to be the only ground-floor room, the house proper beginning at first-floor level. He'd been in the house for less than a minute, but Eugene had already seen enough to know his first impressions were dead on. The place had cost a fortune, and no mistake about it.

To the right of the stairway was a darkly polished half-moon table set flush against the wall. Above the table was an enormous oval mirror. Looking across the hallway, Eugene saw an identical table positioned precisely opposite the other. Again, the table was surmounted by a mirror, the glittering, silver frame exactly matching that of its twin. Shards of light danced between the two revealing a reflected infinity within the glass. 'It's like magic isn't it?' Brittany's voice made Eugene jump. 'Sometimes I get mesmerized standing here,' she continued. 'Look – seems to go on for ever, doesn't it? I've tried counting – but it doesn't work.' She smiled a thousand smiles, and a thousand Eugenes smiled back at her. 'Anyway,' she said, 'come on up.'

The stairs were graceful, sweeping upwards through a wide curve. Wrought ironwork, leaping and spinning exuberantly, rose to follow the upward turn of mahogany banisters, the red-dark wood glowing from the passage of countless hands. The stairs led to a wide circular landing with rooms leading off it, whilst a second flight led on to a higher platform from which more rooms radiated. A final climb – much shorter this time – rose to a mezzanine floor and a single doorway. From the winding stairway, you could see the whole house from top to bottom, and Eugene realized that both staircase and landings were off-kilter. It really reminded Eugene of somewhere he'd been before – but he couldn't quite get it. He gave up and went into the kitchen after Brittany.

The kitchen opened on to a balcony and wooden steps ran from there to the garden below. It was a warm night – warm enough to risk sitting outside. Eugene couldn't believe the place. What was the girl – billionaire's daughter or something? He asked for the bathroom. He needed a line, or two maybe, lift his mood a bit.

As usual, the coke did the trick and he felt back on form. It was OK – drinking champagne, looking at Brittany, talking about nothing. He wondered what she'd be like in bed – and then Brittany asked him if he liked the house.

Eugene took a mouthful of champagne and shook his head. 'It's beautiful,' he told her. 'And I haven't seen half of it – so what's the story? I mean how the fuck did you swing it? Lottery win? International money-laundering? No, hang on – you were married for six months to a ninety-five-year-old Texan billionaire who left you everything in his will. Am I right?'

Brittany said he was extremely wrong.

Eugene shrugged. 'Oh, well, it was always the odds-on favourite anyway. Millionaire daddy's baby daughter. Loads of them running round Ladbroke Grove and that way. So,' Eugene continued. 'Put me on the track. How much did daddy stump up?' He got no reply. 'Come on,' he tried again. 'Don't go all coy. Fuck, I bet you get an allowance as well. I'll make a guess – I bet he gives you . . . what . . . yeah, about ten thou a month. Am I close?'

'Why don't I run and fetch my bank statements – you can check them through, just to make sure? I've probably got the

145

deeds of the house – oh, and I'll bring my credit-card receipts, too, have a good look at the lot, seeing as you're so fascinated.'

'I don't give a fuck,' Eugene said. 'I was only asking. Just something to say. You think I care about that shit? Why'd you ask me round here anyway, check my table manners before you risk a restaurant? Another giddy little middle-class rebel who fancies sleeping with a black man?'

She said nothing. The silence expanding in the darkness. Seconds ticking into minutes. Nothing said, neither of them moving.

It was time to head out, Eugene thought. Stuck-up bitch. He hadn't meant anything, he was only foolin. Fuck her. Just go home.

Eugene stood up. 'I'm going,' he said. She nodded and turned her head sharply away, looking out into the shadowed garden. Eugene walked past her and out through the kitchen. He was halfway down the stairs, when suddenly it came to him. The place reminded him of a treehouse – that was it. A central trunk with rooms branching outwards. As if the house was growing and alive. His father had built him a treehouse in the Haleys' garden. Eugene looked down to the hallway, hesitated, and then he turned round and walked back up the stairs, through the kitchen and out on to the balcony. She hadn't moved. He touched her shoulder, and she turned to look at him.

'I'm sorry.' Eugene spoke very quickly, but didn't duck his head or look away. 'I owe you an apology, big style. I'm nervous. I meant no disrespect. It was meant as a joke, but it wasn't funny. Just stupid and rude. I like you. I'd like to stay, although I know I'm taking a risk with your cooking.'

She cuffed him gently. 'Forgiven and forgotten,' she said. They stayed outside, kissing, for a long time. Afterwards, Eugene could only shake his head and wonder – either he'd really fallen for the girl, or he was losing it and big time.

Apologizing was something he just didn't do. He made a mental note to get a grip.

It turned out Brittany had inherited the money from her aunt. She didn't specify exactly, but it was obviously a major haul. She kept saying how lucky she was. 'Too right,' Eugene thought, although he had the brains not to say it. And it was a brilliant story, Brittany and the old aunt. Eugene loved it. It was like something off the Discovery Channel. That Great Books series they did – it was full of grateful orphans getting surprise inheritances.

In fact the aunt was really a great-aunt – a hundred and one when she died. The old lady had adored her niece, who adored her in turn. Eugene heard how Brittany spent every summer with Aunt Felicity – learning to ride, reading books, playing practical jokes. Dogs, horses, an English country house and tons of money.

To him it was a fairytale – utterly foreign, and therefore all the more compelling. It had all the right ingredients – lonely, neglected child palmed off on ancient spinster aunt of terrifying reputation. Aunt and sad child forge unbreakable bond. Aunt dies leaving everything to beloved niece, thus utterly infuriating niece's cold and neglectful parents. It was magical. Eugene couldn't get enough of it.

Brittany asked if he wanted to see the house. Her excitement made him smile. He drained his glass and took his cue. 'Come on, then,' said Eugene. 'I know you want to. Show me round the dream home.'

It was obvious she'd only just moved in. Most rooms were full of boxes. Paintings were propped against walls and piles of books littered the floor. She hadn't been there long enough to finish unpacking. 'And anyway,' she told him, 'I need to think about it. I want to do it properly, get it right.'

Houses weren't Eugene's thing. He owned a skanky flat down Fin Park, bought a couple of years back – but only for investment purposes. The flat guaranteed him a monthly rent cheque, courtesy of the council. Eugene took the money and never went near the place. The tenants were, inevitably, asylum-seekers – he didn't want to listen to fuckin Albanians whinging about blocked drains and the like. Otherwise he was happy enough living at Wentworth Road.

He couldn't see the point in wasting money moving. All he needed was somewhere comfortable to sleep with a decent bathroom and shower. And you had to have a fridge, plus TV with cable. That was about it. It was all provided at Wentworth Road. And his mum lived at Wentworth Road – which meant first-class food. Not only that, but his mum kept the place clean and decent, and she made sure all his washing was taken care of. He just couldn't see what was to gain going elsewhere.

But as he went from room to room following Brittany through the house, he began to feel a flicker of interest. He caught some of her exhilaration, shared her pleasure in the bizarre layout of the rooms. For some reason, she didn't take him to the room on the top floor. She said it was locked when Eugene asked. When the tour ended, Brittany suggested he look round outside whilst she sorted the food. Eugene walked down the wooden steps and then to the far end of the garden, which was deep in shadow. Leaning against a tree, he thought how quiet it was. He saw an expanse of plants and trees turned silver-green and grey under the pale light of the sickle moon. There was nothing of the city noise, no background of traffic – only a rustling silence prevailed.

Over dinner Brittany asked about where he worked. Eugene was ready for this one: he was an independent financial advisor, he explained. Had an office close to Highbury Corner. Eugene avoided details. 'Come on, even I know it's the world's most boring job,' he joked. 'You really want the gen on pensions, stocks and gilt bonds? I don't think so.' He did however manage to insinuate that he earned a fortune.

Brittany worked for some TV company. Eugene learnt

148

that Rhoda-the-friend-from-hell lectured at Holloway Uni – same place as Belinda – although Eugene made no mention of Ralph's barking-mad wife. Brittany told him her parents were retired and living in France. There were no brothers or sisters, and Brittany saw her mum and dad twice a year, Christmas and August. 'We keep in touch by email,' she said. Eugene thought it strange and sad – a pale pretence of a family, it seemed to him.

When Brittany said, 'What about your mum and dad?', Eugene momentarily floundered. He didn't talk about Wentworth Road, didn't discuss it. That area of his life was private, even with Ralph, who had spent half his adolescence in and out of Eugene's home.

Brittany thought he hadn't heard her. 'So tell me about your family, then,' she said again.

He said there wasn't much to tell. Did a lightning sketch, muttered something about living at home, Mum, Simone, Nero. Just off the Holloway Road. That's about it. Then Brittany asked about his dad, and family life. Was he close?

Afterwards he decided it must have been the coke, making his mouth run on, fuelling the talk. Must have overdone the lines, too much white powder – because once he started he didn't shut up. He told her about Guyana, and how his mum and dad had left for England. He told her all about the Haleys and Wentworth Road. He explained about Ralph, that they were good as brothers, and how they met that first day at school. He said nothing about the Firm and next to nothing about his father's death – he hadn't lost the plot entirely. Instead, he made Brittany laugh by recounting tales of the Minimonster – although he edited out the worst stuff; and she was fascinated when he explained about Simone lap-dancing – especially with her working at SweetHearts.

The mention of SweetHearts led on to the murders – she was every bit as obsessed as Eugene – and he was able to regale her with Simone's version of the 'inside story'. It was dead on midnight when Brittany stood up. 'Would you like to stay the night?' she said. Eugene didn't need asking twice. Once again, he followed her up the stairs – this time to the very top.

The supposedly locked door opened to reveal her bedroom. It was the only room in the house that seemed complete. An entire wall of French windows stood open to the soft night air. Outside, the leaves and flowers flowed over curved trellises, whilst more plants, some dark and shining, others trailing feathery loops of delicate, creamy flowers, were inside the room itself.

The bedroom's walls were deep green. In the centre of the room stood a canopy of twisting silks, tumbling downward, partially concealing the bed beneath, casting liquid shadows across dark satin. They kissed as he undressed her, running his hands up and down the skin of her back, then she wrapped her legs around his waist and they started to move, sliding together, surrounded by glimmering shadows.

Eugene had fantasized a lot about shagging her – been looking forward to it. It turned out his fantasies had been way wide of the mark – hadn't even come close. They slept, spoon-style, legs entwined, his breath against the nape of her neck.

Brittany had to be in work for 10 a.m. Eugene gave her a lift down to Fin Park tube, they kissed goodbye and he asked when he could see her again. Wednesday night seemed a long way off, but he hung cool and arranged to pick her up around 8 p.m. He watched her until she turned into the station and disappeared from sight. Then he let the Puma lope at its own pace, as they headed back home. Singing along to a CD down the Stroud Green Road and smiling to himself all the way. As further proof of fortune's favour he got home bang on time for the start of *Trisha*.

Holloway University stands less than a mile away from Wentworth Road. An ugly combination of concrete and glass built in the seventies and now distinctly tatty. The dilapidated and increasingly precarious 'Glass Tower' is acknowledged as a particular eyesore. The tower's hundreds of windows have not been cleaned in living memory. Opaque brown slabs have replaced the sparkle of reflected sunlight the architect once envisaged. Inside the building, however, one design innovation still cuts the mustard. Attempts by staff and students to jump in and out of the perpetually revolving open-door paternoster lifts still provoke hilarity and painful accidents – just as they did thirty years ago when the tower was opened.

The department of social sciences shares the tower's eleventh floor with race and gender studies. The twelfth and top floor houses the staff canteen, which supposedly enjoys 'panoramic vistas of the capital'. In fact the windows are now too dirty to see out of. For the ten weeks of summer term, 'Al Fresco – rooftop restaurant' opens up out on the terrace, and you can see for miles and miles. If you knew where to look – St Joseph's on Highgate Hill, Archway Tower directly below, Saracen's Head on the corner painted saffron-yellow – you could find Wentworth Road. Maybe even pick out number forty if you spotted the silver Puma idling outside the Burnsides' door.

Inside number forty, *Trisha* was hotting up. The programme's theme was Are You Just a Love-Rat's Doormat? The three accused 'love-rats' protested their innocence and took lie-detector tests. The audience booed. Trisha demanded to know why 'doormat' wives and girlfriends put up with such treatment. One of the women started crying. Trisha – inevitably – recommended counselling, and the studio audience clapped approval.

After the break, on came Gary and Mel. Gary said he was no love-rat; he told Trisha about Mel's obsessive jealousy. How she'd accosted a girl at the works Christmas party – 'Hardly knew the girl,' Gary said. The audience tutted their sympathy. 'Is this right, Mel?' said Trisha. 'Do you really search his pockets and all that stuff? I mean, opening somebody's personal letters is actually against the law.' Gary said Mel should go to counselling. Trisha nodded sagely, the audience applauded. Eugene thought Gary was a cocky little twat.

Then Trisha asked us to welcome Andrea. Seventeen years old and unbelievably dim, Andrea said Gary had been shagging her for over two years. 'We're engaged,' she said and showed her ring. The audience 'oohed'. Gary said he didn't know what the girl was talking about. 'Statutory rape,' Trisha replied. 'But first let's welcome Lorraine, who also says she is Gary's girlfriend.' Utter pandemonium ensued.

Eugene reckoned it was one of the best *Trisha*s he'd seen. He checked the time and went upstairs to sort things and get ready. He was meeting Talus at 11.30 a.m. 'Punctuality is the politeness of princes,' Talus liked to say. Eugene got a move on.

Later that morning, in Al Fresco, a slim, dark-haired woman was waiting for a colleague. It was a glorious day, but the woman ignored the famous Glass Tower view, preferring instead to fiddle endlessly with her mobile. She checked one more time – 10.30 a.m. when she sent the text; the reply came soon after. When her colleague arrived, she wasted no time. 'Have a look at this,' she said, passing the phone across.

CHAPTER THIRTEEN

What warre so cruell, or what siege so sore,
As that, which strong affections do apply
Against the fort of reason euermore
To bring the soule into captiuitie:

FQ: The Legend of Sir Gvyon: II.xi.1

Eugene had written off Friday night – had accepted the inevitable. He'd heard from his star boy at the beginning of the week. The way Ralph told it, Belinda was getting worse, not better. 'She's just blazing, man,' Ralph said. 'Can't tell her nix. Keeps saying how she knows – knows what for fucks sake? She's been screaming and raging all weekend – and I'm talking like every waking minute, E.' Ralph sounded shaky. Eugene told him to cool it. 'She's your wife, star. She loves you – really loves you. Women are always doing stuff like this; you know – hysterics, tears, giving grief. Ride the storm, spar – a day or so and she'll be fine.'

Ralph said he was steady. 'No probs, bro. I'm light and level, just sitting it out. No worries.' If this was an attempt at reassurance, Ralph didn't pull it off – not even nearly. He kept trailing out to silence, his voice disintegrating into a series of fractured gulps. Eugene was petrified. It sounded like Ralph was going to cry. Thankfully he didn't. Eventually Ralph got himself back together, and said he'd better get back to the shop.' 'I'm lost, man,' was the last thing he said. 'Don't know how to handle this.'

Eugene blamed Belinda. It was entirely her doing, his star boy's misery was of her making. Ignorant bitch. It was a total tragedy. Of all the women in all the world – and, statistically speaking, there were millions – his best bro had to fall in love, and fall sky-diving big style, for that mega-mouth snapper. What a fuckin joke. Not that Eugene was laughing any.

He heard no more from Ralph all week. Which he took to mean domestic bliss was more or less back on track. The skanky cow had probably calmed down some by now, Eugene thought. But even so, Ralph was totally unlikely to chance a boys' own Friday night – and thus risk setting the whole thing off again. So in Eugene's book, seeing his star boy – well, it was a certain non-starter. He was already considering alternative plans when Ralph called him midday Friday.

But Ralph wasn't cancelling. He said he'd meet Eugene outside the shop. Bang on 7 p.m. 'Excellent,' Eugene said. 'Brilliant. You know I'd kind of written you off after what you were saying on Monday.'

'Yeah. Good,' Ralph said. 'Look, man, gotta go.' There were people in the shop. Business to attend to. 'Fill you in tonight, E.,' he said, 'and I'll need whatever you're bringing. So check supplies. Catch you later.'

Eugene was puzzled. Of course he knew perfectly well what Ralph meant – the white stuff and plenty of it – but Eugene always had a decent stash, and always made sure Ralph was well looked after. But it was an unspoken thing. Ralph had never asked before – and Eugene was surprised, not because there was anything wrong, but because it was – well – such an un-Ralphish thing to do.

*   *   *

154

At five to seven on Friday, the Puma moved eagerly up the Hornsey Road, leaping over the brow of Crouch End Hill and racing down the slope so fast, Eugene had to check speed quickly, pulling on the curb rein just before they jumped the traffic lights at the bottom. The Puma's skittish high spirits made him smile. He was in a good mood himself. He wanted to tell Ralph about Brittany. About the magical house, and the old aunt. He just hoped Ralph didn't do the 'black and white/can't be right' bollocks. He really wasn't up for it.

His star boy had locked up already and was on the pavement waiting, as Eugene settled the Puma outside DCT. Then the two of them walked round the corner to Verity's wine bar. Eugene slipped a wrap of coke into Ralph's pocket and left him to hit the toilets; meanwhile Eugene sorted the drinks. He thought Ralph looked like shit. Grey-faced and tired. Eugene got a bottle of white and found a quiet table.

When Ralph came back, Eugene left to do his own line. When he returned, and they were settled, Eugene turned to his friend. 'What's up my mainman? You having some problems? Or maybe not? P'raps jus' a bit of a bad day?'

Ralph shook his head. He had clearly taken a serious run at the coke. His eyes told the story, and, like it does, the cocaine made him voluble.

Eugene was totally taken aback. Could hardly credit what Ralph was saying. Belinda had kicked him out. Was talking about divorce. Ralph was staying back with his parents; Belinda had told him she wanted 'time and space to think'. And what really annoyed Eugene was the foolishness, the idiocy of the whole thing. Belinda was adamant Ralph was screwing around. She KNEW, she kept saying, absolutely KNEW, Ralph had at least one regular girlfriend. Because he'd been seen.

'Seen by who?' asked Eugene.

Ralph shrugged. 'She won't tell me. Some friend of hers told her she saw me in Mirrors Bar – Belinda says this fuck-friend told her I was dancing, smooching, she said, with this girl. Supposedly I bought the girl drinks and was kissing and fondling her. Left with her apparently. Blonde girl. Oh, and it was a Friday and you were there too, with another blonde.'

'That's total crap,' said Eugene. 'You never . . .'

'Yeah,' Ralph interrupted. 'You know, I know, but Belinda, she believes every stupid word. Nothin I say makes any difference. I was going to ask you to come round and tell her, but she just laughed at me. "Yeah, get your gangster friend round. Like he's not the biggest liar in London. Like he respects women. Like I'll listen to him."' Eugene raised his eyebrows and Ralph shrugged. 'Yeah. Totally out of order. Sorry.'

And Ralph had more to tell, none of it good. 'What's really convinced her is the phone calls and stuff,' he said.

'What?' Eugene asked.

'Silent phone calls, dropped calls,' Ralph explained. 'Phone rings at home, she picks it up, and whoever's on the other end says nothing and cuts the call. Only happened two or three times. She's convinced it's my fantasy blonde. Then she found some number in my desk, she says. She rang it and a girl answered. But I don't know fuck about it. It'll be some customer or supplier or some fucking thing. I can't remember.' Ralph paused and finished his vodka and Red Bull. Then he looked up. 'I don't know what's happening, E.,' he said. 'I haven't a clue. I think she's going to leave me and I can't do a thing to stop her.'

Eugene let Ralph talk it all out. Kept quiet, listening and asking the odd question. Sensing his spar's need to down-load the whole thing. Cos it sounded like Ralph had had it well rough.

'I tell you, E. – it's been fuckin unbearable.' Ralph looked across at Eugene with his blacked-out, coked-up eyes. 'No joke, man, it was almost a relief when she kicked me out. I mean, the last couple of days – serious – I mean, it was total madness.'

Ralph took a drink and stood up. 'Be back in a minute,' he said, and headed for the toilets. It was closer to five minutes, and when he came back his eyes were popping. Another drink, then back to the story like he'd never left, catching the thread straight off:

'She's screaming accusations the second I walk through the door. Then she runs upstairs. I can hear her. In the bedroom, in the bathroom; sobbing like her heart is breaking. She kicked me out two days ago. You know, E., you know; when she's mouthing off all the fuckin time, and she's shouting and screaming so the whole world can hear. The entire street knows our stuff. Honestly, man, it's a good thing I'm away from there. Few more days and I'd have flipped.'

Ralph looked at Eugene and shrugged, palms upward. 'And, oh shit, E. I can't take it, bro. She's crying like there's no tomorrow. I can't bear it, man. I can't stand to listen . . . Hang on a minute.' Ralph got to his feet, saying something about 'off to the loo'.

'Take it easy, spar,' Eugene said. 'You only went ten minutes back.'

'Yeah?' said Ralph. 'Well, here's a thing. I'm going again.' He came back with eyes glittering, every muscle twitching and jumping. And the boy just couldn't shut up. On and on and on he went. Non-stop drivel. Eugene was utterly sick of it. Was aching to tell Ralph to forget the stupid bitch. Dump her. Leave while you still can – and don't stress about it.

But Eugene listened and kept his mouth closed. Love is blind, they say. Eugene couldn't argue with that. In Ralph's case, deaf, dumb and stupid as well. But there you go.

They left the bar some time after midnight. Eugene vetoed Ralph's nightclub ideas – shoved him in the Puma and took him back to his parents. When he saw Ralph was safely inside, Eugene turned the Puma towards Wentworth Road. He felt exhausted. He'd spent the entire night playing agony aunt – and hadn't enjoyed it. Eugene was not a natural at the therapist/counsellor/supportive-friend thing.

In fact, as he steered the Puma homeward, Eugene reckoned he'd been a regular Florence Nightingale. Encouraging, kind and tactful. Putting up with Ralph's increasingly incoherent Belinda-babble had not been easy. But he'd managed. He was rather impressed with himself.

And he'd never so much as mentioned Brittany's name – although he'd sent her a text when Ralph was on one of his many toilet trips. So far, no reply.

Brittany's mobile was safely zipped up inside her bag, and she wouldn't have heard it ring above the music anyway – which was all to the good, because she was concentrating hard and didn't need interruptions. Her face was shiny with sweat, her hands were damp, and there were dark stains between her shoulder blades where the sweat running down her back had soaked into her blue top. Like everyone else in the room she was watching the demonstration.

'So, everyone is OK? Everyone happy, or you want I do again? Good. Right, get ready, and we do it all together one last time. One second, OK. Brittany, darling, your turn with me. You see, I don't forget you.'

Rhoda mouthed, 'Lucky bitch', as Brittany moved towards the front of the class. Fabrio's favours were fought over – as far as Brittany and Rhoda could work out, he'd slept with at least five of his salsa students and was steadily working his way through the rest.

At 9.30 p.m. Fabrio said, 'Thank you, baby,' to Brittany, and ended the lesson. The lights dimmed and the music got louder. Fabrio – morphing seamlessly into Latino DJ – took to the mike. 'It's gonna be hot-hot-hot in here tonight. Come on, salseros, show me your style, I wanna see floor action at the coolest club outside Colombia. Cicibeo's Club Cali.'

Fabrio paused to turn the music up further before leaning into the mike. 'Soooooooo, saaaaalSA.'

The club was filling up quickly, In the meantime Brittany and Rhoda hit the loos to cool down and re-do the make-up.

Standing side by side in front of the mirror, Rhoda waved her hand before Brittany's face. 'Hello. Anyone home? Calling Brittany, will Brittany Martin come in now, please?'

'Which planet are you on?' asked Rhoda, eyebrows raised. 'As if I couldn't guess after the text you sent. But I want the news in full. Come on, don't keep me in suspense.'

Brittany initially enjoyed the conversation. She wanted to talk about Eugene and didn't need much encouragement – especially as Rhoda had met him, knew what she was going on about. Ninety minutes later she faked a migraine, left Rhoda in the club and taxied home. She'd been desperate to get away from Rhoda and her insinuating, relentless demands for every last detail.

And the woman had been unstoppable. Nothing Brittany tried – jokes, sarcasm, obvious annoyance – nothing had dissuaded Rhoda from her poking and probing. Brittany agreed to dance with anyone who cared to ask, just to get away from it. She was close to telling Rhoda to fuck off and get a life, and just so glad to get away.

She was home a couple of hours before she thought to check her mobile: 'WSH U WRE HRE. MS U & WL RNG TMRW. E . . . XXX.'

Eugene was watching Discovery – a life of Catherine the Great of Russia. The stuff about the horse was unbelievable. Eugene was sure it couldn't be right – OK, she had that special sling thing set up, but even so . . . Eugene was pretty convinced the whole thing would have been physically impossible. He was still thinking it over when his phone beeped and Brittany's reply came through. Eugene read her message and smiled.

CHAPTER FOURTEEN

. . . lawlesse lustes, corrupt enuies,
And couetous aspectes, all cruell enimies.

FQ: The Legend of Sir Gvyon: II.xi.8

After *Catherine the Great* came to an end, Eugene channel-flicked. He was momentarily caught by something on police car-chases – but it turned out to be lots of grainy American CCTV footage of teenage joyriders careering around eight-lane freeways. They took car-theft seriously in the US – police helicopters hovered, spike chains and roadblocks were set up and fleets of speeding squad-cars converged from every direction in mad pursuit of the felon.

Eugene had seen loads of rubbish like this. Remote in hand, he waited for the outcome – God knows why, as he could predict the entire scenario. It was always the same. American car-thieves, Eugene felt, couldn't drive to save their lives. They always, but always, fucked up. Sure enough, less than thirty seconds elapsed before the runaway car lurched sideways, plunged off the road, down a dirt embankment, and toppled on to its side. Pathetic. He hit the remote.

The next hour was taken up watching *Dogs With Jobs*, usually one of the naffest programmes on the network – but this episode was a total gem, all about how dogs can be trained to look after autistic kids. One such wonder-dog was assigned to seven-year-old Patrick. Eugene watched, amazed, as 'Chloë' the labrador did her stuff.

Secured to Chloë on a long lead, Patrick – previously a behavioural nightmare needing constant supervision – was free. He could go to the park, run around and play – do the usual kid stuff – because Chloë kept him off the road and out of danger and brought him home when she judged the time was right. He could attend normal school without an ever-present adult 'minder'. The minder was replaced by Chloë. If Patrick got aggressive with other kids, Chloë intervened. If he became hysterical, she restrained him. But he wasn't as bad as before, anyway, because stroking the dog calmed him down, and he liked the attention and admiration the dog generated from the other children.

Eugene was almost in tears watching little Patrick. Training a dog like Chloë – it was obvious, Eugene thought – cost an unbelievable amount of money. But Patrick's wealthy parents loved him to bits, so paying for the dog was no prob. The parents – euphoric and grateful – were setting up a 'Chloë Fund' now, so poor kids could get dogs, too.

Eugene checked Ceefax. He rang the Chloë Fund line and donated £500 on his Amex. For a nanosecond, he thought of buying Nero a puppy. Then he remembered the incinerated rabbits, the kitten hanging from the washing line. Eugene ditched the idea straightways. The Minimonster was a psychotic little bastard, a malign goblin child – any dog given to Nero would be lucky to survive the first week.

By the time Eugene had finished quoting his credit-card number and doing his bit for charity, it was just gone 3 a.m. He pulled on his trainers and got ready to move. He'd promised Simone a lift home, and if he set off now he should hit SweetHearts dead on time. Car keys in pocket, he killed the TV, clicked off all but the hallway light and opened the door. It was pitch black outside. Eugene paused for a second

161

to let his eyes adjust, and as he did so, something brushed against his thigh, causing him to jerk backwards. He made a grab – and just in time: the small dark figure had almost wriggled past him and off into the night.

Hauled back into the house, Nero's initial windmilling explosion of kicks and punches ended when Eugene slapped him hard on the bum. The little boy opened his mouth to scream, saw Eugene's face, and subsided. 'Lets me go,' he said sullenly. 'Me want sleepies.'

'You little twat,' said Eugene, still holding tight. 'What do you think you're doing?'

Nero was fully dressed – shoes, coat, the lot. It was near enough three-fifteen. What the fuck was the Minimonster up to now? 'I mean it,' Eugene said. 'Where were you going? I want to know.'

Eugene kept it up for nearly ten minutes, but got absolutely nothing. The boy just blanked him. 'It's no fair,' he said – over and over again. 'No fair. I don't go nowhere.' In the end, the only thing Eugene could do was drag the little bastard back to bed and make sure he was well and truly locked in. He was going to be late for Simone as it was. But as the Puma glided down the empty roads towards SweetHearts, Eugene kept going over it in his mind. What the fuck was up with that kid?

When he arrived at the club, Simone was waiting in the foyer with Mae. Eugene said, course he'd drop Mae off on the way home. No bother, practically drove past her front door anyway. 'I thought we'd be picking Angie up tonight,' Eugene said to his sister as they walked across to where the Puma stood idling.

'You got things wrong, as usual, boy,' Simone replied to Eugene. 'Angie come in tomorrow. She's doing party work tonight.'

Angie was one of Simone's oldest friends. Her family lived at the far end of Wentworth Road. The two girls had been friends at school and had remained close. A couple of months past, Simone had put in a word, and Angie started working the weekend bar shifts at SweetHearts. She was grateful for the work because she was saving like mad. 'Her and Martin need at least £8,000 for the deposit,' Simone told Eugene. 'I mean, the wedding's next summer, you know, and Angie's definite that her and Martin aren't living at Wentworth Road when they're married. Can't blame her, can you? You want some independence, some privacy. On top of that, the wedding, reception and honeymoon are costing a fortune. But Angie always wanted a big do, and you know what her mum's like. Angie says they need every penny they can get.'

As they drove through Islington, Mae asked Eugene what he thought of the murders. Eugene said the whole deal was spooky and he hoped the police would do their job right and catch the bastard. 'It's giving me the jitters,' Eugene said. 'And what about yourselves? How's things in the club?'

Mae said it was difficult. The police were on their backs full time, and the girls, especially, were becoming paranoid – which created a bad atmosphere. Mr Barry was under so much stress she didn't know how he coped.

After Eugene dropped Mae off, brother and sister drove in silence for a while. They were less than five minutes from home when Simone spoke up. 'Eugene, you remember Carl. Nero's father – you remember?'

'He was unforgettable, girl. Course I do,' he said.

For a moment, Simone said nothing, then she continued. 'Well, tonight I think I saw him.'

'Where?' said Eugene.

'Outside the club, when I arrived for work. Standing across the road, looked like he was chatting to this other bloke, but I didn't really see properly . . . the other guy, I mean. Y'know, it was dark and that, and across the road, like I said, but I was so sure, Eugene, just so, so, sure.' Simone looked across at her brother. 'You believe me then . . . that I saw him?'

Eugene nodded. 'I believe you, girl.' Then he told Simone about driving back from the Halcyenda party last month. How he was sure he'd seen Carl just turning off the Holloway Road. He said he hadn't got a good view either, but just the same, he'd be certain that it was Carl.

He thought Simone seemed edgy. Almost as if Carl's reappearance had unnerved her. Eugene hoped it had. His worst nightmare was Simone and Carl getting together again – with Carl staying nights at Wentworth Road – bringing his stuff round, joining family meals, moving in. No fucking thank you. That boy was pure pondlife. Glancing across at his sister, Eugene decided not to mention Nero's 3 a.m. breakout bid. Simone seemed upset enough as it was.

Eugene slept in Saturday, dead to the world until gone eleven. The house was quiet. Buzzi Bee had reopened, and Simone had already left with Nero – the Minimonster had yet another psychiatric appointment to attend prior to being dropped at Buzzi Bee. Nero had spent the past couple of weeks undergoing a battery of 'assessments'. Some of the reports were already completed – the experts were in agreement. Nero's obsessive fascination with the Meatman murders showed little sign of abating. He remained totally 'in denial' about his role in the Buzzi Bee breakout: according to Nero, the gate came open and he followed the other children outside. There was no man involved, and he hadn't seen anything. The children who said he'd deliberately pushed the little girl off the climbing frame – she was still in a coma – were liars. 'I never done it,' and 'Don't know,' were his constant refrain.

The various 'child professionals' felt Nero had some 'serious issues to confront' and that 'there was a lot of work to be done.'

Eugene wished them the best of luck with it. In the

meantime, he was just grateful Buzzi Bee had agreed to take Nero back. Saturday afternoons were once again Minimonster-free. He lay back on the sofa and flicked the remote, pausing at some African thing which had started a few minutes earlier. Eugene spent an intriguing half-hour learning about the Ekoi tribe of Eastern Nigeria and Cameroon. The Ekoi were known for their elaborate dance ceremonies and the amazing quality of the masks they carved for ceremonial use. The tribal style was unusually naturalistic – previously, the Ekoi dancers had performed with the decapitated heads of slain enemies strapped on to their own heads in place of a mask.

Eugene kept wondering about the practicalities of it – the weight, and did you pop the corpse's eyes out so you could look through the sockets? How did they dry the things to stop brains and body fluids dripping everywhere? It can't have been easy.

He was deep in thought and faintly irritated when he heard Simone coming in the door. Usually, she spent Saturdays shopping or hanging out with friends, but she told him she was tired, needed to catch a couple of hours' sleep. She had barely been in the house five minutes when the doorbell went. Eugene checked out the window. It was Migsy, Angie's elder brother. What the hell did he want?

Migsy was looking for his sister. She hadn't come home last night and her mobile was off. The family was frantic – they had rung everyone and drawn a total blank. Meanwhile, Migsy was clutching at straws – p'raps Angie had swapped her shifts at SweetHearts? P'raps she was working there and had, y'know, just forgotten to tell anyone?

Simone shook her head. Said Angie had called her yesterday, 'It'd be some time around sixish, just girlstalk, y'know. She said she was doing another party thing and she'd catch me tonight at the club. She wasn't at SweetHearts last night, Migs.'

Even so, Simone had rung SweetHearts, like Migsy asked,

but Simone had been right. Angie was due on shift at 8 p.m. Saturday – tonight. Mae asked all the bar staff, checked the entire club, then she rang Simone back – no one had seen Angie. She hadn't been at the club last night and she definitely wasn't there now.

Anyway, just as Simone had said, Angie had a party booking last night. She did quite a few – taking round trays of canapés, pouring champagne, keeping on top of the washing-up. She enjoyed it, she told Simone. It was interesting, seeing inside other people's houses, checking out what the guests were wearing. And it paid reasonably well.

'Yeah, what about the party people?' asked Eugene. 'They're the ones to ask.'

'I fucking know that man, been trying all fucking day. Can't find where the fuck the job was. She'll have the address in her bag, won't she? And the fucking bag's with her, innit?' Migsy's voice had become a shout.

Eugene held his hand up. 'Cool it Migs. I was only asking.'

'Sorry.' He shook his head. 'Sorry, Eugene. I'm just . . . a bit worked up. It's my sister. Angela. My little sister. If something's happened to her . . . if she's . . . if someone's done something.' He paused. 'Mum reported her missing about an hour ago. They took all the details, then the police rang back and said they were on their way round to interview us. I mean, what's that all about then? Not normal procedure is it? They think he's done another one, don't they?'

'Come on, M.' Eugene put his arm round Migsy's shoulder. 'Gotta keep positive. Keep searching. Look, you go back and sort it with the cops. Then give us a bell when you're through with the police stuff, and we'll take the Puma out and have another look around.'

'Yeah. Thanks, mate. It's all this hanging around – the waiting – it gets to you. Good idea, Eugene. I'll bell you the minute I'm done.'

Eugene stood with his sister, watching Migsy walking back. It looked like the police had just arrived. Two dark-coloured Rovers were parked outside the Caridads' house – and Eugene recognized a third, a red Sierra – they were murder-squad cars. He turned and followed Simone back into the house.

Simone made tea laced with whisky and sugar. Brother and sister sat in silence, looking at each other across the kitchen table. Neither of them said it – almost as if saying could make it so – but they both knew. They knew Angie wouldn't be coming home. The Meatman had got her.

CHAPTER FIFTEEN

But making way for death at large to walke:
Who in the horror of the griesly night,
In thousand dreadful shapes doth mongst them stalke,
And makes huge hauocke, whiles the candlelight
Out quenched, leaues no skill nor difference of wight.

FQ: The Legend of Sir Calidore, or of Courtesie: VI.xi.16

It turned out that the police wanted to interview Simone as well – partly because of Angie's call to her on Friday, partly because the family said she was one of Angie's closest friends. Around 5 p.m., Simone walked down the road to the Caridads' house. Everyone was in the kitchen, the family and Angie's fiancé; tall, blond Martin. Simone said hello, refused a cup of tea and waited for the police to call for her. It was late afternoon now. Shadows lengthened across the grey-lit kitchen. Angie's middle brother – Rafi – was in the front room, talking to the police. No one spoke.

Eventually the kitchen door opened and Rafi returned. A police officer asked 'Ms Burnside' to come through, and Simone followed after him.

DS Scudamour and a uniformed WPC were waiting for her in the front room. The WPC sitting close to the door and taking notes. DS Scudamour reminded Simone of the young

FBI men in *Mississippi Burning* – the same crisp white shirt and tie, the same hair, cut sharp and short. And like the filmic FBI, he was polite.

Simone gave him every last detail she could remember about Angie's phone call. Told him everything she could about Angie's bar work at SweetHearts. Then he moved on, asking what sort of person Angie was, what she was like, where she went. Endless questions, on and on, for ages. Going over the same ground again and again, pushing her to remember, wanting every tiny scrap of information. But Simone did her best. She held nothing back, searched her memory, thought so hard it hurt. It took a long time, but at the end, DS Scudamour said thank you and told her she'd been outstandingly helpful. Simone said thanks in turn and gave him a sideways glance, half-curtained by lashes. He gave her his card and told her to ring if she remembered anything more.

Simone tucked the card away and got up to leave. But somehow her legs didn't make it, and she collapsed backwards in her seat, tears rolling down her face. 'He's got her, hasn't he?' she said. 'I've known her nearly all my life. Oh my God, not Angie. Please not Angie. Oh my God, please no.'

DS Scudamour asked the WPC to fetch tea. He passed Simone a box of tissues, told her to take her time and made her drink the hot, sweet tea. Eventually she pulled herself together. Before she left, Simone thanked the detective for being so kind.

DCI Gale's investigation had wasted no time. When the Caridads' call came through, he forwarded an immediate requisition order for Angie's mobile-phone records. The phone company wasn't keen, talking about data protection and being closed for weekends. But Gale's murder squad insisted, bullied and forced the phone execs into reluctant compliance.

The records revealed that Angie had rung Simone, her

fiancé Martin, and her mum. She had also made and received calls from an unknown mobile throughout Friday. The same number was recorded calling her twice earlier that week. She received a final call from the same unknown number at 9.47 p.m. Friday. After that, no calls were made or taken. Her phone seemed to have been switched off around tennish and was not currently emitting a signal.

The mobile number almost certainly belonged to Angie's party client. As DCI Gale predicted, the number was now dead. The mobile – a pay-as-you-go affair – had been bought six months previously, but had only been activated recently. The only calls made on it were to Angie Caridad.

DCI Gale had precious little to go on. Angie had told her mum the party was in Crouch End. The place was apparently hard to find, so Angie had said the man was going to pick her up by the Archway Tower – it would save her getting lost, he said. Angie said she'd be back around 3.30 a.m. – four at the very latest. But 4 a.m. had come and gone.

It was past eight that evening when Migsy rang Eugene to say the police had finally finished. They'd left a WPC 'family liaison officer', who was staying in the house. Migsy said his mother was in bits and they'd had the doctor out. He asked if Gladys could come down to keep her company. The police had said they could go on searching, and everyone was desperate to get out and do something.

When Eugene and Gladys arrived at the Caridads', Moira Haley opened the door. Migsy was waiting for Eugene; everyone else was out looking. Staying in pairs, like the police advised: Angie's father with the middle brother, Rafi; the youngest brother, Gabo, driving with Martin. Moira looked at Gladys and shook her head. 'This is a terrible business, God love us. Pray God she comes home.' Eugene followed his mother into the house. As Moira shut the door behind them, Eugene saw that a transformation had taken place.

The Caridads' was renowned as the noisiest house on the street. Usually, the three TVs competed against a background of merengue, cumbia and rap, whilst the brothers booted a football round the backyard and their dad José shouted for someone to 'turn that rubbish music down'. Then there were endless parties and summer barbecues with booming salsa and Colombians shouting in Spanish and screaming with laughter.

Now all was silence. The house remained in semi-darkness – stilled and suffocated beneath the unbearable weight of fear and grief. In the front room the WPC was trying to comfort Angie's mother. Maria Caridad was barely listening. Just sobbing, breaking off only to plead for God's mercy and the return of her daughter.

Eugene and Migsy left the women to it. They headed out to the Puma, joining the others looking for Angie. It was gone 2 a.m. when, by general agreement, the searchers gave up and returned to Wentworth Road. Angie's dad insisted Eugene came in for a glass of rum before going home – Martin was staying at the house.

The six men stood around drinking. Nobody said a word about murder. Nobody spoke about the Meatman. But the certainty was growing, minute by minute. As they dashed round and round in their hopeless quest Migsy and Eugene had tried to think of possibilities – what might have happened. Tried out explanations, each more fantastical and less convincing. They wondered if Angie could have fallen, broken her leg, say – fallen somewhere she couldn't be heard or seen. So she could just be lying there, waiting for help. Or she could have fallen and knocked her head, lost her memory and not know who she was any more. Or maybe she'd been accidentally locked in the party house and the owners had gone away on holiday. She might have had a breakdown and gone off to be alone for a while to work things out.

They took comfort in these improbable imagined

disasters. Like children, they were afraid of the monster hiding out there in the dark. But they knew they were simply delaying the inevitable. Soon enough, they would have to come out from behind the sofa.

Because everything pointed the same way. Angie wasn't a runaway, junkie, prostitute. She wasn't a desperado of any kind. She was good fun, up for a couple of drinks and a laugh, but that was it. José and Maria were proud of their daughter. She had just been promoted, to senior administration officer at the TUC Education Centre on Crouch Hill.

She'd met Martin at work. He was one of the earnest young politicos in the research and strategy team – and all the girls were after him. Whenever Martin was forced to visit the admin and secretarial section, the girls would start, Angie included: 'Six foot two, eyes of blue, Brad Pitt's double, we want you' – then uptempo: 'Cos Martin, Martin, he's the best/so much better than all the rest!'

They'd been going out for two years now. And Angie was so in love – couldn't wait to get married. Angie wasn't going to be staying out nights, she wasn't that sort. Someone had made the decision for her, made quite sure she wouldn't be going home.

Eugene got the call around 11 a.m. Monday. He was still groggy from sleep, and grabbed the mobile on autopilot. It was Migsy. Eugene had trouble following; Migsy was crying and breaking off. Finally Eugene understood. Angie had been found – well, most of her – all the bits the Meatman had left.

Almost in the dead centre of Crouch End, a tiny snicket road runs at right angles to the Broadway, between Lloyds bank and Prospero's bookshop. Fifty yards in, the snicket becomes a Tarmacked yard. A high brick wall borders the left side, the four-storey offices of Haringey Council social services department enclose the remaining three sides. At the entrance, the snicket is blocked by a high metal gate fastened by a padlock and chain from 6 p.m. to 8 a.m. The yard itself is mainly used for parking and rubbish collection, housing two enormous round metal bins and a five-foot-high red plastic 'disposal unit'.

All the staff in the social services department had keys for the padlock, and whoever arrived first unlocked the gate and propped it open. But that morning, the padlock wouldn't open. At 8.30 a.m. on a Monday, the social worker wasn't in the mood for this. She banged and rattled at the gate and twisted her key, until it dawned on her. Someone had changed the lock. New security measure, she thought, and the silly bastards forgot to issue keys. After a couple of minutes' fiddling, she gave up on the padlock. As she looked up her eyes travelled across the yard. For a moment she couldn't make sense of the jumble of shapes and colours, for a couple of seconds she stared intently – utterly baffled. Then she realized. 'Oh, Jesus,' she said.

Luckily it was only a matter of minutes before a colleague arriving for work found her slumped against the gate and semiconscious. The colleague phoned an ambulance and helped her stand, avoiding her flailing arms. For some reason, she kept pointing at the yard. Maybe she'd hit her head? Now – embarrassingly – the woman began shouting as well. 'Look! Look! LOOK!' she screamed. The colleague decided it was best to humour her – she duly looked. Afterwards, the two social workers leant against the wall, and each other, whilst they phoned the police.

DCI Gale thought the bastard was getting worse. He'd done a real job on this one. The girl's father had identified the body – although they'd needed to check dental records to be sure. Then there was the boyfriend. They had tried hard to persuade him not to do it. But he was immovable. He wanted to see her. He had to say goodbye. He insisted, so eventually, police and pathologists gave in. DCI Gale shook his head, trying to blank the memory. Her face was terrible enough, but the lad had insisted on seeing the whole thing. He said he wanted to know what had been done to her. If she'd lived and died it, well the least he could do was look, that was what he said.

He kissed her before leaving, what was left of her – stroked the remaining strands of hair. Said he loved her very much. Then the mortuary attendants pulled the sheet over her and covered up the Meatman's leavings. Afterwards, DCI Gale walked with Martin out to the car park. Just after they shook hands Martin suddenly spoke up. 'I suppose that when the bastard chopped off her hands for a keepsake, he took her engagement ring with them, yeah?'

'Yes,' said DCI Gale.

'Thought he must have,' the young man said, then slid into his car and drove away.

CHAPTER SIXTEEN

Then beautie, which was made to represent
The great Creatours owne resemblance bright,
Vnto abuse of lawlesse lust was lent,
And made the baite of bestiall delight:

FQ: The Legend of Cambel and Telamond;
The Flight of Florimell: IV.viii.32

Murder fever was now endemic. On the TV, radio, every newspaper cover, the street, in every corner shop, pub or wine bar, dominating every conversation, top item on all news programmes – it was impossible to escape. The Meatman was everywhere – and he was especially big on Wentworth Road.

The Caridads' neighbours were in demand, police and journalists calling on a daily basis. The Wentworth Road residents weren't used to feeling so wanted – to having friends, colleagues and relatives hanging on their every word. No one admitted it, but it was all rather exciting and enjoyable – being the centre of attention, everyone wanting your views, your take on it all. It was like being a celebrity.

Amongst the denizens of Wentworth Road, Simone was the star attraction. Close friend of the victim and top girl at SweetHearts, Simone was a tabloid dream. The offers flooded in for her 'exclusive' story and pictures. The 'pictures' would be topless, with Simone gyrating around a lap-dancing pole.

In different circumstances Simone would have snatched their hand off. 'Good for my profile,' she would have said. 'What's the problem?' But now things had changed, and Simone didn't hesitate: she could see the problem all too clearly. They could stuff their money. The answer was no.

Simone wasn't coping too well, as it was. Parading across the tabloids topless with a G-string wasn't likely to help her mental state. Nor did it seem the best way to remember her dead friend – the friend who might still be alive, if Simone hadn't encouraged her to take the SweetHearts job.

And it hadn't taken long for Angie's family to reach the same conclusion. José Caridad had said it, shouting and furious, blaming Simone for leading his daughter into the underworld. There'd been no warning. One minute everything was OK; the next, José had flipped – turned on her, yelling at Simone to get out of his house and not to come back. Called her a whore. 'Why'd you have to drag my daughter into your dirt?' he'd said. 'You and that filthy club, that's what got her killed.' Simone had run home sobbing.

Migsy came after her and apologized. 'Dad's just lost it. It's hit him really hard. Take no notice. He doesn't mean it,' he said. But Simone knew different. José meant every word – and Angie's mum, fiancé and brothers probably agreed with him. And worse still, he was right. She had introduced Angie to the Meatman's world – to the epicentre of his murderous odyssey. It was her fault.

She said nothing to her mother and nothing to Eugene – she knew her brother would have gone ballistic. He hated her job, always had done, but that was for him to say, not for anyone else. Dead daughter or not, if Eugene knew José Caridad had called Simone a whore he'd have been straight round there. Faced with Eugene, José would have little choice but to apologize. But what was the point?

Simone was off Monday and Tuesday, but Wednesday she was back to work. She didn't want to go. Didn't want to shimmy around in front of some half-drunk, pot-bellied businessman. Didn't want to stand three feet from her 'client' and pretend to be thrilled as he tucked fifty quid in her G-string, making sure his hands did an ordnance survey before he let go of the notes.

But by eight o'clock on Wednesday night, she was showered and ready to leave, trainers on and kit bag over her shoulder. Eugene gave her the taxi money. Told her to phone a cab and get someone at the club to take the guy's number before she got in. Simone said thanks. She tried to kiss Nero goodbye, and the child hit out at her, catching her face. She almost ran down Wentworth Road and was on the bus heading down the Holloway Road before the tears became unstoppable.

On Wednesday, DCI Gale had the results from the post-mortem on Angela Caridad and immediately called a meeting for two o'clock that afternoon. It was rumoured that there was a breakthrough – of sorts – and the murder squad was buzzing with anticipation. By five to two, every-one was in the operations room, prepared and waiting. Exactly on time DCI Arthur Gale walked in. He was followed by his secretary carrying a stack of documents.

'The Caridad postmortem report,' said DCI Gale. 'Pass them round so everyone has a copy. Fine.' He waited until his secretary closed the door behind her, then turned back to his waiting team. 'Read through the report please,' he said. For the next five minutes the silence was broken only by the rustle of paper. Then DCI Gale began. 'Well, gentlemen,' he said, 'we seem to have some new information.'

DCI Gale's murder squad were an elite group. Despite having to speedread the report, and despite the scientific jargon in which it was couched, they all spotted it – the shocked faces behind every desk made that plain. The information was undoubtedly 'new', so new they were having trouble taking it in.

It was DS Scudamour who spoke up first. 'Her fiancé and family have been eliminated as possible sources, sir?' DCI Gale nodded. 'Yes. And I should point out that the semen splatter traces were on internal body areas – areas exposed and accessible due to the extreme mutilations suffered by the victim. Of course, this means the samples are badly contaminated. They are also too small for comprehensive testing. But on the basic analysis there is no doubt. It's absolutely certain.'

'Will this stand up in court, sir?' said one of the squad.

'The pathologists say they are absolutely confident. Apparently it is very clear cut – almost by definition. They are in no doubt at all.'

No one had anything more to say. The room had gone very quiet. DCI Gale paused, then turned to address his men. The murder squad leant forward in unison. When he spoke, his voice was precise and even: 'Well, gentlemen, this makes sense of a great deal. Discrepancy in the injuries and in the signature markings on the body. The various oddities and interruptions found in the sexual injuries. In fact, there were numerous conflicting signs arising from previous post-mortem results.'

DCI Gale moved across the operations room. All eyes followed him. He pointed to the board, where photographs of Stella Jane Hope, Amy Fiddeler and Angela Caridad were displayed – Socpix, or scene-of-crime pictures – stark, sharp-focused, brightly lit. 'If we apply our new findings to the two previous murders, we can appreciate that a consistent pattern emerges.' He indicated the arcane incisions, bizarre slashes, amputations, knife wounds – a myriad of desecrations and defacements, which, taken in their entirety, reduced each of the three victims to little more than a slimy, glistening heap of disarrayed liquidity. 'Here, here, and again, the same thing here,' DCI Gale continued. 'There is no question in my mind – but I am willing to listen to any alternative interpretations you may wish to put forward.'

There was a profound silence. The murder squad had no alternative interpretation to offer.

'Can I take it that we are all agreed?' said Gale, glancing round the room. Heads nodded in unison.

'So,' Gale said. 'We are chasing two murderers, not one.'

DCI Gale expected his officers to digest this news and return to business. He moved on immediately to discuss the increased level of savagery evident in the murder of Angela Caridad. He suggested this could be 'because the killers had the luxury of a private location, where they were unlikely to be disturbed'. But otherwise – DCI Gale stressed – the murder had all the familar features. 'Once again, jewellery and body parts have been taken, and the usual patterns of sexual sadism and mutilations are present,' he told them.

He also emphasized that, like Stella Jane Hope's, and Amy Fiddeler's, Angela Caridad's body bore strange marks – weird zigzags, dotted lines, strange rips and indentations. Forensics were baffled – could offer no idea what could have caused the various cuts and punctures. The wounds were totally unique. No one had ever come across anything remotely similar. It was unprecedented. 'I've asked Forensics to redouble their efforts,' Gale said.

Eventually, DCI Gale stood up and reached for his brief-case. Before reaching the door, he turned. 'And I would like DS Scudamour and DC Lalibela to prioritize the investigation into the SweetHearts connection.' He signalled to the detectives. 'Could you two come to my office for a briefing in – say – twenty minutes. Thank you.'

Eugene spent Wednesday afternoon with Talus and the Farons – the Firm's executive were discussing the possible expansion of the Nottingham enterprise. Nottingham had gone well. Eventually, it was decided to go ahead. They would target Sheffield and Leeds initially – the Notts boys had existing connections in Yorkshire.

They were starting small. No intention of flooding the market. The Brothers wanted to assess how things panned out. 'We'll have another look around December time, see how the thing's performing and where we go from there,' said Archie.

'Fair enough,' Talus agreed. 'We need to know how things will pan out. That takes time.'

Eugene backed Talus up. They just had to take a risk and see how it worked out, but however many risks you were willing to take, it always paid to take care. Eugene had paid serious attention to matters of security – as he told the meeting: 'The whole deal's set up with a "disconnect" button,' Eugene explained. 'The idea is that, first sign of trouble – that's it. We pull the plug and leave – cleaner than Persil.'

'Well, let's hope trouble doesn't arise,' Archie said smoothly. 'I prefer to leave firefighting to public servants.' Then, he gave one of his strange clown's smiles. 'Nottingham is shaping up very nicely indeed: Talus, you and Geno will obviously take control of the Yorkshire deal . . .'

Archie paused, and turned to his brother. 'You agree, George?'

'Makes sense to me,' George grunted.

Talus said, 'OK with you, Geno?'

'Sweet,' said Eugene. 'I'll bell the Notts boys, get the full read-out, then we can talk Friday?'

Talus nodded.

'How long before we see any returns from our new investments?' Archie enquired.

Eugene had the figures. Spent half the previous night working on getting things ready. 'Taking the most pessimistic projection, it will be three months – towards the end of August – before we recoup our total layout. Another month will see us 11K in profit. There'll be the usual fluctuations but, barring major disruption, we should be looking – after that point – to clear around 25 to 28K a month. Course we could hit lucky and do double that – but I prefer to keep cautious.'

'You're a bright boy, Geno,' Archie Faron said. 'Talus?'

'I've looked through the figures,' Talus told Archie. 'He's done a proper job. And the strategy's right. Start careful. Plenty of time to expand if it works out.'

'Good,' said Archie. 'Well, that seems to be the lot. Anything else, George? George! GEORGE!! For fuck's sake. Pay some fucking attention, will you?'

George had been staring out of the window. When Archie yelled in his ear, he came to with a start. Archie told him they were finished. 'Great,' George said.

Talus needed a lift to Archway, and Eugene offered to take him. Ten minutes later, security were pulling back the iron gates and the Puma was striding smoothly along Hampstead Lane in the bright spring sunshine.

They chatted briefly about business, then Talus looked across at Eugene.

'She's a menace, that woman,' he said.

'Who?' said Eugene.

'Yeah, you wouldn't have seen her – facing the wrong way. Well, you saw George was out the loop?'

'Yeah, right – he blanked out wholesale. So what's the story?'

'It's always the same fuckin story,' said Talus. 'She was lying there in full view – wearing a gold thong – nothing else. Tits out and covered in sun oil. George couldn't take his eyes off her. He didn't realize anyone else could see her – but she knew all right – knew she was giving me an eyeful. The bitch is trouble, and he's fuckin obsessed with the cow.'

Eugene was appalled. 'But – I mean. She can't pull stunts like that,' he said. 'She's his wife for fuck's sake. Not some ten-minute shag. She should remember that. Have some dignity, some class, you know.'

'That's the point,' said Talus. 'George Faron's wife – a slag who can't keep her legs closed. She's an embarrassment, Geno.'

'Yeah,' said Eugene cautiously. Talus was known for utter loyalty to the Farons and the Firm – Eugene wasn't entirely sure what this Gloria stuff was all about.

'You've joined the big boys now, Geno,' Talus said suddenly. 'Which means you get things sorted. She's becoming a problem. You need to understand that.'

Eugene and Talus parked up and went for a drink in the Archway Tavern. They had a lot to discuss. Talus told Eugene about Gloria's penchant for black boyfriends and what she got up to on her many holidays. That had been bad enough, but there was a new development – and this couldn't be tolerated. Gloria had gone too far now and had to be stopped. Simple as that.

Shagging her way through the third world was one thing, Talus said. But now she was shitting on her own doorstep. She'd found herself a black boyfriend who lived local. Had been seen out with him. 'It's only a matter of time before the shit hits the fan,' Talus said. 'Cos it ain't just a personal matter, Geno, you can see that?'

Eugene nodded. 'She's humiliating all of us if she makes George look a cunt. It makes us look crap.'

Talus nodded emphatically. 'That's it, Geno. If George can't keep his wife in order, stands to reason – he can't control fuck all else. Unless we sort this soon – no doubt about it, Geno – there'll be some individuals thinking the business can be taken as easy as the wife. I'm not coping with that sort of fall-out just because some bitch can't keep her knickers on.'

'What about Archie?' Eugene asked.

'I've arranged a meet later this week,' Talus replied. 'Nothing's been said, but Archie's well sharp. He knows the score and he's not happy.'

Eugene and Talus left the Archway Tavern side by side, in

thoughtful silence. 'This is not going to be an easy gig,' Eugene finally said.

In the bright May sunshine Talus's bronze curls seemed almost aflame, turquoise eyes a brilliant, dazzling counterpoint. 'It's a complete pig,' he replied. 'And sorting that whore won't be the worst of it. George worships her. When he finds out what she's up to, it'll destroy him.'

Talus looked at Eugene and shook his head. 'If she'd kept it discreet and tidy – well, fair enough. But half of North London's seen her out and about with this bloke. It's only a matter of time before George tumbles to it. We've got to take control before that happens.'

'No other option,' Eugene agreed. 'Speak Friday then.'

During the short drive home, Eugene gave the Puma its head and thought about Gloria Faron. Talus was right, Gloria was no longer worried about discretion. He thought about the Halcyenda party, walking with her in the tropical conservatory, the tiny clinging dress which quickly became soaked in the steamy heat and visibly shrank yet smaller and tighter against her body.

Eugene was quite sure he was just one amongst many men Gloria had targeted. He felt a surge of anger and disgust. If she didn't like George Faron, well, why go and marry him? The answer was obvious. But if Gloria wanted the money, power and position, well, Eugene thought, she could at least play the part. Instead, she was whoring around in full public view. As he settled the Puma on Wentworth Road, Eugene knew one thing for sure – he didn't want to be anywhere near – in fact make that a million miles away – when George learnt just what his beloved wife was getting up to.

CHAPTER SEVENTEEN

. . . all things in troublous vprore were,
And all men busie . . .

FQ: The Legend of Britomartis: III.x.16

Scudamour and Lalibela arrived at DCI Gale's office bang on time. Gale closed the door behind them and began to speak.

He told the two detectives to interview every member of SweetHearts' staff. To reinterview those previously spoken to. He wanted statements from every last employee, part time or full time, cleaner, dancer, doorman . . . everyone. And anyone off sick should be tracked down at home. Secondly he wanted the two detectives to learn everything possible about the club's 'clientele'. To recheck all the names on the membership lists, to take note of regular faces.

'I also want you in there every night until further notice. It shuts at 3 a.m. Earlier, if it's a poor night. Weekends tend to be later. The licence extension runs until 4.30 a.m. on Fridays and Saturdays. I apologize for the disruption to your lives but I believe it's necessary for us all to do our utmost.'

DCI Gale went on to remind them that the murders had taken place at one and two week intervals, all three victims having been killed between Friday evening and the early hours of Sunday morning. 'I don't think we can rely on this pattern continuing,' said Gale. 'It gives us uncertain guidance. Nothing more.'

The DCI explained the assignment had been cleared with SweetHearts' management. 'The Farons control the club, as you both know,' he said crisply. 'The police investigation into club records has been pulled. Apparently, Archie Faron's book-keeping is beyond reproach. Whatever your opinion of the matter I ask you to concentrate on the job in hand. Any financial irregularities have been resolved – since when the club has been highly cooperative. I should stress that I regard that cooperation as key.'

He told them they'd been assigned a driver. Gale said he expected both men to file daily written reports. They should start immediately. Mr Barry, SweetHearts' manager, was expecting to meet them around 5 p.m. for an initial briefing and introductory tour of the club. That was it.

As Scudamour and Lalibela turned to leave, DCI Gale spoke. 'They will have selected their next victim by now,' he said quietly. 'Some girl is already earmarked for their theatre of destruction. We have no idea who she might be. However, I can assure you, gentlemen, unless we catch these men, we are certain to meet our mystery girl – or most of her – on the postmortem slab in nine or ten days' time. Thank you. I believe your car is waiting for you.'

Minutes later, Scudamour and Lalibela were on their way to SweetHearts. Awaiting their arrival, pacing up and down his office, Mr Barry was at the end of his tether. As he told Mae, he wasn't sure how much more he could take. 'It's the pressure,' he explained, 'the constant pressure. It's getting to me.' Mae sympathized and suggested a brandy might help. Mr Barry was grateful. 'Thanks, love,' he said. 'At least there's one person round here I can rely on.'

And, at present, Mr Barry felt he needed all the help he could get. Yesterday had been a nightmare. And in less than half an hour, he'd have two fuckin coppers to cope with. Brilliant. Just sodding brilliant. Mr Barry had been incredulous when they told him, 'You're bloody joking, aren't you?' he'd said. That wasn't the way you talked to Archie Faron. Mr Barry was hot and clammy at the memory of it. And the moment of silence that followed . . . then that psycho-nutter Gerry Talus standing up and walking across the room.

'Mr Faron's not a comedian,' Talus said.

So Mr Barry had shut it. Had listened to Archie's instructions, briefed Mae and made the necessary preparations and adjustments – got it all sorted. He checked his watch. He'd got time, just about. And God knows he needed it. 'Mae, love, fetch us another brandy will you?' he called.

He'd just got back from cleaning his teeth as reception rang through. Mae picked up the phone, then hit the mute button. 'It's them,' she told him. Mr Barry sat up straight and took a deep breath. 'Right, then,' he said. 'Tell her to bring them straight up.'

Just over an hour later, rehearsals for Harem Nights' key belly-dance scene came to a sudden halt. The music was pulled without warning, leaving the dancers in mid-step, as Mr Barry strode forward, clapping his hands and shouting, 'Girls! Girls!' There was a moment's confusion, then silence, as everyone turned towards Mr Barry and the two detectives.

Mr Barry introduced DS Scudamour and DC Lalibela. He said everyone should do their best to help the police, and that included 'not blabbing about them being here or mouthing off about why they're here'. Mr Barry ended by declaring SweetHearts' only priority was the safety and wellbeing of club employees. No one believed him. Then DS Scudamour stepped forward.

Scudamour explained that the first-floor prop room was now converted into a temporary office where he and his colleague – indicating DC Lalibela – would be based. 'The club has made a real effort to accommodate us,' he said, 'and we appreciate it. I know our presence will be disruptive, but we'll do our best to keep difficulties to a minimum. And as your manager has just explained, this is a semi-covert operation, so we are relying on your discretion.' DS Scudamour's gaze ran left to right along the line of dancers. 'I don't think anyone here wants to tip off the Meatman, do they?'

The last to speak was DC Lalibela. He explained that he and DS Scudamour would be interviewing all SweetHearts employees. Names would be announced over the internal Tannoy system, and the person called should immediately make their way to the detectives' first-floor office. The first person would be called for interview in ten minutes' time.

'Thank you, girls,' said Mr Barry, and the three men departed. Seconds later, the belly-dance music started up and rehearsals continued.

Eugene was due to meet Brittany at 8 p.m. He was meeting her at the house, then they were off for a meal. He was nervous and excited. Desperate to see her again. He'd fantasized about her every night, imagining the feel of her skin, the silky hair slipping through his fingers. Remembering her face looking up at him. She was something serious. No question about it.

And he was glad to be getting away from Wentworth Road. He'd got home early and spent a couple of hours with his mum, watching the TV and the endless murder reports. Moira had come round halfway through, and he'd left the two women together and retreated to his bedroom. It was a relief to be alone, to channel-surf far away from the Meatman and his doings. He found a decent thing on National Geo, all about pink dolphins which only lived in the rivers in the Amazon jungle. The things were really more grey than pink, but they definitely had a kind of rosy sheen. They'd only been discovered a few years ago, which was pretty amazing, Eugene thought.

When the dolphin programme finished, he went for a shower. Downstairs, Gladys and Moira had adjourned to the kitchen. Moira had brought the music with her, because 'Four Green Fields' was rolling out at top volume. 'Shit,' Eugene muttered. As far as Eugene could tell, the Irish sang only about the dead. Luckily, only an hour to go before he was off to Crouch End and well out of it.

Despite the nightmare of 'Mountains of Mourne' and 'I'll Take You Home Again, Kathleen' singalongs, Eugene was more than happy to see Moira. He thought – or hoped – he'd be spending the night with Brittany, and at present he didn't want to be leaving his mother alone. Didn't want to think of her sitting vigil at the kitchen table, eyes on the clock, counting the minutes past 3 a.m. till Simone came home.

Gladys had always worried about her children, all the more so after her husband died – and had continued worrying after Eugene and Simone had left childhood long behind. But since the murder of Angela Caridad, Gladys had gone into paranoia overdrive. She was utterly terrified for Simone. Unable to rest until her daughter was back, safe and sound. Eugene tried to reassure his mum. Tell her not to be foolish. Trouble was, he was almost as frightened himself. Whilst she remained at SweetHearts, Eugene knew, Simone was high risk. His sister was courting disaster, as they said. Dancing with the Devil – and beneath her feet the flowers of evil were in full bloom.

Before he left, Eugene spent ten minutes in the kitchen with Moira and his mum. It wasn't the usual mix of joking and family news – 'Siobhan says you'd best be coming to her birthday do . . . you know their little Rory's an altar boy now? . . . Caitlin's husband got family troubles again' – there was none of that. Instead, they discussed the Meatman. And most of all they talked about the Caridads and – of course – about Angie.

Eugene listened as the two women reminisced – tales of Angie as a little girl. The beautiful frocks her mother dressed her in – little dresses sent from Colombia, a mass of ruffles, lace and satin. 'She always looked a picture,' Moira said. 'And her hair ribbons. Maria spent a fortune on those things. Everything had to be perfect, little shoes to match her outfit. Oh, Gladys, and do you remember, that velvet coat they got her? Gorgeous, it was.'

'Yes, the one with the hood,' Gladys said. 'And she was such a happy child. I can't take it in, Moira. It just doesn't seem possible. Oh, and I found these – pass my handbag, please, Eugene.'

Gladys delved inside her bag and fished out half a dozen old photos. 'Will you look at that!' Moira exclaimed. It was a snap of Angie, aged eight, wearing an elaborate white dress and veil – the day of her First Communion. Eugene passed the photo back – he could hardly bear it: the picture of the smiling child. He decided it was time to go.

As Eugene picked up his keys and jacket, the two women were still poring over photos. 'She was a lovely-looking girl,' his mother was saying. 'And that dress, I remember Maria saying she didn't dare tell José what it had cost. Real lace.' Eugene was turning towards the door when his mother called to him.

'Look at this, son,' she said. It was a photo, of Simone and Angie, hand in hand outside the church. Simone had taken her First Communion the same day – and was decked out, like her best friend, in white lace and ribbons. Eugene took the photo, and handed it straight back. 'Very sad,' he said. 'Sorry, but I've really got to shoot. I'm running late.' He was desperate to get out. He could see it coming – any minute now, his mum would start crying. And Eugene just couldn't face it, couldn't cope – because he was only a whisker away

189

from crying himself. And that wasn't acceptable. Wasn't going to happen.

A few minutes later, the Puma was swooping beneath the trees, bowling down Crouch Hill, the road dappled with the green-gold evening light. He opened the window, grateful for the rush of soft spring air and the Puma's eager speed. Since Angie's murder, Wentworth Road had become increasingly claustrophobic. The street itself choked with cars belonging to throngs of journalists and police, and the narrow spaces between the crush of vehicles endlessly busy with jostling people – an unedifying mix of professionals, residents and gawkers. And down at the far end, like a dead star collapsing inward, was the black hole of the Caridad house.

Maria wore black, her husband likewise. Martin and Angela's three brothers were dark-suited, black-tied. Blinds were pulled down, casting a pallor of shadowy gloom through the house. And the notorious Caridad cacophony of shouting and salsa was gone. Angela's old home was a temple of darkness and silence – as if the entire building were in mourning. It seemed – Eugene thought – as if the grief of the family had now seeped into the very bricks of their home. A contagion of pain spreading outward – hard to resist and impossible to ignore. Agony had moved into Wentworth Road. The new neighbour was unwanted and unwelcome. But like other antisocials, Agony didn't give a fuck. So the neighbours were upset. So what?

As the Puma strode past the Crouch End clock tower towards Brittany's house, Eugene felt a guilty relief to be back in the light, to escape from the Meatman's long shadow. He tried his best to comfort his mother, tried to tell Simone to stop beating herself up, blaming herself for Angie's death – looking after the family was his job. Eugene prided himself on it. But coping with this nightmare wasn't easy. And worst of all – seriously worst – was Nero.

190

Eugene knew he was going to have to sit down with his sister and do some plain talking. His mother was on his side; they'd already discussed it. They were in complete agreement that the little bastard was beyond control or reason and becoming worse by the day. He needed, in acceptable terminology, 'structured development within a secure environment under expert supervision'. Or, as Eugene said, 'some juvie-psycho place where they'll lock him up and throw away the key.'

He was only six years old, but the Minimonster had always been big for his age, and Eugene was starting to worry. He didn't like his mum being left alone with the little git. Nero had begun to physically attack his grandmother and had hurt her badly on a couple of occasions. Simone was upset but defensive. 'He doesn't mean it. It's only play,' she repeated. But Eugene knew different. The Minimonster liked hurting – all his toys bore witness to his fondness for stabbing, twisting and beating. Successive teachers remarked upon his sadistic bent, and no small animal was safe in his presence.

The Burnsides had become used to Nero's predilection for biting, lashing out and kicking, but his talent for violence was escalating. He'd tried to push Gladys down the stairs, and all scissors, knives and sharp implements had to be locked away. And that wasn't the worst of it.

His frenzied excitement and obsessive interest in the Meatman murders had been disturbing from the very first. Now, in the wake of Angie's death, it had become intolerable. Every time the news came on, every time Angie's name was spoken, the Minimonster erupted, high-pitched and insistent: 'I wanna see what he did. Did he carve her up? Lotsa blood, and see inside her tummy? Yes? Let's go see, please, please PLEASE PLEASE! I wanna see. She wa mummy's friend, yes? Wanna see the dead friend. Please. Now NOW PLEASE!'

191

The boy kept it up night and day. He was utterly engrossed, possessed, by the killings. Angie's death only exacerbated his passion. Gladys tried to reason with her grandson, tried to explain that murder wasn't exciting. But she got nowhere. Simone had reached the point of breaking down in tears every time Nero began shouting about 'Mummy's dead friend.'

Eugene wasn't putting up with any more of it. Now, every time the Minimonster kicked off with his Meatman routine, Eugene went into action. He didn't bother with explanations or argument. He grabbed the little sod straightways and locked him in his bedroom. Nero raged, thrashed and threatened as he was carted off. 'My Daddy gonna kill you dead. Yeah. Dead, you gonna get dead for this.' Eugene ignored the little bastard and went back downstairs to watch TV in relative peace. Nero's insistent kicking and thumping and his screams of rage and fury were audible throughout the house, and even Simone seemed relieved to be rid of him.

Luckily, there was a handy space bang outside Brittany's house, where Eugene settled the Puma. He was early, so he spent ten minutes wandering along Crouch End Broadway before retracing his steps to number three.

She looked fabulous. Classy and fabulous. He said so, and then they headed for the restaurant, Eugene walking on the outside, as his father had taught him.

They went to an Italian five minutes from the house. The place was OK, Eugene thought. He couldn't remember the last time he'd taken a girl out for dinner. If ever. But this was all right. Better than he thought, really. The food was decent, and quite quickly he'd begun to relax, and even to enjoy himself.

He'd been worried about being alone with her – no music, no TV, no distractions. But it had been totally fine – an absolute breeze. Within minutes of arriving at the restaurant,

Eugene had relaxed; by the time he'd got halfway down his glass of champagne, he was positively blooming.

Checking his watch as they left, Eugene was amazed. Over two and a half hours they'd been in there – and it had seemed like ten minutes.

Eugene decided he was obviously a natural sophisticate, taken to it like a duck to water. Of course his mum had always been a stickler for table manners. 'You'll thank me one day,' she'd said repeatedly and, as usual his mum was right. Knowing the 'outside in' cutlery rule hadn't struck him and Simone as a worthwhile use of their adolescent time. Gladys had drummed it into them, nonetheless. And in doing so had saved her son from making an idiot of himself in front of the woman he desperately wanted to impress. It just goes to show, Eugene thought. You think you know everything, but you don't.

They walked back to her place hand in hand. It was a clear, starry night. As a little boy, Eugene's father had lifted him up to sit on the bedroom window ledge. He had leant against his dad and listened as Jean-Baptiste spoke about the eternal dance of the stars, teaching his little boy how to recognize the great constellations and planets. Through the cold clear nights of winter Eugene learnt about the Pole star and the Plough, Orion the Hunter, Cassiopeia, the Great Bear, and Sirius, the Dog Star. He told Brittany about it. How he'd felt like an apprentice magician, those nights with his dad. And how he'd loved the mystery of it all, the naming of the stars: Arcturus, Procyon, Betelgeuse and Bellatrix, Castor and Pollux.

'Show me, please,' Brittany asked. 'Show them to me.' So, tripping over their own feet, and holding on to each other as they stared upwards, they made their way homeward as Eugene showed Brittany the starry Plough and the belt of Orion. As they reached the house, Brittany said she hoped he would stay.

*   *   *

The next morning, they woke early, turning to each other as the pale sun pierced through the blinds and a cacophony of tuneless birds screamed their way through the dawn chorus. Eugene couldn't get enough of her, was almost dizzy with desire and happiness. As before, he gave her a lift to the tube. Before she got out, they arranged to meet up on Saturday evening; then she leant across and kissed him goodbye. Again, Eugene watched her until she disappeared into the underground before turning the Puma in the direction of Wentworth Road. Heading up the Stroud Green Road, Eugene rummaged for his mobile and rang Ralph on the hands-free. He was badly in need of help and advice. He had fallen in love.

CHAPTER EIGHTEEN

Full large he was of limbe, and shoulders brode,
But of such subtile substance and vnsound,
That like a ghost he seem'd, whose graue-clothes
    were vnbound.

FQ: The Legend of Sir Gvyon: II.xi.20

Eugene spent Thursday morning at home. 'Something's put a smile on your face,' Gladys said. 'Or is it someone, maybe?'

Eugene grinned, looked at the floor and shrugged. 'Maybe,' he replied. Then ducked out of the room.

Gladys paused, eyebrows raised. She had never seen Eugene remotely approaching bashful – he didn't do un-dignified. And although he was never without at least one girlfriend on the go, anyone who lasted beyond two weeks with Eugene was considered long-term. Gladys had met a couple of them, back when he was a teenager. She hadn't been impressed. 'Flashy and cheap,' she'd told her son. Over the last ten years, she had seen no evidence that he'd changed his taste. As far as Gladys could tell, what passed for romance in Eugene's life had been a nameless, faceless parade of one-night stands.

If some girl had rocked him back on his heels, then so

much the better. Gladys didn't care who she was – rich, poor, black or white, didn't matter where she came from, Gladys was even prepared to overlook religion, at a pinch. 'All I want is a decent girl who loves him and makes him happy,' she told Moira on a regular basis. Which was a neat way of asking for nothing and everything.

Eugene didn't have long to indulge in daydreams of Brittany. Talus rang just after midday. He was in the car, on his way up to Archie's place in Finchley. Unforeseen business difficulties had arisen – Archie wanted Talus to deal with the problem.

'New importation fuck-up?' Eugene enquired.

'Had to be,' Talus replied. 'And didn't we see this coming. Told George, but he wouldn't have it – now he's in bleeding Marbella with the missus. Not back till late tomorrow. Which means me and Archie have to clean up the mess.' Talus swore at the traffic. 'Come on, you dickhead. You'd get a tank through there—' There was a pause, then Talus was back. 'Yeah, as I said, the deal's gone seriously moody and needs sorting before there's any more damage. I'll be out of town till tomorrow, but we're still on for our meet, yeah?'

'Four p.m. King's Head. Sweet by me,' Eugene said.

'Sound. Right, and I want you to stand in for me today on a job. I should have gone down there myself, but now you'll have to take it.'

'What is it?' Eugene asked.

Talus laughed. 'Oh, you'll love this, Geno – you really will. You need to drop down and see that crazy cunt, Shifter.'

'Oh fuckin not,' Eugene moaned.

'Yeah, mate, I know,' Talus said. 'He's a weird bastard, and as for the old bags . . .' Talus laughed again.

'They're worse than him,' Eugene said. 'And the fuckin dogs give me the creeps. Can't someone else do it?'

'Nah, mate. Archie says he wants you. End of story, I'd

196

say.' Eugene resigned himself to his fate and listened carefully as Talus outlined the business in hand.

A little later and less than a mile away down the Holloway Road, two women were walking towards the notorious Glass Tower lifts. Each negotiated the paternosters competently, riding all the way up to the top floor of the tower, where both jumped free. It was sunny, but not yet summer, so they took an inside table at the far end of Al Fresco, which ensured their conversation wouldn't be overheard.

They clearly had plenty to talk about, and it was something worth discussing, judging by the animated expressions and emphatic hand gestures. At first, the black woman did most of the talking. Her white companion listened intently, occasionally shaking her head in apparent disgust or disbelief. The two women stayed for over an hour. Both of them looked angry – though one seemed ashamed and the other satisfied.

Eugene could sense the Puma's reluctance as he turned up to Acre Row; he didn't complain – the unwilling progress exactly mirrored his own mood. He left the Puma in a sidestreet, a two-minute walk away from the Camden Council 'no vehicles' gate barring the entrance to Shifter's cul-de-sac. He was round the corner and into Acre Row proper when it hit him with an almost physical force – the smell of death, rot and decay hanging over Shifter's street like a sodden blanket. Eugene began to gag, his mouth filling with saliva. For a minute, he thought he might vomit; luckily, he didn't.

He was convinced it was getting stronger, the awful meaty stench of decomposition roiling round Acre Row. And the weed-choked gardens seemed worse as well – the vegetation humming with shocking vitality. Eugene walked on the road; it seemed safer. Muscular creepers traversed the pavements. Strangulating fibrous loops wrapped around

197

lamp-posts and dangled from gutterings. The creepers in turn were enmeshed by coiling vines with slender tendrils perpetually stretching out eager, spiral fingers.

The plant life of Acre Row always made Eugene uneasy. The frantic, pell-mell pace of growth and decay unnerved him – and there were other oddities. All plants were green – but not livid, toxic, Day-Glo green. And the size of the stuff was another thing. The plants were too big, too fat, Eugene thought. He saw a leaf wobble slightly as a huge slug began to gorge, and shuddered. The entire road repelled him. He determined to get the Shifter business over as quickly as possible.

The sound of the dogs' nails clicking on the hall lino was the first thing he heard after ringing the doorbell. Seconds later, Shifter appeared. 'Well, well, well,' he said. 'Home comes the hero. Just look who we've got here, my boys. Such a pleasant surprise. Do come in. What a treat this is.'

Shifter led Eugene down the hall, the dogs padding after them. 'Here he is, Ladies,' Shifter sang out. 'The one we've been waiting for.' He turned and winked at Eugene. 'So exciting for them,' he whispered conspiratorially. 'When Talus rang, I couldn't wait to tell them the news. Absolutely thrilled they were, especially Dolly, but then she's such a bubbly personality.' Shifter paused and gave Eugene a nudge. 'They've been closeted upstairs all week, you know. Special project. Working their fingers to the bone, and such tricky materials. It's a gift of course.' He tittered and nudged Eugene again. 'But the minute I told them you were visiting – well, that was it. You're honoured, my boy. They don't interrupt upstairs work for anybody, you know.'

Eugene nodded. Shifter waited. The silence lengthened. 'Great,' Eugene said eventually.

'I knew you'd be pleased,' Shifter trilled. 'Come on, then.' He walked forward, ushering Eugene into the kitchen. 'Sit down, make yourself comfortable. Just like old times, isn't it?'

'Yeah,' said Eugene. 'Pity I won't be able to stay and socialize like I used to.'

Shifter smiled. 'I'm sure you can spare the Ladies a few minutes, Geno. Not too grand and important for that.'

Eugene's reply was completely drowned out by Dolly's welcoming screams of ecstasy.

'I'll make the drinks, shall I?' Shifter said. 'What do you fancy? I'm Manhattan and Dolly's doing Wallbangers. What shall it be? Name your poison – as they say.'

In the end, Eugene compromised. He insisted on getting the business done first, then – he said – when things were sorted, he would have time for a quick drink. 'If that's all right with the Ladies,' he finished.

'Yes,' Letitia said impatiently. 'Go on, then, Malcolm. Stop playing the fool. Give the man what he's come for.'

Shifter and Eugene adjourned to the back room where Shifter had the merchandise. 'There you are, my friend, exactly as agreed. Three quarter keys. Three grades, all labelled. Personally, think you'd be mad to say no. Superior quality, beautiful stuff. Have a taste, here you go, don't be coy.'

Shifter suddenly produced a small mirror with a couple of lines ready and waiting.

Back in the kitchen, sipping his caipirinha cocktail, Eugene reflected that Mal Shifter was right. The gear was top notch, so good it even made sitting with Shifter and sisters seem bearable.

Dolly was singing along to Shaggy, giggling suggestively at every sexual innuendo whilst surreptitiously edging her chair ever closer to Eugene. The elder sister was in her customary iron-backed seat at the head of the table. Laid out before her were various shapes cut out of pale leather, which she was deftly matching and pinning together. Eugene asked her what she was making.

'Gloves,' she said, with a hoarse laugh. 'For Malcolm.

Gloves fit for an emperor. Softer than kid, they'll be, and smooth as butter. Made to measure as well. Each hand is different. Left and right need separate fittings.'

'She's a *non-pareil*,' Shifter said admiringly. 'I tell you, Geno, money couldn't buy that sort of quality.'

Letitia shrugged. 'Oh, Malcolm gets carried away,' she said.

'Nonsense,' cried Shifter. 'Praise where praise is due, eh, Geno? Those gloves will be a work of art – soft, flexible and fitting like' – he paused and giggled – 'like a second skin.'

'That's enough, Malcolm,' Letitia snapped. 'One day you'll wake up with your mouth sewn shut.' Shifter subsided immediately.

'How are you at the moment? Health improving?' Eugene asked Letitia, purely to break the silence which followed.

'So-so. Picked up verrucas from somewhere.' Letitia raised an eyebrow and looked across at Dolly, who snatched back the hand inching towards Eugene's thigh and busied herself with her drink. 'Troublesome things,' Letitia continued, 'but small beer. No. The real news is the osteoarthritis. It's spread to my left hip and the knees are worse. Got crepitus as well.'

'I'm sorry to hear that,' Eugene said.

Letitia cackled. 'Know about crepitus, do you?'

Eugene hadn't the faintest idea.

'Listen to this,' Letitia instructed. 'Turn that music off, Dolly.' Once all was quiet, Letitia gripped the table and slowly levered her body upright, then paused and steadied herself as Shifter rushed to pull back the iron chair to ease her progress. After cracking her knuckles, Letitia took a deep breath and released her hold on the table to hobble a few steps across the kitchen. She reached the sink and rested against it for a few seconds, then limped slowly back. Her every movement accompanied by a loud, eerie, creaking sound – a sinister noise which ceased abruptly the moment she lowered herself into the iron chair. The silence which followed Letitia's odyssey provided a dramatic counterpoint to the penetrating screams of rusty protest from her deformed joints.

'That's crepitus, boy.'

'Learn something new every day,' Eugene said.

Dolly felt it was her turn in the limelight and breathlessly told Eugene that her thrush had returned and developed into pruritus. Eugene said it sounded serious. Dolly said that wasn't the half of it. Because, due to a 'fissure', the pruritus had spread. 'The consultant said I was a highly unusual case,' she confided. 'Very rare to have them both. Pruritus vulvae and pruritus ani. The consultant's thinking of writing a paper about it. Doctor Kildare, I call him, though it's not his real name. But he's got the look, you know – distinguished, with brushed-back hair, just going silver at the temples . . . ooh.' Dolly gave a theatrical shiver. 'I'm seeing him again Monday. Another examination. Exploratory internal. Can't wait, Gorgeous! Ooh, those cold fingers!'

'Shut your filthy mouth,' Letitia snapped. 'And, Malcolm, go upstairs for me.' Shifter rose immediately whilst Letitia checked her work. Eventually, the pale grey eyes snapped up to Shifter's face. 'Are you listening, Malcolm? You'll need to be. Right: I need two straw needles and a wedge point. The blue awl and the seam-ripper. Got that? And get me a grabber while you're at it. Go on, then – don't just stand there like a wet weekend.'

Shifter moved immediately, the three dogs padding silently in his wake. In the kitchen Shaggy had given way to Ricky Martin. Eugene said he didn't fancy dancing; no, he really didn't. Dolly grabbed his hand and tried to pull him to his feet. She was a lot stronger than she looked. Eugene was rescued by Letitia rapping the table. Dolly disengaged and pirouetted away. 'La Vida Loca' was one of her favourites, she told Eugene. He was a total spoilsport.

Dolly flung herself into bursts of abandoned dancing,

punctuated by lisping complaints. 'I'm a disappointed girl, Gorgeous. You've made me really miserable, but you don't care, do you? You're ruthless.' Then back to wild hip-thrusts and hair-tossing.

When Shifter returned, Dolly told him that Eugene was 'a heartbreaker. I begged him, just take me in your arms and dance. But he wouldn't budge, not even to oblige a lady.'

'How very ungallant,' said Shifter. 'And I thought you people loved to dance, innate rhythm and all that. Is that just a myth, then, Geno?'

'I don't think enough reliable data exists to decide,' Eugene replied. 'From what I've read, there's been real trouble setting internationally agreed parameters for academic surveys on the question. Apparently there's a major difference of opinion between Princeton and Oxford professors on what constitutes good and bad dancing. You can see the problem, Mal?'

Shifter's smile was razor-thin. The dogs bunched up behind him, staring at Eugene with hot eyes, their lips starting to wrinkle back from the long white teeth. 'Very good, Geno, very funny, you're quite right. These things aren't scientific, just based on experience. And your sister certainly seems to like dancing, she looks like she's really enjoying herself. Very uninhibited, and such . . . energy. Quite a sight, it really is.'

Eugene leant back in his chair, looking past Shifter, focusing behind him, concentrating on the dogs standing rearguard. He knew Shifter wanted him to lose it, and he wasn't going to oblige. He studied the dogs, trying to tell one apart from the other, waiting for Shifter's insinuations to end.

'She's very popular, I understand. Known for her athleticism, so I'm told. I do so admire that about you darkies, totally uninhibited, in touch with nature, with our primeval . . .'

'It's their collars, isn't it?' Eugene interrupted.

Shifter stared at him. So did the sisters. Everything suddenly still and quiet.

'That's how you tell the dogs apart,' Eugene continued. 'By their different collars. Am I right? Sorry, Mal, what were you saying? I missed it. Anyway, lovely to see you all, but I've got to move.' Eugene stood up and pocketed the three cocaine samples. 'Bye, Ladies,' he said, walking out of the kitchen and down the hallway, Shifter and the dogs in close pursuit.

Eugene opened the front door, and paused, to allow Shifter to catch up. Then, feeling Shifter's physical presence closing in on him, he grabbed him by the throat and waist, spinning them both outside, slamming the door smartly shut in their wake. Inside the house, the dogs flung themselves forward, their bodies smacking impotently against the solid wood of the door. Eugene laughed and rapped at the door with his free fist, causing the dogs' frenzy to hit crescendo level. 'Fuck all you can do about it, you rabid bastards,' he said, then turned back to Shifter and punched him twice straight in the face, breaking his nose.

'You ever speak about my sister again and I'll kill you. You understand?'

'Yuslsh,' Shifter said, through a mouthful of blood.

Eugene banged Shifter's head back against the door, causing another flurry of thuds as the canine trio hurled themselves forward. 'And let the fuckin hounds of hell after me and I'll kill them, too, enjoy it, in fact. Clear, is it? Follow my argument?'

Shifter nodded.

'I want an answer, fuckwit.' Eugene slapped him hard again.

'Yush,' Shifter said. 'Itsh clar. Vay clar.'

Eugene released his hold. 'Funtime is over, Mal,' he said.

CHAPTER NINETEEN

Some for vntimely ease, some for delight,
As pleased them to vse, that vse it might:
And all was full of Damzels, and of Squires,
Dauncing and reueling both day and night,
And swimming deepe in sensuall desires,
And *Cupid* still emongst them kindled lustfull fires.

FQ: The Legend of Britomartis; Castle Ioyeous: III.i.39

The Puma sped away from Acre Row, then leapt north-
wards up the Holloway Road and skittered across
Archway Roundabout, before bowling up Highgate Hill,
escaping the long shadow of the Archway Tower which
reached almost to St Joseph's Church. The Puma slowed to
a law-abiding dawdle through Highgate Village, picking up
pace over Three Boroughs Junction and speeding on to
Finchley. It was a perfect gold-green evening, trees floating
with blossom, leaves unfurling, sun bouncing across the
Puma's flanks, a pinpoint effervescence of silver light fading
in its wake.

Eugene was in no state to appreciate any of it. He
was miles away, and if the Puma hadn't recognized Mago
Drive and slowed accordingly, he'd more than likely have
missed it.

Archie's house stood at the far end of Mago Drive, a detached, red-brick affair with double garage, recently built, and identical to every other house on the road. Inside was functional, and immaculately clean and tidy. Archie had employed an interior designer, an effete young man who had unwisely attempted to ignore Archie Faron's elliptical instructions and impose his own radical and exciting ideas.

Marco's initial 'conceptual space' earned him a visit from Talus. Their dialogue gave Marco a much clearer understanding of Archie's original brief. 'Keep it plain, smart and simple,' Talus told the designer. 'Stop poncing about and wasting our time, unless you want me round for another chat.' This was absolutely the last thing Marco desired, so he'd duly dumped the *trompe l'oeil* effects, the 'walls of light' and the innovative use of sand and straw floor-cover.

The final result was a success – at least in Archie's eyes. Marco took the money and ran, having learnt that self-preservation supersedes artistic integrity. The place always reminded Eugene of a dentist's – the same mixture of cleanliness and threat, shiny white walls and discomfort.

Eugene delivered the cocaine samples and talked Archie through matters of price, quality and quantity. When the main business was sorted, Eugene explained about his run-in with Shifter. Archie listened carefully. Not that Eugene was telling him anything new – Shifter had been on the phone seconds after Eugene's departure.

'"An unprovoked attack," Mal told me,' Archie said. 'Quite difficult to understand him – sounded like he'd had half his teeth knocked out. But his feelings regarding you were clear enough. Getting worked up like that could give him a heart attack at his age. Told him he needed to calm down.'

'He needs to learn how to behave,' said Eugene. 'I've put up with shed-loads of shit from Mal Shifter and never raised a finger. But you know the rules, Archie. Family is out of bounds.'

'You're not wrong, Geno,' Archie said softly. He paused a moment and walked across the monochrome room. The outside wall was made entirely of glass, a permanent water-fall running over it, catching prisms of light in a constantly flickering pattern. If you tried looking through it, grass, trees and buildings all submerged into a single distorted, formless image, so that the world seemed to melt and dissolve under your gaze.

'I'll have a personal word with our friend Malcolm,' he said, at last. 'You're right, Geno, boundaries have to be recognized. He needs to understand that. Yes, I'll have a word. No worries.'

As the Puma turned out of Mago Drive and loped home-wards, Eugene couldn't shake Shifter from his thoughts. The picture of him hanging round SweetHearts. Leaning against the corner of the bar, giggling and licking his lips, sipping courtesy cocktails. Smirking and sliding his hands into his pockets. Standing quietly in shadows – enjoying the spectacle.

Eugene knew Shifter was the authorized SweetHearts wholesale supplier.

All the drugs discreetly available on the premises came from Shifter. Cocaine, skunk, crack, Ecstasy and Viagra were on the menu. Whenever stocks ran low, someone at the club would ring Shifter and tell him fresh provisions were needed.

The retail side of SweetHearts' internal drugs market was handled by Firm-approved dealers. The trade inside the club was carried out quietly, under the protection of SweetHearts security muscle. The heavies kept things in order, and – more importantly – ensured the Farons received their rightful dividend from the profits accrued. The cut was 50 per cent. An entirely reasonable demand, given that the Firm provided merchandise, business premises and commercial security.

And SweetHearts' 'alternative services' were very popular.

The cocaine and Viagra lines were the punters' preference. The girls – who had a 'staff discount' – bought coke, skunk and crack. Simone admitted to 'doing a few lines backstage', plus 'the odd glass of champagne', but vehemently insisted that was it. Eugene wanted to believe her.

Despite regularly dropping by the club on Firm business, Eugene had never seen his sister 'perform'. He had watched other SweetHearts dancers do their stuff, though. Seen them time and time again. There were personal variations, a trademark spin, a particular pole-gimmick or dance routine but, basically, once you'd seen one, you'd seen them all. Really, there wasn't much chance to express your unique appeal in a three-minute musical strip. And there wasn't much point in trying. The punters were usually drunk – they wanted tits 'n' arse and bump 'n' grind. So the girls tried their best to oblige.

The dancers did the drugs and drink backstage. It was part of the preparation to face their public. Then, kitted up and ready to go, it was through the 'stage door' and out there.

As Mr Barry was fond of saying, 'the performance starts the minute you walk through that door.' On show: limbs oiled, make-up perfect, big smile. They began by strutting around the floor, posing in costume – naughty nurse, school-girl slut, red brocade, black satin, corsets, hot pants, tiny skirts – hoping to catch the attention of some sweaty git who would beckon them over.

Then the girl would sashay across, ask for champagne and engage in a few minutes' chit-chat. Once the dance was bought and paid for, she'd signal to the DJ – all the dancers had favourite songs – and when the music started, she was off into her routine. It was always the same – some did it well, some couldn't dance for toffee, but the moves were universal. Rotating hips and jiggling breasts, bending over, legs akimbo, stripping off bit by bit – wriggling out of her G-string last of all.

The more 'tables' asking you to dance, the more

money the girl – and the club – made. Stars, like Simone, commanded £100 per dance. But none of the girls came cheap. £50 a pop was rock bottom. There were also – cue Tina Turner, Mr Barry's favourite artiste, 'a true survivor and a towering talent' – two rooms set aside for 'private dances'.

A private dance lasted fifteen minutes and cost a small fortune. Table-dance routines were governed by strictly enforced rules – no touching, always maintain a minimum one-metre clear physical distance from the client, no use of 'lewd words, gestures or movements'. And – most importantly – 'no exchange of personal telephone numbers or any contact details.' So, no chance of arranging to meet after closing. And – hopefully – no chance of SweetHearts' licence being lost. Mr Barry was very tough on this. 'High-class table-dancing emporiums are places of fun and relaxation,' he said repeatedly. 'At SweetHearts we provide a luxurious and friendly atmosphere, top-level international cuisine and entertainment courtesy of some of the world's most beautiful and sensual women.' The Farons appreciated Mr Barry's eloquence – the quote was included on all SweetHearts promo literature.

The reason private dances were so outrageously pricy was that all the boring rules and dutiful nods to legality, licences and moral probity could be dispensed with in double-quick time. Out on the main floor everything was on view. Many of the tables were set in demi-booths, giving the impression of seclusion. But in reality everything that occurred was open to public and management scrutiny. Any customer who laid a finger on a girl – or tried to – was immediately pounced on and carted away by security. Any girl trying too hard for a tip would find herself summoned in front of Mr Barry the moment she got her clothes back on. The most serious misdemeanour was anything suggesting an assignation. 'I will not turn a blind eye to sexual commerce in this club,' Mr Barry said – and meant it.

But inside the private rooms lay another world entirely. Not free of surveillance – the mirrored wall which allowed the client to appreciate every angle of the girl's 'artistry' was two-way, and monitored by closed-circuit TV. The device ensured swift rescue for the dancer if matters got out of hand. It was supposedly viewed only by Mr Barry, or by SweetHearts' head of security – but the tapes were copied and regarded by SweetHearts' male employees as a genuine perk of the job. Went down a storm at parties.

The girls all knew this. And knew what 'private dances' entailed. And knew how much they'd be paid, and how much was on offer if they were minded to meet the man – and his friends, perhaps – after work. So it was a very nice calculation. The weighing-up of pros and cons.

Simone didn't need to do the private stuff. She was the girl in demand anyway, could easily pull ten, twelve tables a night. Made more than enough money . . . but who ever made enough money when it was so easy to make more? And they all asked, all wanted her to do it. So inevitably the nightly temptation proved too much.

She finally said 'yes' to one of her regulars. A white guy in his thirties – an executive in 'the music industry' who spent his money with careless cool. She'd turned him down a dozen times, but he just kept on upping the bids. The other girls said, 'Go for it,' told her to think of the money, and helpfully offered tips on the best moves to keep her face clear of the CCTV.

And, to be fair, it wasn't that bad. She'd even done a couple more of them, had pocketed the money and felt OK. She'd been off her head at the time of course. The crack, smack and skunk cocktail made her feel sexy – made the dancing easy – allowed her to enjoy herself. To tease and twirl and laugh as she pirouetted away from the grasping hands. At the time it was OK. Afterwards, back in Wentworth Road, things were different. She couldn't shake loose from the memories, from the feel of hands sliding inside her knickers, pulling at her nipples, probing, pinching, exploring fingers, dirty voices saying dirty words, and her own manic laughter.

It was no surprise that most of SweetHearts' dancers did drugs of one sort or another. Eugene liked naked girls as much as the next man, but he couldn't get off on the SweetHearts brand of sexy. It was partly because of Simone. The thought of his sister doing that stuff was horrible. And praps that had ruined the whole experience for him, because nowadays it made him wince, watching a nineteen-year-old crack addict from Kiev stripping off in front of a table full of rowdy City boys. It was worst at the end, when the music stopped and the girl, naked except for four-inch stilettos, had to fish around on the floor for her discarded clothes, trying to ignore the comments and obscene jokes, grabbing her stuff at top speed before sprinting naked for the safety of the 'stage door'.

When he got back to Wentworth Road that Thursday night, Eugene found he was home alone. Simone was at work. Gladys, Moira and the rest of the gang were off at the bingo. The Minimonster was staying overnight with one of Simone's friends, Tanya, another single mother, who regularly looked after Nero. Eugene knew Tanya from school – had slept with her a few times. He thought she deserved to be nominated for sainthood, the way she put up with the psycho-toddler.

In the quiet of the house Eugene tried to get a grip and stop obsessing about Shifter. He microwaved the dinner Gladys had left for him, collected a couple of beers and trotted upstairs. He needed to relax, he thought, let himself unwind a bit. To this end, he had high hopes of the Discovery Channel. 'Thursday night is Crime Night!' and so it was. Wall-to-wall murder and mayhem till 1 a.m. Eugene settled down happily.

Ten minutes later, he was moodily channel-flicking. *The*

FBI Files – normally one of Eugene's sure-fire faves – was concentrating on 'the demise of the international drug barons' – and had dedicated the entire night's programming to the same.

Eugene had no desire to watch his professional colleagues getting turned over. Trouble was, as he flicked top speed from channel to channel, there was fuck all else to watch. In the end, he settled on Channel 4 and *Time Team*. Quite entertaining, really. The 'Team' were all labouring away in the mud and rain on top of some Dorset hill. Dead sure that – according to aerial photos and some complicated soil-sampling – they were about to discover the spectacular remains of a Roman villa. The big mad bloke with ginger hair and short-arse Tony were both gibbering with excitement.

Eugene watched with only half his attention. His mind repeatedly flicking back to Shifter's. Something about the whole weird scene kept snagging his attention but couldn't quite catch it.

Whatever it was, it was driving him mad. And, like picking a scab, Eugene couldn't leave it alone. It was when he was sitting in the kitchen and Shifter was going on . . . fuck it. He wasn't going spend his entire night thinking about Shifter. He picked up the remote and ran through the options. A thing about killer whales caught his attention. Orca, hunting in the deep – Eugene thought it sounded worth a try. Seconds later his mobile rang.

The last thing, the very last thing Eugene felt like was a sex and drugs extravaganza round at Lucy's. He said sorry but he was too knackered to be up for it. Lucy wasn't having any. She pushed, cajoled, pleaded. Turned out Lucy's dealer had let her down. It wasn't so much Eugene she wanted as the cocaine. He said he'd shoot over and leave her a couple of grammes – which was a total pain in the arse, but probably easier in the long run. Eugene had a feeling that Lucy wouldn't give up until she got what she wanted.

At that very moment, 10 p.m. Thursday, Scudamour and Lalibela were through the majority of the interviews and were preparing to leave their newly requisitioned office. The club was filling up, and it was time to mingle with the punters and start surveillance.

It was their second night out on the SweetHearts floor. Mr Barry had told them that Thursday night would be 'well busy', and the two detectives watched a constant flow of arrivals. Mostly the men were in little knots and groups of three and four – out for a laugh, wanting to unwind a bit after work. There was also a surprising number of lone punters. Some were clearly foreign – tourists, or more likely travelling execs, putting the expenses budget to good use. Then there were the obvious weirdos – some bold and reptilian, staring with hungry unblinking eyes at the flesh displayed – other singles were more furtive, their gestures jerky and nervous, gaze darting and sliding from side to side, waiting for the alcohol to work, when they could finally relax and enjoy.

Perverts, sadfucks, tourists, minor celebs, sports stars, lawyers, politicians, out-of-town business men and nobodies who'd saved up for six months, SweetHearts had the lot – drunken boys of all ages and professions. But Scudamour and Lalibela were looking for a pair of serial killers and saw nothing worthy of comment.

The two detectives skirted the mirrored dance floor – the surrounding tables were all taken – and headed upstairs: the Balcony Bar offered a good vantage-point. Scudamour scanned the people below whilst Lalibela went to the bar. Quite a few of the girls were still backstage, preparing to face their public.

Scudamour and Lalibela hadn't had a particularly productive day of it. In their police interviews they had asked each girl to think back carefully over the past few weeks. The detectives wanted them to concentrate on the clientele. Yes, of course it was hard to remember, and yes, six weeks was a long time, but they wanted the Meatman caught, didn't they? So, could they try again – starting with Friday and Saturday nights. The weekend before Stella died. The weekend the clocks changed to British Summer Time – yes, you got it now? Great, take your time, don't leave anything out, even small things can be vital.

Who were the regular weekend punters? Description? Anybody behaving oddly, anybody especially creepy, threatening, odd or obsessive? Anyone showing particular interest in the victims – hanging round Stella, or Canday Sweete's flatmate, little Amy? Any men seen trying to chat up Angie, the dark girl who'd started doing bar shifts? Angie – Simone's friend. You know her, yes, she was getting married, that's the one.

'Like pulling teeth,' was DS Scudamour's verdict. DC Lalibela concurred. 'I don't think most of them can remember much anyway,' he said. 'They don't know what day it is. Just making it up as they go along, is my take.' Scudamour nodded agreement.

The girls' interview statements were near useless. Sifting through, the detectives earmarked a couple of regulars as possible suspects, though neither seemed exactly right. They had the strong feeling that many of the girls weren't telling everything they knew. But that was no surprise – Sweet-Hearts' management didn't believe in encouraging a culture of openness.

Scudamour looked across the dance floor. All the girls were out now, bar one. Top girl always made the final entrance. The detective watched as the DJ announced her, and then, swaying across the floor to a welcoming chorus of whistles and cheers, Simone appeared. 'That girl is something,' Lalibela said in his ear. Scudamour nodded, eyes still fixed on the beautiful face below him.

CHAPTER TWENTY

Her face right wondrous faire did seeme to bee,
That her broad beauties beam great brightnes threw
Through the dim shade, that all men might it see:
Yet was not that same her owne natiue hew,
But wrought by art and counterfetted shew,
Thereby more louers vnto her to call;

FQ: The Legend of Sir Gvyon; Lucifera: II.vii.45

Eugene snapped his mobile shut and headed straight over to Lucy's. The quicker he went, the sooner he'd be back, he reasoned. And he'd told her on the phone that he was pushed for time – that it would be a case of 'in-out, can't hang about'. 'OK, I'll shoot over to yours,' he said, 'but I'll have to drop the gear and split.'

But as the Puma skimmed down the Holloway Road, Eugene's resolve began to waver. There was nothing he had to get back for. Lucy had persuaded and cajoled. Surely he could manage to stay for a quick drink and a line? she'd asked. It wouldn't kill him, just thirty mins or so? They could have a laugh. Come on – what was his problem?

Lucy was sure he could put off whoever was waiting on him, it couldn't be anything that vital – ooh, and whilst she remembered, could he buy a bottle of Bollinger and some brandy on his way round? She'd give him the cash, course, but the shop was aeons away, so it would be brill if he sorted it.

Eugene did as required. Walking back to the Puma, he decided Lucy was right. Half an hour or so – it was no big deal. He definitely, absolutely definitely, was not getting involved in another marathon, all-night extravaganza. That was a hundred per cent certain. But a couple of lines and a drink would be fine – kill an hour or so, specially as the telly was so crap. And seeing as he'd bought the champagne, well, he may as well stay and help to drink it.

He told himself it was no big deal. Sex with Lucy was past history. He wouldn't be going there any more. He was just doing a friend a favour. And anyway, he wasn't staying long. Brittany would understand, he was sure of it. No, if she knew, she'd be totally cool with it. But there again, Brittany would only find out if Eugene were to tell her, which he had no intention of doing.

He opened the champagne when he arrived and told Lucy he'd managed to put a couple of things on hold, so he wouldn't have to rush straight off after all. Lucy said, 'Way cool,' and 'Fab,' and applied herself to chopping the cocaine.

Three hours later, Eugene was still there. The champagne was long gone; they'd moved on to the brandy and were halfway down a third gramme of coke. Lucy was curled next to Eugene on the sofa, her legs over his thigh, bare feet resting in his lap. She was rolling another spliff. Eugene asked her where she got the skunk from. It was seriously good. She said something about Carlos or Marlon, or someone, but Eugene wasn't really listening. He was telling himself that he wasn't meeting Talus till 4 p.m. – which was late enough – and, otherwise, he was clear. Lucy kept wriggling her toes, and Eugene felt less and less inclined to drive home. Lucy started to cut out two more lines, leaning forward to reach the table, her white shift dress rucking up as she moved. She wasn't wearing knickers. As Lucy snorted her line, Eugene ran his hand up her leg. He was under her skirt when his mobile shouted.

He grabbed it and checked. It was Ralph. Eugene hesitated a split second, then pressed 'accept'. Ralph wouldn't be phoning gone midnight unless the boy had a reason. Five minutes later, Eugene grabbed his car keys and told Lucy he had to split. 'Sorry, babe. Emergency. Take care now.' Then he was out of there and gone. The Puma shot away northward, flying down the empty road.

Eugene got to Ralph's just before 1 a.m. He ignored the lifts, which, true to form, functioned admirably as public toilets but were otherwise useless, and took the stairs two at a time, heading for Ralph's parents' flat. Eugene had spent half his adolescence hanging round the Palmers' place. On the second floor of a low-rise seventies council block, handily situated bang next to Seven Sisters and the Holloway Road, the Palmers' flat had become Eugene's second home. Walking along the familiar landing, level with the tops of the plane trees planted in the street below, reaching out to touch the leaves, Eugene could almost believe he was fourteen again.

Ralph had buzzed him through the main security door downstairs, and was waiting for him, the light from the flat's open front door spilling diagonally across the landing. Eugene thought his star boy had lost weight. In fact, to tell the truth, Ralph looked like shit.

'Thanks for coming, spar,' Ralph said, as Eugene approached.

'No sweat,' Eugene replied. 'Come on. Inside and tell me what's going on.'

The Palmers' flat was just as Eugene remembered. New paint, different wallpaper – and brand-spanking kitchen units which Ralph and his dad had laboured to install the previous summer – but still the same feel. The gilt-framed 'studio portraits' of Ralph and his sister – aged eight and six respectively – were in their familiar place, joined by wedding photos now: Ralph's sister Constance and her husband standing in a hail of confetti with huge smiles; Ralph with his arms around a radiant Belinda, just married, and eyes only for each other.

Ralph was on his own in the flat. His parents were staying with his sister up in Leeds, not due back till Monday. 'I tell you man, they've lost it. Not just my mum, it's both of them. Totally flipped they have.' Ralph rolled his eyes as he handed Eugene a beer. 'I mean you should have seen what they're taking up there – spent a small fortune, I tell you. Never seen so much pink and white fluffy stuff in my whole life.'

Eugene laughed. 'Oh, come on. First grandchild, isn't it? I bet your mum's away with it.'

'Just a bit,' Ralph said. 'And Dad's nearly as bad. He's taken the camcorder up.' Ralph shook his head at Eugene. 'Yeah, very funny, bro. They're going to come back with a million hours of film. And Uncle Ralphie will be stuck with watching the entire lot. Five times over.'

'Look on the bright side,' Eugene said. 'Simone dumped me with the fuckin Minimonster. If you think home vids are bad, just imagine living with that little troll twenty-four seven.'

They chatted on for a while. Ralph fetched another beer and talked about work. He told Eugene about some deal with an upmarket Turkish hotel chain. Eugene said it sounded sweet. Ralph explained how the chain was part of a wider conglomerate with access to the fledgling Eastern Europe tourist industry – where there was real money to be made. Eugene nodded. 'Yeah, looking good.'

'Well, you've got to get your foot in, y'know – soon as the door opens,' Ralph said.

Eugene nodded approval.

'Yeah,' Ralph said, and subsided. The silence stretched.

Eugene searched for something to say, then, suddenly, abruptly, Ralph got up and left the room. He came back holding a file, from which he fished out a piece of paper. 'I got this,' he said, passing the folded sheet to Eugene. 'Arrived two days ago.'

It was a lawyer's letter. Couched in the usual obfuscation and legalese, but its meaning was clear enough. Belinda's brief was obviously right-on feminist from hell, thought Eugene. Every line of the letter quivered with aggression and hostility. Every sentence flung a splatter of new accusations. It took Eugene a couple of read-throughs, but eventually he got the gist. Belinda was instigating divorce proceedings on the basis of adultery and mental cruelty.

'Shit,' Eugene said.

'That's right,' Ralph nodded. 'Oh, and then there's this fucker. Arrived this morning. I couldn't believe it, E. Couldn't believe she would do this, like I'm some psycho-street-trash or something. I've never touched her, man. Never would. Then she gives me this shit.'

Ralph passed over another letter, bearing the same legal heading as the first. It warned Ralph and his family to cease all contact with Belinda and to make no attempt to visit the house – Ralph's marital home. Such actions would be seen as harassment and would precipitate an immediate application for a legal injunction against all members of the Palmer family.

Eugene looked at Ralph in total incomprehension. 'What the fuck?' he said. 'What's she on about, bro? I don't understand, what is this bollocks?'

The explanation took the best part of an hour. Ralph told Eugene how he'd tried to talk to Belinda. 'She said she wanted space, so I said OK. I thought it'd be a few days me sleeping at Mum and Dad's, and then back to normal. I knew I loved her, thought she loved me. Thought it'd all be sorted out in no time. Well, I got that one wrong big style.'

Ralph went through the arguments, the phone calls ending

in rows and tears, the meetings over coffee which got nowhere. Belinda wouldn't believe a word he said any more. He was a liar and a cheat, she said. She knew about his girlfriend, knew what he got up to on Friday nights, running round town with his drug-dealing friend. He could say what he liked, she wasn't hearing him. She knew the truth.

Ralph had tried and tried. But it was useless. Finally his mum took matters into her own hands. She went round to the flat without telling Ralph. She'd always been close to Belinda, always got on well with her daughter-in-law. Mrs Palmer thought she might be able to get to the bottom of this nonsense.

Ralph told Eugene that his mum had talked to Belinda for hours. Both women had ended up in tears, but Belinda wouldn't budge. Mrs Palmer learnt that all the 'proof' of Ralph's supposed infidelity came via a friend. The friend had 'seen' Ralph and Eugene in a nightclub – seen them with girlfriends, cheap, tarty blondes. Belinda's friend had said nothing at the time. Then, a couple of weeks later she'd spotted Ralph again – out with the same girl. That's when she'd made up her mind that she had to speak to Belinda.

And Belinda – remembering the dropped phone calls, the scrap of paper with the scrawled mobile numbers, how her man went out with Eugene and came home wired at 2 a.m. – well, Belinda believed everything her friend had to tell her: it all made perfect sense. And nothing Mrs Palmer could do or say made any difference. Except that his mum said Belinda had been very upset – and now Ralph had a lawyer's letter.

Eugene didn't know what to do – other than sit quiet and listen. And that's what he did as Ralph talked on about his misery and desperation, and how hopeless he felt, and how much he hated Belinda's bitch of a friend, and how he couldn't get his head round why someone should want to fuck up his marriage, why someone would lie like that, and why the hell Belinda believed all these lies. Why didn't she trust him, believe what he said, stand by the man she married and supposedly loved instead of throwing it all away on the say-so of some cow who pretended to be her friend? Ralph went round and round in endless circles. Eugene nodded and made occasional noises of support and agreement.

At around three-fifteen, he phoned Simone's mobile and told her he was staying at the Palmers' and he'd be home in the morning, and would she leave a note for Mum. He'd expected the usual backchat, but for once his sister was sweetness and light. He checked how she was getting home – turned out one of the police guys had a driver waiting and, seeing as they were going the same way, the copper had offered her a lift. Eugene was relieved. At least one worry was off his plate.

It was another hour before Ralph had talked himself out. Once or twice he'd been close to tears. 'What's happening to me?' he kept asking. Eugene had no answers. Ralph had never looked at another woman, as far as he knew. Eugene thought it was clear as daylight that a major wind-up was going on. Someone out there was having a real laugh. And he would make it a personal priority to find Belinda's so-called friend, who was so full of information. Although, to Eugene's way of thinking, the poisonous girlfriend was only half the trouble. What he wanted to know was why Belinda had been so quick to believe such nonsense in the first place.

When Ralph finally stopped talking and hit the pillow, Eugene settled down in the spare room and did some serious thinking. He'd had Belinda down as many things, but stupid wasn't one of them. He knew what he was going to do, knew he had to keep it quiet – but he wasn't going to just sit by and watch his star boy get filleted. He knew that for sure.

When Eugene surfaced on Friday it was past 2 p.m. Ralph was long gone, heading out to work at 9 a.m. and leaving

Eugene a note about locking up and posting the keys back through the door – and reminding him that they were hooking up at around 8 p.m. Eugene admired the boy's stamina – personally, he felt like death.

He headed back to Wentworth Road. Then, showered, shaved and feeling generally brighter, he turned the Puma off the Holloway main drag, down the Cally Road, coming to rest outside the King's Head. He was early, as he'd planned. As yet there was no sign of Talus.

Vinnie unlocked the door and welcomed him in with all the charm and warmth Eugene had come to expect. Vinnie's vestiges of human affection were exclusively saved for – in descending order – George Faron, Archie Faron and Talus. That was it. As far as Vinnie was concerned, the rest of humanity was disposable scum, and he made no attempt to pretend otherwise.

Eugene had brought a copy of the *Sun* with him as an insurance policy. Talus was always on time, but – as befits the junior partner – Eugene was five minutes beforehand, and even five minutes making small talk with Vinnie was an unthinkably grim prospect. So, once inside, Eugene commandeered a corner table, grabbed an ashtray and his bottle of Becks and immersed himself in the paper. He read it back to front, starting on the sport and the three pages dedicated to the complexities of the football transfer market. Real Madrid and Arsenal were competing for the favours of Gildasio – a seventeen-year-old Brazilian prodigy. Manchester United were also rumoured to be interested. The teenager's price was leaping £10 million at a time. Eugene passed a few minutes calculating how long it would take the lucky buyers of Gildasio to recoup the teenager's transfer fee.

He eventually decided there were too many variables to factor in on Gildasio, gave up, and turned the paper round. The headline dominated the front page – heavy black letters in block capitals: 'MEATMAN WILL STRIKE AGAIN, warns murder-squad boss.' The news story on pages one and two was supplemented by 'full analysis of Meatman Murders, pages 8–11.' Eugene was utterly engrossed. It was only when he finished reading that he glanced at his watch – 4.25 p.m.: what the fuck was Talus playing at? Eugene contemplated the showbiz-gossip pages – some unheard-of boybander was shagging a girl from *EastEnders* – riveting. He checked the time again. Talus was never late. Something must be going down. Eugene decided to ring. He couldn't just keep on sitting there like he was waiting for Christmas. He fished in his pocket for his mobile, and was just hitting the number when Talus walked through the door.

'Sorry, Geno. I'll explain. We've got a lot to talk about, my son. Some serious business. Get us a couple of beers, Vinnie, will you?'

Vinnie did Talus's bidding, then locked the doors and made himself scarce. Talus waited till he'd gone, then took a couple of sips of his beer before turning to Eugene. 'We've got a problem, Geno. That's why you've been kept hanging. I've been trying to straighten it out – as far as possible. What a fuck-up. That bitch has really excelled herself.'

Eugene listened in silence. It was the classic story, sad and predictable. Destined to end in tears and pain. George Faron and his wife had been due to fly back from their 'Spanish break' on Friday morning. But Gloria had told George that Spain was really doing her the world of good. The sunshine and fresh sea air, and all the time she spent in the hotel gym. She fancied a couple more days of saunas and massages, workouts and swimming in the pool. She would be 'raring to go' when she got back. George happily agreed. It was fair enough, he'd got a ton of work to catch up on back home. And he knew Gloria would have something special for him when she came home. Some things are worth waiting for – as they say.

So George had arrived at Heathrow solo. He'd gone back to the Halcyenda for a sleep, then rung his brother. When the Farons finished talking shop, Archie had asked after Gloria, and George filled him in about what a great time they'd had in Spain and how 'Glor' was staying on and not due back till early Sunday. The moment he got off the phone, Archie rang Talus. The thought of Gloria unchaperoned on the Costa del Sol was a total nightmare.

So, Talus went to work. Spanish associates were phoned and instructed to earn their money, whilst two of the Firm's full-timers went straight to Heathrow and took the next flight out. Not a man to do things by halves, Talus also instigated a computer check, which took several hours but revealed that a Mrs G. Faron had flown out of Malaga Airport on a first class Iberia ticket earlier that afternoon, due to arrive at London Heathrow at 4 p.m.

Talus sent a posse hurtling round the North Circular to Heathrow with instructions to collect Gloria – willing or otherwise – and drive her straight to Archie's place, if they managed to make it in time. Unfortunately, the Iberia flight landed bang on 4 o'clock and the boys were too late. 'Missed her by a good twenty minutes,' Talus told Eugene. 'Now she's fuckin vanished.'

'With the boyfriend, I'd guess,' Eugene said.

Talus nodded. 'Archie's thinking about the best way to handle George. Everyone else is out there looking. It's a complete balls-up.'

'What do we know about Loverboy?' Eugene asked.

'Near enough fuck all. We know what he looks like – well, just about. This is off the CCTV – came from the Bower Bar in Kentish Town.' Talus fished inside his jacket and passed the grainy print across to Eugene. 'Quality's crap,' he said.

The definition was fuzzy, but Gloria was instantly recognizable. Skin-tight trousers, gold halterneck, her dark hair hanging halfway down her back. Standing, arm round her waist, was a tall black man, his face half turned, almost as if he'd registered the camera watching him.

Eugene remained silent for a long moment, looking down

at the photocopy, saying nothing as the seconds ticked by. But there was no doubt. It was him. He turned to Talus and spoke. 'I know the fucker,' he said. 'His name's Carl. He's the father of my sister's kid.'

Talus took another look at the grainy print. 'Sure, are you?'

Eugene nodded. 'No mistake,' he said.

CHAPTER TWENTY-ONE

There he tormenteth her most terribly,

FQ: The Legend of Britomartis: III.xi.17

'Well, there's a turn-up,' said Talus. 'So, what do we know about him?'

Eugene gave a slight shake of the head. 'Near enough fuck all. He's your regular Disappearing Man. My sister was seventeen when she got knocked up. Almost seven years back. She met the cunt in a club up Tottenham way. Only ever knew him as "Carl". They were together off an' on for maybe two, three months. Simone thought she was in love. Next thing I know is that Prince Charming has vanished and Simone's in floods of tears. Personally I thought she was well rid. Except a few weeks later it turns out Simone's pregnant – and tosspot Carl is the only possible candidate. So, obviously, I went looking for him.'

Talus nodded. 'Only thing to do,' he agreed.

Eugene shrugged and nodded. 'But I got nothing,' he continued. 'Not even a fuckin proper name. No address. Found out he used to stay nights in a squat down Camden Town. Right dive, it was. Full of hippies and anarchists and shit. Our boy Carl paid his way by dealing a few grammes of coke. They called him Charlie, the other blokes in the squat.'

Eugene paused and took a mouthful of beer before resuming. 'Yeah, "Charlie", as I said. Anyway, the only other lead I got was a girlfriend, up in Tufnell Park. He'd kipped at her place on and off for a couple of months. Told her he was an Angolan refugee – she called him Carlos – complete bollocks, of course.'

'He's got a very fertile imagination, our boy,' Talus said. 'Have we any idea who he really is?'

Eugene shook his head. 'Not really. I wouldn't bet on Carl being his real name either. He sounds like a Scouser or a Manc, for what it's worth. I tell you, the guy drifts around like smoke on the wind. Gives everyone a different story. When I was out looking for him it was like chasing shadows. I got hold of five or six mobile numbers for him – all useless.'

Eugene took another swig of beer. 'Basically, that's it. I was getting nowhere and back again, so in the end I jacked it in. To be honest, I wasn't that sorry. I met him a couple of times when he was out with my sister – and I had him down as real pondlife. Her kid's six now, but Carl's not been anywhere near.'

'So it looks like Mrs Faron's pulled a winner, then,' said Talus.

Eugene shrugged and nodded, 'Oh yeah,' he said. 'He's a real specialist, is our boy. Oh, and by the way – it's not much, but you never know.' Eugene went on to tell Talus about the sightings of Carl. How he was near certain it was Carl he'd seen turning off the Holloway Road some time after 2 a.m., the night of the Halcyenda party. And how a week past, Simone had been sure she'd seen Carl hanging outside SweetHearts.

Talus digested the news. 'If he's sniffing around after Gloria, it would make sense, him hanging round. Makes me wonder if they're somewhere local. Sounds like our boy's happiest North of the river.'

Eugene considered. 'Yeah. Maybe so. Still gives us enough territory to cover, though.'

Talus nodded and checked his watch. 'More than enough,' he agreed. 'And we're running out of time, Geno. George is expecting his loving wife to come skipping off the plane 10 o'clock Sunday morning. Sending one of the boys to pick her up. My guess is the bitch'll spend Saturday night getting shagged senseless somewhere. But I'll bet you, come Sunday, she'll be trotting out of terminal three fresh as a daisy, ready to give George a load of bollocks about her lovely time in Spain and how much she's missed him.'

'I'd say it's a near certainty,' Eugene replied.

From the Firm's point of view, there were a number of difficulties with this scenario. For a kick-off, Archie had several points he was keen to discuss with his sister-in-law – points which were better discussed in private – before she made contact with George.

More seriously, there was the problem of the next forty-odd hours, when Gloria – plus boyfriend – could well be out and about in North London. If the Firm's business competitors spotted Gloria making a fool of her husband, there would be serious trouble. George Faron's humiliation would be widely enjoyed, and interpreted as a sign of weakness and lost control. The fall-out would be immediate and bloody. There was little doubt that the Firm would reassert their dominance, but as Talus said, 'Why should half a dozen blokes get shot up just because that selfish cow can't keep her legs together?' Plus the fact that the damage to George's reputation would not be easy to undo. Gloria's infidelity would ensure George Faron became a standing joke for years to come. That couldn't be allowed to happen.

When Eugene finally left the King's Head and headed for home, it was gone 7 p.m. Half the Firm were out in pursuit of Gloria and Carl, there'd been countless conference calls to Archie. All they could do now was wait and see. Eugene felt depressed and tired. In exactly forty-five minutes he was meeting up with Ralph, which was the last thing he felt like doing. But letting Ralph down in the current circs was a total non-starter. As the Puma skidded to a halt outside Wentworth Road, Eugene leapt out, sprinted up the steps and straight into the shower. He hoped he'd feel better once he'd cleaned up and taken a couple of lines.

On his way out of the house, he paused to say a quick hello to his mum and sister. He kept quiet about Carl. Firm business was nothing to do with Simone and, more importantly, he simply didn't see the point in upsetting her. What with Angie's murder, the stuff going down at the club and dealing with the Minimonster – well, in Eugene's view, his sister had more than enough on her plate.

Eugene was right, although he didn't know the half of it. As he shot out of the house on his way to Ralph's, Gladys got up to pour more tea, settled herself back at the kitchen table and nodded across to her daughter. 'Go on, my girl, tell me the whole thing, from start to finish,' she said.

Gladys had been out shopping that afternoon. She and Moira were doing most of the Caridad family meals. Maria Caridad was now confined to bed and under sedation. Every time the drugs wore off, she began screaming. The menfolk had retreated into a trance-like silence – plodding to work and back like zombies, sleepwalking through the days, oblivious to all around them. So, Gladys and Moira had taken charge, doing what they could to keep the house in some sort of order, making sure the meals were on the table.

Back with the shopping, Gladys had called for Moira and they'd spent most of the afternoon round at the Caridads'. Simone, meanwhile, had been home alone with Nero. When Gladys finally got back to the house, she was greeted by a cacophony of kicking, banging, screaming and swearing. Nero had been locked in his room. Walking down the hallway, the noise reached an absolute crescendo, the hammering of feet and fists punctuated by threats and strings of swear words. It was then that Gladys noticed the bloody handprints on the bedroom door, the door handle sticky with coagulating blood and the drips all over the carpet, leading, splash by splash, to the bathroom, where Simone was standing over a basin of blood-red water.

Simone told her mother the story of the afternoon. Nero had been fine in the beginning. She had taken him up to the park. First, they'd fed the ducks, Nero hurling his bread pellets like missiles, with all the force at his command. But the ducks were unfazed, and Simone had enjoyed watching them squabble and scoot across the water. Then, they moved on to the fenced-in play park. It had a special springy floor, swings, a slide, roundabout, climbing frame and so on. Nero enjoyed himself on the swings and behaved well. OK, he'd tried to push another little boy off the slide, but that was his sole transgression, and less than nothing, by Minimonster standards.

But as the afternoon wore on he'd become increasingly hyper and out of control. Simone said he'd pinned one little girl to the ground. 'Her mother went mad,' she told Gladys, 'and you can't blame her. The little thing's elbows were all grazed and her dress was filthy.' That was bad, but it was going to get a whole lot worse. Simone told her mum how she had been mid-apology to the child and her mother when she'd heard a scream. Turning round, she saw Nero with an Asian girl, his little fist wrapped in her long dark pony-tail. 'Mum, I can't tell you, he was dragging her around by her hair. She was shouting and crying, and before anyone could get to them, he pulled her over. Then he tried to drag her along the floor.' After the grown-ups had separated Nero from his victim, the Asian girl's father had threatened to call the police. Simone had grabbed Nero by the hand and forcibly marched him out of the play park, Nero struggling and shouting as he went.

Getting her son home had been a nightmare. He'd thrown a total tantrum, lying down on the ground, refusing to walk, kicking out at her when she came near. She'd attempted to carry him – big as he was – but he'd punched her in the face, tiny fists flailing. Eventually, she grabbed his hand and had to semi-carry him down the street, in front of an enthralled and disapproving audience of Friday shoppers.

When she'd finally got him back in the house, Simone had tried to calm her son. Nero was shouting and hitting out whenever she came near him. Simone decided the best thing was to take him to his room. But that was easier said than done. The child fought every step of the way, and when Simone released one hand to open his bedroom door, Nero seized his chance. Turning his head, he sunk his teeth into the underside of Simone's arm, just below the crook of her elbow, and refused to let go. He only released his grip after Simone smacked his legs and he opened his mouth to yell with shock and outrage.

Once Nero was secured behind his bedroom door, Simone turned to clearing up the damage. Blood had poured in torrents down her arm, and she'd taken any number of kicks and punches. Her legs, stomach and lower back were discoloured and very painful. She knew from experience that a warm bath, embrocation and body make-up would sort that. The bite, however, was another matter. No matter how tight the bandage, the blood kept seeping through.

For weeks now, Nero had been getting worse. As Simone said, he'd always been a handful, a bit too high-spirited. But, recently, things had changed. Simone used to make excuses for her son, to gloss over the worst of his behaviour. But she couldn't fool herself any more. And her mum was really the only person she could talk to. Because Simone and Gladys both knew the truth. Nero was getting bigger and older. And he had started to frighten them.

And Nero's ratcheting violence wasn't the only thing on Simone's mind.

She was the only dancer yet to be interviewed by Scudamour and Lalibela. Simone guessed this was down to the fact that Scudamour had already interviewed her at length after Angie's murder. She thought they probably wouldn't bother to speak to her again – just wasting everyone's time going through the same stuff, really. In part, Simone was relieved, because she was under enough pressure as it was, and she really didn't need any more problems, thanks.

In fact, DS Scudamour was simply biding his time with Simone. The detective wanted to collate whatever new information could be gathered from the other dancers first. He had an instinctive feeling that talking to Simone was his best – possibly only – chance of getting the real picture.

Scudamour knew that, unlike most of the other girls, Simone had no fear of being sacked. She was way too popular for that. Far too much of an attraction for the club to mess with. Scudamour had also noted Simone's friendship with Mae. In his opinion, Mae knew far more about the club than anyone, including the manager. And there was another factor influencing Scudamour's tactics: Simone was sharp, clever; she kept her eyes open and picked up on things. And the Meatman had killed her best friend.

Simone was haunted by Angie's murder. But all the girls had been touched by the Meatman. The earlier, slightly larky, black humour had been replaced by genuine terror. No one wanted to wait for nightbuses, no one was willing to take risks with men outside the club. Within SweetHearts' walls they felt safe; outside, anything could happen. After Angie's murder, there was no room for doubt. It was obvious, wasn't it? And that's why the cops were there – because the Meatman was targeting SweetHearts, wasn't he? And everyone had heard the rumours – the awful stuff he'd done to the victims – cutting and slicing. The word backstage was that they were tortured first, before they died. And that the police had kept the worst of it back, the really terrible things. So it was no surprise that the dancers – and the waitresses, kitchen staff, barmaids; even the cleaners

231

and office day-girls – no surprise that the lot of them had got well jittery.

But despite the nerves and the nightmares and the horrible calculations of who might be next, despite all of it – as the detectives knew full well, the dancers weren't telling Scudamour and Lalibela the whole story. Nobody talked about Shifter, nor about the half-dozen dealers who sold drugs in the club. Nor were police told of the regular customers who were keen on 'outside favours' or the men who 'liked to party' and paid well for girls prepared to party with them. Nothing was said about the ones who wanted to handcuff, humiliate, hurt – and paid top dollar to do it.

The girls agreed amongst themselves that there was no point in causing trouble, of bringing loads of shit down on your own head. So certain things were kept quiet. Cos the blokes involved were basically harmless. Bit pervy maybe, but nothing sinister. They told each other that they knew what they were doing, that you developed a sixth sense for danger in this job. 'Can spot a loony from twenty paces,' one girl said, and they all laughed and agreed.

But Simone was beginning to worry, was thinking long and hard about it. Thinking about someone in particular, and about talking to the police. The man in question was creepy, everybody said so. And he was a real regular, especially at weekends. But SweetHearts was full of creeps, and Simone had never taken much notice of the man – not until after Angie died anyway.

Simone still blamed herself for her friend's murder. Night after night she woke drenched in sweat. The same nightmare repeating itself so that she'd become scared of sleep. In the dream, Simone saw herself in Crouch End with Angie. Knowing her friend was in terrible danger, Simone's dream self tried frantically to lead Angie away from where the Meatman was lurking. But every time the same thing happened. She would finally persuade Angie to come with her, taking her by the hand and walking to safety. But when they were almost there, Simone would get the same feeling of utter dread. Angie's hand was still linked with hers, but as she turned around, Simone could see Angie in the distance, waving to her with the stump of a handless arm. Then Simone would scream and scream as she tried to drop the disgusting, cold thing she held. But no matter how hard she tried to shake it off, Angie's dead hand clung to her and wouldn't let go.

CHAPTER TWENTY-TWO

Greatly thereat was *Britomart* dismayd,
Ne in that stownd wist, how her selfe to beare;

FQ: The Legend of Britomartis: III.xi.22

Eugene pulled up outside the Palmers' flat bang on 8 p.m. He thought he'd done bloody well to turn himself around in thirty minutes flat. As he walked towards the security entrance for Ralph's block, he looked up and saw his star boy leaning over the railings above him.

'Stay where you are, E. I'm coming straight down, bro.' Seconds later, Ralph appeared beside the Puma and slid into the passenger seat. 'Take a look,' he said, passing Eugene a glossy folder. 'New club. It's opening tonight. They've sent me a couple of comps. Think we could drop by and check it out, yeah?'

'Sounds good to me,' Eugene said, as the Puma leapt forward. 'So why'd you get the freebie?'

'What do you mean, "why me?"' Ralph said. 'S'obvious. I think you'll find they targeted me as "a prominent member of North London's thriving independent business community". Their words, not mine.'

'Fantastic,' said Eugene. 'I always knew you were a top man, but "prominent" and "thriving"? – I'm a bit overawed, spar. You sure it's cool taking me with you? I'm not going to let you down, damage the profile of . . . what was it? . . . yeah, damage the profile of the independent business community?'

'Gave it serious thought,' Ralph said. 'But I'm going to introduce you as my work-experience boy – that way no one'll expect too much of you.'

Eugene shook his head. 'Almost funny, bro, keep practising. I mean, you're a long way from slick, but the hard work's definitely paying off – stick at it. Anyway, smart-boy, where to now? If we're hitting this grand opening thing, we got a couple of hours to kill first.'

'Down to Stroud Green Road,' Ralph suggested. 'This club's somewhere up the top end of Green Lanes, so we may's well head that way.'

Eugene concurred and shortly afterwards bagged a space bang outside Wild Hart wine bar. He settled the Puma and followed Ralph inside. The place was semi-full but not heaving, and they managed to grab a table with minimum fuss. After the drinks were sorted – and after they'd both completed the inevitable trips to the toilets – Eugene asked Ralph if he'd heard any more from his wife. He hadn't.

'Let's not go there, man,' Ralph said. 'Tonight, I want to relax and enjoy. Tomorrow morning I'll wake up alone – and it'll hit me like it does every morning. She's left me, and it don't look like she's coming back. I think about her all the fucking time, going over and over the same things. So tonight I decided to try and stand back from it. Get some perspective and talk about something else for a couple hours.'

Eugene was relieved. He didn't like what was happening to his best bro.

Since his wife had kicked him out, Ralph had become one of the walking wounded – as if losing Belinda had drained the life out of him. Any attempt to re-engage with cheerful

235

normality had to be a good thing. So Eugene said, 'That's cool,' before asking Ralph if he'd caught the latest episode of *Supernanny* on Channel 4.

Ralph asked Eugene if he reckoned Jo – the supernanny in question – would have any luck with the Minimonster. Eugene said, possibly, but only if she could stop Simone being so soft with the little bastard. Ralph said it would be great TV – watching Supernanny trying to tame Nero and sort out Simone's dodgy parenting skills. Eugene wondered if he should write in and volunteer Nero for the next series. He told Ralph about the massive bruise he'd spotted on his mother's leg. 'Minimonster kicked her, didn't he? It's his new thing. My stupid sister bought him these kiddie boots. Now he won't take them off. Spends all day kicking out at things. You know he's nearly four foot six now? And well solid with it. I don't like leaving Mum alone with the little psycho.'

'And he's getting bigger every day,' Ralph pointed out. 'Look, 10 p.m., bro – another drink, then make our move?'

'Spot on,' Eugene agreed.

Half an hour later, satisfied the Puma was safe, Eugene and Ralph walked down Green Lanes towards the pulsating neon sign advertising the opening of Amazon Zone. As usual, the Firm's security boys were on the door, but Eugene stayed quiet, letting Ralph show his comp tickets. The two of them were ushered through and directed upstairs. 'Wow,' Ralph shouted above the music, 'talk about top dollar. They've really gone for it. Grab the drinks, then take a stroll, yeah?'

Holding complimentary bottles of Brazilian Bramah beer, the two of them sauntered round. It was as if they had parachuted into the middle of a tropical rainforest, the club sheltering beneath a vast, overarching canopy of tall trees. Fifteen feet above their heads a mass of broad leaves waved and swayed, supported by giant treetrunks marching asymmetrically across the place like the pillars of a Gothic cathedral. Thick Tarzan-style rope vines trailed from the high branches whilst, closer to the ground, giant ferns and scarlet-orange gingevra clustered. A final touch were the laser projections, making it appear as if birds, lizards and monkeys were flitting, chasing and climbing through the treetops. Every time the music stopped, bird calls and jungle noises abounded.

The dance floor itself resembled a jungle pond. Its surface covered in strange silvery tiles that appeared to move under the lights, mimicking liquidity so the entire space seemed to ripple and flow. And, unbelievably, there was a genuine Amazonian river, three metres in width, snaking through it all – curling and undulating its way across the floor. The river was stocked with fish – including piranhas – and separated from drunken reality by a layer of toughened glass.

Their beers half drunk, Ralph and Eugene headed upstairs to the VIP section. Security recognized Eugene and waved them straight through into a plush haven of air-conditioning and comfort, where Brazilian samba-girls in G-strings and feathers were serving free caipirinha cocktails. Looking over the balcony to the main floor below, Eugene could see the club filling up. The DJ was apparently from São Paulo, and the watery dance floor thronged with yet more barely dressed samba-girls, who'd clearly been instructed to get the party moving. Gradually, more and more people sidled across and joined in the dancing. Everyone seemed to be in an infectious good mood.

Despite the lack of sleep the night before, the coke was keeping him buzzing, and Eugene was enjoying himself. The place was amazing, and he was content just to sit back and take it in – the banks of ferns and orchids, the simulated flash of hummingbirds. 'Good choice, bro,' he said to Ralph.

'Yeah. This is well slick,' Ralph replied. 'Must have cost an unreal amount of cash to set all this up – hey, fancy another one of these?' Before Eugene had chance to reply, a girl wearing a two-foot headdress of pink and yellow feathers, with matching bra and G-string, arrived with two more caipirinhas.

'Service for real,' said Eugene. 'I'm seriously impressed.'

Ralph grinned. 'You can always rely on me to show you a good time, E. You know, I feel it's my mission, to educate you about the finer things in life, to kind of raise your social standards.'

'Yeah, yeah, star boy. What you planning for next week, tea at the Ritz or a short course on ballroom dancing?'

Ralph considered. 'Well, you could definitely use some better dance moves. I'll see if I can find a decent beginners' class. It's going to be a real challenge trying to find you a partner, though.'

They carried on in similar vein, laughing and messing. Eugene thought it had been weeks since he'd seen Ralph looking this good.

Afterwards he would pinpoint the exact moment when it all started to go wrong. It was quite clear – looking back – that the nightmare began the precise second she arrived. When he felt her long hair tickling against the nape of his neck and her voice whispering in his ear. Next thing, she had slithered over the arm of his chair and was in his lap.

'Come on, Mr Loverman. Introduce me, then.'

Eugene looked helplessly across at Ralph – who was goggle-eyed with incredulity. 'This is Ralph,' he said lamely. 'Ralph, this is Lucy, a friend of mine.'

Lucy giggled. 'Yeah, we're very good friends.'

Ralph said he was pleased to meet her. Lucy blew him a kiss, then turned her attention back to Eugene.

And no matter how he tried, he couldn't get rid of her. He tried polite but pointed remarks about being with his best friend, how the two of them needed to talk – privately. Lucy said, 'Don't mind me,' and blagged a wrap of free coke.

Blunt requests didn't work either. Lucy giggled and blithely carried on as before. Eugene didn't know which was worse – when he sat down, she immediately draped herself across his lap, lips nibbling at his neck and ears, hands running up his thighs and stomach; standing up risked her dragging him on to the dance floor, where Lucy became more intimate still.

When Lucy headed to the ladies for the third or fourth time, Eugene grabbed Ralph and told him they had to get out of there. 'Come on, man, let's move it. Lose her while we still can.'

Ralph raised his eyebrows.

'Yeah, I know,' Eugene said impatiently. 'I'm not being a gentleman and all that. I've tried asking nicely but she's sticking tighter than a limpet, and I'm not getting stuffed with giving her a lift home – and all the rest of it. Fuck, I made a mistake getting involved with her in the first place. I'm not risking some mega-scene going down. I'm out of here. I'm splitting.'

They were jogging downstairs towards the doors when Lucy caught them. Eugene wondered just what she'd been doing in the toilets. She was flying, eyes like saucers and body jittering.

Eugene said he'd tried to say goodbye, but couldn't find her anywhere. Lucy said, 'Way cool,' and demanded one last dance 'as a forfeit, for running out on me. And I think, y'know, it's only fair you give me another wrap. Then I'll definitely, totally forgive you. S'okay, yeah? Deal, yeah?' Her voice was becoming louder.

'Deal,' Eugene said and led her back into the club.

The minute they hit the floor, he regretted it. It was a slow song, and Lucy had left her few inhibitions back in the ladies. Eugene was rigid with embarrassment and anger. When the song finally ended, he slipped half a gramme into her hand and told her they were off. 'See you later, alligator,' Lucy replied, and headed straight for the toilets.

Eugene walked over to Ralph, who was leaning against one of the 'trees' – in fact, Ralph seemed to be looking at something or someone.

'What a fuckin nightmare,' Eugene said. 'She's a total basket . . . what's up, spar?'

'Nightmare's about to get serious,' Ralph said. 'Take a look, E. Over there by the edge of the dance floor.'

Eugene turned, following Ralph's direction. He couldn't believe what he was seeing. Standing side by side, they looked back across the dance floor, staring straight at him. The shock almost took his voice. Eugene turned back to Ralph. 'Oh no,' he said. 'Please no.'

Like Eugene and Ralph, Rhoda and Brittany met up that Friday evening at 8 p.m. Like Eugene and Ralph, the two women had tickets for Amazon Zone. And just like Eugene and Ralph, they had gone to a wine bar before heading for Green Lanes and hitting the club. And that's where the similarities had ended.

Rhoda had been waiting for a chance to have a proper talk with Brittany – to put her friend in the picture – for some time. She'd been positively looking forward to it. Yes, Rhoda couldn't wait to tell Brittany, to let her know the unpalatable truth about her wonderful new boyfriend.

Rhoda knew of Eugene long before he'd walked over to her and Brittany that night in the Mirror Bar. She'd heard a great deal about him, and none of it pleasant, courtesy of her friend Belinda. Attached to interlinked departments, Belinda and Rhoda were both based on the twelfth floor of the Glass Tower, and the two women had become increasingly close over the past year.

As Belinda's marriage rapidly disintegrated, Rhoda had provided her workmate with a shoulder to cry on. She had listened to Belinda's tales of angry suspicion, heard about Ralph's Friday nights with Eugene, his gangland

240

buddy. Rhoda sympathized, thought Ralph's friend was a bad influence, and said that Belinda deserved a man who valued and respected her.

Rhoda and Ralph had met on a couple of occasions. It was Rhoda who spotted Ralph out with Eugene and the fabled blonde girlfriends. And Rhoda who broke the news to a stricken Belinda. Courtesy of a Lebanese grandmother, Rhoda had dark hair and brown eyes and regarded herself as 'black identified'. Belinda had been impressed and comforted by Rhoda's fierce condemnation of Ralph's behaviour – and had taken her advice on how to deal with it.

When Brittany was walking on air after her first night with Eugene, she sent a text to her friend Rhoda, saying how happy she was, how it had all been wonderful. That she was seeing him again very soon. Rhoda was at work when she got the message. She read it, then called Belinda. Said she needed advice on behalf of a good friend. Half an hour later, the two women met for coffee in Al Fresco.

Over coffee, Belinda told Rhoda everything she knew about Eugene, plus all the stuff she imagined to be true – cos the guy was capable of anything, Belinda was sure of that. She described Eugene as a violent gunman, with babymothers scattered across London. He was notoriously promiscuous, with three or four 'girlfriends' on the go at any one time. The man was serious bad news, a gangsta and a jailbird. 'Your friend has no idea what she's getting into,' Belinda said. Rhoda shook her head and awaited her chance.

So on Friday night Rhoda suggested that she and Brittany meet in a quiet bar on Green Lanes itself prior to hitting the nightclub – anyway, the bar was just a couple of hundred yards down from Amazon Zone. After twenty minutes of chit-chat, Rhoda told Brittany she had something serious to discuss with her. It was gone 11 p.m. when they left for the club. Walking up the road, the two women made an odd couple. Brittany's face was devoid of expression, her complexion pallid and bloodless. But her companion in the dark red dress was full of animation and energy – once inside the club, she became more vibrant still. Her good night was just about to get even better.

CHAPTER TWENTY-THREE

Daunger without discretion to attempt,
Inglorious and beastlike is: therefore Sir knight,
Aread what course of you is safest dempt,
And how we with our foe may come to fight.

FQ: The Legend of Britomartis: III.xi.23

Mid Saturday morning, Eugene was en route to the King's Head. Talus needed to see him, pronto. The Puma fretted and bridled, frustrated by the crawling stream of shoppers. Inching towards the Cally Road, Eugene knew it was all going to get worse. Everything was going wrong, and he was quite certain there was plenty more trouble ahead. He was desperate to see Brittany. To explain things, to win her back. But he was needed elsewhere. The Gloria crisis had escalated, and something had to be sorted. If – when – that was done, there was no shortage of other problems clamouring for attention. There was Ralph for a kick-off. And then there was the situation at home. Eugene was determined to speak to Simone. To talk to her about Nero and make her see sense, because it couldn't continue. He wouldn't allow it.

*   *   *

Nero was getting even worse. After last night's debacle at Amazon Zone, Eugene had gone back to Ralph's to talk things over. He'd arrived home a bit after 3 a.m., and walked straight into another catastrophe. His mother was sitting with Moira, drinking tea and whisky. Gladys looked shaky and her right arm was in bandages from shoulder to elbow. A dark bruise was spreading across her cheekbone and she had the beginnings of a black eye. Nero was in his room, but Gladys had needed to enlist Moira's help to get him there. Moira had got a split lip for her trouble. The women were playing CDs – Daniel O'Donnell, no less – above which shrill screams of rage and abuse occasionally surfaced, accompanied by the frantic pounding of small fists and feet.

Gladys told Eugene that Simone had put her son to bed and left for work as usual. Nero must have woken around midnight. 'I was putting my nightie on,' Gladys explained, 'when I heard him. Running like the wind he was. Good job the door was locked, otherwise he'd be gone.' She managed to grab the child as he struggled to turn the front-door key, then the real trouble began. 'He turned on me like a little demon, hitting out in every direction, he was. It took all my strength to hold on to him, but I couldn't get him back up those stairs, try as I might.' Eventually, Gladys had rung Moira – who came straight round. 'Honestly, Eugene, he was shocking. Some of the things he said – God alone knows where he's heard such words. And we had the devil's own job to get him in his room. Hit Moira straight in the mouth, and sank his teeth into me.'

Before he left to meet Talus the following morning Eugene had persuaded his mother to unwrap the bandage encasing her upper arm. When he saw what the Minimonster had done to her, Eugene was glad his nephew was out the house, and thus out of his reach. If Nero had been around when Gladys finally revealed her arm – a bloodied mess of multiple bites and tears – Eugene wondered if he'd have kept control of his temper. Or if he'd have given in and played Nero at his own heedless game, inflicting pain and damage because he could. He was glad not to have been put to the test.

Instead, he rang his mum's GP and insisted on an emergency home visit. The doctor on call sounded less than thrilled, but after a brief chat with Eugene bucked his ideas up, agreed that it was totally unrealistic to expect Mrs Burnside to come to evening surgery, and promised to be round some time before noon. Eugene was relieved. His mum was wincing in pain, and he thought the bites showed the beginnings of infection. He wanted to be sure she was properly cared for. Antibiotics, surgical dressings, something for the shock – Gladys was still a bit shaky and had stayed in bed pleading a headache till Simone and Nero left for Buzzi Bee.

He also jogged down the Holloway Road to get flowers and a bottle of Bell's for Moira. It was the least she deserved. When Moira answered the door, Eugene got a shock. His mother's best friend looked like a victim of collagen implants gone wrong. Her whole mouth was swollen, the top lip especially so, ballooning lopsidedly over the cut on the left. Eugene was horrified. The injuries looked obscene. Such disfigurements belonged in the realm of teen street-fights, or drunken lads on a Saturday night. Like his mum's black eye, Moira's cut and swollen lip seemed utterly out of place disfiguring the face of a grandmother.

He stayed for a quick cup of tea whilst Moira talked about Nero's outburst. It was clear that the child's attack had shaken her. 'The boy was a terrible handful, son. I'll tell you straight, he's not safe. When he goes like that – it's like the child's possessed. He frightened me, I don't mind telling you. Six years old or not, he frightened me.'

Eugene apologized again, and thanked her for helping his mum. 'Don't worry, Auntie, I'm going to talk to Mum and Simone and sort things out,' he said. 'Put a stop to this nonsense, whilst we still can. I mean, he's out of control now – imagine what he'll be like in a couple of years' time, never mind when he's thirteen or so.' Moira said it didn't bear thinking about.

The Puma swung into the King's Head carpark just ahead of Talus. Vinnie opened the door with a thin-lipped smile and promptly relocked it as soon as they were through. Eugene settled himself in what was becoming their usual corner, whilst Talus got a couple of beers. Then it was down to business. The news wasn't good. Not good at all.

Talus said the pursuit of Gloria was getting nowhere. There had been one Friday-night sighting – a barman on the payroll had spotted a couple fitting the description of Carl and Gloria leaving a restaurant on Upper Street. As Talus said – the bare-faced cheek of it was unbelievable. Upper Street was Islington's main thoroughfare, packed full of wine bars and clubs and the like. It was also smack in the Firm's territory – and Gloria must have known there was a real risk of running into someone who knew her. She was clearly willing to gamble and, so far, her luck was holding. Although the boys had arrived less than five minutes after the barman's tip-off, Gloria and her man were gone.

There had been another tip-off – one of the security boys at the Camden Palais rang in around midnight with a report of a woman with long dark hair walking in with a black guy. But the tip was less than reliable, especially as the security guy saw three people – not a couple. A black guy, an older white guy and a good-looking woman with long thick hair, hanging to her waist. 'Yeah, it sounds like the missing Mrs Faron,' Talus mused, 'but there must be other women in London with hair like that, eh?' Anyway, whether or not the Camden sighting was genuine hardly mattered. Because they'd heard nothing since and got nothing more to go on, despite the round-the-clock efforts.

'What a fucking nightmare,' Eugene said.

Talus agreed, and said that Gloria seemed to have a deathwish, because not only was she openly parading her boyfriend around the Firm's North London fiefdom, she was totally ignoring her supposedly beloved husband – something that had never previously been known.

'Archie's having a hell of a job,' Talus told Eugene. 'George is going bananas. Can't understand what's happened. She – Gloria – always phones him when she's away. Every day, without fail. Wherever she is, always rings him. Except this time. George has heard jack shit since he arrived back on Friday morning. Archie and I keep trying to tell him to calm down. It's only twenty-four hours, for fuck's sake. But he's frantic. My Sandra's had to fly out to fuckin Marbella to handle the hotel, cos Georgie-boy is ringing them every five minutes, demanding to speak to his wife. What's really done it is that both her mobiles are switched off.'

'It's no wonder that George is going mental,' said Eugene. 'What the hell is she doing?'

'She's playing with fire,' Talus replied.

Eugene spent the rest of the afternoon working with Talus to try and find George Faron's missing wife. They had no luck. Nor did anyone else. Archie was down at the Halcyenda with his brother. He was the only one who could make George see a modicum of sense – it was Archie who prevented George from getting the next flight out to Marbella. Archie told his brother to stop acting like a prat. Gloria was landing at 10 a.m. tomorrow. If he was that keen, he could meet her at Heathrow; in the meantime, there was no point in overreacting.

Eugene finally headed home around 7 p.m. His mum and Simone were in the kitchen. The Minimonster was watching TV. Eugene checked in on him: the child was sitting, very close to the screen, one little hand clutching the remote.

He was so absorbed, he didn't hear Eugene open the door, his attention entirely focused on *Forensic Detectives*.

Gladys said she had taken her painkillers and was off to bed for an hour, as Moira was due round at nine. Eugene told his mum he was planning on a night in as well. The relief at this news was plainly written on Gladys's face.

He made another pot of tea as he waited for his mother to go upstairs. Eugene was not looking forward to confronting his sister. Simone worshipped her son and consistently explained away his behaviour as 'high spirits'. His aggression was always the fault of other children, usually Nero's unfortunate victims, who, Simone was sure, had provoked his outbreaks of ultraviolence. He was pretty certain his sister would go ballistic when she heard what he had in mind for her adored little boy.

Eugene wanted Nero out. He was seriously worried about Gladys, and about Simone, for that matter – Eugene had noticed his sister's accumulation of cuts and bruises over the past few weeks. And now there was the biting to contend with. Within the space of a couple of days, Nero had taken chunks out of his mother and his grandmother. Eugene saw uneasily that the child had targeted the same place each time – the inside of the arm, just below the elbow joint. It was a good place to pick – soft skin and plenty of blood vessels close to the surface. Nero was fast turning into Vampire Child.

Hearing sounds of his mum retreating upstairs, Eugene poured the tea. Simone told him she'd been round to see Moira in the afternoon. 'Have you seen her face?' she asked.

Eugene nodded.

'I wanted the ground to open up and swallow me,' said Simone. 'It was terrible. I just didn't know what to say.' She lapsed into silence. Then suddenly, abruptly, she spoke up: 'I've rung his social worker, told her what's happened. He needs to get away from all this murder shit – he's obsessed with it. It's making him worse. I talked it through with social

248

services – they think it's the best option. They're coming to collect him tomorrow morning. About 10 a.m. It's only temporary.'

Eugene was stunned. 'Where's he going?' he asked eventually.

'Temporary specialized secure foster placement,' Simone replied. 'It's only temporary. Because of all the murders – it's upset him.' As far as Eugene could recall, rather than being 'upset', the Minimonster had positively revelled in the Meatman's doings, but he said nothing. 'It won't be for long,' Simone said. 'He just needs to calm down a bit. I can phone him every night. And I can go and see him. It'll be all right.'

Simone left for work just after nine, leaving Eugene and Gladys to deal with Nero. Everyone agreed Simone had made the right decision, especially as Nero was so hyperactive he bordered on hysterical. Simone usually put him to sleep before she went out – but lately there was no chance of that. Short of tying him down, there was no possibility of the Minimonster remaining in his bed. He played up so relentlessly that the Burnsides took a family decision to allow him to stay up and watch TV, providing he had his bath and put on his pyjamas. Nero didn't seem to think this was much of a deal but, eventually, he was parked in front of the screen, channel-flicking and giggling happily.

Simone arrived a good half-hour early for the Saturday-night opening. She wanted to think things through, to have some time alone to search her memory and make sure. First, though, she had to slip across the road to buy cigarettes – club prices were exorbitant and Simone had no intention of paying them. So she went out via the backstage door, turned right on to the main road and straight in and out of the newsagents' on the corner. She was about to shoot back over the road, when she stopped dead. Framed against the

249

backstage doorway were three figures. A tall woman with long dark hair hanging almost to her waist – the woman was a stranger – but she recognized the two men immediately. Nero's father and Mal Shifter – talking together like the best and closest of friends.

CHAPTER TWENTY-FOUR

There she him taught to weigh both right and wrong
In equall ballance with due recompence,
And equitie to measure out along,
According to the line of conscience,

FQ: The Legend of Artegall, or of Ivstice: V.i.7

E ven as Simone started with the shock of recognition, the
threesome broke up. Shifter disappeared inside the club
whilst the other two turned towards the main road. Within
seconds, Carl hailed a black cab, and he and the woman
vanished into the night. Simone paused a moment, then
followed Shifter, through the backstage door, and upstairs
into the club.

She passed Shifter, who was talking to one of the security
heavies. As she walked by, she heard low whistles and
shared laughter. She ignored it, it was par for the course –
but all the same, she decided to change tack and headed for
the bar. She ordered a glass of white – large – needed it to
steady her nerves. Like the other girls, she hated Saturday
nights. OK, you could make a pot of money but, Christ, did
you have to work for it. On Saturdays, the club was always
packed. The clientele – with no work tomorrow – drank
enthusiastically and consequently became more demanding

and unreasonable. Saturdays, the bouncers earned their money – dealing with the trouble which inevitably kicked off as the night wore on.

Simone took her glass backstage to the changing-rooms. There was someone she had to talk to. It was just a case of waiting for her to turn up. As yet, no one else was around. Simone bagged her usual place by the big corner mirror and began to prepare. First, the body moisturizer, then the 'Bronze Shine' body make-up. Next, a final top coat brushed on to finger- and toenails. Chipped nail varnish was a no-no – as Mr Barry was fond of saying, 'Nothing looks cheaper or more unsightly on a woman.' When she finished, Simone carefully sat down and waited for her nails to dry and thought it all through.

It had started a couple of days ago, when Detectives Scudamour and Lalibela arrived, and the whole club was once again abuzz with Meatman gossip. Mae sent a text asking if Simone fancied a coffee, and the two of them had slipped out of SweetHearts and gone over the road to the café.

They'd talked about the police and about the Meatman. Mae said Mr Barry was pushing himself too hard, and his workload was crazy. She thought he was punishing himself, still heartbroken because of what had happened to Stella.

Over a second cup of coffee, Mae had told Simone – in strictest confidence – the full story of Stella's secret romance with the SweetHearts manager. How Mr Barry was guilt-wracked because he hadn't known about the baby. How he couldn't forgive himself for the time he'd told Stella to lose weight, at rehearsals, in front of everybody. But the thing that really got to him, Mae had said, was that on the night she was killed, Stella should have been with him. But Mr Barry had cancelled.

'That Saturday, he sent me downstairs with a message for her,' Mae explained. 'They were supposed to be going back to his place together, but he cancelled. Said he couldn't meet her and he'd be in touch next week.' Mae paused. 'This is just between the two of us – yes?'

Simone nodded. 'On my word,' she said.

'Thanks,' Mae continued '. . . because he's really upset and, well . . . they'd been together quite a while, you know? Mr Barry told me they had this routine worked out. Stella always waited for him to finish up on Saturday nights. Then Stella would say goodnight and walk out the front as if going home. But, really, she'd just wait round the corner, or down the road. He'd tell her where they'd meet up – different places, always somewhere close, but out of sight. Then he'd hop in a taxi, and tell the cab to stop and pick her up, and off they'd go.'

'I never even suspected,' Simone said.

'Don't think anyone did,' said Mae. 'Anyway, Mr Barry's in a terrible state over it all, because she should have been going home with him. He keeps on about it – how he dumped her that night, left her to find her own way home.' Mae had another sip of coffee. 'They showed him the pictures of her, you know, after she was dead? They shouldn't have done that. He was gutted, still has nightmares, you know.'

The conversation somehow caught in Simone's mind, like cloth snagging on brambles. It wasn't that she shared Mae's compassionate concern for the angst-ridden Mr Barry . . . but something kept on pulling her attention. It was irritating, a persistent, unscratchable itch – a sense that Mae's gossip had sparked off something of importance, something that remained just out of reach.

Nero's vampire behaviour over the next couple of days had subsequently claimed Simone's attention, and she had largely forgotten about her conversation with Mae. After dropping Nero off at Buzzi Bee as usual on Saturday morning, she'd spoken to her son's designated social worker and spent a laborious hour going through the paperwork needed to process the Minimonster's temporary respite care placement. Simone arrived back at Wentworth Road just in time to catch the lunchtime news.

The top London story concerned a little boy, missing for thirty-six hours. The newsreader announced that 'Little Lee is safe.' Police had found the toddler in woods, a quarter of a mile from home – cold, hungry and crying, but basically OK. He'd simply wandered off and got lost. There were pictures of his mum sobbing with happiness, and then an interview. Lee's mum said the past two days had been 'a living hell.' She'd been terrified, unable to sleep, eat or even think straight. Then she gave a big smile. 'But all's well that ends well,' she'd said.

And Simone remembered: a recollection so vivid she could almost see little Stella standing in front of her, smiling, just like the woman on the TV. Stella pulling on her jacket, saying 'All's well that ends well,' as she left to meet her boyfriend on Saturday night.

And quite suddenly, it all started coming back – a helter-skelter of remembered incidents, of snapshot images and throwaway lines. On the night of Stella's death, Simone had been booked for a private dance. She had psyched herself up to do it in the usual way, by getting totally blitzed.

That Saturday night – it was about five weeks ago, back in early April – Stella's troubles had barely registered with Simone. The combination of crack, skunk, alcohol and panic had ensured a mental wipe-out. But now, with the benefit of hindsight and a clear head, the events of that night began to make a macabre and terrible sense.

The week before her death, Stella had been in a bit of a state. Simone remembered a string of minor incidents: the time Stella had suddenly broken down in rehearsals, had just sat on the floor, sobbing. Stella pulling on a baggy T-shirt, trying to disguise her tummy during work-out. And, then, when Mr Barry had a go at her in front of everyone, she'd burst into tears again and run out.

All week Stella had been like that, crying at the drop of a hat. Then, on the Saturday, Stella told Simone what was going on: her boyfriend had chucked her. 'He says he doesn't want to see me tonight, says he wants to be on his own, that he'll ring me after the weekend.' She'd been crying again, and Simone, chemically blitzed and fighting a totally insane urge to giggle, had tried to comfort her. Simone had passed tissues and given Stella a cold flannel to stop her eyes swelling up. They'd had a girls' chat, about men being crap. It was all flooding back; Simone remembered it exactly. She'd advised Stella to keep her head up. 'Show him you're not bothered. Come on, girl, wipe your face and smile. Believe me, he'll come back.'

Simone had still been off her head when she'd run into Stella, just after closing. The girl was bouncing – happy as a lark. 'What's changed with you, hey?' Simone couldn't believe the difference – Stella was transformed, all smiles, eyes shining. She told Simone she couldn't stop – had to do her make-up – but it was all all right now. 'He sent a message, asking if I'd still meet him tonight, so I said to tell him OK. I'm just going to get ready.'

And Simone had been waiting for her lift in the entrance, when, ten minutes later, she saw Stella for the last time. Tip-tapping in five-inch heels as usual, smiling and flicking back her long blond hair. Simone had waved, said something about having a good weekend, and Stella had laughed, crossed her fingers and said, 'All's well that ends well.' Then she was gone – out through the doors and into the night.

Except there was no boyfriend waiting. Mr Barry had cancelled – had been beating himself up about it ever since. Whoever had given Stella the 'message' and pretended to deliver her reply had set her up. And Simone was certain it had to be someone inside the club – someone who knew about Stella and Mr Barry's top-secret relationship. Someone with the access to come and go.

Simone could see it quite clearly: Stella waiting in her high heels at 3 a.m., teeth chattering with nerves and cold. Still smiling, waiting for him to arrive, as promised. Then the sweep of the car headlights, and Stella's face lighting up in a warmer smile of welcome, before the back door opened and she was dragged inside. That would be the moment when she realized that she'd made a mistake – that Mr Barry wasn't coming after all.

Back at the Burnside home, Eugene was having a seriously bad time. Moira had come over for her usual Saturday night with Gladys, and the two women were ensconced in the kitchen, tea and whisky on the go, Christy Moore on the sound system. Moira's lip had gone down a bit, although it still looked bad enough. She was having to sip her tea from the corner of her mouth, and smoking was 'the devil's own job', but Moira said she'd be 'right as rain' in a day or two for sure. Eugene had told the two women to relax. He would deal with the Minimonster. No worries.

His mum and Moira hadn't argued: they'd both had more than enough of Nero for the moment, and their relief was plain. Gladys said what a wonderful son he was, staying in – on a Saturday night as well – just to take care of his mother. Moira agreed, telling Eugene he was 'one in a million', and asking Gladys, 'Isn't the boy more like his father every day?'

The shower of praise and thanks mollified Eugene, made him feel a bit more positive. He reminded himself that he was the head of the family, had a role to fulfil, people relying on him. Seen in that light, a night devoted to Minimonster damage-limitation was bearable – the sort of responsibility you had to shoulder. His duty.

So Eugene returned to guarding Nero with a fractionally lighter heart. He tried not to dwell on what should have been – because that really was a guaranteed downer. He was supposed to be meeting Brittany – they'd had it all arranged. Saturday night. They'd discussed going out for a dance, maybe somewhere locally – Brittany didn't share Eugene's *laissez faire* attitude to drink-driving. Afterwards, they would go back to her place. Talking on the phone, she'd told him all about the front room, how it was nearly straight, all the painting done. She wanted to see what he thought.

The debacle at Amazon Zone had put a dead stop to all of that. He'd tried to explain about Lucy, tried to tell Brittany it wasn't like it seemed, but she'd scarcely listened. And Rhoda's constant sarcastic asides had made matters worse, interrupting and mocking Eugene as he tried to plead his case. Eugene tried to ignore her, to talk only to Brittany, but Rhoda was so in his face it was nigh impossible. Then – out of nowhere – Ralph intervened. Told Rhoda to 'shut up' and stay out of other people's business. Eugene had been surprised at Ralph's sudden vehemence. Rhoda immediately went ballistic. She rounded on Ralph: who did he think he was? She didn't need his permission to speak and, anyway, what did he know? He was a fucking misogynist, and no wonder his wife had got rid. For a split second, Eugene thought Ralph was going to punch her. Then the moment passed. Instead, Ralph told Rhoda she was a 'poisonous jealous bitch', and the two of them began a full-scale row.

Eugene thought things couldn't get much worse – then, Lucy turned up, off her head and giggling uncontrollably. Brittany said she was leaving. 'I'm sorry,' he'd said. 'I'll ring you, sort it out.' Against the backdrop of the music, Ralph and Rhoda's screaming, and Lucy's coked-up laughter, it was hard to hear, but he'd got her next words crystal clear. 'Please don't bother,' Brittany said, and walked away.

Then it had taken God knows how long to extricate Ralph from his shouting match with Rhoda – and even longer to get rid of Lucy. Eugene was adamant that he was not walking out of the club with her. He wanted Brittany back, and leaving with Lucy was not going to help his chances. Lucy was equally determined to blag a lift home.

Predictably, another scene ensued and Eugene had wait for Lucy to make her umpteenth trip to the toilets before he and Ralph got out of the club and away.

He had rung Brittany after leaving the club, and he rang her the minute he woke up Saturday. He carried on ringing her – with the same dismal result. Brittany rejected every call. His text messages were ignored. She didn't want to talk to him. Eugene was desperate. He suddenly understood Ralph's utter misery over Belinda. That it didn't matter how many other beautiful women were out there – no matter how dazzling or how fine they were – because it wasn't about a quick jump any more – it was about her. Love, Eugene discovered, was specific. No one else would do, because she was unique, singular. And this pearl beyond price was – it seemed – lost, thrown away. Except that Eugene wasn't going to let that happen. He'd made mistakes, but nothing that couldn't be put right. He wasn't going to give up. He was going to fight to win her back. And he had a strong idea who he'd be facing in the battle – Rhoda Gunne, the Red Queen.

Eugene had disliked the woman straight off – marked her down for blagging drinks off him, for not having the tact to give her friend some space. Then she came on to him on the dance floor – which was beyond cheap, it was bargain basement – especially as she reckoned to be Brittany's bestest, closest friend. But, according to what Ralph had told him, Rhoda had another 'best' friend – Ralph said she and Belinda were always together, always on the phone. Ralph thought Rhoda was instrumental in the break-up of his marriage. Suspected she'd encouraged Belinda's paranoia, talked up her fears. Eugene thought he could well be right, and something else occurred to him: the popular Rhoda was Belinda's colleague and close friend, Brittany's constant companion and confidante. It didn't take a genius to make the connection – Eugene knew that Belinda loathed him. He had little doubt that Rhoda had quickly realized his connection to Ralph. No doubt she'd asked Belinda what she knew about this man, Eugene, her friend's new lover. And Eugene could well imagine Belinda's response. Rhoda must have been gleeful when she passed on Belinda's X-rated horror stories to Brittany – he could almost hear Rhoda's voice dropping to a sincere whisper: 'It's about Eugene. I'm only telling you because I don't want you to get hurt.' As if that wasn't enough, Brittany then had a perfect view of Lucy's Royal Command Performance madness at the club. No wonder Brittany wasn't taking his calls.

'Stop that now!' Eugene's thoughts of Brittany skidded to a halt as he suddenly caught sight of Nero. Taking advantage of Eugene's reverie, the child had crawled across the front-room floor and, shielded by the curtains, had been working assiduously to undo the window lock. Eugene crossed the room in two strides and bodily swung Nero across the room, plonking him back in position on the sofa.

'Don't even think about trying that again,' Eugene said. 'Sit down and behave. In fact, next time you move, you're off to bed.'

'Noooo. Don't want. No go. Noooo.' Nero was bouncing on the sofa, shouting at top volume.

'Shut up. I said "SHUT UP,"' Eugene yelled in turn. 'Stop creating or you're going upstairs now and straightways. Understand me?' Nero subsided into sullen silence. 'Good,' said Eugene, going over to rescrew the window lock. 'Good. You're dealing with me now. So, start kicking or biting and you'll seriously regret it.'

They had just settled back into an uneasy truce on the sofa when Eugene's mobile went. He'd been expecting the call – it was Talus. The news wasn't good. Gloria's mobile was still switched off. George Faron was going mental. Talus was directing operations whilst Archie was tied up nurse-maiding his brother. There was still no trace of Carl or Gloria although half the Firm were out looking. 'The lady's going to have some explaining to do when she finally turns up tomorrow morning,' Talus said. 'Anyway' – he paused – 'I'll bell you straight off if anything develops. Otherwise, hook up in the morning as planned.' The line went dead.

This was bad enough, but between times he had somehow to cope with the Minimonster. By 11.30 p.m. the kid was still watching TV and refusing to go to bed – and getting more hyper by the minute. Eugene stayed in the front room with him. He wanted to keep an eye on the child, who seemed to be increasingly excitable – although, theoretically, he should have been exhausted and fast asleep. Nero insisted on watching his favourite *Forensic Detectives* – it was hardly suitable for a six-year-old – but Eugene couldn't be bothered to argue, partly because he knew Nero would throw a massive tantrum, partly because he was rather partial to *Forensic Detectives* himself.

The crunch came at midnight. *Forensic Detectives* had given way to *Serial Killers*. The first instalment was set in Louisiana. The raped and mutilated bodies of five young women had been discovered floating in the local swamps and bayous. Eugene was fascinated but had to tear himself away. This was plainly not appropriate bedtime viewing for a six-year-old boy. Nero thought otherwise.

'That's it,' Eugene announced. 'It's way too late anyways.' He flourished the remote high above Nero's grabbing hands and switched the TV off. 'Right,' he said, 'bedtime.' Nero stared back, eyes unfathomable beneath spider-leg eyelashes.

'Wanna milk,' he said. 'Gass milk.'

Eugene said OK, tucked the TV remote in his pocket and headed for the kitchen. He'd just got through the kitchen door when it happened. The noise was so overwhelming that Eugene, Gladys and Moira all froze, suspended in a split second of shock, then Eugene turned and pelted back and through the front-room door.

The window was smashed to bits. The front room was empty. Eugene went straight through the broken window and hurled himself in pursuit. As he sprinted across the Tarmac he caught sight of a tiny figure in the darkness, running full tilt before disappearing round the corner.

CHAPTER TWENTY-FIVE

And all the while she stood vpon the ground,
The wakefull dogs did neuer cease to bay,

FQ: The Legende of the Knight of the Red Crosse: I.v.30

As the changing-room filled up with girls getting ready for the Saturday-night stint, Canday Sweete finally walked in – late as always – and Simone gave a sigh of relief. She was about to signal to the girl, when she realized Canday was waving to her and on her way over.

'Hi, got something for you. He's, like, waiting, so I said I'd go and get you straightways. It's Mal, y'know. He's at the door, said would I tell you he needs to talk. He's got this message, yeah? Sorry an all that.'

'Fine,' Simone said. 'Hey, Canday, I want a word. Give me five minutes before you hit the floor?' It was more a command than a question. Simone was top girl, and Canday was anything but. The girl nodded. 'Sure. I'll be here . . . oh, shit. I knew she'd fucked up, told her the glue wouldn't hold them, I bloody told her . . .' Canday got down on the floor and picked up a blonde hair-extension.

'There's two more over there, where you put your bag.' Simone pointed on her way to the door as Canday swore some more and gathered up the synthetic hair. Simone shook her head. 'Be careful, girl. You don't want that happening out there on the floor. Mr Barry'll have a fit.'

Simone went out into the corridor that separated the changing-room from the Artistes' Door which opened on to the general public. She was irritated to see that Mal Shifter was already through the first door and waiting in the corridor.

'Ah, the delectable Simone, Queen of the Tables, Pole Princess, the Dusky Diva of Dance. What a vision you are.'

Simone didn't bother to acknowledge Shifter's greeting. 'Heard you got a message for me,' she said.

'Indeed, indeed I have,' said Shifter. He stood back and looked at her intently. 'You really are a superb specimen, you know,' he said. Simone winced and Shifter smiled fleetingly before continuing. 'First time I've had chance to study you in mufti – so to speak. Beautifully put together. Of course it's the movement that puts you a cut above. Spectacular body, without a doubt, but in my opinion it's the way you use it, the dancing, that's what gets the men in a sweat. That's my conclusion anyway. And it's based on a great deal of observation and study. Oh, yes. I make very sure I watch all your . . . er . . . performances . . . that's the polite word, isn't it? Yes, know every inch of you by now. Know you inside out . . . as we say – well, very nearly.'

Simone leant against the corridor wall and folded her arms. She was on the way to a panic attack, she could feel it. Her heart was leaping and banging, and she wanted to cry. To slide down the wall, wrap her arms round her body and sob – to have her mum and brother take her home and look after her and tell her she never never ever had to do this shit job ever again. Instead, she kept silent, took deep breaths, finally steadied herself. 'Canday said you had a message for me?'

'Oh – of course!' Shifter trilled. 'As always, the very sight, the very scent of you, makes me forget everything. Must get a grip on myself, eh? After all, I'll be seeing plenty more of you later, won't I? Yes. My friend Carl would like to see you. You are the mother of his child, after all, isn't that right?' Simone ignored this, so Shifter continued. 'He needs to talk to you about his son, and his son's future. He knows you work . . . what should we say . . . night hours? So he suggests perhaps an early drink? Tomorrow evening or . . .'

'Don't bother with the dates,' Simone interrupted.

'Oh?' said Shifter. 'So you're happy to see him any time, is that it?'

'Tell Carl that I'd be really happy to see him,' Simone said. She was calm now, voice light and steady. 'And there's no prob whatever about me bringing his son along, too. It's great he wants to do all the father stuff. Brilliant.'

Shifter smiled. 'That's very positive, very commendable. And he can get in touch any time, you say?'

'Yeah,' Simone agreed. 'Just a couple of hours' warning maybe. And course I'll need his phone number, and address, and full name. Now, if you've got them.'

'Sorry?' said Shifter.

'Because I'll need to get in touch with social services, and the Child Support Agency, and I'll probably need his bank details as well. Because before he sees me, or his son, he'll be wanting to put right the six years of contributions he's owing towards paying for Nero. It's great he wants to be a dad. I'm dead pleased, and dead pleased about the money for sure – you know kids, they cost a fortune, right? But I don't want Carl getting ripped off, so best way I figure is to talk to social services and that lot, cos they'll know how much he owes and what instalments he needs to pay.'

'Top girl,' said Shifter quietly. 'You and your brother, eh? You make quite a pair, you really do. Well, if that's your answer I must pass it on. I trust you're being careful by the way, not taking chances, playing safe? Wouldn't want you to end up keeping company with the Meatman, would we? Yes. Look after yourself, that's my advice.'

Simone kept perfectly still until Mal Shifter had gone and

the Artistes' Door closed in his wake. Then she took three or four deep breaths and turned back to the changing-rooms. She hoped Canday was still there, as promised. She badly wanted to speak to her.

Eugene pelted down Wentworth Road at top speed, skidding round the corner just in time to see the Minimonster running full tilt towards Hornsey Road. He was gaining on Nero, stride by stride but, all the same, the little bastard was moving like lightning, his small pyjamaed legs powering on like mini pistons. Eugene shouted at him to stop, but the child never as much as turned his head, just continued helter-skelter through the darkness.

Nero hit the Hornsey Road and turned northward. By now the Minimonster was obviously tiring, and Eugene was less than ten metres behind him. At the intersection with St John's Road Nero didn't hestitate, sprinting straight across. An oncoming driver was forced to stamp on the brakes, slewing the car sideways. Eugene didn't pause for apologies. Nor did he try any more shouting, instead he turned it on, increasing his speed and closing the distance stride by stride until he was within grabbing distance. Nero feinted and swerved, Eugene tried for him and missed, went for it a second time and snagged the Minimonster's pyjama collar. There was a loud tearing sound as Nero flung himself out of Eugene's grasp, leaving the pyjama jacket behind. Eugene dropped the jacket and was straight after him. Half a dozen strides and he'd closed again – this time he had no option, he took hold of a fistful of hair. Nero yelped with pain. Then he turned and attacked, kicking, biting and flailing in a desperate attempt to get free.

Like all the Burnside family, Eugene was an old hand at child-restraint procedures, and in short order had Nero under some sort of control. Then he took him home. Nero screamed and fought every step of the way. 'Wanna watch, lemme watch. Fucka you, fucky wanks. Wanna go see. I hate you. Gonna die, make you die, soon.' By the time they reached Wentworth Road, Eugene's ears were ringing.

Inside the house, he didn't pause but carried the furious Minimonster straight up the stairs and into his bedroom. After locking the door, he proceeded to change Nero into clean pyjamas and put him to bed, resolutely ignoring the continuous screaming and intermittent physical attacks. Then he walked out, making sure the door was firmly locked. The furious pounding and shouting followed Eugene downstairs. He wondered how the hell the 'respite care' foster parents were going to cope with the brat. He wished them luck – they'd need it.

DS Scudamour insisted on giving Simone a lift home. It meant pissing off his driver, who had to wait near on an hour, whilst the club closed and Simone showered, changed and wiped off the make-up. Scudamour didn't care. He'd watched the man watching Simone. Kept an eye on him all night. Shared his suspicions with Lalibela, and Lalibela agreed. The man had never taken his eyes off the top girl. Whichever section of the club Simone was in, you could be sure the man would be there, never more than a few feet away, his gaze focused and intent, stripping the clothes, and then, when the clothes had been shed, the skin, from her body. Scudamour regarded himself as a dedicated professional, a career man. Only the elite were chosen for DCI Gale's squad. Scudamour was acutely aware that he was close to overstepping the mark – allowing personal feelings, emotions, to dictate his actions.

DC Lalibela had another take on it. 'Look, sir, this guy's a suspect, right?'

Scudamour nodded.

'And he's been trailing this girl all night. We know the murders have a SweetHearts connection. It's our duty to detect crime, and if possible to prevent crime?' Scudamour nodded again and Lalibela made an open-handed, Well,

QED, there-you-go gesture. 'I'm happy to put on record now, sir,' he said, 'that I am entirely in support of your proposed action.'

So, some time after 3 a.m. Simone and Scudamour once more shared the backseat of the chauffeur-driven police Rover.

Simone had endured one of the worst nights of her SweetHearts career. She had talked to Canday, and afterwards had managed to snatch a fifteen-minute coffee break with Mae and talked some more. She was now pretty certain. She had to tell the police, of course, and quickly. But first she wanted to talk to her brother. And before any of this could be sorted, there was her little boy. It was his last night – tomorrow morning, social services were picking him up. Part of Simone itched to cancel the whole deal. To pull back and keep her baby with her, where he belonged, at home. But she'd gone over and over this, talked with her mum for hours. So there'd be no going back. She'd packed his little case before going to work – clothes, favourite toys, school stuff. A framed picture of the two of them taken a year ago. She didn't want him to forget her.

Once social services had done their stuff, then she'd be able to concentrate. She knew she had no time to waste. And she wanted to talk to Eugene about other stuff as well, because this job was making her sick, was doing her head in. And that bastard tonight, following her round – every table she'd danced for, he'd be there, a couple of yards away – looking, always looking at her. There was no point asking security, they couldn't help her. Mr Barry ditto. She wasn't risking a taxi tonight. She was thinking of phoning Eugene – he wouldn't be pleased, but he'd do it. And then Mae had appeared, smiling knowingly. 'Chauffeur-driven Rover awaiting your ladyship,' she'd said. Simone was so thoroughly rattled she just stared at Mae. 'What?'

Then Mae had told her about the lift and asked her if she was OK; she looked pale, jumpy. Simone said she was fine.

267

Could Mae say she'd be as quick as poss and thanks? Fifteen minutes later, she was sitting next to Scudamour, sliding on the leather upholstery as the Rover glided through the darkly silent streets. At every corner, they bumped against each other, hip to thigh.

Scudamour instructed the driver to turn round in Wentworth Road and wait whilst he escorted Simone to her door. They walked in stride, close together, hands brushing. When they came to number forty, Simone hesitated, then asked if it would be possible to contact him tomorrow. There was something she wanted to discuss, something about the murders. Scudamour gave her his card, his home and mobile number scribbled on the back. He said good-night and waited until she was safely inside the house before returning to the car. For the rest of the journey home, he was silent, thinking about her.

It was almost 4 a.m. when Simone got in, but no one was in bed. Eugene and Gladys were in the kitchen. As Simone walked through, her mum was standing by the kettle making two cups of tea with whisky. Her brother was alternating tea with iced vodka. Both looked exhausted. There was no need to ask why they were up. The noise from Nero's room was indescribable – his normal banging, kicking, shouting protests were nothing compared to this furious avalanche of sound.

'Don't go in,' were Eugene's first words. 'He can't hurt himself, he's safe. But leave it, Sis. He'll wear himself out eventually. We've had the police out twice – neighbours complaining about the noise. Next door on the other side are going bonkers, can't blame them. He's gone completely mental.'

As Simone sipped her whisky tea, Eugene filled her in on the events of the night. She went through with him to see the front-room window – now boarded up. 'Got a firm coming tomorrow morning to put new glass in,' Eugene said. Simone started to cry, and he put an arm around her. 'It's not your fault, little sister. You get that straight. You did your best, and your best is a class act – you understand? I don't know what you could have done different, or Mum, or me.'

They walked back into the kitchen. In the light, Simone saw that her brother's arms were covered in scratches and marks. Eugene laughed and told her it was nothing. 'Minor war wounds,' he said. Simone learnt that on the second call out, just before three, the police had brought along a social worker, and she had insisted on seeing Nero and going in to assess him, despite Eugene's warnings. Predictably, the Mini-monster had attacked. Eugene and two police officers had pulled Nero off her, and received a fair battering in the process.

'But you ought to have seen the state of that poor woman,' Gladys said. 'You wouldn't have believed a child could do it.'

Nero had done his now usual vampire trick – the woman's inner arm had been covered in bites and spraying blood everywhere. Then, apparently bored with biting, he'd gone for the social worker's hair. Luckily, she kept it short, but he'd still managed to pull out a couple of handfuls. 'Roll on tomorrow,' said Eugene. Simone looked at the floor and said nothing.

By the time they'd finished talking it was gone four-thirty, and Nero was noticeably quieter. Chaperoned by Eugene, Simone went in to say goodnight and was able to tuck the exhausted child in bed. As they left the bedroom, Nero opened his eyes. Straightening his first two fingers so they resembled the barrel of a gun, he pointed at Eugene. 'Hate you, fucky kill you, bang, bang. You fucky die.' As they shut the door, they heard the boy giggling. Eugene raised his eyebrows and looked at Simone.

'I know,' she said. 'I know.'

*   *   *

Three miles northward, another pair were getting ready for bed. Like Eugene and his sister, the two men were tired. For them it had been an exciting and fulfilling night, but all good things must come to an end, and once 4 a.m. had come and gone, the fun was largely over. By four-thirty everything was finished and they were packed up and ready to go, their spoils carefully stored and everything accounted for. They tidied up, left the place as they found it – with one important addition – and went away quietly. Even when safe in the car and heading for home, discipline was maintained. Everything kept low key, unremarkable and entirely normal.

It was only when they were inside the house and basking in the toasting and fêting of their admiring audience that their trophies were revealed and inspected. There were squeals of excitement and grunts of approbation, congratulations all round. Even the silent animals seemed to catch the mood, their claws scratching on the lino as they raced round kitchen and hallway. One of the two men – the white man – suggested a celebratory drink, and after taking orders from those present began to mix the requested cocktails. Whilst he chopped limes and mint, speared olives and maraschino cherries, the other – the black man – set up the sound system. Despite the late hour, no one bothered about the neighbours. As the sound of Abba's 'Dancing Queen' filled the kitchen, one of the women got up and began to move suggestively. Seconds later, the black man accompanied her.

Back in the place the two men had come from, everything was quiet. The rows of plants, all sorted and labelled, carried on growing silently and slowly, untouched by the scenes so recently witnessed. In the garden furniture section, wooden benches and wrought-iron tables remained unperturbed. And only some drag marks and a kicked-over terracotta urn indicated anything unusual had occurred in the area devoted to garden ornaments. That was the initial impression anyway. Come daylight, the pathway would bear

270

many other signs, all testifying that a struggle had taken place earlier. Experts reading the footprints and scuff marks would see that a woman had been fighting against two men. Fighting with fierce desperation. But, judging by the evidence, the experts believed the men had overpowered her.

Past the urns and pots and hanging baskets was the 'statuary', as it was rather grandly called. There were concrete Neptunes spitting water, fat little plaster cupids in every conceivable pose and row upon row of classical figures: Diana, Juno, Venus, Apollo, Poseidon – even copies of the horses from the Elgin Marbles. All were here, in vast numbers – with a choice of finish: marble, bronze, granite, to name a few.

And over at the left corner was a group of three – Diana and Venus flanking one of the lesser goddesses, or perhaps a nymph, positioned between the two deities, held up by their supporting arms. All three figures were naked. But whilst the two plaster goddesses shone gleaming white, some other material had been used on the nymph. Marble, perhaps? The figure appeared veined and mottled and, on coming closer, it looked like vandals had been at it. There were any number of chips and scratches, some quite large. However, the worst damage was to the head and face. Presumably, some accident had caused the top portion of the head to split away, and a number of facial details had been destroyed, possibly at the same time.

The moonlit darkness shrouded the strange trio, lending an aura of mystery and grace. Muted silver light picked out round shoulders, whilst moonbeams slithered across the slope of collar bones and emphasized the shadowed hollows of the throat. Arms around each other, moonlight flowing along their corresponding curves, the three figures waited silently.

CHAPTER TWENTY-SIX

Als in her lap a louely babe did play
His cruell sport, in stead of sorrow dew;
For in her streaming blood he did embay
His litle hands, and tender ioynts embrew;
Pitifull spectacle, as euer eye did view.

FQ: The Legend of Sir Gvyon;
The Bloudy-Handed Babe: II.i.40

Social services arrived bang on 10 a.m. Eugene was relieved to see they'd come mob-handed. Six of them, to be precise – four women, two men. 'Sorry about this,' one of the men had said to Gladys as she was handing out cups of tea. 'I'm Dave. And I really think it's totally over the top, I mean, sending a squad of us like this. You can blame the director. Honestly, bloody suits and pen-pushers.' He gave a disparaging laugh and shrugged his shoulders, suggesting to Gladys that they were on the same side. Gladys asked if he wanted sugar. 'Oh, no, no thanks. I mean, invading you like this – and the director says he's read the little guy's case notes and talked to the police . . .' He paused here to roll his eyes. 'I mean, he's never even met the child . . . hello.'

Eugene had come into the kitchen. 'Hello,' he replied. 'His

stuff's all packed and in the boot. Simone's got everything sorted. She says he's ready. There's no point in hanging about – you may as well get going. He's OK at the moment. Knackered after last night's kick-off.'

'Ah, yes. I heard something about that,' said Dave, as everyone stood up and prepared to leave. 'Unfortunately, all I've got is the police report. The poor kid must have been so distressed.'

Eugene nodded. 'Yeah. Well, let's get moving before the little bastard gets distressed again.'

Luckily Dave had real empathy with black people, and understood perfectly that Eugene was using bravado to cover up his genuine feelings of guilt and loss. Five minutes later, the people-carrier trundled down Wentworth Road with six social workers and Nero on board. The child had gone off happily, barely bothering to say goodbye to his mother and grandmother and favouring Eugene with a malevolent stare. As the vehicle turned on to the Holloway Road, Dave told his team he was very concerned about the way the child had been demonized. He was obviously prone to outbursts of hyperactivity and had been diagnosed with acute Attention Deficit Disorder. But instead of addressing these problems, the system had labelled the kid as some sort of little monster. He was going to take up the matter internally. Everyone nodded.

Dave privately felt that the kid's problems probably stemmed from the Burnside family's inadequate parenting skills. However due to ethnic sensitivities he kept these thoughts to himself, but determined to have a tactful chat with the foster parents when he arrived at Nero's temporary new home in Cricklewood.

In the event, Dave and two of his colleagues had to be dropped off at the Royal Free Hospital's outpatients unit. Nero spent the rest of the journey to his foster home under restraint, as the police and Eugene had advised in the first place.

Within minutes of the Minimonster's departure, Eugene's mobile rang. It was Talus.

'Geno, I'm on my way to the King's. Get yourself there as quick as you can. It's gone seriously pear-shaped. George is out at Heathrow doing his nut. There's no sign of her.'

Eugene checked his watch – just coming up to 11 a.m.

'Is everybody off the plane?' he asked.

'Yeah. Well, we knew she wouldn't be on it anyway, but I thought she was guaranteed to turn up – keepin up appearances and all that. She knew she'd be met at the airport. She might be a slag and a chancer, Geno, but the woman's not fuckin stupid. She had to be there. But she isn't. So where the fuck is she?'

'I'll shoot straight over,' Eugene said.

'Sound. I'll see you there.'

Eugene raced round the house apologizing and mumbling about an emergency at work. Simone grabbed him just as he was on his way out the door. 'I need to speak to you,' she said. 'About the murders.'

Eugene glanced at his watch – eleven fifteen. 'Take your mobile and I'll bell you. We'll hook up afternoon or maybe evening – early doors – that all right?' Simone nodded. 'Sorry, Sis. Promise we'll speak today, yeah? Yeah?' Simone nodded again, unconvinced. Eugene put his arm round her. 'Look, I know this morning's been torture, and I know I shouldn't be running out, but something seriously bad has kicked off and I've got to go and sort it. But I give you my word, I'll bell you before . . . say, six? At the latest. And we'll arrange a meet, tonight. If you think it's important – well, that's good enough for me. I won't let you down, promise, seriously.'

Simone patted his shoulder. 'Don't. Cos I'm relying on you, and I'm telling you, "seriously".' She smiled at him.

'Yeah, yeah, yeah – take the piss – my baby sis,' Eugene responded.

Simone laughed. 'Please, bro, never, just never go near a public mike. I'd die of shame.' Then she was back sombre and straight. 'Anyway, keep your promise, I need to talk to you. So call me.'

Eugene promised he would.

The Puma bounded out of Wentworth Road and fairly flew the short distance to the Cally Road and the King's Head. Vinnie opened the door and Eugene went straight in. Talus was already there, talking on the mobile, a shaft of sun lighting up the close-cropped bronze curls so they resembled a gladiator's helmet. As Eugene approached Talus clicked off the call and put his phone on the table. His face seemed very pale for some reason, making the aquamarine eyes more vividly shocking than usual.

Eugene sat down. 'Any more news?' he asked.

Oddly, Talus laughed, a short, dry rasp of laughter. 'Yeah. You could say that. It's only just come through – the call I was on when you arrived. It was one of the plods on the payroll. Well, I say "plod", but he's Serious Crime. Anyways, he says his murder-squad mates have all been busy today. Looks like the Meatman's got another one.'

Eugene could feel himself going cold. He thought immediately of Simone but realized with relief that he'd only just left her. Then he looked across at Talus and suddenly understood. 'It's her, isn't it?' he asked.

'That's right,' Talus said quietly. 'Gloria's dead.'

'Oh, Jesus Christ,' said Eugene. 'Where's that fucker Carl?'

'We'd all like to know that,' Talus replied. 'Got people chasing, though I wouldn't hold your breath.'

'He's involved,' said Eugene. 'Positive of it.'

'Yeah.' Talus nodded. 'I'd say so. So we'll keep looking till we find him.'

There was little time for further discussion; too much

needed doing. First off, Eugene and Talus had a lengthy three-way conference call with Archie. Followed by more calls soliciting information from police and forensic contacts. Once the facts were more or less established, Eugene and Talus launched into long chats with selected friendly journalists – the story of Gloria's death would be major news. It had to be made clear to reporters that Gloria was the daughter of a highly respected lawyer and her grieving husband was a prominent London businessman with a wide portfolio of interests. Eugene and Talus implied – off the record – that Gloria had probably been snatched from her car whilst driving back home. George Faron was said to be 'devastated', quote. There was absolutely no mention of Carl, Marbella or boyfriends.

When that end of things was satisfactorily wrapped up, they checked in again with Archie, who had by now spoken to DCI Gale. By early afternoon, things were more or less under control, but two problems remained. First off was the matter of ID'ing the body. From what the police were saying, it wasn't going to be a pleasant task. The obvious person to do this was George. But no one, police included, thought this a good idea. George was in a state. There was a doctor on standby waiting for his arrival at the Halcyenda.

There was no other option: Ali Acrasiafi – Gloria's dad and Firm lawyer – was roped in for the job. That problem solved, there was only one immediate difficulty – what the fuck were they to do about George?

'One thing at a time,' said Talus, as he and Eugene headed to Finchley to collect Gloria's father and drive him to the morgue at St Pancras, where the remains awaited identification.

'So have the murder squad said any more?' Eugene asked Talus. 'Bring me up to speed, before her dad gets in the car.'

Talus nodded. 'They've still got no idea how she got up to

the Ally Pally, or what the fuck she was doing there. They've found her jacket and one shoe up by the palace itself. Rest of her stuff is missing.'

'So how far's this garden centre from where they found the jacket?' Eugene asked.

''Bout quarter of a mile downhill – not far. The place is locked up at night, opens at 9 a.m. on Sundays, but the coppers say the gates would be easy to climb.'

'They think they killed her inside the place then?' said Eugene.

'Not clear – they're waiting on forensics. First off they want the formal ID out the way. Feel sorry for her old man.'

'He made a mess of her,' Eugene said.

'Yeah. They won't commit themselves yet, but they say so far it looks like classic Meatman . . .' Talus broke off. 'Well, here we are.' He pulled up outside a smart, well-maintained house. Mr Acrasiafi must have been waiting as he was already locking the front door.

The journey to the morgue took no more than half an hour and was passed in silence. Mr Acrasiafi's empty, stricken face didn't invite conversation.

When they arrived at the morgue, Ali Acrasiafi asked Talus and Eugene to accompany him. 'Her mother's dead. I would appreciate it. I don't want to do this alone,' he said. So all three men walked into the cold, windowless room. The body, covered by a green surgical sheet, lay on a metal gurney. Apart from two orange plastic chairs positioned against the far wall, the room was entirely bare.

Immediately after their arrival, DCI Arthur Gale came into the room and introduced himself. He talked through procedure and assured Mr Acrasiafi he was welcome to take as much time as he wanted. He asked her father if he knew of any identifying marks his daughter had? Any moles? Tattoos? Operation scars?

Ali Acrasiafi shook his head; he seemed bewildered by the question.

DCI Gale spoke softly. 'I must warn you, sir, your daughter's killer has badly mutilated her features. In particular, he has removed her scalp and hair. It's not going to be easy for you to make a positive identification.'

When they turned back the sheet the thing revealed seemed barely human. Fifteen minutes later the formal identification was completed, and Eugene and Talus had to half-carry Gloria's dad back to the car. They drove back to the Acrasiafi house, where two of Gloria's aunties and a cousin were waiting – all dressed in black. Eugene thought of the Caridads as he watched the women support the grey husk of Al Acrasiafi into the darkness of the house.

'We won't let this lie,' Talus said, as he drove Eugene back. 'This can't go on.'

'Was she dead before he started on her?' Eugene asked.

'Have to wait for forensics and postmortem,' Talus replied. 'You know George is insisting on seeing her?'

'Oh Jesus,' said Eugene. 'He's got to be stopped. Archie's got to make him see sense. He doesn't want to see . . . especially . . . he's got to be stopped.'

'Told Archie on the mobile,' Talus said grimly. 'Said her face was a total mess, told him about the scalping and all the other stuff. Not that Archie needs persuading. He's trying to talk George out of it, but he's insisting. Says he wants to say goodbye. Fuck me . . .' Talus subsided, concentrating on the road, staring blankly ahead.

For Eugene the rest of the long afternoon spiralled into one nightmare after another. Try as they might, they got no further forward in the hunt for Carl. Just as before, Carl seemed to have evaporated into thin air. As if sorting this out wasn't trouble enough, George was causing havoc. He demanded to know what the fuck his wife had been doing.

When had she left Spain? Why had she lied to him? What had she been playing at? And who, and where, was the bastard who killed her? Because – as George repeatedly swore – when he got his hands on the bastard, he would pull him to pieces, joint by joint, bit by bit, until there was nothing left worth talking about.

Worse still he insisted on seeing the body. Nothing anyone could say – police, family, close friends – made the slightest dent upon his resolve. Even Archie couldn't talk him out of it. George told his brother that he had to see his wife, no matter what had been done to her. He wouldn't rest until he said a proper goodbye.

Talus and Eugene likewise tried everything to dissuade him, without success. In the end Talus drove George down, and stood with DCI Gale whilst George sobbed, shook and ranted beside his wife's mutilated corpse. Finally, Talus persuaded George to come away, and drove him back to the Halcyenda. George spent the journey in tears, breaking off sporadically to ask Talus unanswerable questions or to say, over and over again, that he loved his wife. Loved her so much. Loved her more than anything in the whole world.

When they got to the Halcyenda, Archie had the family doctor on standby. George didn't argue and accepted the sedation with something akin to gratitude.

Eugene had rung Simone as promised and told her he would be home around nine. She said fine. In fact, he only just made it – rolling down the Halcyenda driveway at eight-fifty and allowing the Puma free rein to carry him home. He was so exhausted, he almost fell asleep on the way. The only thing lifting his mood was that home was now a Nero-Free Zone. No screaming, shouting, kicking or biting. Total bliss.

It was just after nine when he settled the Puma on Wentworth Road. His mobile beeped to show he had a message. He prayed it wasn't work. He'd had enough and more than enough. He wanted a hot shower, a good dinner and a long sleep. Nonetheless, he had to check. There was a faint outside hope that it could be Brittany. It wasn't. It was about the last person in the world he expected to hear from. He would think about it tomorrow.

CHAPTER TWENTY-SEVEN

Yet was thy loue her death

FQ: The Legend of Britomartis;
The House of Busyrane: III.xi.36

Eugene couldn't believe it. He'd just that second clicked off the message service when his mobile rang again. He was halfway across the road and heading for his front door – but no rest for the wicked, as his mum frequently said. He checked the number – it was Talus. Eugene cursed but immediately took the call.

'All right, Geno. I've got some news.' Talus, as always, straight to the point.

'Tell me,' Eugene replied.

'Just had a bell from our boy in Serious Crime,' said Talus. 'He tells me Gale's murder squad are looking for two men – not one – two fuckin serial killers, working together.'

'Jesus,' said Eugene. It took him a moment to digest the implications.

'It's the forensics,' Talus continued. 'The body of the girl they did in Crouch End . . . the third one . . .'

'Angie,' said Eugene. 'Angela Caridad.'

'Yeah, that's right,' said Talus. 'Angela. They managed to extract DNA material from her. I'll spare you the details –

bloody revolting – but the pathologist played a blinder apparently, and the copper says the results are a hundred per cent – no question. Samples show there were two men doing the girl – no doubt about it.'

Eugene could scarcely credit it. 'Two men doing it?' he echoed.

'Yeah. A regular double act,' Talus affirmed.

'So, what now?' Eugene asked. 'We still after that toerag Carl?'

'Dead right. We've tipped off the murder squad about him – given them everything we've got. But "everything we've got" amounts to fuck all.'

'What about that bloke who thought he saw Gloria in Camden then?' said Eugene. 'She was with two men, yeah?'

'Been back there to check it out,' Talus replied. 'No certainty it was her, but the clothes and hair were dead on. She was seen walking with a black guy and a white guy, right?'

'S'right,' said Eugene.

'I'll get one of the boys to go back and see if there's more in it. OK,' Talus said. 'Meet tomorrow – Archie wants to see us. Round at the Halcyenda, about ten-thirty, yeah?'

'Sweet,' said Eugene. 'How's George?'

'Awful,' was Talus's succinct reply.

When Eugene finally got through the front door, he found Simone home alone. She told him Gladys was down the Saracen's on the corner, with Moira, Gerry Q and the usual crowd. The two women had scarcely ventured out since Nero's attack, but Gladys's bruises were fading and Moira's lip, though still swollen, had subsided to the point where they both felt fit to show their faces in public. Eugene was pleased – a few drinks with old friends would do them both good.

Simone was watching something about the pharaohs –

Ancient Egypt was another Discovery Channel perennial, and Eugene reckoned himself something of an expert on Akhenaten and the experiment with monotheism. He opened a beer and collected a Bacardi Breezer for Simone, and settled down to watch. In fact, the thing wasn't about the pharaohs at all but about genetics and inheritance. The Egyptians got a mention because of the incestuous marriages between brother and sister, or half-brother and sister. Politically, it made sense, Eugene could see that – keeping power in the family and so on. Unfortunately, it also created a genetic nightmare of knock-kneed, snaggle-toothed nutters – witness Akhenaten – but 3,000 years ago, they didn't know that.

What really caught Eugene's attention was the race stuff. They did this genetic profile of two Americans – one black, one white – and tried to trace back their origins. It was unbelievable, Eugene thought. It turned out that your white guy – and he was really white: red-haired and freckled with paper-white skin – had more black genes than the black guy, who turned out to owe the majority of his ancestry to somewhere in Germany. The black guy was a full-on Belinda-style 'race activist', and he'd gone into the whole thing because he was desperate to know which 'tribe' he'd come from. 'The Lederhosen Burghers of Bavaria tribe, in the main' was not the answer he was looking for – especially as his carrot-top cohort turned out to be 40 per cent Ibo, genetically speaking. Eugene found it fascinating. Unfortunately, Discovery then switched to the perennial standby of Mount Everest. Eugene wondered if there was somewhere he could email a complaint? Everest and the Second World War were doing his head in. He flicked to Discovery Civilization, which looked half OK: *Bedlam – A History of 500 Years of Mental Illness*.

Simone said she'd prefer something less depressing, and after a couple of minutes they ended up on BBC cable something or other – a rerun of *The Blue Planet*. David

Attenborough was whispering on about the predators of the open seas. Eugene asked Simone if she'd heard anything from Nero.

'I spoke to him on the phone,' Simone said. 'And the foster woman as well – Mrs Redmayne. She was all right. Nice enough. Told me not to worry, he'd settled in and everything was fine. He was a bit hyper, but he seemed OK. Course, kids are so adaptable, aren't they? Probably hit me harder than it's hit him.'

'So he's not jumping off just yet?' Eugene asked.

'No, no trouble at all, they said,' Simone replied. 'They said I could ring whenever I wanted to. Made me feel a bit better, knowing I'm still in touch, y'know?'

Eugene nodded. Personally, he would have felt better knowing the Minimonster was currently en route to the Australian outback with no hope of contact for the foreseeable – but Nero's mother obviously felt differently. Eugene glanced up at the TV; David Attenborough dominated the picture. 'Anyway, Sis, to change the subject, you said you wanted to talk to me, 'bout the murders?'

Simone nodded and hit the mute on the TV remote. 'It might be all something and nothing. But I wanted to talk it through, to get your take on it – cos I'm thinking I should maybe pass this on, y'know, talk to the detectives in the club?'

Eugene told her to go ahead. For the next half-hour he listened intently as his sister sat cross-legged in front of the plasma screen. Framed by the flickering blue backdrop of orca pods, shark attacks, barracuda, sword- and sailfish, Simone told her story.

She began with Stella and her secret romance with Mr Barry. The Saturday-night tryst that Mr Barry had broken. And how someone inside the club had conned Stella – someone who knew about Mr Barry's secret romance. Someone who knew Mr Barry, someone Stella believed to be close to the SweetHearts manager. Simone explained how she'd checked up with Mae, who'd told her that Mr Barry blamed himself for Stella's murder, because he'd left her to find her own way home and she'd walked straight into the Meatman. And she told Eugene about waiting in the foyer for her lift on the night of Stella's murder, how Stella had said, 'All's well that ends well,' and had clattered off on five-inch heels to wait for her murderer.

Simone explained how she'd started to really think about the murders, to try and piece things together. And so she took the next step: she talked to Canday, the one-time best friend and flatmate of the second murdered girl – fifteen-year-old Amy Fiddeler.

Canday talked a good deal about Amy's secret boyfriend, how she had changed after meeting him. 'She went on and on about him – no details, of course, cos mystery man had told her to keep it secret,' Canday told Simone, still plainly upset at the way her supposed best friend had cut her adrift. 'Silly cow never asked him, like, why? What's the big deal?' Canday continued. 'Just went along with it. Did whatever he wanted, as far's I can see.' Canday said she'd been upset by Amy's attitude. 'Y'know, she's like stayin in my place, I'm lookin after her an' that, puttin work her way, and we're supposed to be tight. Then she meets him and thinks she can just burn me off.' Beneath the angry bravado, it was easy to see that Canday was hurt. Essentially alone in the world, the two teenagers had clung together. Canday told Simone over and again how they'd been 'like sisters, dead, dead close'. They had a 'special bond', told each other they were 'soul mates'.

Almost overnight, the arrival of Amy's boyfriend changed everything, and Canday felt betrayed. 'She meets some bloke and goes on about him like he walks on water, and me – I'm like nothing. She can't be bothered being mates – spends all her time with him – said she wasn't interested in working with me no more. Like, thanks a lot, sister.' Then Canday told Simone what she hadn't told the police.

Canday explained that Mal Shifter arranged clients for her and Amy. 'We earned loads of cash. We did the schoolgirl thing, both of us in school uniform. Some of them would just watch, some would want to join in.' Shifter sold the girls drugs at discount and would drive them to and from jobs. Once a client requested a threesome, and this friend of Shifter's, a black guy, joined in with them. Then Amy got this new boyfriend, and the work with Shifter started to drop off. Amy wasn't around at nights, out with the boyfriend. But Canday became suspicious. 'Amy always had shedloads of money, and she was, like, really stoned twenty-four seven.' Canday thought her friend had done the dirty on her. 'I mean, I fuckin introduced her to Mal Shifter. She only got the work cos of me. And then she goes behind my back and betrays me like that.' Canday told Simone she was pretty certain that Amy's new boyfriend was the same black guy they'd met working for Shifter. Canday was sure that Amy and the boyfriend had provided Shifter with a new double-act to tempt his clients. That's why she – Canday – was out of a job. 'Fuckin disloyal,' was Canday's take on it.

Simone shrugged. 'Who knows whether she's right,' she said to Eugene. 'But she should have told the police all this stuff. And if she won't, then I will. Oh, and just wait till you hear this, bro.' Simone quickly told him how Mal Shifter passed on Carl's 'message' that he wanted to meet his son and her response.

'Good one,' Eugene said – but his mind was racing. Simone knew nothing of Carl's involvement with Gloria. Nor that Gloria was almost certainly the Meatman's fourth victim – or the Meatmen, because it now seemed there were two of them. Simone was telling him about her argument with Shifter, and Eugene was suddenly attentive.

'Then he tells me to be careful, says to watch out for the Meatman. He's sick, I tell you. Honestly, Eugene, we get plenty of weirdos in – but Shifter is one of the worst.

'And it's spooky, y'know,' Simone went on. 'Because

before all this, I nipped out to grab some cigarettes, 'bout half an hour before opening, and as I'm coming back round the corner, I stop dead. It was like seeing a ghost, really made me jump, y'know. Cos standing by the backstage door, there's this little group chatting away: Manky Mal Shifter, and Carl with his arm round this tall girl. I only saw her from the back, she had long dark hair. Carl and her went off in a taxi and Manky Mal went back upstairs.'

She didn't tell her brother how, afterwards, Shifter had dogged her from table to table – every time she was paid to dance, there he was. Watching her as she shimmied and stripped. Tongue licking his dry lips, his pale eyes almost unblinking, slowly scrutinizing every inch of flesh. Hovering in the shadows behind the raucous paymasters at the table. Staring at her, like some lurking reptile. She knew Eugene would be furious, would more than likely cause trouble – which would probably make things worse in the long run.

As Simone's voice ran on, the plasma screen behind her head showed a hammerhead shark circling slowly in green, tropical waters. Smaller fish in brilliant stripes of blue and yellow darted for cover. Eugene shook himself, and dragged his attention back to his sister, who was looking expectantly at him.

'So what do you think then, bro?' she said. 'Should I go to the police or just forget it? What's your take on it?'

Eugene knew he should probably have checked with Talus and Archie, but he didn't bother. He knew what he thought and guessed the Firm would agree with him. If not, well, it was too bad. 'You should pick up the phone straightways, Sis,' he said. 'Talk to the DS you know at the club, or whoever you think is sound. Tell them everything. I think it's important. And . . . hang on a minute, I've not finished—' Simone was already ferreting in her handbag for Scudamour's card, mobile in hand. She stopped rummaging and turned her attention back to Eugene.

'And you need some level of protection, in the club

and getting home. You're at risk, no point in pretending different. I don't want you anywhere near Shifter and Carl. I don't want you taking minicabs, and double ditto, don't dream of going near tubes and buses. If the police won't take you to work and back, then I will. You clear on this?'

Simone nodded. She was unexpectedly unnerved. She had been waiting impatiently to tell her brother everything she'd found out – and she had expected, half hoped, that clever, cynical Eugene would dismiss her fears as ridiculous, demolish her shaky theory and tell her that Shifter was a weirdo, but a harmless weirdo, and she'd got it all wrong. Instead he seemed to think she was more or less on the nail. Simone was taken aback. She checked the time – it was gone 10 p.m. 'Maybe I ought to leave the detective till tomorrow, bro?' she said. 'It's pretty late to be calling.'

Eugene shook his head. Monday's papers would be full of the Meatman's latest victim – once the story was out, his sister would understand the importance of her testimony. She needed to tell the police, and as soon as possible.

'No. Phone him now and ask him to come down and take a statement,' he said firmly.

'You got to be jokin, Eugene. At this time on a Sunday night? To listen to a few stories from SweetHearts' changing-room and rubbish like that? No way.'

Eugene raised his eyebrows and pointed at the phone. 'Yeah, I hear you. You think it's overkill and you'll end up looking foolish. Trust me on this, what you told me is important, and I know the police will see it the same way. No argument. So come on, hit those buttons and get some-one over here.'

Twenty minutes later, DS Scudamour was heading the short distance from his flat to forty Wentworth Road; he'd arranged to meet DC Lalibela outside the Burnside house. Simone had sounded hesitant, a little embarrassed, on the phone. She told him she was at home, with her brother,

Eugene. Scudamour knew all about 'Geno', the senior Firm operator without so much as a parking ticket against his name. The word was that Geno was 'a clever bastard'. DS Scudamour had no time for people like that. He was equally dismissive of lap-dancers with a taste for recreational drug abuse – or rather, he used to be, before he met Simone.

In the event, the detectives were tied up for two hours at the Burnside house, first listening to Simone's story, then taking her statement. Despite the late hour, neither Scudamour nor Lalibela had a problem. Both agreed that what Simone had to say was well worth the time.

It was Scudamour's first time inside number forty. Previously, he'd interviewed Simone at Angie's parents' house. He knew enough about Simone's background – not to mention her brother, Geno B., the Firm's rising star, right-hand man to the utterly notorious Gerry Talus – to predict what he would find behind the front door. He guessed it would be a mix of filth and ostentation: state-of-the-art giant TV sitting opposite threadbare sofa with broken springs. Kitchen chock-full of expensive gadgets, with last week's washing-up and a mountain of takeaway tins piled high on the marble worktops. He didn't like the thought of it. Try as he might – and seeing as she was possibly the most unsuitable woman on the planet, he tried bloody hard – he couldn't dismiss Simone as a slapper. Couldn't countenance her as one of the Candays, Trixies, Storms and Xanadoos who were her SweetHearts colleagues. In his mind, she was different. Special. As Scudamour got out of his car in front of number forty, he had a sudden flashback to the previous night. Simone, at the end of one of her dances, picking her clothes up, graceful and unhurried, untouched by the stink and corruption she moved through – or so he wanted to think.

DS Scudamour's last serious relationship had ended eighteen months ago. Jill was a solicitor, keen to get engaged, settle down. Scudamour had ended the relationship for the very good reason that he no longer found her remotely attractive. Nonetheless, several friends and colleagues felt he was being a fool. Scudamour winced when he imagined what they would make of Simone. Fortunately, this train of thought was interrupted by the sweep of DC Lalibela's headlights. After a brief chat, the two men strode up to the door of number forty.

Afterwards, Scudamour and Lalibela drove the half-mile down to Holloway police station for a quick cup of coffee before typing up their report ready to give DCI Gale first thing. They were both excited by what Simone had had to say. 'The brother wasn't what I expected,' Lalibela said, as he finished his coffee. Scudamour mumbled his assent. House, brother – nothing had been as he expected. The plasma screen was the only thing he'd got right. And he couldn't stop thinking about her. Picturing her, sitting close to her brother, looking anxious – and, to Scudamour's eyes, immensely fragile.

CHAPTER TWENTY-EIGHT

There were full many moe like maladies,
Whose names and natures I note reader well;
So many moe, as there be phantasies

FQ: The Legend of Britomartis: III.xii.26

Eugene was beginning to feel the strain of coping – the avalanche of problems seemed unending. Every day a new disaster to be dealt with. And each successive nightmare brought with it an entire retinue of associated smaller difficulties, all aggressively demanding action, all having to be sorted. It was exhausting and Eugene's temper was beginning to fray. Cocaine was fine to keep awake with, but he knew from experience that cocaine plus stress tended to turn you into a paranoid nutter, dithering over every minute decision and prone to pointless rages. Eugene was supposed to be taking executive control of the mess, not adding to the casualty list. So the white stuff was kept firmly under control – meaning he was sane, but utterly knackered.

Once the police had departed he was desperate for bed. But first there were things to do. He nipped upstairs and made a rapid but vital call to Talus explaining new developments. Then it had been hot-foot back down to chat it all through with his sister and reassure her she'd done the right thing. Then his mum and Moira had returned, so they went through the whole rigmarole again. He was dead on his feet when he finally headed to bed, but the torture wasn't quite over. Almost the second he hit the pillow, his mobile started beeping insistently. Another text had come through. He read it quickly and realized the earlier text had been re-sent. He checked his watch – 1.40 a.m. – keen wasn't the word. He thought a while, then decided to answer it. Otherwise, he had a depressing feeling, the text would continue re-sending until he gave in and replied.

He was so tired he hit the wrong button and deleted his first attempt. Swearing furiously, he tried again: 'GT YR MSSGE. SORRY, NOT POSS.' The answer came back immediately. 'THINK YR MKG A MISTKE. IF BUSY THS WK, WHT ABT NXT? RHODA.'

'Oh for God's sake – give me a fuckin break,' Eugene said. Sighing with irritation, he simply re-sent his first message. 'Now piss off . . . please,' he muttered, collapsing back on to the bed.

Eugene was wakened from what felt like less than two minutes' sleep by his mother. 'He's done it again,' she said. 'The Meatman – they're saying he's got another one, up at Alexandra Palace.' Eugene noticed his mother's hands were shaking as she put down his tea. Tiredness forgotten, Eugene was dressed and downstairs in short order. Gladys and Simone moved up to make room on the sofa, and the three of them watched as the horrors unfolded on their screen.

Eugene, of course, had seen it all for real. It was shocking, listening to the description of Gloria's wounds, but Eugene recognized that this was very much the edited account, cleaned up and made palatable for mass consumption. A tame, abridged version of the horrors revealed when he stood alongside Al Acrasiafi and the green morgue sheet was pulled back on Gloria's remains.

He said he'd go to the newsagents', see what the papers

were saying. Gladys got up, saying she'd get some tea and toast going. Simone said nothing. Eugene thought his sister looked genuinely frightened. He wasn't surprised. He was frightened for her.

Once Gladys had left the room, Simone grabbed Eugene's arm. 'That woman, Eugene. Gloria Faron, the dead woman.' Simone's voice was shaky, high-pitched. 'That's the one I saw Carl with. Her hair's the exact same. The clothes and everything. Look, they say she died around 3 or 4 a.m. on Sunday. I saw him with her Saturday night, just a few hours before.'

Eugene had discussed this with Talus last night. There was no way to stop Gloria's infidelity becoming public. Any attempt to do so would eventually collapse and, in the meantime, Carl would be the only beneficiary of short-term confusion. But that meant somebody telling George how his wife had spent her last weekend on earth. And telling him soon, before he found out from Sky News or the *Daily Mail*. It wasn't a prospect to relish.

And there was no denying that the Meatman (the media were still thinking singular) was massive news. Looking along the headlines stacked up in the corner shop, Eugene could see that every single front page was devoted to Gloria's death. Eugene was at the counter with the *Mirror* and the *Mail*, when his phone buzzed again. Juggling money, phone and papers, Eugene answered. He expected Talus but got Ralph.

'Hey, Eugene. Seen the news?'

Eugene rolled his eyes. Did Ralph act this stupid deliberately? 'Course I've seen it. What'ju think? I'm off up the Farons' any minute now. It's a fuckin nightmare.'

Ralph, apparently oblivious to the sharpness of Eugene's tone, carried on. 'It's a nightmare all right. And they don't seem any nearer finding the bastard. Jesus, Eugene, I mean, the thing's so local. When I caught it this morning on the radio, I knew you'd be full-on, but I had to bell you. First off, there was Angie. Now you've got to deal with George Faron and you must be worried sick about Simone and that. I'm sorry, man, I know there's nothing I can do about it – but any time you want to talk, or not talk . . . whatever, well, I'm here, understand?'

Eugene was grateful. Thankful that his best friend had read it right . . . got it dead right, in fact. It made him feel better. ''Preciate that. Thanks, bro. I might be taking you up on that,' he said. Then, 'Anyway, how's it going?'

'More of the same,' said Ralph. 'Worse, to be honest. I'm off to meet with my lawyer. Belinda wants the divorce pushed through. She won't take no for an answer. Still convinced I'm shagging mystery blondes, with your help, of course.' Ralph tried to keep it light, but sounded anything but.

'Still refusing to talk to you?' Eugene asked.

'Got it in one,' said Ralph. 'Communication strictly limited to lawyers' letters. I tell you, Eugene, I have to pinch myself to be sure this is real. This is my wife we're talking about. I would never, like, *never* cheat on her. I love the woman. Can't she get that? And now, all the fuckin hours we worked, and she helped plenty with the business, I'll tell you, and everything we went through, and it's all going to come to shit. Her lawyer says I've got to sell the shop, sell the flat and split the proceeds. Business can't survive that, man. Don't want to even think about it, but I've got no fuckin choice. I'm off to my bloody lawyer now. Throw a bit more money away. I can't believe this is happening.'

Eugene chatted on for a few more minutes, then told Ralph he'd be in touch later and wished him luck. Then he rang him back. 'Sorry, bro, just a couple of quick questions.' Luckily, Ralph was still in the flat, so he found the info Eugene needed in short order. Eugene said goodbye again, and reiterated his promise to be in touch soon.

Forty minutes later the Puma was striding down Hampstead Lane towards the Halcyenda. Eugene really ought to have foreseen it, but his mind was so full he hadn't given it a thought. So he came upon them completely unawares. The Puma flipped skittishly over the small rise and round the corner – and there they were: for a second, Eugene was almost blinded as the murky light beneath the elms guarding the Halcyenda gates exploded into nuclear white-out. The Puma stopped dead, and waited. The light faded, and Eugene's eyes readjusted. There were hordes of them, hundreds of them, milling outside the gates wielding cameras of every size and description. TV blokes, journos with radio recorders, newspaper journos with notebooks and Dictaphones, people with microphones; English, American, French, German, Spanish, Danish – you name it, they were there. Eugene hit the auto-lock system and allowed the Puma to edge nervously towards the gate. The throng parted slowly and with reluctance, cameras jammed up to the windows melting Eugene in the heat and light of the flashes. Behind the lights was a babble of noise, a shouted dissonance broken by milliseconds of clarity: '. . . think . . . family . . . murders . . . know her . . .' Eugene prayed for the gates to open.

He hadn't seen the police uniforms but, eventually, they managed to push the heaving pack far enough aside to let the Puma wriggle through. Then the gates slammed shut behind him, and Eugene breathed again. Inside, all was silence. The Puma went forward at an even pace, halting just to the left of the house. Eugene could see Talus standing in the doorway.

'All right, Geno,' Talus said quietly. 'Ran the gauntlet, did you?'

Eugene nodded. 'Don't think they got my good side, y'know.'

Talus laughed. 'Hundreds of the cunts out there. Bedlam,

innit. Let's move – Archie wants a word before Gloria's dad gets here.'

They went straight through and found Archie standing by the French windows. It was early May and the garden was beginning to explode. Wisteria and festoons of yellow-gold roses chased along the trellises, whilst George's Afghan hounds – Lady and Tramp – were gallivanting across the pale-green velvet lawns. Archie turned as they came in. 'God knows why he bought those bloody things. Thickest animals I've ever come across. Untrainable. Stink when it's wet. He should have stuck to his guns.'

Archie shook his head, then motioned Eugene and Talus to sit down. 'Right, Geno. I want to run through everything you and Talus can tell me about Gloria and the man Carl. I want to get the full story before Al arrives. He knows most of it, but he doesn't need to hear it again, and he doesn't need details. Poor bastard's gone through enough.'

It turned out that Archie had spoken privately to DCI Gale the previous night. It was agreed that, in the afternoon, Gloria's father would do a press appeal for witnesses to come forward. Police were going to use CCTV footage of Gloria and Carl in the pub. They would also place the couple outside SweetHearts on the strength of Simone's Saturday-night sighting and credit the Camden witness as having probably seen Gloria with two men. They were setting up phone lines for anyone who might have seen anything suspicious in the area of Alexandra Palace. The police were also working with *Crimewatch*, who'd got a couple of Gloria and Carl lookalikes and were filming a reconstruction package to go out on Tuesday night with a major public appeal.

'Sounds like the coppers are doing their job,' Talus said.

'Yeah,' Archie said. 'It's a slick operation. Can't fault it.'

So far, Archie hadn't mentioned his brother, and the meeting seemed to be at an end. Archie was back at his post by the window, staring at the dogs, who were joyously engaged in digging up great clumps of herbaceous border. The lawn was now scattered with mud and the broken reeds of flag irises. Archie suddenly snapped out his mobile. 'Terry? Right. Get up here and get those fucking dogs out of my sight. Do it quick, before I shoot the stupid fuckers . . . Hang on, yeah. And don't let them near the fucking house in that state.' The phone clicked off.

Eugene and Talus exchanged glances. Eugene gave Talus a nod. Then he spoke up. 'How's George?' he said.

Archie turned away from the window. 'Terrible, Geno.'

Eugene shook his head. He decided the only way was to go straight for it. 'Does he know she flew back to London on Friday? Does he know about Carl?'

Archie closed his eyes momentarily and gave an oddly gentle smile. 'George doesn't know yet. I'm going up to tell him when Al arrives.'

There was a long moment of dead silence. 'The doctor's here?' Talus asked.

Archie nodded. Then the silence resumed and they waited. All three staring through the window at the exhilarated Afghans, now running full tilt in great sweeping circles and effortlessly dodging any attempt at capture by the pursuing security men.

'Glad to be out of that stinking club for a couple of hours,' said Lalibela. 'I don't know which is worse, day or night.'

Scudamour laughed. 'You're right there,' he said. 'The daytime makes you sad, the night makes you angry. And I'll tell you what really winds me up is idiots telling me how fucking lucky I am.'

'"Best job in the world,"' Lalibela chanted, adding, '"You don't mean to say they actually pay you to do that?"'

'Yeah,' said Scudamore. 'Not forgetting the never-heard-before lines about girls "assisting with inquiries" and, of course, the ever-popular "Do you get to take down their particulars then?" It drives you mad.'

297

'Yeah,' Lalibela agreed. 'And sometimes it makes me wonder about people, you know – these murders are all over the TV and papers: is everyone talking about the Meatman because they're shocked and horrified? Or maybe they're excited, titillated, turned on by the idea of all that sex and sadism. Would probably like a go themselves but don't have the balls to do it.'

By now they had reached the top of the stairs. The two of them filed into the operations room and took their seats alongside their murder-squad colleagues. Two minutes later, at exactly 12.30 p.m., DCI Gale arrived. As usual he was accompanied by his secretary carrying a stack of papers. 'Please ensure all my detectives have a copy of the praece document, constable, and then could you return with the illustrative material we prepared this morning,' Gale said.

'Yes, sir,' said the WPC, already moving swiftly and efficiently around the room. Seconds later, she had disappeared, returning with a much smaller stack of coloured photocopies, which DCI Gale indicated she should leave on the front desk.

'Thank you constable,' he said. 'That will be all.'

He then turned his attention to the room. 'Well, gentlemen, we have a great deal to ponder. The document before you has a number of short sections dealing with current progress on the murder investigations. You have five minutes to read through. As you will see, we are making concrete progress.' He paused. 'Detective Sergeant Scudamour and Lalibela have done particularly useful work; I would like your views on the statement of Ms Simone Burnside. We also have to discuss the need for protection, to ensure Ms Burnside's future safety. I am also looking for any comments regarding the *Crimewatch* appeal, and the press conference we are running this afternoon. It is now confirmed that Aldir Acrasiafi, father of the deceased, will read out an appeal for information.'

A minute or so later a detective raised his hand. 'Sir?'

'DS Grice, yes?' said Gale.

'Looking at the address, is this Simone Burnside connected to Geno B.?'

'She is his sister,' Gale said. There were a series of low whistles around the room. Somebody stifled a laugh.

'It's all getting a bit murky, isn't it, sir?' the detective continued. 'Geno B. and his lap-dancing sister, Acrasiafi, king of the bent legals, George Faron. All we need is a couple of Yardies and Reggie Kray and we'd have a full house.'

Gale waited for the scattered laughter to subside. 'What is your point, Grice?'

'Well, how far can we trust this bunch? The Simone Burnside statement, Acrasiafi and the Farons. How do we know they're not leading us by the nose?'

'I see,' said Gale. 'I should make the following entirely clear. We are working on the assumption that Gloria Faron is the fourth London victim of the two men we refer to as "the Meatman". Every single piece of evidence in our possession indicates this is the case. Secondly, I have studied Ms Burnside's statement and believe it to be important and valid. I should also say that I will not tolerate any lack of respect towards witnesses, and will take a very serious view of any behaviour running counter to this. Thirdly, until we catch our Meatmen and stop the cycle of torture, rape and murder currently terrorizing Londoners, everything else is immaterial. So far, the Farons have fully cooperated. Don't any of you dare to dream of undermining that cooperation. And, finally, to those who found DS Grice's remarks funny, I ask you to recall what you can of the postmortem results of previous victims. Gloria Faron suffered as much if not more. Her father and husband – whatever their faults – apparently loved her very much. Suffering is not solely the prerogative of the virtuous.'

DCI Gale looked round the room. 'I expect my officers to adhere to certain standards. Anyone unable to comply should see me this afternoon and request a transfer to a less demanding unit. Is that clear? Right, let's stop wasting time.'

It was a lengthy, exhausting, but ultimately productive meeting. It was agreed that tracking down the mysterious Carl was top of the agenda. Scudamour and Lalibela were to offer Simone a nightly escort home and to prioritize her safety within the club. The evidence against Mal Shifter was interesting but didn't amount to a great deal. DS Grice and DC Fradubio were assigned to interview Shifter and check his alibi.

'And finally,' DCI Gale announced. 'We have something of a breakthrough from forensics. They have done some excellent and important work. You will recall, gentlemen, the reports from scene of crime officers. Preliminary post-mortem reports have endorsed their initial findings. We can confirm that Mrs Faron had silicone breast enlargements. Both breasts were mutilated, and one silicone implant appears to be missing. The second was found still in place. I understand that a partial fingerprint has been recovered from the silicone.' Gale held up his hand as his men began to clap. 'There is more to say.'

He switched on the overhead lights illuminating the scene-of-crime pictures taken from Alexandra Palace garden centre and the subsequent postmortem shots. 'As you know, living skin does not hold fingerprints. But if a body is handled after death, prints may, very occasionally, be retained.' He used his pointer to mark a place below the nape of Gloria's neck and, passing to another frame, marked the left and right temples. Lastly, he pointed to the depression of her breastbone. 'The lab reckons there are possible prints in these locations. They think the sites on the head and neck originate with one of the killers holding the head steady whilst the other carefully removed the entire scalp and hair. They surmise that the marks on the breastbone come, similarly, from an attempt to steady the corpse whilst carrying out mutilations in the breast area.'

'That's fantastic news, sir,' said Scudamour. 'When do they expect a result?'

'They estimate a couple more days. They've already gone through the fumigation tent and saturation, plus the dusting-down. It's a case of waiting for the latex to fix now, so any prints can be lifted off. I don't have to tell you how failure-prone this process is, but the lab tells me it is hopeful.'

DCI Gale gave a rare smile. 'And that's not all, gentlemen. Our scientific colleagues have yet another breakthrough to offer us.' He picked up the colour-photocopied sheets and gave them to the nearest detective. 'Two sheets each. Pass them round quickly.

'As you know, we've been unable to identify the tools used to inflict many of the mutilations suffered by the victims. Each of the corpses carried a pattern of strange marks, cuts and indentations. Marks which appeared to have been made with a premeditated purpose in mind. Since the discovery of Stella Jane Hope's body, forensics have searched to identify the tools responsible.'

DCI Gale paused, looking down at his own copy of the colour illustrations. 'The list is not finite, gentlemen. There may be more, but the implements shown have all been positively matched to the victims: we have leather-shears, pinking shears, a thread-clipper and a rotary cutter. The sharp punching tool is an awl. Many of the peculiar diamond and triangular marks were made by small, sharp-pointed scissors, whilst the perforations are due to the use of a tracing-wheel. The two smaller tools you see on page two, in the bottom left corner, are, respectively, a seam-ripper and a stitch-ripper. The residue of markings and lines on the corpses comes from wax chalk, used by tailors to mark out patterns. All of the implements you see here are particular to tailoring, sewing or dressmaking.'

CHAPTER TWENTY-NINE

The messenger of so vnhappie newes
Would faine haue dyde: dead was his hart within,

FQ: The Legende of the Knight of the Red Crosse: I.vii.21

Gloria's dad rang to tell Archie he'd been delayed. He was faxing over a copy of the statement he was due to read out at the afternoon press conference. He told Archie he saw no problems with it, and to ring back if he had any worries. Otherwise, he'd be at the Halcyenda at 2.30 p.m. They could talk in the car on the way to Holloway police station. Archie said fine. He suggested that, instead of coming to the Halcyenda, Gloria's dad should wait up in the carpark of the Spaniard's Inn, just up the road. 'No point in trailing up to the house,' he said. 'It'll be quicker this way. Fine. See you then.' Archie turned to Eugene and Talus. 'Don't want to put the poor bastard through the ordeal of the gates,' he said. 'Press'll be all over him, and he's in no state to cope with it. Right.' Archie left his post by the window and headed across the room. 'I'm off to see George. Don't know how long it's going to take, but we should be leaving around two-fifteen. Yeah, that's about right. May as well take the Merc. So I'll see you here two-tenish.'

'Sweet,' said Talus. 'Think Geno and me'll head up the Spaniard's, get something to eat.'

'Good idea,' Archie replied. 'You've got the key for the back?' Talus nodded. 'Good, you can walk over and miss the vultures at the gates.'

'That's the plan,' Talus agreed. 'We'll see you back here at two-ten. OK, Geno?'

'Sweet with me,' Eugene replied.

The three men left the room together. Their footsteps echoed on the polished-parquet hallway which led to the front door. As they left the house, Talus turned back to Archie. 'Tell George my Sandra's written a letter for him.' He passed the envelope across to Archie. 'It's about her and Gloria and the holidays they had together.' Archie looked questioningly and Talus responded with a tight smile. 'Sandra's written about all the good times they had, and how much Gloria missed him. She's told him how Gloria used to talk about him all the time. Says anyone's entitled to one mistake, but he should remember it was him she loved.'

'Sandra's one of the best,' said Archie.

'I've always known it,' said Talus. 'OK, let's get going.'

Eugene and Talus walked across the stone terrace, through the laburnum pergola, and past the conservatory to the back of the house. A strange howling could be heard, steadily becoming louder – it seemed to come from the stable block. The sound was agonized, redolent with misery and loss. Motioning Eugene to follow, Talus followed his ears and tracked across the lawn, under the clock arch and into the stable yard. The cries had redoubled; Eugene found the noise traumatic. He wondered if George or Gloria's dad . . .

'It's those fuckin stupid dogs,' said Talus.

Lady and Tramp were tied up in the yard. Terry was supervising, whilst a group of his minions were busily engaged in washing the dogs. It was hard to say which party was the more miserable. The dogs were transformed into a mass of soapsuds, and were doing their level best to avoid the hosepipe-wielding security men. Terry's expression was murderous.

'OK, Tel. Doing a good job there,' said Talus.

Terry nodded. His suit was filthy. 'George wants to see the dogs,' he said. 'Archie said to get 'em cleaned up first. And dried. And brushed. It's a bastard.'

Talus and Eugene left them to it, the eerie howling gradually fading behind them.

It was a relief to hit the cheerful normality of the Spaniard's – the one-time residence of both the sixteenth-century Spanish ambassador and, subsequently, Dick Turpin – or so legend had it. Eugene and Talus ordered food, then took their drinks outside into the beer garden. They sat in a distant and secluded corner, heavily screened by vegetation. Being spotted by lunching journalists was not on the agenda.

When they were settled, Eugene asked Talus for a favour. He needed a trace on a couple of numbers, mobile and land line. Didn't Talus have a contact who specialized in this stuff? Talus did. Asked Eugene what he wanted, then rang it through. The bloke said he'd have it all sorted by 5 p.m. the next day. Eugene was well pleased.

The food arrived and looked good. Talus set off in search of ketchup, and Eugene took the opportunity to tap out a message at top speed. 'Y CNT WE TLK? I CN EXPLN + NT WHT U THNK. PLS RPLY. LOVE E x.' Brittany ignored his entreaty.

DS Grice and DC Fradubio had snatched a plastic canteen sandwich for lunch and were en route for Acre Row. Grice spent most of the journey complaining – he was fed up with DCI Gale, 'an arrogant uptight bastard', who, Grice felt, had no understanding of 'real' policing. Grice's anger had been further fuelled by the praise of Scudamour. DS Grice had his eye on promotion and was well aware that DS Scudamour had similar ambitions. As DC Fradubio drove towards Camden, Grice denounced Scudamour as an 'arse-licker', a 'crawler' and 'a college boy'. The last half-mile of the journey was spent rubbishing Simone Burnside – 'some gangland tart who drops her drawers for money' – and her 'bollocks' statement. Bloody Gale had sent the two of them on a wild goose chase.

Tommy Fradubio 'mmn'd' and 'yeah'd' in response to his sergeant. He'd found the Burnside girl's statement interesting and thought it well worth looking into. On the other hand, the DS had a point – she wasn't exactly great witness material, and you couldn't rule out an ulterior motive. He was keeping an open mind. It was no use contradicting a senior officer – which was worrying Fradubio, because he knew Grice had directly contravened the DCI's instructions.

DCI Gale had told them to go over to Camden and surprise Malcolm Shifter. Have a look around the house and get him to describe his whereabouts on the murder nights. But the minute they left the meeting, Grice had gone back to his office, got Shifter's number and put through a call. Shifter had agreed to meet them. Grice said they'd be round in an hour, 'Just for a chat – it's a routine inquiry, sir.'

Fradubio was shocked. He considered reporting DS Grice, but wasn't sure whether to or not. He was the youngest member of the unit, and the least experienced. Perhaps this sort of stuff went on all the time? But they'd just given a key suspect the equivalent of an hour's warning, and that couldn't be right. In the end, he tentatively raised the matter with Grice. The DS told him he was a 'silly twat'; he – Grice – wasn't going to waste all afternoon sitting in a bloody car waiting for the guy to turn up – the man might be anywhere. Fuck that. Now, they knew the man would be in, and waiting, and they could get the job done in double-quick time. 'Which,' Grice said, 'means we can spend the rest of the afternoon working on something important, instead of this load of toss.'

And, afterwards, as they drove back to headquarters,

Grice felt vindicated. Shifter had been helpful and co-operative. And the alibis were rock solid – the two . . . aunts? . . . he'd have to check that, but 'elderly relatives' would do, confirmed everything the man told them. Said how guilty they felt about the situation. Their illness and infirmity meant they couldn't really be left alone. Malcolm, they said, was their full-time carer. He was marvellous but he had so little life of his own, well, it wasn't fair. But he wouldn't hear of paid help – said you read so many horror stories about what can happen.

Grice was satisfied. All done and dusted in under forty minutes. So much for Scudamour's breakthrough.

Tommy Fradubio didn't share Grice's satisfaction. Something about the man Shifter had made him uneasy. He found the two old ladies unconvincing, stagey somehow, as if they'd over-rehearsed their lines. And the dogs which snuffled and scratched behind a door in the hallway. It was odd, Fradubio thought afterwards. The road, the house, the old women, Shifter himself – everything seemed, well, diseased. He wondered if he should speak to DCI Gale. He couldn't make his mind up. He decided to sleep on it.

Eugene and Talus got back to the house slightly early. They hung round awkwardly in the hallway, not quite knowing where to put themselves, each harbouring an unspoken dread of running into George. There was absolute silence in the house – a heavy blanket of stillness, oppressive and stifling, which Eugene felt settling over him as he waited.

The sound of footsteps announced Archie's arrival. He came slowly down the stairs, his face expressionless. They followed him as he walked past them and out of the door.

'I'll drive,' Talus said. Archie nodded, and they sat, once more unspeaking, as the Mercedes glided down the drive-way, out of the gates and through the swarm of press and media waiting outside. Al Acrasiafi was waiting by the entrance to the Spaniard's carpark. Talus swung the Merc around and began the short journey to Holloway police station.

The press conference was absolutely packed. There was a raised podium, backed by a blue screen carrying the insignia of the Metropolitan Police. In front of the screens was a table covered by a blue cloth. On the table, a carafe of water, three glasses, pens and paper. DCI Arthur Gale sat on the right, the Met Police Commissioner on the left. Between them, his grey suit draped over him like a shroud, was the gaunt, shrunken figure of Al Acrasiafi.

Eugene, Talus and Archie stood at the back of the room. Whilst Gale and the Commissioner were talking, Eugene looked around the room. At the front were the TV cameras and press photographers, behind them serried ranks of journalists, around the walls a number of police, standing with wary eyes and arms crossed. Then something caught Eugene's eye. Someone had waved at him, a discreetly raised hand and half-smile, the gesture in keeping with the circumstances. Eugene looked across and returned the wave – it was Angie's brother, Migsy, and standing next to him was tall, blond Martin. Eugene wondered why they had come, but then he thought he could understand it. The desire to act, to do something, anything, however painful or mundane. Because, otherwise, you gave yourself up to grief. Stumbling through, your life defined by misery and inertia. That's why bereaved parents were forever setting up campaigns, establishing charities, lobbying for this or that change in the law, he thought. It gave them an escape route, allowed them to run away from the anguish patiently waiting in the shadows.

Al Acrasiafi was the last to speak, standing under the glare of camera lights, reading from his prepared statement. He kept it short. Eugene could see the effort it cost him. The man had to stop a couple of times to avoid breaking down. He spoke personally. Gloria had been his only child. 'Idolized' by her parents. And after her mother died Gloria was 'the centre of my life'. He asked the public to search their memories, to look at the police photos, to watch tomorrow's *Crimewatch* reconstruction. If they had seen anything, anything at all, they should ring the police immediately. 'Somebody has suspicions,' Mr Acrasiafi said. 'Somebody has seen the killer of my daughter and all the other poor girls. I'm begging you, please contact the police.'

As the press conference ended, the pack surged forward, and the three men on the podium disappeared beneath a mass of journalists. Talus went off to look after Gloria's dad, and Eugene took the opportunity to say hello to Migsy and Martin.

They told him DCI Gale had notified the family of Gloria's death, and then rung them to tell them about the press conference. Migsy's mum, Maria, was still confined to bed and showing little, if any, sign of recovery. 'It's hit her very hard,' Migsy said. 'Dad's not much better. He's raging the whole time. Looking for someone to blame, someone to punish.' Migsy told Eugene he thought his dad would only start to recover when someone had been arrested. When there was a named, tangible culprit to focus his fury upon. 'He keeps going on and on about life back home,' Migsy said, shaking his head. 'Saying how if this had happened back in Medellin, he could have sorted it. He'd have got hold of Tio Diego, Tio José, and God knows which cousins, gone round mob-handed and carved the bastard who hurt Angie into a hundred pieces.' Migsy shrugged and looked at Eugene. 'You know how it is, Geno – he's talking shit to make himself feel better. To feel like a man again. Me and Martin have tried to get through to him. Told him he'd be better off looking after Mum and helping the police. But he prefers to go drinking down the Unicornio with his Medellin mates, hatching mad plans of revenge against the Meatman. It's fuckin hopeless.'

'I'm sorry, man,' Eugene said. 'I know everyone says it,

but if there is anything I can help with, just give us a bell, yeah?'

'That's appreciated, Eugene. Thanks, man. But your family's been fantastic, from the first. Your mum and Moira Hayley are round every day, man. Cooking, cleaning, looking after Mum. They've been brilliant. We're dead grateful, aren't we?'

The question was addressed to Martin, who nodded in agreement. Eugene asked him how he was doing? 'Bearing up,' Martin half-smiled in response. 'Glad we came today,' he added. 'Me and Migsy and the brothers, we're just trying our best to get the bastard caught. Thought we should come along and listen, see if it triggered anything, you know, little forgotten details. It's a long shot, but you never know. Poor, poor woman,' he said suddenly, and then turned to Eugene. 'You know the family, don't you?' Eugene nodded. 'Where's the husband?'

'He's not here, Martin,' Eugene explained. 'He loved her to bits. Absolutely adored her. He's under the doctor, back at the house. I'm not sure he's going to get through this. His wife was his whole world . . .' Eugene paused, struck by what he'd just said. Possessed by an odd compulsion to speak the exact truth, a pointless desire to be precise. 'What I mean is, she was the best part of his world. He called her his queen. Sounds stupid, but when you have someone special, well, it's not stupid, is it?'

Martin shook his head. 'It's not stupid at all,' he said quietly. 'You know, Angela thought I was special. She used to joke about all the girls at work being jealous of her, called me her knight in shining armour, and, yeah, it does sound stupid when you say it out loud, in the daylight, in ordinary talk. But it wasn't stupid when she said it to me. In bed, or at night watching telly together, sitting next to her on the sofa, her legs over mine, head on my shoulder.' Martin's blue eyes were bright, but the tears didn't spill over, and the voice stayed firm.

'If you get the chance,' he said, 'tell George Faron I understand. I lost my queen, too. I wanted to go out and do great things for her, you know that?' Eugene nodded. 'I was so fuckin proud of her. And I knew she was proud of me, and that gave me the strength, the will to do just about anything.' He stopped and looked away for a moment. 'She was the kindest person I've ever met, Eugene.' He laughed, a short caustic cough of laughter. 'Killed by kindness, that was Angela. We'd got enough money for the deposit on the house. The wedding was half paid for and would have been OK. But her mum and dad were so chuffed about it all – and so was she, to be fair. They wanted the aunts and uncles and cousins over for the wedding. I suppose they wanted to show off, to say "Look, we've done all right over here." And that's not wrong. Not a sin, is it? I hated her doing the Sweet-Hearts stuff, hated her doing the parties, and every bloody penny she earned from it went into the pot. She used to make a joke, "Working for the AFF", she'd say – the Air Fare Fund – to pay for the relatives' tickets over. So they could come to the wedding.'

Martin took a deep breath. 'I didn't like it. But I reckoned it was her decision. Used to joke about it with her. "You know your AFF-ing relatives won't be using their return tickets," I'd say. "They'll be staying put," told her Wentworth Road would soon be known as "Little Medellin". She said "no chance", that she'd personally hire a minibus and ship them back to Heathrow.' Martin smiled wryly. 'Well, luckily, the AFF won't be wasted. The relatives have all been in touch, clamouring for their tickets to come over for the funeral – when the body's finally released and we have a date. "Life goes on" – as they say.'

Eugene could only say what everyone repeats on such occasions, commiserations, offers of help – inadequate but heartfelt attempts to reach out to those marooned by grief.

Just before saying goodbye, Eugene asked Martin about his ring. It had caught his eye when he first went over, and he was sure he'd seen it somewhere before. Martin wore it on his wedding-ring finger – a gold band with a large heart-shaped ruby in a claw setting, topped by a blaze of small yellow diamonds and topaz.

Martin told Eugene the ring was a copy of the engagement ring he had made for Angie, which was stolen when she was murdered. He took it off and handed it to Eugene. 'It's meant to signify a heart in flames,' Martin said. 'It's supposed to be a symbol of extreme passion. I had another made.'

'It's beautiful,' Eugene said truthfully. 'What does this say inside – the engraving?'

Martin took the ring back. 'Amor vincit omnia,' he said. 'Love conquers all.'

CHAPTER THIRTY

And is there care in heauen? and is there loue
In heauenly spirits to these creatures bace,
That may compassion of their euils moue?
There is: else much more wretched were the cace
Of men, then beasts.

FQ: The Legend of Sir Gvyon: II.viii.i

Talus and Eugene took a minicab back to the Halcyenda.
Archie was taking the Merc home to Finchley and
dropping Al Acrasiafi back at his house en route. Talus said
taking a cab was no bother. Best for Archie to take care of
the old man who – as Talus pointed out – was looking
seriously shaky. Eugene concurred. Gloria's dad was in an
awful state, grey-faced and tremulous. The sooner he got
back home, the better.

And, anyhow, it was only a fifteen-minute journey.
They got the minicab to drop them off by the back gate,
which Talus locked shut before the two of them cut
across the perfect velvet of the lawns and headed back to
the house. As they walked, Talus raised the question of
Shifter. What did Eugene think? He knew Shifter pretty well
– what was his take on this business of Shifter hanging
round with Carl? Did Eugene seriously reckon that Mal

Shifter might be involved with the Meatman?

Eugene said he was far from happy with Shifter. Simone's testimony could be relied on absolutely – which proved nothing but undeniably suggested that Shifter knew Carl and that the two of them were close. Added to which, Shifter seemed to have been loosely involved – hovering in the background – having something to do – with all of the murder victims. Eugene suggested giving Omar a ring. Omar – the unfortunate Somalian guy who'd taken over as the Firm's link with Shifter – might have something useful to tell them. Talus said that he'd do it tonight. He was minded to agree with Eugene: Shifter's involvement merited further investigation.

'I'll talk to Omar, and I'll have a word with Archie,' Talus said. 'Then you and I can meet up and talk it through. Look, my bloke's coming back with that phone stuff for you tomorrow afternoon, yeah? So why don't I bell you once I've got the necessary? I'll gee him up a bit – with a bit of luck should be in touch around threeish.'

'That'll do me,' Eugene agreed. 'And thanks for sorting the numbers. I owe you one.'

'Forget it, Geno. Every good boy deserves a favour, or so they tell me.'

Talus smiled, showing sharp white teeth. 'OK, here's my motor. Catch you tomorrow.' Talus waved and headed off to his car. Eugene shouted his thanks and waved back, then he turned his attention to the Puma. Being left behind, while Eugene disappeared in the Mercedes, had obviously gone down badly. The Puma sidled and fretted the whole way home, spooking at shadows and acting the fool. Eugene was grateful to get back to number forty in one piece.

Simone was the only person at home. Gladys and Moira were doing the weekly shop for the Caridads, after which they'd be staying on to cook a family meal. Simone said their mum was expected back around ninish. She'd left a casserole and a pan of rice, and salad in the fridge. Eugene smiled – his mother was a star, no denying it. Simone also told him there was an hour-long documentary about a Pakistani serial killer at nine-thirty, which looked pretty hot. She'd sort the food, and they could eat whilst they watched the prog.

'Sounds good to me,' Eugene said. 'I'm off for a shower.'

'That's fine, bro. Get yourself down here and ready to eat by, say, nine-fifteen?'

'I'll be there,' said Eugene, and headed for the stairs. Before he hit the shower, he took a minute in his room. Making sure the door was firmly shut, he sat on the bed and called Brittany. She was still refusing all his calls. As soon as his number came up, she hit the 'straight to answerphone' key. Any 'number withheld' tricks got exactly the same treatment. Eugene was desperate to speak to her; he knew that, if only he could get to see her again, then he could explain that night at Amazon Zone. He could tell her about Lucy, tell her the truth. And, hopefully, he could show her that he wasn't the sort of shag-'em-and-run mega-bastard that her bitch of a friend had made him out to be.

He had snagged Simone's mobile from the kitchen table. Brittany wouldn't recognize the number and, hopefully, she would answer. Afterwards he would drop Simone's phone back in the kitchen and she'd be none the wiser. That was the theory.

Reality proved to be a major disappointment. Brittany did answer, but the moment she realized it was Eugene, she put the phone down. Eugene had deleted Brittany's number and was heading downstairs to replace the phone, when he ran straight into Simone, who told him she'd spent the last ten minutes searching for her mobile. Taking the phone out of his hand, she asked what the hell he was doing borrowing her belongings without permission? What was

314

wrong with his own phone? Had he gone mad? Eugene mumbled incoherent apologies whilst Simone shook her head and suggested he grow up.

When Eugene came out of the shower, Simone was on the phone herself. 'You've got my numbers,' she was saying. 'Right – yeah, I see what you mean. Well, either way. OK. Could I just say goodnight to him? Right, well, can you take the phone upstairs, then, please? I'm sorry 'bout that, but it was agreed this was a temporary measure because of the murders and so on. I need to keep a connection with my son. No, no, it won't take a minute, I've explained, I want to say goodnight. No, he's not asleep. I could hear his voice when I rang. Look, I don't want to argue about this. Right, thank you. I'll hold.'

Eugene raised his eyebrows and Simone rolled her eyes in return and silently mouthed 'wankers'. Seconds later, her whole face brightened. 'Hi best-boy. How are you, are you OK? Mummy's missing you so much . . . so what have you been doing, eh? . . .' Eugene left his sister to it and went in to watch TV. A few minutes later she joined him.

'What was that all about, then?' Eugene asked.

'I'm getting straight on to social services tomorrow,' Simone said furiously. 'That was Mr Fuckin Redmayne. I mean, what's his problem, trying to stop me speaking to my son? What's he trying to do? Tells me' – Simone put on a sanctimonious voice – '"Nero's probably asleep by now." Well, no, he isn't, mister, cos I can hear him clear as day in the room behind you. Him and his wife need to remember what's going on here. This is temporary care. I'm the boy's mother, right? Once they catch the Meatman, things will be getting back to normal, and their role will be finished. I'm not putting up with being messed about, no kidding, Eugene.'

'So, never mind the fuckwit foster-folk,' Eugene interrupted. 'How's the boy?'

Simone smiled. 'He sounded good. Said he missed home and wants to come back. Sounded like these Redmayne people are a bit too strict. But he was fine. You know, Eugene, I really miss him.'

Eugene nodded noncommittally. His sister seemed to have forgotten why Nero went in the first place. It was fair to say that Eugene and Gladys had no desire at all to see the return of the small vampire-in-the-making to Wentworth Road.

Brother and sister settled down to eat in front of the TV. They watched the story of Javed Iqbal, son of a wealthy businessman in Lahore. Iqbal was also a paedophile rapist who, predictably, turned to murder. He gave himself up in 1999, having killed an estimated 140 runaway street-boys aged between eight and sixteen years of age. He put the bodies in plastic containers filled with acid and poured the subsequent sludge into the town sewers. Eugene and Simone watched in disbelief as the story unfolded. Iqbal had taken Polaroid snaps of his victims, kept their clothes and written about them in his diaries. Which was fortunate in terms of identification – because not one of the 140 children had been reported missing.

On Tuesday, Talus rang just after 2.30 p.m. to say he'd got the info Eugene wanted. He suggested meeting in the King's Head for three, if Eugene could make it. Eugene said he'd be there. Luckily, the Puma had calmed down and threw no more fits of temperament, striding smoothly down the Holloway Road and the Cally before halting in the King's carpark. The pub, as usual, appeared totally closed, but when Eugene rang the bell, Vinnie opened the door and motioned him to the corner where Talus was sitting. He got Eugene his usual bottle of beer before disappearing. 'Is he OK?' Eugene asked. 'He looks terrible. Is he ill or some-thing?'

Talus shook his head. 'He's not too good. Vinnie worships

George, spoilt him rotten as a kid – George was the apple of his eye. Now, he's worried sick about him.' Talus paused and looked across the empty bar, then continued. 'It'll be all right, George'll pull through it. But it's going to take time, plenty of time. Archie says the doctor's still at the house. Every time the pills start wearing off, George tries to fly after Carl. Archie's had to make sure someone's keeping an eye on him, twenty-four seven. Sometimes he's dead quiet, or he spends an hour or more looking at pictures of Gloria, just crying. But then, with no warning, he just goes off on one. Screaming and shouting and crashing about. Losing her has crucified him. He can't bear it, but he hasn't got any bloody choice, has he? He'll have to bear it, somehow.'

'Anyway,' Talus said, signifying a change of subject, 'here's the info you wanted. Check it through – I think it's all there.'

Eugene scanned the sheets of printed A4. Exactly what he'd hoped for. 'Sweet as a nut. Brilliant. Thanks.'

'No worries,' said Talus. 'Now, about our weirdo friend, Malcolm.'

'Yeah,' said Eugene. 'So what's your thinking?'

It turned out that Talus had done his homework. He'd got a tame copper to pull Shifter's file, which had some unpleasant material recorded in it. Questioned regarding the rape and murder of a nineteen-year-old prostitute in Liverpool. Discounted due to strong alibi. Case unsolved. Arrested in connection with apparent drug overdose of Kelly Winter of St Helens, Lancashire. The body of fourteen-year-old Kelly had been found in a multi-storey carpark. She appeared to have been sexually assaulted after death. A known drug-user, her death had not initially been regarded as suspicious until forensics came back. The girl had been the victim of vicious anal and vaginal penetration with some sort of object – speculation it may have been a wine bottle. She had a massive amount of high-grade heroin in her system, far superior in quality to the drug sold on St Helens' streets. Shifter had been seen with the girl on the night of her death and was named by other prostitutes as their regular drug-supplier. He had refused to answer questions and, with no real evidence, police were eventually forced to release him. His most recent brush with the law had taken place nearly eight years ago. He had been living in Stockport, Manchester, sharing a flat with a black guy known only by his street name of Iceman. The two men were both questioned informally in connection with suspected drug-dealing. Once again, nothing came of it. Shortly afterwards, Shifter was believed to have left the North-West, which, Talus said, would more or less tally, as the Firm had been doing business with him for around six years or so.

'Jesus,' Eugene whistled. 'Not one you'd take home to meet the family, by the sounds.'

'Nasty little fucker, isn't he?' agreed Talus. 'I'm willing to look on the bright side . . . you know, innocent until proven . . . and all that, but our Malcolm's cv is throwing up more shit than your local sewage plant. Plus, the mystery black guy—'

'Yeah, what a coincidence. And what about Omar?' Eugene asked. 'Did he have anything useful?'

'So-so,' Talus replied. 'Went on about the two old bats and the dogs. He was terrified of the dogs.'

'Can't say as I blame him,' Eugene said, his memories of Hopeless, Faithless and Loveless still vivid.

'Only thing he did say was that one of the old girls told him about a million times how he wasn't anything like as much fun as "the other one". Apparently, she was talking about another black guy. The old dear went on and on about how fuckin marvellous he was, so handsome, so charming, how much she enjoyed his visits. Omar thought it was you.' Talus laughed. 'He thought you might still be dropping round or something.'

'Is he mad?' Eugene said. 'Dropping round there for a fuckin social call – what? I don't think so.'

'Exactly,' Talus continued. 'Could Mr-Charming-the-Grannies'-Darling be our mate Carl is what I wonder?'

They talked it through for twenty minutes or so and finally came to an agreement. Eugene was going to drop round on Shifter, unannounced, on Wednesday night. Anything linking Shifter to the Firm would be removed, by force, if necessary. Really, there was only one thing bothering them – the Firm had lent Shifter a state-of-the-art, highly expensive set of ultrasensitive pharmaceutical scales. It wasn't the money – the scales could be replaced – it was the certainty that fingerprints belonging to George, Archie, Talus and Eugene, plus a few lesser mortals, could most probably be pulled off the equipment. Fingerprints that could lead to a twelve-year-plus stretch for importation and dealing of a class A drug. That had to be sorted. Eugene told Talus he'd be in touch the minute he got out of the place.

'That's sound. OK, but just hang on a minute before you split,' Talus asked, punching a number into his mobile as he spoke. Five minutes later, a car pulled up outside and someone knocked at the door. 'S'OK, Vinnie,' Talus shouted, 'I'll get it.' It was one of the boys, carrying a padded envelope. 'Here you go, boss,' he said, and handed it over. The next minute Eugene and Talus were alone again. Talus slid a Glock with a silencer out of the bag. 'Take it with you, Geno. It's clean. Use it if you have to. No one will hear a thing.'

Eugene examined the gun, checked the safety-catch and slid it back inside its envelope.

He nodded. 'I'll stay cool. But if he wants to take me on, well, I shan't be shy.'

Shortly after, the two men went their separate ways. Eugene headed back to Wentworth Road. He had a full night ahead of him, and a lot on his mind. Not least of which was tomorrow's confrontation with Shifter. He wanted to go to Shifter's house for one last time. He hadn't told Talus, but there was something nagging at the corner of his mind, something connected to the house. It was important, but he couldn't quite get it, and like a name almost remembered, it was driving him mad. He would go back tomorrow and have a last stab at recognizing it – whatever it was.

CHAPTER THIRTY-ONE

Said *Guyon*, See the mind of beastly man,
That hath so soone forgot the excellence
Of his creation, when he life began,
That now he chooseth, with vile difference,
To be a beast, and lacke intelligence.

FQ: The Legend of Sir Gvyon: II.xii.87

Simone left for work early on Tuesday. In the middle of all the murder and mayhem, rehearsals for Harem Nights were still in progress. Mr Barry was understandably worried. Everyone involved in the production wanted out: the dancers, in particular, had lost their sparkle. The last runthrough had been a disaster. 'The show is supposed to transport you to the sensuous heat of the Turkish seraglio,' Mr Barry told the performers. 'You lot transported me straight to a psychiatric daycare centre. You're meant to exude sexual promise. I've seen more promise outside the bingo hall. Suki – you've got to stop that shaky, trembly stuff. Take some fucking beta-blockers or something. Cleo, whatever you're taking, stop it. You're half asleep, girl – that's not dancing, that's bloody sleepwalking. And Canday – that business with your eyes makes you look like a mental case. Pack it in. As for the rest of you, you were all crap as well. Come on. Put a bit of bloody effort in.'

Mr Barry had little hope of this week's runthrough being any better. Both he and the Farons were happy to pull the show, but it wasn't that easy. Lucrative contracts had been signed – there was a five-page photo-shoot for a glossy lads' mag, plus a promo competition offering readers the chance to win an all-expenses-paid trip to watch the show. Then there was an interesting and hugely profitable deal with a Turkish-based syndicate who planned to market a Harem Nights photo calendar throughout the Middle East. Mr Barry had been intrigued by that one – he had a vague idea it was against their religion or something. And, last but not least, an Anglo-American cable company were going to film the entire show to broadcast on 'adult' TV channels.

In the current circumstances, the Farons were prepared to forfeit the likely financial bonanza from Harem Nights. Unfortunately, their various business partners felt very differently. For them, the Meatman was a stroke of luck. The likely profitability of their various endeavours had gone through the roof. The Turkish calendar kings had even enquired about using the victims – were there any publicity photos of Stella Hope? Topless would do, nude would be much preferred. Mr Barry had gone ballistic. He told Mae afterwards that he'd felt like sending the Turkish twats one of the postmortem pictures – 'make them realize what we're dealing with,' he'd said, adding that he hadn't gone through with it. 'I realized they'd probably be grateful – put it in the fucking calendar, wouldn't they?'

The Farons' lawyers were picking through the various contracts for get-out clauses but, for the present, the dreary business of Harem Nights had to go on. Simone, in the starring role, hated it as much as anyone but, like everyone else, had little choice but to continue plodding through.

Eugene waved his sister off to work and made her promise

to get a police lift home. He and Gladys watched the *Crimewatch* special and taped it for Simone. He and his mum agreed that the black actor looked nothing like Carl – although, as his mum had seen Carl only twice, both times on the street, and that over seven years ago, Eugene wasn't sure she was qualified to pass an opinion. Gloria, Eugene thought, was spot on. He wondered if George was watching. From the back, especially, the actress was almost indistinguishable from his dead wife. What was it like to watch this, to see her walking down North London streets with 'Carl's' arm around her. Eugene hoped Archie had been able to keep his brother away from the TV.

The bits with the lookalike Shifter made him almost snort with laughter. Gladys was disapproving. 'It's not a comedy, son, the girl's dead. What's funny about that?' Eugene had quickly pulled himself together and apologized. His mother was right, of course, but if Shifter was watching, he was not going to be a happy man. Eugene didn't know where the police had got their description – but it had certainly done Mal Shifter no favours. True enough, Shifter was a weirdo, but this made him look like everyone's idea of a child molester. And the actor playing him had obviously been out of work too long – he went at the role with undisguised relish, sidling crookedly down the street, leering and ogling, talking to the Carl character in a sinister sideways mutter. Eugene thought, any minute now, he'd burst into a verse of 'Gotta Pick a Pocket or Two'.

Back in the studio, Nick Ross spoke earnestly to camera. Eugene wondered if the public appeal would do any good or simply tie up hours of police time, answering calls from attention-seekers, nutters and helpful souls who 'might have seen something'. Who knows? It was time for him to move. He said goodbye to his mum and headed out.

It took less than five minutes for the Puma to reach Crouch End. Eugene looked up at the flat and saw the lights were on. Belinda was in. He left the Puma safe and walked up to the front door – he hoped she was alone.

When Belinda answered the door her face was a picture. Eugene kept his own expression carefully neutral. 'Hi Belinda, how you doing?' he said. 'Can I come in please? It's important.'

Belinda looked like she wanted to say no but was too stunned to think how to do it. Eugene followed her into the front room. Belinda switched off the TV and turned around. 'Why have you come here and what do you want?' she asked, hostility and aggression evident in every word.

'I want to talk to you, and it's going to take time. All I'm asking is that you hear me out – just listen to me. I wouldn't be here unless I needed to be. And, before you ask, Ralph has no idea I've come to see you.' He paused, looking meaningfully across the room at Belinda's half-full glass of red wine. 'Any chance of me joining you in a drink before we get started?' he asked.

Belinda nodded and poured him a glass of wine. 'This had better be worth listening to, is all I'm saying.'

Eugene pulled out his pieces of paper and began to talk. 'You and me need to do some growing up . . .' he began.

At police headquarters, DCI Gale and his squad prepared for the onslaught as the *Crimewatch* programme ended. Almost the second the credits rolled, the phones began to ring. The reconstruction had gone well. Gale thought the lookalikes convincing enough to jog the memory, although the idiot who was supposed to be Shifter seemed to think he was playing panto. But the trouble was, most people around the pub and club areas of North London at that time on a Saturday night were – to put it kindly – not at their most observant or reliable. The murder squad were resigned to wading through hundreds of well-intentioned time-wasters on the off chance of the one call that threw up the vital link or key witness.

On the other side of the room, DC Tommy Fradubio was on duty, checking through the calls deemed of possible importance. He felt increasingly uneasy. That morning, DCI Gale had handed out copies of Mal Shifter's previous form. It didn't make happy reading. The litany of sexual violence and alleged drug-dealing had really worried Fradubio. He'd gone back – had checked over the Burnside girl's statement again. Gone through it meticulously, line by line. It didn't look like 'rubbish' to him – on the contrary, everything Simone Burnside said appeared more and more believable.

But he was DS Grice's junior partner. And he knew that Grice had already filed a report of the visit to Shifter – Grice had given it to him, told him to put it on Gale's desk. He had obeyed, although he had felt, as one of two officers present, Grice should have consulted him, or at very least given him the chance to read the report before handing it in.

Throughout the day the feelings of guilt and unease steadily increased until Tommy Fradubio decided he had to say something. He didn't want to be a 'grass', didn't want to drop Grice in it. But he kept asking himself how he would feel when the next girl died. And it *was* 'when' not 'if' – until they caught them. He was off duty in half an hour, p'raps then would be—

'What's up? Guilty conscience?' DS Grice's hand on his shoulder caused Fradubio almost to jump off his chair. 'Gaffer's told us to get off home. Says there's plenty of uniforms here to hold the phones, and tomorrow could be a long day.'

Fradubio forced a smile. 'Brilliant. Need the sleep.' He looked across the room. Gale was over the far side, deep in conversation. He would just have to leave it till tomorrow to speak to the boss. He would definitely do it then. Anyway, another night wouldn't hurt.

At SweetHearts, Scudamour and Lalibela were back on duty, up in their customary lookout eyrie, viewing the scene below with some surprise.

'It's bloody Tuesday night. Look at the ghouls.' Scudamour pointed below. Every table was taken. The club was thronging. It couldn't be denied – the Meatman was certainly pulling them in.

'They can't get enough of it, can they?' Lalibela said. 'It's a turn-on, a real novelty. Just think of the thrill – the girl stripping in front of you tonight could end up on the Meatman's block tomorrow. Gives them a hard-on just thinking about it.'

'You're right.' Scudamour scanned the floor with disgust. 'You can see it in their faces. Wondering which one will be next to cop it.' He turned to his junior officer. 'We don't have to be like that, do we? Like slavering animals, waiting to devour the next piece of meat.'

'No sir.' Lalibela spoke quietly. 'We can fly with the angels or root with the pigs. It's our choice. Flying is harder to do, but that would be my aspiration; I have no wish to spend my life grubbing in the mud.'

At that moment, the door opened and Mr Barry appeared. The manager looked harassed and unhappy.

'Look at 'em,' he said. 'Bleeding vultures. Two hundred and thirty percent increase on our normal door tally. Tuesday night should be bloody empty. Not any longer. Bloody great sales gimmick, eh, getting a few girls butchered. And we're pulling a fortune over the bar and with the dancers. Dirty bastards.'

Scudamour and Lalibela swapped glances. 'We were just saying the same thing,' said Scudamour.

'Yeah, well. Shouldn't turn down the custom, but . . .' The manager shrugged '. . . well, nuff said. Sorry to disturb you, gents, but we've had a change of policy. We've taken on a taxi firm, drivers all licensed and vetted, police-checked – all that bollocks. From tonight, all the girls will be driven home. That OK?'

'It sounds excellent,' said Scudamour. 'But I do have specific instructions regarding Simone Burnside . . .'

'No bother,' said Mr Barry. 'I'll send a message to Simone that she's coming home with you.'

Mr Barry left. DC Lalibela looked across at his boss but said nothing.

Belinda couldn't take it in at first, what Eugene was telling her. She looked repeatedly at the itemized phone bills, incredulous and nonplussed. She ran her finger down the columns, stopping at the entries that Eugene had marked up and highlighted. She went off and came back with her diary and her own phone bills, tallied up the dates and times and saw that they matched. Then – with some embarrassment – she pulled a crumpled piece of paper from the zip section of her purse.

'That the number you found on Ralph's desk?' Eugene asked.

Belinda nodded. 'I rang it. A woman answered, with a really squeaky, breathy voice. "Hi! Is that you . . . ?" I thought she was expecting Ralph on the line because I used the office number. She wouldn't tell me her name. It was just about the last straw.'

Belinda checked the scrap of paper against Eugene's bill sheets. It was a mobile-phone number, issued just six months previously to a Ms Rhoda Gunne. In that entire period, only a handful of calls had been made on it – all of them to Belinda and Ralph's numbers. And only one call had been received – the call from Belinda herself.

Belinda poured more wine for the two of them, then went through the whole thing again, making her own notes, checking and rechecking, collating times and numbers and dates. It was pointless, because the whole thing was screamingly obvious. But Belinda felt compelled to keep studying the neat lines of numbers which offered stark, incontrovertible evidence that her best friend deliberately set out to wreck her marriage.

She couldn't believe her own gullibility. 'As if I wanted him to be guilty,' she said. 'Was just waiting for the inevitable betrayal to happen.'

They talked for over an hour before Eugene checked the time and said he had to go. He got up and walked across to Belinda. 'Here,' he said, passing his mobile over. 'Let's start sorting out this mess.'

Ralph was at his parents' house when his phone rang. Two minutes later, he was out the door and heading home.

Back at SweetHearts, Mr Barry had been doing some serious thinking. He'd been quite impressed by the swash-buckling young copper – 'specific instructions regarding Simone Burnside'. Oh yeah? Specific instructions my bum, thought Mr Barry. But the boy had class; it was a smart move.

Mr Barry stared out of his office window, lost in thought for two or three minutes. Then he made his mind up. 'Who dares wins,' he said to himself, and headed downstairs on his mission. He found Mae checking till receipts on reception and asked her for a word. Mae, of course, already knew about the new business with the taxis – she had organized it, in the main. She also knew that Tuesday was early closing night. Mr Barry took a deep breath and asked Mae if she'd share his taxi. 'Back to your place?' she asked. Mae instructed one of the reception girls to cancel her cab. Winked at Mr Barry and said she'd see him later. The reception girls exchanged amazed looks.

Mr Barry ascended the stairs with a macho swagger. He couldn't believe he'd had the balls to do it. Couldn't believe she'd said yes – just like that, happy for everyone to know it. Mr Barry's shoulder swing became way over the top – 'Who dares wins,' he said to himself once more, and then began whistling 'Lady in Red' .

Scudamour and Lalibela watched the manager's progress with astonishment.

'Something's made him happy,' said Lalibela.

'You're not kidding,' Scudamour agreed.

Both Eugene and Gladys were in bed when Simone came home from work in the early hours of Wednesday morning. If either of them had been up, they would have noticed immediately that something out of the ordinary was going on. Simone didn't so much walk as float into the house, her beautiful face vivid with happiness and excitement.

CHAPTER THIRTY-TWO

All in a canuas thin he was bedight,
And girded with a belt of twisted brake,
Vpon his head he wore an Helmet light,
Made of a dead mans skull, that seem'd a ghastly sight.

Maleger was his name, and after him,
There follow'd fast at hand two wicked Hags,
With hoarie lockes all loose, and visage grim;
Their feet vnshod, their bodies wrapt in rags,
And both as swift on foot, as chased Stags;
And yet the one her other legge had lame,
Which with a staffe, all full of litle snags
She did support, and *Impotence* her name:
But th'other was *Impatience*, arm'd with raging flame.

FQ: The Legend of Sir Gvyon; Maleger and Hags:
II.xi.22, 23

B rittany was home by 7.30 p.m. The late-May evening was filled with a soft, gold-green light, filtering through the trees, which were now in full leaf. She should have enjoyed the ten-minute walk from the bus stop, eyeing the shop windows on Crouch End Broadway, before turning right up the hill and along streets shaded by lines of lime, cherry and ash. But Brittany wasn't currently enjoying anything very much.

Less than a week ago and you'd have found her constantly touching wood, thanking God for her blessings, almost nervous of the euphoria she felt. Superstitious that this perfection couldn't continue. That surely such luck couldn't hold?

And then on Friday night it had all crashed to the floor. Rhoda – the 'friend' she was increasingly irritated and repulsed by – had told her, with unmistakable relish, that she was being taken for a fool. Rhoda's source was impeccable: Eugene's best friend – 'You remember the guy. We've met him, right? Well, him.' His wife, Brittany learnt, worked with Rhoda, was a close friend of hers. 'She knows all about Eugene,' Rhoda explained, 'and told me. She said I had to put you straight. Said she couldn't bear to see another woman turned over and hurt by this guy. He's a junkie, Brittany, and a criminal and, most of all, he's got at least three other girls on the go – one's pregnant.' On and on it went, the litany of Eugene's sins. The time in jail, the bullying violence, drug-fuelled madness, staggering promiscuity and, the *coup de grâce*, the two neglected kids (shortly to become three) he had by two different (shortly to become three) 'babymothers', as Rhoda termed them.

And Brittany felt like her world had fallen around her ears. Tried to defend him, but Rhoda had been relentless: 'Belinda's known this guy for years. Look, Brittany, her own marriage is on the rocks because of his influence. Her husband follows the man like a lamb to the slaughter.' Rhoda's manner softened, her voice becoming quietly sympathetic. 'I know he's gorgeous, and sexy, and probably great in bed' – raising a questioning eyebrow, Rhoda waited for a response; getting none, she ploughed on – 'but let's face facts, Brittany – he's treating you like shit, cheating on you already. Probably telling his friends about his latest conquest. You've too much self-respect to take that.' And there was more, lots and lots more, of the same, until at last the pub called last orders.

Standing on the pavement Brittany said she was going home, but Rhoda wouldn't hear of it, grabbing her arm and pulling her along. So, the two women had walked into Amazon Zone: and there – straight in front of them – was Eugene, in a dance-floor clinch with some hardly dressed model girl, and behind him was Belinda's husband, as Rhoda told her, the ever-loyal sidekick.

There was nothing more to say. Brittany was no one's fool. Had no intention of being sweet-talked into bed another time. Which was clearly all it had ever been about, for Eugene at least. So she deleted every text he sent, cut every call, tried to persuade herself she'd got off lightly. That it was just one of those 'learning experiences' that life will throw at you.

But she hadn't got off lightly. She had been in love. She was certain of it. The intensity of emotion was unnerving and exhilarating – at least when she had believed it was mutual. Now she hated herself for being so naive, so stupid, and for crying over him – after all she knew – crying over that bastard.

She hadn't been out since Friday night. Rhoda had rung twice, and she'd switched both calls to answerphone. It had occurred to her over the past couple of weeks, before it all crashed to the ground, that Rhoda might be slightly jealous – that maybe she'd fancied Eugene for herself. Now, Brittany simply couldn't bear to hear her voice. She resented Rhoda's evident pleasure in delivering the bad news, telling her she was just one of Eugene's many shags-about-town. To Brittany's ears, the messages on voicemail and answerphone were almost worse. Rhoda spoke as if Brittany had just come out of hospital or suffered a major bereavement. Should she come round? she enquired or was Brittany up to a night out? But maybe it was too early? If so, Rhoda entirely understood. 'But if it would help to talk about it,' Rhoda assured her friend that she was 'always here'. Brittany felt an overwhelming desire to slap the woman. But the thing that really infuriated her was the enquiry repeated at the end of each and every message – a would-be casual throwaway – 'Oh, and by the way,' she would say, as if she'd almost forgotten to mention it, 'has he tried to get in touch?' or 'Don't suppose you've heard from him since?' Why did she want to know? Brittany couldn't see it was any of her bloody business.

But now Brittany came to think about it, Rhoda had always had a prurient obsession with other people's relationships – and other people's boyfriends, come to that – which she justified in ideological terms. Rhoda condemned marriage and romance as 'servitude made palatable by self-delusion'. She proselytised that 'transient sexual interchange' was the only 'realistic and healthy option' in the contemporary socioeconomic context. Such fatuous nonsense became rather less risible, Brittany supposed, when Rhoda targeted your relationship for some 'transient sexual interchange'. Brittany realized that for a long while she had tolerated rather than enjoyed Rhoda's 'friendship'. Now it seemed a pointless waste of time.

Intent on her thoughts, Brittany hadn't noticed the car parked outside her house, nor that a man and woman, both black, got out the car on seeing her approach. She had turned her key and was halfway over the threshold when she heard a woman say, 'Excuse me, but we really have to speak.' Startled, she spun round and saw the couple now standing by her front gate. The man introduced himself, and his wife – she'd already recognized him; then the woman again insisted: 'We have to talk.' She had an educated voice and a firm, determined manner. 'I'm sorry,' the woman continued, 'but it really is important.' Brittany didn't have much option other than to invite them in.

It had been Belinda's idea to go to the house. Belinda who said they had to talk to Brittany Martin. Ralph, in a haze of happiness, was pleased to comply. He'd spent most of the previous night making love to his wife, both of them revelling in the return of lost joy. They'd talked so much about themselves that Ralph wasn't entirely clear about it, but it seemed like Eugene had managed to convince Belinda of what Ralph had been telling her all along: that her friend Rhoda was a lying, conniving bitch, and that he, Ralph, had not been remotely unfaithful. How his best star boy had achieved this was a mystery. Belinda hadn't gone into much detail. Just told him that her and Eugene were making a new start, putting things behind them. She also told Ralph he should be grateful for a friend who loved him the way Eugene did. Ralph had in fact been grateful since the age of four, when they met in the Seven Sisters primary school playground, but he just smiled and said, 'Too right.'

So when DCT Travel Agency shut up shop that evening, Ralph had fished the address off the office computer, and they'd driven down to Brittany's house. She wasn't in, but Belinda insisted on waiting. There were things she had to put right, past behaviour – words and deeds – troubling her conscience.

It was awkward at first. Brittany made coffee and Ralph stumbled through what had happened that night at Amazon Zone. But eventually Ralph hit his stride, stopped stammering and began to make sense. By the time he'd finished, Brittany was half inclined to believe him. Then Ralph said something about a business commitment, and Brittany and Belinda were alone. In fact, Belinda had prearranged this. She had told him she needed to talk 'woman to woman'. In truth she felt it would be easier for both her and Brittany without her husband, and Eugene's best friend, as an audience.

Ralph was fine with that. He had stuff to do anyway. He told Belinda to ring him when she wanted collecting from the house. He was beginning to get anxious when, finally, he got Belinda's call, a few minutes past 11 p.m.

Eugene waited till after 9 p.m. before heading off to Shifter's. He left the Puma just behind the traffic barrier at the top of Acre Row. The sky was fading from dusk to dark, and a pale full moon glowed above the orange glare of the street lights.

Acre Row's vegetation was reaching its yearly zenith. Even in the monochrome night, the tumescent plantlife's vivid green was unmistakable. Eugene quickened his pace – as always, he found something hateful about the place, something that whispered of disease and decay. He could hear music coming from Shifter's. Looking along the side of the house, he could see the kitchen window ablaze with light. Eugene paused: it was possible Shifter had visitors – Carl amongst them. Eugene decided to check it out. He skirted silently to the left, then began to edge quietly down the side wall of the house, towards the illuminated kitchen which shone out about two-thirds of the way along. He could feel the reassurance of the Glock under his waistband, but Eugene wasn't some half-wit gangbanger. Shoot-outs were not his style and, first off, he wanted to know just what he was walking into.

As he approached the kitchen the music got louder. It was some sort of awful compilation they were playing at top volume: Eugene could have done without 'Bat Out of Hell', but, for the moment, noise, any noise, was a gift. The dogs would hopefully be deafened. Dealing with Hopeless, Faithless and Loveless was absolutely the last thing he needed. But it seemed the luck was with him. Meatloaf was bawling at multidecibels, and Eugene made it to the window entirely undisturbed. Then he flattened himself against the wall and, very cautiously, looked inside.

Time was suspended. He almost screamed aloud, so great was the shock. It was impossible. Unable to believe his own eyes, he risked another look and, at that precise moment, she spun round to face him, eyes half closed, singing along as

335

she shimmied and wiggled to the Meatloaf rhythm. Eugene forgot all about noise, forgot about everything other than getting away. He stumbled backward, gagging and retching as he went, a trail of vomit in his wake. When he got outside on to the road, he threw up for real, emptying his stomach into the surrounding undergrowth. He went on retching – the bile stinging his throat and sickening him further, his gut going into spasm, heart racing, until he was doubled up and gulping for air. Listening to Cliff Richard singing 'Devil Woman', Sonny and Cher, 'I Got You, Babe,' Cyndi Lauper, 'Girls Just Wanna Have Fun'.

He had no idea how long it took him to clean himself up and stand upright again. He had to go back to the Puma to dump his jacket and put on a spare. He steadied himself, then turned back to Acre Row. Billy Joel, 'Uptown Girl', was booming out of the kitchen. Eugene was already beginning to doubt what he'd seen. And that was no good. He had to make sure, to be absolutely certain. He took a deep breath and moved quietly down the side of Shifter's house and back to the window.

The kitchen was alight with fairy lights and paper lanterns. Letitia was in her usual chair, engaged in needle-work, as always. Eugene couldn't see what she was working on, for which he was grateful. Mal Shifter was – as usual – mixing yet more exotic drinks, whilst Dolly, clad in clinging gold lamé, was dancing. And it was Dolly, although at first he hadn't recognized her. At first, he thought he'd seen a ghost – the heavy, silky dark hair falling halfway down her back, the gold dress. It was only when Dolly spun around, and he'd seen her face, incongruous beneath the wig, gobbets of skin and blood still attached beneath the spiky fringe falling on Dolly's forehead – it was only then he'd understood. Eugene watched a moment longer, then ducked beneath the window and walked quietly back to the road.

Once back on Acre Row, he gave himself a moment, then he allowed his footsteps to ring, marched through the front gate and leant on the doorbell. It took some time before the tell-tale scratching of nails announced the dogs, shortly followed by Shifter. 'Malcolm,' Eugene said, smiling. 'Sorry to surprise you like this. Bit of a social visit, plus a little bit of business.' Eugene walked forward. 'Can I come in? Thanks.'

The dogs stiffened the moment they saw him, lips wrinkling, hair rising. 'Oh, dear, oh, dear,' said Shifter. 'I don't know why, but they've really taken a dislike to you, Geno. But don't worry, my boy, I'll keep a close eye on them. Well, anyhow, this is a really unexpected treat, an unlooked for delight. Do, do come in.'

'Thanks,' said Eugene. 'And how are the Ladies? I hope I'll have the pleasure?'

'Oh, of course, of course,' trilled Shifter. 'Letitia is awaiting you, and Dolly will be down in a moment. She's just upstairs attending to her toilette – you know what the Ladies are like, appearance is all. And she does have something of a soft spot for – how should I put it – well, those of a dusky complexion, yes?' Shifter dropped his voice to a whisper. 'I think she finds something rather delicious in the idea – forbidden love and all that. I'm sure you know what I mean.'

Eugene smiled. 'Yes, I think so,' he replied.

As he followed Shifter down the hallway towards the kitchen, the three dogs bunched at his heels. Shifter was right, Eugene thought, the fucking things hated him.

Letitia was in her usual chair and her usual grey cardigan. The needlework he'd seen in front of her had vanished. Of Dolly there was no sign. And the music had been killed. The only sound was the click, click of the dogs' nails as they continually paced the lino, three pairs of piggy eyes continuously fixed on Eugene.

'So sorry to disturb your evening,' Eugene said to Letitia. 'Business, unfortunately, but it won't take long. I feel bad about barging in on family time like this.'

337

Letitia cackled. 'So sharp you'll cut yourself, young man. Feel bad, do you? But not too bad, I'll warrant. Smart as a whip, this one, Malcolm. You better watch him.'

Shifter smiled unpleasantly. 'Oh, yes,' he said. 'Our Geno is a clever boy all right. Quite the leading light nowadays. Done very well for himself. Lost something of civility on the way, but there again, nobody's perfect, not even Geno.'

'You're right, Mal,' Eugene agreed. 'But I'm working on it.'

Shifter gave a bark of laughter. 'You see what I mean? Ooh, he's quick on the uptake, this one. Well, let's try and keep the proprieties, despite past provocations.' He turned his attention to Eugene. 'Would you like a drink before this oh-so-rapid business? Or are you too busy and too important for ten minutes' socializing?'

Eugene said a drink would be fine. He picked a cuba libre. Shifter was on his way to start mixing when a breathless shriek announced the arrival of Dolly. 'It's Mr Gorgeous! So you still care about me. I thought you'd deserted us. Lost and gone for ever is what I said. Then you arrive, in the middle of the night, out of nowhere. Oooh' – Dolly paused for a theatrical shiver – 'it's just soooo romantic. I love surprises, you know.'

'Hi,' said Eugene. 'Sorry to turn up unannounced. Work stuff, you know.'

'Men's business,' said Dolly, tossing her head.

She had changed out of the gold lamé into a purple wrapover. Her hair, which she shook constantly, appeared damp. As Shifter devoted himself to the cocktails, Dolly checked through the music on offer and, after some deliberation, picked Prince. Eugene said it was a great choice, one of his favourites. Dolly duly turned it up louder. Then, as Shifter chopped cocktail garnish, Eugene stood up, 'Mal, I'll just nip out in the corridor. Text from Talus. He might want to speak to you. If he does, I'll bring the phone through, but I've got to ring him back.'

Engrossed in his cocktails, Shifter barely raised his head to nod.

Once he had shut the kitchen door behind him, Eugene went straight up the forbidden stairs, shouting imaginary conversation with Talus as he went. When he reached the upstairs landing, he looked around. He hadn't got a clue where Dolly's room was, but he was lucky. The second door down was partially open, lights blazing. He pushed the door and walked in – Dolly's room, had to be. Rows of frilly dresses were hanging up. Festoons of pink net at the window, mirrors a-gogo and a dressing table groaning with make-up. And there it was – unmistakable: Gloria's hair, and scalp, hanging up on the metal bedpost. Still wet and bloody.

Eugene grabbed a pillow and pulled off the pillow slip. Wincing, he picked up the scalp and put it inside, rolled it up tight and zipped it inside his jacket. Then he went straight downstairs, still shouting into the fake mobile call. He waited in the hallway long enough for Shifter to come out. 'Yeah. No – he's cool with that I'm sure. Yeah, I'll tell him. Sweet. Half an hour? I should make it. See you.'

Eugene smiled at Shifter. 'Sorry, Mal. You can imagine how things are at the moment – you know, Gloria and everything. Lot of stuff to sort out. Bit frantic. Listen, you know those scales?' Shifter nodded, cagily. 'Problem with the ones we've got. So Talus needs the ones you're using. In here aren't they?' Without asking further permission, Eugene opened the door on his left and walked in. He'd known for a long time that this was Shifter's 'powder room' and, just as he remembered, the scales were sitting right there on the table. Eugene picked them up.

Shifter had followed him into the room, flanked by the dogs. Now, they were in front of Eugene, blocking his path, Shifter smiling, leaning against the door, whilst the three animals, hackles up, teeth skinned, walked slowly forward.

'I think you'd better put those scales back down on the

table, young man,' Shifter said. 'I've come to rely on them –
essential, you might say. I think you'd better go home, tell
your bosses you made a bit of a hash of things.'

As Shifter spoke, Eugene had his eye on the dogs. All three
continued to inch towards him, all three appeared to be
looking at . . . Oh, fuck, Eugene suddenly realized. Jesus, no.
The fucking things can smell it, the blood and stuff. They're
going for my pocket. Eugene took a sidestep behind the
table, his eyes still fixed on the canine trinity. He heard
Shifter laugh and risked a glance at him.

Shifter had cottoned on at the same moment. He was
staring intently at Eugene, talking to the dogs. 'What's he
got, my bold, bad boys? Something you want? Something
that doesn't belong to him maybe?'

Eugene switched his attention back to the dogs. On the
table was an Anglepoise lamp and, as the hounds continued
their stiff-legged advance, the lamplight hit them and, for
a split second, their red coats shone gold against black
shadows, as if the ghost of Rembrandt had descended. The
light reverberated from the ivory teeth, turning the dripping
saliva to threads of silver and, from one of the beasts,
something else, a blaze of red and gold, caught the eye, the
colours bright and immutable, before the animal moved
back into the shadows.

Shifter's smile was broader now. He spoke to the dogs in
whispers. 'Do you want to go hunting, eh? Hopeless? Do
you want a little blood in your mouth, my Faithless? Do you
want to shake and tear, Loveless, feel the bones rattle? Shall
I send to you battle, my three? Shall I . . .'

'You'll shut the fuck up.' Eugene had the Glock pointed
straight at Shifter's face. 'I'm leaving here with the scales,
now. You say one word and I'll kill the fucking lot of you.'
Eugene looked back at the dogs and took the safety-catch
from the gun. Shifter whimpered something, which Eugene
ignored. He gestured with the gun and spoke slowly and
clearly. 'Take these three mutants and get in the kitchen.

Shut the door behind you. Fuckin move it.' Eugene walked forward and Shifter retreated.

'Kitchen, boys,' he whispered. The dogs obeyed and Shifter followed.

Eugene backed down the hallway and out of the house. He shoved the gun in his belt and sprinted down Acre Row. The minute they were reunited he gave the Puma its head, and they shot away.

The Puma leapt down the darkened streets at top speed, finding its own way. They stopped outside the King's Head. Eugene picked up his phone and told Talus he needed to see him, now.

'I'm on my way,' said Talus. 'Be about ten minutes. Geno . . . everything OK?'

'I've got the scales, and I've got Gloria's hair and scalp in my pocket,' Eugene said.

'I'm on my way,' Talus repeated.

Two minutes later Vinnie appeared and beckoned Eugene inside the pub. 'Talus said to get you,' was the only explanation offered. Then Vinnie plonked a brandy in front of Eugene and retreated back to his usual corner and silence.

The brandy helped Eugene snap out of it. He stopped staring into space, and the adrenalin overload was subsiding. By the time he heard Talus's car pulling up, the initial shock had given way to anger and revulsion.

He must have still been a little off kilter though because for a fleeting moment he started hallucinating. Over by the doorway a mythic figure appeared – bronze armour and an iron flail in his hand – it was Talus, burnished curls tight against his head, eyes blazing. Eugene shook his head and everything returned to normal.

Talus looked at Eugene carefully. 'You OK?' he asked.

'Ten minutes' quiet, and this' – Eugene pointed to the brandy – 'seem to have done the trick.'

'You've done well, Geno. Going back in there after seeing

341

that . . .' Talus gestured to the pile of dark silk beside them. Inside the King's Head, Eugene had taken Gloria's scalp from the pillow slip and, borrowing Vinnie's copy of the *Sun*, had attempted to lay it out straight on the adjoining table. He wanted her free of Shifter and sisters, every last piece of her.

It took under fifteen minutes for Eugene to talk Talus through what had gone down at Shifter's. Then Talus stood up and said it was time for him to make a move.

'I'll come with you,' Eugene said, also standing.

Talus shook his head. 'No, my son. You'll go home – which is where you've been all night. Am I right?'

Eugene nodded. 'But . . .'

Talus smiled. 'No problem, Geno. Now go home.'

Before they left, Talus and Eugene gave the scales to Vinnie. They wrapped the hair carefully in leftover Christmas paper which Vinnie had managed to root out. Then Vinnie reverentially carried the package behind the bar.

After Talus and Eugene had departed, Vinnie set about his task. He cleared the DVDs and paperbacks from the shelf in his living room, which he dusted, then washed down with Flash. Then he left the place to dry and nipped out to the twenty-four-hour shop on the Cally Road. He came back and polished the shelf, changed cloths and polished the silver-framed wedding picture George had given him. The picture he positioned behind the Christmas package. Next he arranged the flowers on either side, and lit the fat cream church candles he'd bought. He knew George would have wanted that.

CHAPTER THIRTY-THREE

His name was *Talus*, made of yron mould,
Immoueable, resistlesse, without end.
Who in his hand an yron flale did hould,
With which he thresht out falshood, and did truth
    vnfould.

FQ: The Legend of Artegall: V.i.12

DC Fradubio, along with the rest of the murder squad, was working around the clock. *Crimewatch* had produced a torrent of 'public assistance', most of which could more correctly be termed 'public obstruction'. There were half a dozen callers within a whisker of being charged for wasting police time. And one sad, lonely, persistent soul who kept ringing for 'a chat'. But, mostly, the calls demanded checking out – just in case. As Fradubio waded through them, his worries burgeoned. Mr Malcolm Shifter, or someone amazingly like him, came up repeatedly in callers' sightings. Fradubio now seriously doubted DS Grice's confident dismissal of Simone's testimony as 'all bollocks'.

As midnight passed and Wednesday became Thursday, Fradubio's break-time relief arrived. He handed over, stood up, rotated his cramping muscles, then headed for the coffee machine. Double espresso in one hand, he decided to stretch his legs out in the corridor. Five minutes later, and better for the limited exercise, he wandered back to the murder-squad HQ. He glanced across at the 'victims' board'. DC Fradubio looked at Stella, Amy, Angela and Gloria – he knew DCI Gale was right: there'd be another name on the board soon. Within a couple of days – maybe this coming Saturday night – another girl would be in their hands and at their mercy. Like every member of the squad, Tommy Fradubio knew what that meant, what had been inflicted and what had been suffered. He chucked his plastic coffee cup in the bin and walked across to the DCI's station. 'Sorry to interrupt, sir, but could I have a word, sir, and in private?'

They were in the kitchen, as usual, when he arrived. Shifter and the sisters – making plans. The first they knew was an almighty crash. Shifter ran into the hallway, dogs at his heels. In front of him – where the front door should have been – was a rectangle of night sky. The door's twisted brass hinges lay scattered. The door itself flat on the ground. Standing in front of it was Talus.

Shifter yelped. Then started to babble. 'Don't understand. It's that crazy black boy – he's . . .'

'I haven't come to talk,' Talus said, then shot the three dogs, one by one. Shifter screamed and ran upstairs. Talus walked into the kitchen. 'Goodnight, Ladies,' he said.

His last call was upstairs. There were things Talus needed to know, about Gloria, about Carl. Shifter did his limited best, after which the matter was ended. A further few minutes were spent gathering an eclectic assortment of instruments and artefacts – Talus used surgical gloves and deposited his odd collection into a plastic bag.

He worked for another half-hour or more, fetching, carrying, arranging. When he was satisfied all was in place, he picked up his plastic carrier-bag and left. He was over a mile away when the explosion came, but he heard it right enough and smiled. He checked the time and drove on. It was nearly an hour later, when he was relaxing back at Archie's place, when he picked up the phone. 'DCI Gale? Gerry Talus here. I think it might be worth us having a quick chat. I've got some evidence to hand over – quite important evidence, by the looks.'

DCI Gale had listened carefully to DC Fradubio and assured the young detective he had done the right thing. In fact, Fradubio's account had confirmed Gale's own suspicions. By now it was gone 1.30 a.m., and Gale pondered whether to call DS Grice to his office or leave it till morning. He was interrupted by the phone. DCI Gale listened in astonished silence.

'I'm on my way,' he said.

The entire murder team fell silent as the DCI marched out of his office. He named two teams of detectives, telling them to follow him to Mal Shifter's house, Acre Row – Camden NW1 6DK. He wanted the crime-scene people down there as quickly as possible, and the forensic pathologist alerted and told the same. Three bodies at the scene, possibly more.

'DC Fradubio?'

'Yes, sir.'

'You can drive me. Come on, we're leaving.'

Before he went, DCI Arthur Gale looked carefully at each member of his squad. 'I don't know what we're dealing with here,' he said, 'but if one word, just one tiny word, of this reaches the ears of the press before I've spoken, the man responsible will wish he'd never left the womb. I will annihilate him. Am I clear, gentlemen?'

'Yes, sir. Clear, sir,' the chorus snapped back. Gale disappeared out of the door, DC Fradubio running to keep up. Seconds later, they were speeding towards Camden, blue light flashing on top of the unmarked car.

They drove straight into Acre Row. The gate blocking the road had been unlocked by the firemen. Fradubio drove carefully down the cul-de-sac. The squashed plants covering the road caused the car to slip and slide and the torrents of water made it hard to see the kerb.

Two fire engines were there. Firemen on hydraulic lifts were sending jets of water pouring over the roof and upper storeys, which were still partially aflame. It seemed the gas explosion had torn through the house and caused the mains water pipes to split asunder. Bits of the property kept collapsing inward. It was a scene of utter devastation. 'My God,' said DCI Gale. DC Fradubio was too shocked to speak.

When Eugene left Talus he'd gone straight home. The Puma looked after him, navigating carefully, making sure he wasn't jolted or jarred, keeping the pace smooth and eschewing its usual fondness for speed and skidding round corners. Back at Wentworth Road, Eugene said thanks, stroked the Puma's silver rump and tottered through the door.

It was around 1.30 a.m., and Eugene was surprised to see his mum still up. Dressed in her nightie, slippers and quilted dressing-gown, Gladys was sipping tea and whisky. She fussed about after him, asked how he was, said he looked like he'd had a hard day and asked him if he wanted tea. Eugene accepted gratefully. He was far too hyper to sleep and far too worried about the dreams awaiting him.

When the tea was sorted and Eugene had poured them both a tot of whisky to go with it, Gladys spoke up. 'Had a bit of a shock earlier, son.'

Eugene almost smiled. The perfect end to a fun day. Then he looked at his mother's troubled face and made himself get a grip. 'Go on, Mum,' he said, knowing full well what was coming.

'Well, I'd just gone to bed. Not long after eleven o'clock, I think it would be – anyway, I was just drifting off, when the phone went. When I got to it, it turned out to be Mr Redmayne, you know, Nero's foster father?'

Eugene nodded. Right first time. He knew it had to be about the Minimonster and, sure enough, it was. 'What's happened now?' he said.

Gladys shook her head. 'You know, there's something wrong with that boy, Eugene, there really is.'

Eugene nodded. He'd known that for years.

Gladys went on. 'Mr Redmayne rang me from the hospital. He was there with his wife, waiting to see the consultant. He said they thought she might have to stay in overnight. It sounded quite serious.' Gladys took a sip of tea and continued. 'He said Nero attacked Mrs Redmayne, just like he went for me and his mother. But from what he said, this time was even worse. Awful, absolutely dreadful. The poor woman was getting him ready for bed – well, you know what he's like. He wanted to stay up watching TV. Anyway, Mrs Redmayne said no and tried to take him upstairs. That's when he went for her. He bit her arm and cut through an artery.' Gladys paused for breath and took a drink of tea.

'An artery? He bit into her artery?' Even Eugene – never one to underestimate the malignity of the Minimonster – was taken aback. 'That's just unbelievable. Are you sure that's right, Mum?'

Gladys put down her tea and nodded. 'I wrote it down, son, on the phone pad. I'll show you.'

Eugene got up. 'I'll get it, Mum.' He was back in seconds. His mum was right. In her careful script she'd written, 'Mrs Redmayne – doctors say partial severing of left radial artery.'

'That's it,' Gladys exclaimed. 'Radial. Like the tyres. Mr Redmayne said their house is a shocking mess with blood everywhere. He phoned 999 and held his wife while they waited for help. And all the time the blood was pumping out of her arm in great spurts, spraying all over. She was unconscious when the ambulance got there.'

'Bloody hell,' said Eugene. 'Sorry. Excuse me, Mum. But

that's just terrible. I mean, the woman could easily have died. She was lucky her husband was around when it happened.' Gladys nodded. Then Eugene asked about his sister's reaction. 'So what's Simone say about the latest escapade?'

Gladys took another drink of tea. 'Simone doesn't know yet. She's not home from work till gone four. There's nothing she can do, and I couldn't see what good it would do to get her all upset. I thought it would be better left till she gets home, eh?'

'Spot on, Mum,' Eugene agreed. 'I think you're dead right. Like you say, there's nothing she can do anyhow.'

'Well, the child's safe enough for now,' Gladys said. 'Mr Redmayne called social services, and they came straight away and took the boy. They're looking after him tonight – the social – and Mr Redmayne thinks they'll be ringing Simone first thing tomorrow morning.'

'OK,' said Eugene. 'He's in local authority care for the moment, yeah?'

Gladys nodded. 'Mr Redmayne said he was sorry but he didn't want him back under any circumstances.'

Eugene nodded. It was no surprise. Who could blame the man? 'So what now, Mum?' he asked.

Gladys looked unhappy. 'I know he's my own flesh and blood – but I can't have him back, Eugene. I don't want him here any more. That Mrs Redmayne – the foster woman – the doctors said she could have died. He's getting bigger every day, and he's getting worse. You know, son, I daren't go downstairs unless I know where he is. He keeps pushing and tripping me, trying to make me fall. I'm beginning to worry.'

Eugene nodded again. Told his mum he agreed. They would have to talk to Simone. As Nero was effectively in care already, p'raps they could just make the arrangement permanent. But, as Eugene knew, Simone wouldn't like it. Gladys thought she could talk to her daughter, make her understand. Eugene wasn't so sure. They would just have to cross that bridge when they came to it. As for now, he was too tired to think straight.

'Bed?' said his mum. Eugene nodded and followed her up the stairs. Two-thirty. He wondered where Talus was and what had gone down. Before he hit the pillow, he put his mobile on his bedside table, just in case.

DCI Arthur Gale had witnessed many strange scenes in the course of his career, but none that came close to the bizarre sequence of events currently unfolding on Acre Row. As the firefighters battled to control the flames leaping from the upper storeys of Shifter's house, their hosepipes added to the burgeoning torrents of water pouring out of the lower half of the building, which was already half submerged. Outside, gigantic weeds waved and swayed in the deluge. The flashlights set up to help the firemen intermittently picked up the flotsam and jetsam floating out of the house – embroidered cushions, an upside-down sofa, and the red-brown bodies of three dead dogs.

The scene-of-crime people had to wait for the firemen to finish and the building to be certified safe to work in. Gale hoped that the twin forces of fire and flood hadn't removed every viable trace of evidence – but he was very far from optimistic. Then, as he gazed at the building fast becoming a ruin, a shout went up, 'Sir! Here sir! We've got a body.'

She had floated out of the hole where the kitchen window once was. Crime-scene specialists donned waders and set out to retrieve the corpse. Someone reported to Gale that the pathologist had just arrived. A minute later, the body was stretchered out – an elderly woman dressed in grey, a bullet hole in her temple.

'You know what to do,' Gale said. 'Get her under cover as quickly as possible – pathologist's already here, he's getting changed over by the barriers. What the hell . . . !' There was a crack like thunder, followed by an enormous rumble –

everyone leapt for cover, the firefighters swivelling clear on their hydraulic platforms, their colleagues on the ground quickly retreating. There was a second thunderous roll, then a whole right-hand section of the house collapsed inward with an almighty roar.

As the full weight of the building toppled, a great black curtain of roiling dust flew upward from the ruin – and hovered there. A dense, dark shape, its massive bulk looming above them. Momentarily, it seemed to those watching below that the Angel of Death himself had appeared and was stooping over the house to reclaim his own.

A second later and the shadow was gone, falling back to earth and disappearing into the fast-rising murky waters. This was followed by another cry of alarm, and again everyone was forced to retreat at speed as a new danger became apparent. The massive weight of the newly fallen masonry displaced a tidal wave of water. The swell started slowly, then gathered pace and size, slopping from side to side until the mass and velocity became too much for the house to hold. As firemen scrambled and sprinted for cover, a low roaring began. Louder and louder the sound became, until the roar changed pitch and became a scream of vengeful fury. The thunderous noise caused everyone to step back still further, which proved to be a wise precaution. A second later there was a huge crash. The torrent of water flung itself through the skeleton of the house, overturning anything and everything in its path. Battering through the remaining doors and windows, snapping furniture and floor-boards like matchwood before it burst out into the garden.

Like a miniature tsunami, the wave of water raced forward bearing a flotilla of tables, chairs and the occasional smashed-up cupboard. For a heartstopping moment, it seemed as if the water would just keep on coming, submerging police and firemen in its wake. But its colossal energy finally began to fade. The water crashed over Shifter's garden fence and then started slowly to subside and draw back. As the great swell of water eddied outward, the odd plastic mixing bowl could be spotted, bobbing jauntily on the swirling, rotating current. And there was something else – the figure of a woman lying on her back, eyes open. The powerful current had pulled her clothes half off and tangled the plume of red hair floating behind. As they watched, one of the spirals of eddying water caught her trailing hand and pulled her in, spinning her round and round in a kind of aquatic waltz.

'The minute it's safe, get her out of there,' Gale said. And then his mobile started to ring. It was Talus.

DCI Gale listened carefully, told Talus he was on his way to have a look. This case was becoming more surreal by the moment.

Following directions, Gale had Fradubio drive him a quarter of a mile or so to the north of Acre Row. They turned left on to a small sideroad and then left again into Vesica Mews where, just like Talus said, a small row of lock-up garages could be found. Talus told them Shifter rented the one at the far end. Gale instructed DC Fradubio to smash the lock, which was easier said than done, but ten minutes later they were in.

The first thing they saw was an old grey Mazda, which an immediate computer check verified as belonging to Shifter and registered in his name. Everything inside the lock-up was tidy. In one corner there were shelves full of car stuff, spare parts, cleaning materials and so on. And half-hidden, behind the T cut and cans of de-icer, two-thirds of the way along the middle shelf, was a large plastic bag.

It took less than fifteen minutes for the crime-scene technicians and back-up DCI Gale had requested to arrive. The arc lights were set up and a sterile area prepared. 'Right, gentlemen,' Gale said. 'Let's see what Mr Shifter's been hiding, shall we?'

First, there was a dog collar. In fact, there turned out to be three dog collars in all. A pair of gloves, a handbag, and what, when unrolled, turned out to be a large tapestry.

There was also an old metal box, which contained a comprehensive range of needlework implements.

'Nothing to get excited about here, sir?' Fradubio ventured. 'It's odd stuff, though,' he mused. 'All home-made by the looks, and lots of unusual . . .' Fradubio didn't finish his sentence, but remained staring fixedly at the little collection of oddities. Once, he opened his mouth, but nothing came out. Then he said, 'Oh no, oh no. Sweet Jesus, help me,' and fainted. DCI Gale got behind him just in time. 'Sweet Jesus, help us all,' he said, mainly to himself.

The gloves had been crafted by Letitia. Made from the skin stripped from Angela Caridad's hands. The handbag was originally the skin on Amy Fiddeler's back and shoulders. On the night of her death, Amy had worn coral earrings in the shape of a cross. The police had never publicly released the fact, but her killers had cut both her ears off and taken them. One ear, neatly hemmed, pleated and gathered, with the earring still in place, made a striking and novel fastening for the handbag. Amy's other earring could be found embedded in one of the three dog collars, the one made from her skin – thigh, this time. Another of the collars had been fashioned from Stella Hope's skin, thigh, once again. And Mr Barry would have immediately recognized the little ivory anchor sewn into the 'leather' collar. He'd bought it for Stella on a daytrip to Brighton, and she had worn it on a silver chain around her neck. The third collar was Angie's skin. A dispassionate eye would allow that this collar was a far more complex endeavour. And in terms of design and execution, exhibited a remarkable level of skill. The centrepiece was an exquisite medallion of embroidery which served as a de facto mount for a large ruby cut in the shape of a heart. Above the gem, yellow diamonds and topaz leapt up to indicate a blaze of passion – a heart aflame.

Eugene had noticed it. That time Shifter was talking about Simone and Eugene had made a show of ignoring him.

Blocking out Shifter's innuendoes by fixing his attention elsewhere. The burning red and yellow stones had caught his eye. He kept thinking he'd seen something similar. But couldn't think where. Subsequently, it niggled at him – one of those infuriating things, like a loose tooth that you can't leave alone.

He'd been standing in Shifter's powder room, scales in hand, the three dogs advancing when a flicker of light had hit the stone and, for a moment, the dog's throat was ablaze with fire. At that precise moment, Eugene recognized the ring. As he told Talus, he had come very close to killing Shifter then and there.

The largest piece of evidence was a tapestry. Rolled up, and clearly unfinished, it was ambitious in scale, being around four feet square. Using an impressive variety of techniques, from sumptuous embroidery to rich appliqué work, the tapestry utilized physical remnants from all four dead women. It appeared to be based on an abstract design. But, on closer examination, the canvas had been subdivided into a number of discrete boxes, each depicting individual and graphically explicit scenes of rape and murder. Painstakingly rendered, the figures were represented in perfect physical detail. Around half of these tableaux had been completed; the remainder were no more than outlines. The Ladies were doubtless awaiting fresh materials.

Pornographic necrophile needlework – it seemed like a joke, DCI Gale thought. Except the obscenity of this stuff would be more than a match for anything the internet had to offer. The more so when you were aware of the materials used in its creation – and when you found out what had become of Stella Hope's unborn baby.

Gerry Talus had told him Shifter's fingerprints, and the sisters', would be all over the stuff. DCI Gale believed him. His officers had reported the discovery of a third – male – body. The pathologist wouldn't commit himself – quite correctly – but told Gale his immediate impression was of a double murder followed by a suicide. 'I think he shot the two old ladies. And the dogs, of course. Then did himself. Wounds are consistent. Anyway, I'll tell you better tomorrow.'

DCI Gale had no problem with such an outcome. It made sense. Shifter/The Meatman panicking as the net closed in. Taking his nearest and dearest with him. Gale was, however, perfectly well aware that Shifter and co. had died in very different circumstances. And he was satisfied that justice had been done. Or, at least, in part.

Talus had spoken about Carl. In his final moments, Shifter had told him Carl was still in London but was leaving soon. Shifter said Carl mentioned some girl in Bristol he could stay with. Talus didn't care how far Carl travelled – he would catch up with him.

After his chat with Talus, DCI Gale had put through a call to the Met Police Commissioner. It was just gone 3 a.m. The Commissioner listened to Gale's report. He decided to hold the press conference within the hour, as Gale suggested. Before the leaks and rumours started running. The Met's head of publicity was woken up and given fifty minutes to set up a major press conference at Holloway police station. Five minutes later the press went gaga with excitement.

Arthur Gale would deliver a version of the Shifter drama which would serve to satisfy public and press that the Meatman was no more. DCI Gale disliked such obfuscations and sleight of hand, but not as much as he disliked the thought of arresting Gerry Talus for the murder of Malcolm Shifter.

After talking to Gale, Talus rang Eugene and gave him the full rundown. Eugene was awestruck. 'You don't like doing these things by halves, do you?' he said.

'I don't believe in being half-hearted about anything,' Talus replied.

Afterwards, Eugene pulled on his sweats, splashed his face

354

and went downstairs to watch TV. Everything felt surreal, a little offcentre. As if he'd accidentally stumbled into a film set or something. Eugene thought about it. He wasn't sorry about the deaths. He was worried that Carl was still alive.

Eugene was switched to BBC News 24, reckoning it the best bet for first coverage of Shifter – especially at this hour of the morning. He was right. Some dreary correspondent in Washington was banging on about 'the likely fallout from forthcoming primaries', when suddenly the dreary guy disappeared, to be replaced by a woman in a red suit, her expression midway between shocked and serious. 'We interrupt this item to bring you breaking news: we are going live to an extraordinary, perhaps unprecedented, press conference called by the Metropolitan Police. Just a moment—' She paused to listen to her earphone. 'Yes. Well, things are very unclear just now, but what I can tell you is that following a massive explosion in Camden, North-West London, between 1.30 and 2 a.m. this morning, police can confirm that the Meatman is dead. Clearly, something dramatic has occurred, and I understand Detective Chief Inspector Arthur Gale, murder-squad chief, is about to speak, so let's go live to Holloway police station.'

At that very second the door banged and Simone came in. She bounced straight into the front room and gave Eugene a huge grin and a thumbs-up. He returned the gesture and pointed silently at the screen. Simone plonked herself down beside him, and brother and sister gave their full attention to DCI Gale.

DCI Gale was dark-suited, white shirt and, once again, black tie. He gave the story straight, with no hint of triumph, and he kept it short: 'At around 1.30 a.m. we were alerted to a large gas explosion originating at Mr Malcolm Shifter's house in Camden, North London. The explosion triggered a fire in the upper storeys of the house and burst the mains water-pipes, causing flooding at lower levels. It took the fire service some time to bring the situation under control.'

Gale paused here to pay tribute to his colleagues in the fire service, two of whom were being treated for minor burns. 'Three bodies were discovered on the premises,' Gale continued. 'Two women, believed to be Mr Shifter's elderly relatives, and the body of Malcolm Shifter himself. All had perished due to gunshot wounds, and a gun has been recovered from the remaining upper storeys of the house. Initial analysis by police forensic pathologists indicates that Mr Shifter murdered his elderly relatives and proceeded to turn the gun upon himself and end his own life.'

Journalists scribbled furiously and held up recorders; photographers, gathered around the speaker's podium, snapped away, and a dozen TV cameras trained their attention, and blinding, boilingly hot lights straight on to DCI Gale's face, determined to capture every nuance for the morning news. The Met Commissioner clearly felt the effects of the 4 a.m. call to arms. He kept mopping his face and downed copious amounts of water. Gale was entirely unperturbed. Untouched by lights, heat or media frenzy, he carried on, calm and level and completely self-possessed.

'Shortly after 2 a.m., myself and a number of murder-squad officers went to a lock-up garage close to Mr Shifter's home. The garage was rented in Mr Shifter's name, and contained a Mazda car registered to him. Hidden in the lock-up were a number of items, which are currently undergoing forensic investigation. I am not prepared to go into detail at present, but I will say that amongst the items are artefacts that appear to contain body parts and a collection of tools which we think may have been amongst the weapons used in the Meatman murders.'

Absolute pandemonium broke loose. The press pack surged forward, shouting questions and waving microphones. The Met's head of publicity waved his stewards into action and eventually things quietened down. Gale leant across to the Commissioner, who listened, nodded, and rose to his feet.

'Please listen, ladies and gentlemen, because we won't be taking questions, and there is only a limited amount we can say at this moment in time.' The Commissioner held up his hand for quiet and the noise slowly subsided.

'Thank you,' said the Commissioner. 'Now, I have just a few things to add.'

'Firstly, I'd like to congratulate DCI Arthur Gale and his murder squad on a first rate job. You are all familiar with the so-called Meatman murders – and know that we kept the worst of it out of the public domain. The torture and terror inflicted on these women is the most extreme I have come across in over twenty-five years' experience. DCI Gale and his team have lived and breathed this horror, day and night. Their strength of purpose and truly marvellous detective work has made the streets of London safe again. We should all be grateful for their selfless dedication.'

Gale looked at the floor as the press pack broke into applause. The Commissioner got back into his speech: he talked about the 'appalling' nature of the forensic evidence, and said police were 'very confident' tests would 'establish beyond doubt that Malcolm Shifter murdered Stella Jane Hope, Amy Fiddeler, Angela Caridad and Gloria Faron.' And, in addition, police were 'investigating the probability that Malcolm Shifter's elderly relatives, believed to be his aunts, were his close accomplices in the crimes committed.'

Uproar broke out again. 'Just one more minute, please.' The Commissioner waited until order was restored. 'Finally, we will, of course, be making further announcements the moment forensic test results are received and will be keeping you up to date on the post-mortem results. We would also still very much like to interview the man known as Carl – in connection with the death of Gloria Faron. He is a black male aged late twenties to early thirties. You'll find an artist's likeness in your press packs. We would stress that the public should not approach this man. Right, ladies and gentlemen, I'd just like to thank you on behalf of DCI Arthur Gale and myself for turning out at this ungodly hour of the morning.'

The news switched back to the studio. The red-suited woman said something about 'these amazing events in London . . . and, now, we can go over, live, to our correspondent, who has just left Holloway police station . . .'

Inside the police station, away from journalists and cameras, the Commissioner turned to Gale. 'You think this Carl will be at it again, eh?'

Gale nodded. 'Until he's locked up or dead, sir, he will keep on killing. I also believe he will search out a replacement for Shifter. He likes a partner. For him, it's part of the enjoyment.'

'Then I can rely on you to keep after him, Arthur,' the Commissioner said.

Back at Wentworth Road, Eugene and Simone were talking about Angela Caridad and the other girls – how the killers could seriously want to reduce them in that way, humanity boiled down and sewn up to produce a few dodgy trinkets.

Eugene saw quite clearly the innate idiocy of it all. Angie's beautiful engagement ring had – Simone told him for definite – cost an absolute fortune. But now he understood the point of it – perceived that for Martin, for her lover, the ring was merely an emblem – a representation, of an infinitely more precious reality. And those stupid bastards stuck it on a dog collar – which just about said it all.

Simone went off to make some tea, and Eugene channel-hopped without much attention. He was thinking about his sister.

He hadn't told Simone about Nero's latest outrage yet – they had both been too obsessed with the news about Shifter. But he was also reluctant to break her mood. She had come into the house glowing – very different from the usual stroppy, surly, don't-mess-with-me mood she normally came home in. Even now, as she drifted back with the tea, she had an aura of dreamy contentment that was definitely not your usual Simone. Eugene was intrigued. 'So what's with the smiles, little sister?' he asked. 'Won the lottery or something?'

Simone laughed, giggled really.

Eugene was still more surprised. 'Well?' he said. 'Come on, what's going on?'

It took a while to get it out of her, and lots of totally uncharacteristic shyness but, eventually, she spat it out. Eugene was taken aback. Inclined to be angry, but knowing there was nothing for him to be angry about. And as he heard about her detective – the hand-holding, the tentative discussions – his anger dissipated and, very slowly, he too began to smile. He decided to leave the subject of Nero till morning.

It was gone 5.30 a.m. when brother and sister went upstairs. The phone started ringing at precisely ten past six. Jerked out of heavy sleep, Eugene at first didn't realize what was happening. Then the phone stopped, and one minute later started again, just as loud. Cursing, Eugene dragged himself out of bed and stumbled downstairs. The shrilling of the phone was doing his head in; he was halfway down when, mercifully, it stopped.

There was silence, and then Simone's voice talking to the caller. Then Gladys shouted up. 'Eugene, get yourself down here, son.'

The call, it turned out, came from social services. They, in turn, had been rung by the director of the children and families section. She'd had a call from the principal of Woodlands Secure Residential Centre – or not-so-secure, as it turned out, because some time after his late-night arrival and before their 6 a.m. morning check and roll call, Nero had disappeared. No one seemed entirely sure how long he might have been gone. It was agreed that the best thing the Burnsides could do was to remain at home. Eugene said nothing but shook his head. Home was the last place the little bastard was heading. Eugene's own bet was that social services should get down the police morgue – they'd probably find the Minimonster hanging round the dissection table, agog with excitement and begging to join in.

Eugene had given up any hope of sleep and was making toast when his mobile rang again. He let it ring, and checked the clock – nine-thirty. Who the hell was it now? Eugene wished people would just get off his case and leave him alone. Give him some peace. Then he looked down at caller display and his heart started banging . . . 'Hello,' he said nervously. 'Hello?'

'Hello. It's Brittany.'

EPILOGUE

The Puma skittered, played and bucked with exuberance in the June midday sun, its silver flanks gleaming in the light. Eugene clicked his tongue in pretend exasperation at the high jinks, which too closely mirrored his own mood to cause him much annoyance.

They leapt over the brow of Crouch Hill, skimming down towards the Clock Tower. Brittany told him that, once, a stone cross had stood on the same site. All of Crouch End, Archway, Hornsey, Tottenham and, of course, Wood Green had once been unbroken forest. An aristocratic hunting-ground, game park and outlaws' hideout. And in the middle of this ocean of green, in a forest clearing, where several bridlepaths converged, had stood the cross, signifying the boundary of the Bishop of London's land. Crouch End, Crux End – the land of the Cross. Eugene liked it.

Brittany must have been ready and waiting, cos she was downstairs and locking the front door within a minute of him ringing the bell. With light Sunday traffic, it took them less than five minutes to Wentworth Road, arriving bang on 1 p.m.

'I'm nervous,' Brittany said, as they walked up to number forty.

'Don't be.' Eugene put his arm round her. 'It's only my mum and my sister. You'll get on fine.'

Eugene opened the door and escorted Brittany inside. 'Mum, Simone, we're back,' he called.

DCI Gale surveyed the report on his desk. Sent up from Cardiff. Serious Crime Unit was dealing with the body of a girl. Identified as eighteen-year-old Evie Semper, a known drug-abuser with convictions for prostitution. The file had been sent to DCI Gale because the killing bore marked similarities to the Meatman murders. The same ludic brutality, and – more importantly – the same DNA from semen found near the body. Tellingly, from Arthur Gale's point of view, the trademark weird patterns and indentations were missing. Mal Shifter's signature no longer flourished. However there was another, and notable, addition to the murderer's MO. DCI Gale noted with puzzlement and no little concern the proliferation of tiny punctures, like miniature bitemarks, all over the body. Sometimes the incisions clustered in apparent frenzy, around the crook of the arm, for example; at other times, they appeared random.

Of course, the Cardiff police had sent the strange marks out for analysis. In the dossier before DCI Gale was a report from the Welsh Forensic Odontology Unit. They were confident that the wounds specified were the bitemarks of a male child aged between six and eight years. They added that the bites were inflicted both pre- and postmortem.

Right in the middest of that Paradise,
There stood a stately Mount, on whose round top
A gloomy groue of mirtle trees did rise,
Whose shadie boughes sharpe steele did neuer lop,
Nor wicked beasts their tender buds did crop,
But like a girlond compassed the hight,

362

And from their fruitfull sides sweet gum did drop,
That all the ground with precious deaw bedight,
Threw forth most dainty odours, and most sweet delight.

FQ: The Legend of Britomartis;
The Gardin of Adonis: III.vi.43

ACKNOWLEDGEMENTS

Thanks to the following people: Maurice Mcleod, David Blackall, Deborah Orr, Suzanne Sinclair, Tad Williams, Steven Raymond, Matthew Johnson and Professor Robin Hedlam Wells.

I am particularly grateful to Helen Windrath, Alex Startup and my editor, Simon Taylor.

Especial thanks to my agent, Stephanie Cabot.

And thanks also to the Arts Council for their support during the writing of this novel.